Half Agony, Half Hope

BOOK 1

JANE AUSTEN'S MEN

JOY MICHELLE AUSTIN

Copyright

Half Agony, Half Hope
© 2025 by Joy Michelle Austin
All rights reserved.

This novel is a work of fiction. Any resemblance to actual persons,
living or deceased, is purely coincidental, except where historical or
public figures are referenced. The characters, events, and locations
are either products of the author's imagination or used fictitiously
for the purpose of storytelling.

This book was inspired by the characters of Jane Austen and
reimagined in a modern setting, as well as the true story of
Elisabeth Fritzl, whose strength and survival in the face of
unimaginable darkness deeply influenced the themes of endurance,
faith, and redemption in this novel.

Scripture quotations are taken from the ESV Bible (English
Standard Version), copyright © 2001 by Crossway, a publishing
ministry of Good News Publishers. Used by permission. All rights
reserved.

For permissions, inquiries, or to connect with the author, e-mail:
thejoyousauthor@thejoyousliving.com

First Edition: May 2025
Printed in the United States of America

Table of Contents

Triggers

This novel explores dark and difficult themes, and while every effort has been made to approach these topics with respect and sensitivity, some content may be distressing for readers.

Content Warnings Include:
- Kidnapping & Imprisonment – The protagonist is held against his will, enduring long-term captivity.
- Sexual Assault & Coercion – The novel includes non-consensual situations, manipulation, and psychological abuse. These scenes are not graphically detailed but are deeply impactful.
- Psychological & Physical Abuse – Depictions of gaslighting, humiliation, control, punishment, and physical violence.
- Religious Manipulation – The abuser weaponizes faith and scripture against the protagonist, distorting spiritual teachings for control.
- Child Endangerment & Neglect – While no direct harm comes to the children, they are raised in captivity with emotional distress, malnutrition, and lack of proper care.
- Emotional & Psychological Trauma – Themes of hopelessness, survival, PTSD, and forced submission.
- Dubious Consent in Intimate Situations – Survival-based submission is a recurring element.

This story is a dark exploration of endurance, faith, and survival under unimaginable circumstances. The intent is not to romanticize abuse, but to give voice to those who have suffered and fought for freedom.

Every scene has been crafted with deliberate care, ensuring that the focus remains on the survivor's journey rather than glorifying suffering.

If you are sensitive to any of these topics, please prioritize your well-being. Some readers may find certain passages overwhelming, and that is completely valid.

If you choose to proceed, know that this is ultimately a story of resilience—of a man that refuses to be broken, and of a spirit that fights to reclaim itself even in the face of overwhelming darkness.

For those who need support:

If you or someone you know is in a dangerous situation or struggling with trauma, please seek help. You are not alone. Resources are available, including my companion devotional, *Half Agony, Half Hope but Wholly Free*, that will be coming soon, and your story matters.

Reader discretion is advised.

For Dad—

You have always been one of my greatest supporters, my wisest counselors, and the best beta reader I could ever ask for. Your insight—as a father, as a man of God, and as someone who leads with quiet strength—has shaped not just this book, but the way I tell stories.

Thank you for your patience, your wisdom, and your unwavering belief in me. Your guidance has meant more than words can say.

This book is for you.

With all my love,
Joy Michelle Austin

- "It's Not Over" by Daughtry
- "Start of Something Good" by Daughtry
- "Brother" by NEEDTOBREATHE
- "Rescue" by Lauren Daigle
- "Home" by Daughtry
- "No Longer Slaves" by Bethel Music
- "Scars" by I Am They
- "You'll Be in My Heart" by Phil Collins
- "Raise a Hallelujah" by Bethel Music
- "My Testimony" by Elevation Worship

Part I: Half Agony

I have forgotten the feel of the sun on my skin,
but I still remember what love is.
If love is all I have left, then I will endure.
For her.
- Rick's Journal

Prologue

Rick Wentworth had learned to survive the cold, the hunger, the suffocating darkness. He had endured a decade of chains, of nights spent in restless agony while the weight of captivity pressed against his ribs. But nothing had prepared him for this.

His daughter was slipping through his fingers.

She lay in his lap, her frail body wrapped in every blanket he had, but she still shivered violently. Sweat dampened her curls, her face pale beneath the fever's flush. Each cough rattled her tiny chest as if every inhale was a question and every exhale was an answer slipping further away.

Rick rocked her gently, whispering against her curls, "Stay with me, Sweetheart. Just hold on."

She barely stirred.

His throat burned. He tilted his head toward the small red light in the corner—its unblinking glow the only sign that someone, somewhere, was watching.

She *had* to be watching.

Rick swallowed hard. His voice, hoarse but firm, cut through the silence. "She's dying." His grip on Lily tightened. "You want me broken? You won. But please, don't let her die."

Nothing.

His breath turned ragged. Desperation sharpened the edges of his control.

"Damn it," he ground out, his voice cracking. "She's just a little girl. Do whatever you want to me. But help her."

The silence stretched, thick and unmoving.

Then, a shift.

A click.

Rick's entire body went rigid as the steel door groaned open.

The sharp echo of footsteps followed—measured, deliberate. He braced himself, adjusting Lily in his arms, and forced his voice to remain steady.

"She needs a doctor," he said, swallowing the tremor that had crept beneath his words. "She won't last the night."

A sigh. The kind meant for inconveniences, for spilled drinks and interrupted conversations—not for life or death.

Then, "You always exaggerate, Ricky."

Rick clenched his jaw. "Look at her."

A pause. He felt her gaze shifting, appraising, weighing the moment as if Lily's life was just another decision to be made.

Then, another sigh. "Fine. I'll call someone. But don't think for a second that this changes anything."

The footsteps retreated.

The door swung shut.

Rick stayed frozen, the weight of Lily pressing against his chest.

He wanted to believe that help was coming.

But he knew better than to hope.

Chapter 1

Ten Years Earlier

> Some people fit neatly into the world they're born into. Others have to fight for a place. And some—some are never meant to belong at all.
> – Rick's Journal

The Elliot dining room was elegant, grand in a way that felt too polished to be comfortable. A chandelier glowed overhead, casting warm, golden light over a table set with fine china and gleaming silverware. The scent of rosemary and garlic still lingered from dinner, but Rick barely tasted anything.

Walter Elliot's gaze flicked toward him now and then, sharp and assessing, as if he were still deciding whether Rick had any business being here at all.

Rick had been sitting at this table for four years now—invited as Anne's boyfriend, barely tolerated as Walter's guest. And yet, every meal still felt like a test.

Tonight was no different.

"You're really set on working at a clinic?" Walter asked Anne, his voice calm but edged with expectation. "I just don't see the point of stopping your education when you could do more."

Anne, sitting beside Rick, calmly set down her fork. "I want to work," she said, measured but firm. "I'll have my nursing degree in May. Rick and I want to settle down in Croft Beach after our wedding."

Walter sighed, swirling the wine in his glass. "You'd be wasting potential."

Anne's smile tightened. "Maybe I don't need an advanced medical degree to do what I love."

Across the table, Louisa set down her napkin, watching her sister with quiet amusement. Louisa and Anne were identical in appearance—same golden hair, delicate features, piercing green eyes—yet Rick prided himself on never mistaking one for the other. Anne's presence was warm, steady. Louisa's?

Calculated.

"You'll be in Croft Beach then?" Louisa asked, tilting her head. "That's where your friend Darcy lives, isn't it, Rick?"

Rick nodded. "Yes, Darcy's family home is near the coast."

Walter's expression barely shifted, but Rick caught it—that subtle flicker of approval. He liked Fitz Darcy. Darcy was the kind of man Walter respected—from the kind of family he approved of.

Rick? Not so much.

He was never allowed to forget that he was the son of farm laborers, had been raised in an apartment instead of a house, and depended on two jobs and a scholarship to pay tuition, all while he could not afford the one-carat diamond ring Walter and Louisa expected Anne to wear.

Anne took a sip of water. "You remember Darcy, Lou. He and his family attended Aunt Russell's charity gala at Christmastime.

Louisa hummed, tapping her fingers against her wineglass. "Vaguely. Though I think we were at separate tables, weren't we?"

Walter let out a quiet chuckle. "The Darcys have a certain exclusivity about them."

Rick fought the urge to roll his eyes. Walter spoke as if the Darcys were snobs, but if Fitz Darcy had been sitting here instead of him, Walter wouldn't have had a single complaint. He'd probably be offering him a place at his law firm.

Louisa leaned forward, resting her chin in her hand. "And you, Rick? Any plans yet?"

Rick hesitated. He had plans—or at least the start of them. He'd been promised an internship at the marina, something that could lead to real work in conservation. But sitting here, across from Walter and Louisa Elliot, justifying himself felt exhausting.

"Still figuring it out," he said instead.

Walter made a quiet noise—not quite disapproving, but far from encouraging.

Anne exhaled, setting her glass down just a little too hard. "Rick doesn't need to have his whole life mapped out tonight, Dad."

Rick glanced at her, a flicker of surprise tightening in his chest. Had she always been this quick to defend him?

Louisa just smiled. "You've always liked the ocean," she mused. "I recall you mentioning the tide pools at Croft Beach once. You made them sound almost... magical."

Rick glanced at her, caught off guard. Had he really told Louisa that? He didn't remember.

Anne's fingers brushed his under the table.

Walter, apparently losing interest in marine biology, turned his attention elsewhere. "Louisa, what about you? Have you decided if you'll accept the offer from Musgrove Electronics?"

Louisa smirked. "I have options. A few firms have reached out, but I haven't made any decisions yet."

Rick knew she was getting her degree in engineering. He couldn't deny being impressed—she was likely going to be valedictorian in May.

"I'm still focused on my senior project," she added. "Been putting a lot of work into it."

Anne chuckled. "You mean the cellar?"

Rick's brows pulled together. "The what?"

Louisa's lips curved. "It's nothing. Just needed space to work on a few things, so I converted the basement into a little project area. A personal lab, you could say."

Rick raised an eyebrow. "You built yourself a lab in the basement?"

Louisa shrugged lightly. "I *am* an engineer, Rick."

Anne laughed, shaking her head. "She's always been like this. She had to have her own space for everything when we were kids. Even when she was little, she'd disappear for hours into the treehouse, engrossed in whatever project she was working on."

Walter dabbed his mouth with his napkin. "If I recall correctly, Anne, you were the one who hijacked that treehouse and turned it into a dollhouse."

Rick glanced at Anne, expecting her to laugh—but something flickered across her face before she schooled her expression.

"That's not how I remember it," she said lightly.

Walter huffed a chuckle. "Memory's a funny thing, isn't it?"

The shift in the air was subtle, but Rick felt it.

Before he could make sense of it, Anne straightened, pushing her plate away. "Dad, before we finish dinner, I think we need to clear something up."

Walter lifted his gaze, expectant.

"I am not naming my firstborn Lily."

The silence was immediate.

Walter's expression darkened. "Anne—"

"No," she said firmly. "I know you and Mom always expected that, but Rick and I have our own plans for our future. Children are not part of our five-year plan. And even if they were, we would never name our daughter Lily."

Rick blinked. That was news to him.

He had always imagined them having children together someday. He could picture it—a little girl with Anne's golden hair and bright green eyes. The idea had never felt like something he needed to question. Now, he *was* questioning it.

Louisa swirled her wine, watching them with quiet amusement. "That's a shame," she mused. "Doctor Lily Elliot would've liked a namesake."

Rick glanced between them. Something unsaid lingered beneath the words.

"Guess we'll just have to wait and see who makes Daddy happy," Louisa added, a slow smile curling at the edge of her lips.

Anne exhaled sharply. Too sharply. Then, she let the conversation drop, but Rick couldn't shake the feeling that he was missing something.

Making their excuses, Rick and Anne stepped onto the balcony. The night air was cool, carrying the scent of the gardens, a welcome contrast to the stifling weight of the dining room. Rick exhaled slowly, feeling like he could finally breathe again.

Anne leaned against the railing, tilting her face toward the stars. "That went better than I expected," she murmured.

Rick huffed a quiet laugh. "That's a low bar."

She turned, offering a small smile. "You handled it well."

Rick shook his head. "Your dad and Louisa will never approve of me."

Anne's smile faltered. "They don't get to decide my life."

Rick studied her, his chest tightening. "Are you sure?"

She hesitated. A breath. A glance away. "I don't want Boston," she said finally. "I don't want med school. I don't want a handful of children. I just want us."

She reached for his hand, squeezing it tightly.

Rick swallowed against the pressure in his throat. The words should have reassured him. But they didn't.

Something still felt off.

Chapter 2

> There's a kind of silence that isn't peaceful. It presses against you, thick and cloying, making you aware of every breath, every shift of air. The Elliot estate was full of that kind of silence—like a whisper of something waiting beneath the surface.
> — Rick's Journal

The morning sunlight streamed through the high chapel windows, casting golden halos over the congregation. It should have been comforting. But even here, at Camden Methodist Church, something felt off.

The hum of the organ swelled, filling the space with rich, familiar notes. Families had gathered in their Easter best, pastel dresses and neatly pressed suits, making the room look like something out of a painting.

Rick adjusted his cuffs, glancing sideways at Anne. Her lavender dress caught the light, a picture of elegance and calm. But her fingers—always so steady—fidgeted at the hem of the fabric.

She caught him looking and arched a brow. "Stop staring," she murmured.

Rick's lips twitched. "Can't help it," he said, keeping his voice low. "You're beautiful."

A faint flush touched her cheeks, but she didn't look away—not right away. Instead, she smoothed his shirt, then turned her gaze back to the front of the church.

The hymn began. Anne sang quietly, her voice pure and steady. Yet something in it wavered, just beneath the surface.

As soon as the service ended, the church lawn buzzed with conversation. The crisp spring air carried laughter as children darted between adults exchanging pleasantries. It should have felt warm, inviting. And yet, something left Rick uneasy.

The sharp, measured click of polished shoes against stone cut through the noise. "Anne," Walter said briskly from behind them. "We need to discuss the seating arrangements for the luncheon. You'll ride back with me and your godmother."

Anne's fingers curled briefly against Rick's side. "No, I'll drive back with Rick."

Walter didn't acknowledge her words. "This isn't up for debate."

Anne turned to Rick, cupped his face, and kissed him. When she pulled back, her gaze flicked past Rick's shoulder.

Walter's expression remained unreadable. "We'll leave now," he said.

Anne let her hand linger on Rick's chest, then turned to follow her father and godmother.

Rick exhaled.

The scent of a woman's perfume reached him a moment later—faint but distinct—as Louisa stepped up beside him. "Guess it's just you and me."

The drive was quiet at first.

Louisa traced patterns along the window with the tip of her finger. "Nice truck," she mused, her gaze drifting over the interior.

Rick focused on driving.

"Didn't think Anne was the type to ride in something so... rugged."

"She doesn't mind."

Louisa hummed. "Of course she doesn't. She always gets what she wants."

Rick kept his hands steady on the wheel. "She's worked hard for what she has."

Louisa let out a quiet laugh. "Worked hard? Sure. But do you yet understand what it's like when Anne decides it's her way or the highway?"

Rick kept his eyes on the road.

Louisa exhaled softly. "Must be nice."

The cab felt smaller than it had a moment ago.

At the luncheon, Rick let the hum of conversation fade into the background. Beside him, Anne leaned in, her expression warm, full of light. Across the garden, Louisa stood near one of the floral arrangements, watching them.

Anne followed his gaze and sighed. "She's watching us again, isn't she?"

"She is." Rick's voice dropped slightly. "But who's that with her?"

Anne's gaze settled on the tall, well-dressed man speaking with her twin. "Tom Musgrove," she said. "His family owns Musgrove Electronics."

Rick raised an eyebrow. "The same Musgrove Electronics offering Louisa a job?"

Anne nodded. "That's the one. Tom's on the executive track—he's supposed to take over one day."

Rick studied them. Tom's easy demeanor softened Louisa's usual sharpness. Then Tom said something and gestured toward Rick and Anne. Louisa's gaze shifted—sharp, assessing.

A prickle of unease slid down Rick's spine.

Later, after the luncheon, Rick stood at the guest room window, tugging the curtain aside. Below, near the stone steps, Anne stood with her back to the house, the last slant of sunlight catching in her golden curls. He almost called out. Then she moved. A slow, deliberate pace—too controlled, too precise.

Rick exhaled, rolling his shoulders.

Something about the way she held herself felt... off.

She turned slightly, the light skimming across her face. For a fraction of a second, a voice in the back of his mind whispered, *That's not Anne.*

His pulse kicked.

Then the light shifted, softening the sharp edges of her features, and the moment passed. Of course, it was Anne. Rick let the curtain fall. The house was too quiet now. He exhaled slowly, running a hand through his hair.

It was going to be a long spring break.

Chapter 3

> I used to think love was something solid, something unshakable. But now I know the truth. Sometimes, it's not ripped away. Rather, it dissolves & slips through your fingers before you even realize it's gone.
> — Rick's Journal

Outside, the Elliot estate stood pristine and untouched—a place where everything had its proper place. Except for him.

The afternoon sun filtered through the trees, throwing jagged shadows across the stone steps. Rick glanced at the clock. Fifty-six minutes.

Anne had said five. She had not wanted him inside. The thought unsettled him more than the wait itself. Then the door opened, and Rick's stomach dropped.

Anne stepped outside, hesitating at the top step, her hands empty except for her mobile phone. No luggage. She scanned the driveway—not searching for him, but checking if anyone was watching.

Rick climbed out of the truck, striding toward her. "Anne?" His voice was even, but tension coiled in his chest. "What's going on?"

She didn't meet his gaze. "We need to talk."

Rick's pulse kicked up. "Then talk."

Anne lifted her phone, tapped the screen, and turned it toward him. A photo. Him and Becca.

Rick barely glanced at it. His eyes snapped back to Anne. "So?"

Anne's jaw tightened. "Explain this."

His fingers curled. "Why? You already made up your mind."

Her chin lifted slightly. "You've been spending all this time with her. You didn't think I'd notice?"

Rick's patience thinned. "I work with her, Anne. We've talked about it."

She crossed her arms. "Would you have told me about all these meetings if I hadn't seen this photo?"

Rick's lips parted, but no words came out. He was too angry. Anything he said, he'd regret.

Anne gave a slow nod. "That's what I thought."

His jaw tightened. "Sounds like you've already decided what you're going to believe. So why bother asking me?"

Anne exhaled sharply. "I'm going to Harvard."

Rick's muscles locked. "Since when?"

"An hour ago."

The ground shifted beneath him, and Rick let out a sharp breath. "An hour ago?" His voice was low, controlled. "You made a life-changing decision in an hour?"

Anne held his gaze. "Yes."

His fingers curled into fists. "You—" He exhaled, running a hand down his face. "Last weekend at dinner, you told your father you weren't going back East. You wanted to work at the clinic in Croft Beach. You—" He exhaled, steadying himself. "You said you were happy."

"I was."

Rick scoffed. "And now, suddenly, you're not?"

Her eyes flickered. "This isn't sudden," she said carefully.

Rick folded his arms. "Then why didn't you tell me?"

Anne swallowed. "I didn't know."

Rick let out a humorless laugh. "Bull crap. If you didn't know, you wouldn't be standing here with a decision already made."

Anne didn't flinch. "I needed time to think."

"And you couldn't bother talking with your future husband about this?"

Silence.

"Louisa said—"

Rick exhaled slowly. "Don't do that."

Anne blinked.

Rick's voice was quieter now, but firm. "You don't get to hide behind Louisa. This is your call. Own it."

Her jaw tightened.

Rick stepped closer. "You didn't want to be a clone of Doctor Lily Elliot." His voice cut through the silence. "You didn't want to name your daughter after her. You swore you'd never follow in her footsteps."

Anne's fingers twitched.

Rick's pulse hammered. "So, tell me—who is this decision really for?"

She held his stare, and for the first time, something cracked in her expression. But only for a second.

Anne took a slow breath. "It's for me."

Rick's jaw clenched. "And I wasn't even worth a conversation?"

Her face faltered, but her voice remained steady. "I couldn't let you talk me out of it."

Rick let out a slow breath. "You didn't even give me the chance to try."

Anne swallowed hard. Then, she reached for her engagement ring and twisted it free. She held it out. "I can't."

Rick's fingers twitched—but he didn't reach for it. After a long pause, Anne placed the ring on the hood of the truck. Rick didn't look at her. Anne lingered for a moment, then turned and walked back toward the house. The truck door hung open, but Rick didn't move. The engagement ring sat in the fading light, a small, shining thing against the steel of the hood.

Anne was gone. And she wasn't coming back.

Chapter 4

> Some mistakes you can walk away from. Others pull you under before you even know you're drowning. I should have seen it coming. I should have listened to my gut. But by the time I realized the trap was already set, it was too late.
> – Rick's Journal

The sun was sinking behind the Elliot estate, painting the stone walls in deep amber, but the shadows along the path felt different tonight. Wrong. Rick's truck rumbled to a stop in the driveway, but he didn't shut off the engine right away. The message on his phone still glowed on the screen.

> A: Can we talk?
> Come to the
> back patio.
> Please.

Three months of silence, and now this.

He shouldn't have come. He hadn't even told Darcy where he was going. He didn't want to hear his best friend tell him what he already knew—that driving eight hours north to see Anne after the way she ended things made him look weak. But if there was even the smallest chance that Anne regretted it all, he had to know.

The gravel crunched beneath his boots as he crossed the patio, his breath unsteady, his heart pounding with something he refused to name. The scent of cut grass and jasmine lingered in the warm night air, wrapping around him like a memory.

His breath hitched.

Anne.

Relief surged through him, loosening the knots in his chest. His steps quickened as he rounded the corner, and there she was, bathed in soft light, golden curls catching the glow. Sitting at the wrought-iron table, just like she used to do.

She hadn't left for Boston.

The second she turned, he was moving before he could think, before doubt could creep in.

"I'm sorry," she murmured, rising from the chair. She reached for the glass on the table—homemade lemonade, like always—and held it out to him. "Let's talk," she said, her voice low, coaxing.

Rick hesitated for only a second before accepting the glass, his fingers brushing hers. He took a deep swig—tart, sweet, ice-cold—before setting it down, barely tasting it. It didn't matter. Nothing mattered except the woman standing before him. Everything seemed to be right again when she stepped closer and lifted her chin for a kiss as the light caught the soft curve of her lips.

She was here. She was his.

He didn't wait. His hands found her waist, pulling her to him with a desperation that made his body ache. She didn't resist. Her lips met his, soft and familiar, and the world righted itself.

She was here. She had come back.

He exhaled against her mouth, his grip tightening as he kissed her, as if he could erase the past few months with touch alone, as if he could anchor himself in this moment and never let go.

But something was off.

The way she molded to him was not quite right. The way her fingers curled against his chest was too eager.

His stomach twisted. Then he smelled it.

Vanilla. Thick, cloying—too sweet to be real. His body locked up. Anne never wore vanilla. His pulse hammered, a sickening wave rolling through him. Rick staggered back, his breath coming in sharp, ragged bursts as nausea surged through him.

Louisa smiled. Slow. Serpentine. "Hello, Ricky."

Rick's breath came in ragged gasps, his mind spinning as he grasped for reality. "Where—" His voice cracked. He swallowed hard, forcing the words out. "Where is Anne?"

Louisa's gaze flickered, something dark dancing behind her eyes. "Out to dinner with Dad," she said, her voice velvety smooth. "But let's not talk about her."

Rick's blood ran cold. His entire body tensed, fight-or-flight kicking in too late.

Louisa took a slow step toward him, tilting her head. "You're shaking," she murmured. "You always did have a soft heart, didn't you?"

Rick's fists clenched. "I'm leaving," he ground out, turning back towards the way he had come from.

Yet, the moment he moved, his vision wavered. His stomach clenched. His limbs felt heavy.

The lemonade.

He barely had time to process it before his legs buckled beneath him.

Louisa sighed. "Honestly, Ricky," she murmured, stepping forward as he staggered. "You should have known better. Couldn't you tell us apart?"

His breath hitched, panic rising as he grabbed for the wrought-iron table, trying to steady himself. His fingers slipped. His knees hit the ground.

Louisa crouched beside him, brushing his damp hair from his forehead. "It's all right," she soothed, her voice lilting. "I'll take care of you now."

Rick tried to push her away. His arms barely moved as he reached for the table, his fingers gripping the wrought iron, his breath coming in ragged gasps.

Closer now, Louisa whispered in his ear. "That's it," she soothed. "Just let go."

His head lolled against her shoulder, his fingers twitching, grasping at nothing.

Anne. He had to find Anne.

But Louisa's touch was gentle, coaxing.

She shifted him, moving him with a practiced grace that sent ice through his veins. He tried to resist, to push away, but his body wouldn't cooperate. His limbs were unresponsive, sluggish.

Then—he felt it. Metal. Cold against his back. A faint creak. A shift in balance.

A wheelbarrow.

Louisa eased him down onto it, settling him carefully, her fingers smoothing his hair from his damp forehead as though she was tucking him into bed.

"There," she whispered. "That's better."

Rick's mind screamed at him to move, to fight, to do something—anything—but the weight pressing against his chest was too much to bear. His pulse pounded in his ears, his breath coming in slow, heavy drags.

The wheelbarrow lurched forward.

The gravel crunched beneath them, a sound that should have sent adrenaline spiking through him—that should have kept him tethered to wakefulness.

But the motion rocked him. Soothing. Dizzying. Pulling him under.

And then—

Rick's body lurched backward as Louisa shoved him, gravity pulling him down. He braced for the impact—stone, cold and unyielding—but instead, a thin mattress broke the fall, softening the impact.

The cellar.

She had thrown him down the stairs.

His body screamed in protest, but nothing moved. The drug still coursed through his veins, pressing down like dead weight. He couldn't even lift a hand, couldn't roll onto his side, couldn't do anything but listen as her footsteps echoed behind him.

She descended the stairs after him with the patience of someone who had all the time in the world. Her heels clicked against the stone, each step a cruel metronome.

Rick's pulse thundered in his ears.

A soft hum filled the silence. Louisa's fingers trailed over his shoulder as she reached him. "You're heavier than you look, Ricky," she mused. "Hope you didn't mind the crash landing."

She knelt beside him, laughing as if she'd said the funniest joke as she wrestled the mattress from under him and carried it across the room to a small twin-sized cot lined up against the wall. Finally, she returned and tugged him up with surprising ease. The pain in his ribs burned, his breath coming in sharp, uneven drags.

"Here you go," she soothed, helping him or rather dancing him across the room.

Rick's knees buckled several times, but she always caught him before he could collapse, leading him toward the cot.

His body sank back onto the thin mattress, too weak to resist. Then, there was the cold kiss of metal against his skin. His breath hitched. His fingers twitched, grasping for nothing.

Click.

The collar locked into place.

Panic surged, hot and suffocating. His pulse roared in his ears, his breaths coming in sharp, useless gasps as he clawed at the chain trailing from his throat.

Louisa stepped back, admiring her work. Then, without hesitation, she turned toward the door.

Rick tried to force his body to move, but he was still too weak.

She glanced over her shoulder, that infuriating smile never faltering. "Sweet dreams, Ricky."

The light clicked off, and darkness swallowed him whole.

Chapter 5

> Some wounds heal, while others rot. Some pain you learn to live with. I don't know where this will lead. I just know I'm not the same man I was yesterday. I don't think I ever will be again.
> —Rick's Journal

Rick's body ached. A deep, raw soreness pulsed beneath his skin, every breath a reminder of the fall. His whole body was raw and tender.

And yet, the worst pain wasn't physical. It was the collar. The weight of it. The way it sat snugly around his throat, a cruel mimicry of possession.

Louisa stood over him, arms folded, watching with a satisfied smirk. "You look uncomfortable, Ricky."

Rick gritted his teeth. The cot beneath him barely deserved the name—thin, lumpy, pressing painfully into his back. He longed to shift, to ease the pressure off his ribs, but any movement sent pain flaring, sharp and hot.

Louisa crouched beside him, her fingers brushing over his forearm. A featherlight touch that was both mocking and deliberate. Rick jerked away, pain flaring. He clenched his jaw, swallowing the grimace threatening to surface.

Still, Louisa caught the movement. "Still fighting?" She tilted her head, studying him like a puzzle she intended to solve.

Rick said nothing.

She reached for him again, her nails dragging over his skin with sickening familiarity. "You'll learn."

Rick clenched his fists, forcing his breath to steady. The chain rattled as he shifted, the sound bouncing off the stone walls.

Louisa's smile deepened. "I think you need time to adjust." She stood, stretching like a cat. "After all, change is hard."

She moved toward the kitchenette—a small sink, a hot plate, a compact fridge tucked against the far wall. Rick forced himself to take in the room again, searching for details he might have missed that could help him escape. The cellar wasn't large, but it was disturbingly functional.

Louisa had planned this. The realization settled like a weight in his stomach.

She hummed softly as she pulled something from the fridge. "You must be starving. Want something to eat?"

Rick kept his mouth shut.

Louisa sighed, shaking her head. "So stubborn." She pulled out a plate and carried it toward him, placing it on a small table near the cot. "You'll come around."

Rick's gaze flicked to the plate—simple food. Bread. Cheese. Some sliced fruit. His stomach twisted, a mix of hunger and something else.

Louisa sat beside him again on the edge of the cot. She was way too close. Her fingers skimmed his bruised wrist before sliding up his arm. "Do you feel that, Ricky?" she murmured, her voice a sick parody of intimacy.

Rick turned his face away, his breath tight in his chest. "I—" His voice cracked, useless.

He had no words. No way to explain the deep, aching humiliation clawing through his chest.

Louisa's fingers trailed lower, her nails scraping lightly over hypersensitive skin. "You're shaking," she observed, amusement laced in her tone.

Rick clenched his jaw. *Because of you.* He wanted to say it. Scream it. But his throat locked up, the words refusing to come.

Louisa hummed softly, her fingers trailing lower until they closed around him, firm and possessive.

Rick flinched, his entire body seizing as her nails scraped against bare, vulnerable skin.

"That's how I know you're ready for me," she whispered, her grip tightening.

Rick's stomach turned violently. The words barely registered before his body seized in panic, his limbs jerking in weak, sluggish protest.

No, no, no.

Louisa saw it. The exact moment he realized what she was about to do.

She smirked. "You didn't think I'd stop there, did you?"

Rick lurched, his shaking arms straining to shove her away, but she caught his wrists with ease. His strength was still gone. His body too weak, too disoriented, too drugged to fight her.

He felt her weight shift. The slow, unbearable slide of fabric. "Louisa, don't—!"

His voice broke completely as she straddled him, her nails digging into his chest to hold him down.

Rick gasped, his heart hammering against his ribs.

She was bare. And she was lining herself up with him.

"Please," he rasped, his voice shaking violently.

Louisa smiled. "This is how it's supposed to be," she whispered.

And then she sank down onto him.

Rick convulsed. His body arched involuntarily, his hands gripping the sheet so hard his knuckles went white. It was happening.

She was taking him. Stealing what he had kept for so long. His first time. His *only* time. The moment that was supposed to belong to his bride.

It was gone.

Louisa sighed softly, her nails scraping across his skin as she took her time, savoring every second.

Tears burned hot against his cheeks. His muscles strained, every part of him locked in resistance. But it didn't matter. The drugs and the hands on his skin were doing their job.

She leaned down, her breath warm against his ear, a twisted, satisfied purr in her voice. "See, Ricky?" she cooed, trailing her nails down his chest. "Your body doesn't lie. You want this."

A choked sob broke from his throat. He shook his head, his body trembling violently beneath her. "No," he rasped.

Louisa hummed in mock sympathy. "Oh, but you do. Look at you." Her nails scraped against his scalp, her fingers weaving into his tangled hair, yanking just enough to make him flinch. "You can cry all you want, but this?" Her free hand drifted lower, making him convulse with shame. "This tells me everything I need to know."

Rick's breath hitched, his whole body shaking as fresh humiliation crashed over him like a tidal wave. He wanted to fight, to shove her off, to do something. But the drugs and throbbing pain in his body made it impossible. He could barely move, his limbs heavy and useless, his body turned against him. Tears blurred his vision as he sucked in a shattered breath.

She laughed softly as her lips brushed his temple in a mockery of affection. "Poor Anne." She sighed dramatically, nails dragging over his skin like a predator savoring its meal. "She had no idea how easy you are to break."

Rick's breath hitched. *Anne.*

The name alone sent a fresh wave of pain crashing through him, deeper than the bruises, sharper than the chain biting into his neck.

She had been his everything. Anne was the future he built in his mind. The only arms he ever wanted to hold him. The only body he ever dreamed of claiming as his own.

And yet—she had been the one to leave him. The one who had tossed his love aside. The one who had sent the text.

Rick's stomach twisted violently.

Come to the back patio. Please.

He had read those words over and over, memorized them in the glow of his phone screen, clinging to them like a lifeline. Three months of silence, and then suddenly—Anne wanted to talk?

Except she hadn't. She had never reached out. Never wanted him here. Louisa had sent that text. Louisa had used Anne's number, Anne's voice, Anne's face.

The last scrap of hope he had clung to—the belief that Anne regretted walking away—wasn't even real.

Rick clenched his jaw, his vision burning. A broken sound tore from his throat. He wasn't sure if it was a sob or a curse. Maybe both.

Louisa smiled. "That's it," she murmured. "Just let go, Ricky."

He squeezed his eyes shut, his body shuddering beneath her. He tried to disappear. To slip away from his own skin. But there was nowhere to go. Nowhere to hide. Just the darkness pressing in. And Louisa's voice whispering in his ear—

Lies. Lies. Lies.

And then his body betrayed him.

When it was finally over, Rick lay motionless, his body wrecked, his soul hollowed out.

Louisa stretched like a satisfied cat, her fingers brushing over his heaving chest. "Tired already, Ricky?" she teased.

Rick turned his face away.

She giggled, pressing a kiss to his temple. "You're perfect," she murmured.

And then, just like that, she slipped off the cot, humming as she pulled the sheet back over him.

Rick curled into himself, his body still shaking. He could still feel her.

Chapter 6

> Survival isn't about strength. It's about endurance. About how
> much pain you can carry without breaking. But everyone breaks
> eventually. I just didn't think it would happen this fast.
> — Rick's Journal

The collar jerked. Rick sucked in a sharp breath as the chain yanked against his throat, snapping his head back slightly before slackening again. It was just enough to cruelly remind him he wasn't going anywhere. Every breath dragged fire through his ribs as Rick helplessly retreated to his cot, conscious he could not even reach the toilet without Louisa's permission.

Footsteps. Then the scent of vanilla.

Rick swallowed hard, the rawness in his throat making it feel like swallowing glass as he looked up to see his jailer.

Louisa stood over him, rolling the chain through her fingers, testing its weight. A slow, pleased smile spread across her lips. "Time to get cleaned up."

She dangled a key from the chain around her neck and slid it into the lock, releasing just enough slack for him to move.

Not far. Not enough to matter. Just enough to let him know she had the power.

Rick didn't move.

Louisa tilted her head toward the far corner of the room where a small stall, little more than a pipe and a drain stood beside the toilet. "Go on," she said. "The shower's waiting."

There were no comforts. No dignity.

"Well?" Louisa leaned against the wall, her arms crossed. "Would you rather stay filthy and wet your bed?"

Rick's jaw tightened.

She sighed, shaking her head as she reached into a basket at her feet and pulled out something dark and folded. Clothes.

Rick's body stiffened.

Louisa twirled the fabric between her fingers, smirking. "I was going to be nice. Give you these after you bathed. But maybe you don't deserve them yet."

Rick held her gaze, refusing to let her see the way cold air licked at his bare skin and the way humiliation sat heavy in his gut. Still, he didn't move.

Louisa studied him, then sighed, feigning disappointment. "Fine," she said, tossing the bundle back into the basket. "Stay naked, then."

Rick's stomach turned as she gestured toward the stall again.

"Shower," she commanded. "Now."

He didn't move. The click of metal made his breath stop. His eyes flicked to the far side of the cellar. A locked cabinet.

Slowly, deliberately, Louisa pulled out a taser. Sleek. Black. She turned it over in her palm, like it was nothing more than a casual accessory. With a flick of her thumb, electricity crackled.

Rick's pulse slammed against his ribs.

Louisa tilted her head, watching him struggle with the choice. Move, or she'd make him move.

Rick forced himself to stand. His legs trembled beneath him, the pain from his prior fall rippling up his spine. He took a slow, measured step forward. The stone was cold under his bare feet. He reached the stall and hesitated.

Louisa smiled. She reached past him, turned the knob. Water burst from the showerhead. Freezing. Rick flinched, his back hitting the stone.

Louisa laughed, light and teasing. "Don't be dramatic. You'll get used to it." Then she stepped closer.

Rick's breath hitched.

Her fingers skimmed over his ribs, down his stomach, pausing at his hip. Too close. Louisa's fingers hovered just below his waist, where a waistband should have been. Of course, he had nothing—because she had taken it. Her fingers drifted lower, slow, taunting.

"Don't want to come out and play?" she asked, her voice silky with amusement. "I liked you better last night." A pause. Then, a whisper near his ear. "You were so eager to please."

His chest tightened. He couldn't breathe.

She leaned in. And for a split second—he saw Anne.

The damp walls faded. The cold vanished. Anne's soft blonde curls, delicate smile, and gentle hands. Everything safe. Everything that was supposed to be his future. His breath caught, his body frozen in place, desperate for it to be real. His body responded before his mind. Heat pooled low in his stomach, his pulse kicking up.

Then she smiled, and it wasn't Anne's smile at all. Rick's breath choked out of him.

Louisa. The monster.

His body had betrayed him. Horror flooded his veins. A sick, nauseating shame.

Anne. He had only ever dreamed of her.

And now, his body had responded to Louisa. He wanted to rip his own skin off.

God, Anne, I'm sorry.

Rick staggered back. His heel caught the drain.

Suddenly—his balance was gone. He hit the floor hard. Ice-cold water cascaded over him, stealing his breath, his control, his strength.

Louisa crouched beside him, her hand slipping into his damp hair, gripping tight. "Are you crying?" she asked, delighted.

Rick clenched his jaw, forcing down the panic rising in his chest. But the walls were too close. The collar too tight. His mind screamed, trapped between past and present.

Hadn't Walter said Anne had taken over Louisa's treehouse? Rick squeezed his eyes shut. Maybe she'd take this from her too. Maybe she'd find him.

God, help me.

The words weren't spoken. They weren't even fully formed. They lived in the hollow space between his heartbeat and his breaking point.

He didn't expect an answer. Didn't even know if God was listening. But he reached for Him, anyway.

Then—he broke. A sob tore through him, his body curling inward, trembling against the stone. It was too much.

Louisa hummed, brushing her thumb over his cheek, catching the tears before they could fall. "There it is," she murmured. "That's what I wanted to see."

Rick shut his eyes, pressing his forehead against the wet floor.

Louisa stood, drying her hands on a towel. Then, with a satisfied little hum, she picked up the basket with the clothes, turned, and walked toward the stairs. "I'll bring dinner later," she called over her shoulder.

The lock slid into place.

Rick stayed curled on the shower floor, his entire body shaking, his sobs muffled against the stone. The collar around his throat felt tighter. The walls felt smaller.

Chapter 7

> I used to believe in justice. That the innocent were protected. That the strong defended the weak. But in this place, there is no justice. Only power. And she has it all.
> – Rick's Journal

Time didn't exist here. Only control. The damp chill of the cellar clung to Rick's skin, burrowing deep into his muscles, curling around his bones like a parasite. The weight of the chain at his throat was heavier today, or maybe that was just his body sinking further into exhaustion.

There were no windows low enough to reach. Only the stone walls pressing in, the suffocating darkness reminding him that this place—this prison—was the only world that existed now.

Some days, she was merciful. A few extra inches of slack. A mockery of freedom. Enough to let him sit at the table, to wash the filth from his skin, to feel like something more than a caged animal. Perhaps she'd allow him to have a piece of fruit or a cup of coffee.

Other days, the chain was tight. Too tight. His body curled in on itself, his lungs straining against the weight at his throat. A leash. One she held. One she'd never let go of.

The lock rattled. Rick's entire body stiffened.

The cellar door groaned open, the sound crawling down the stone walls. Then he heard her heels on the stairs. Slow. Measured. Each deliberate step dragging him deeper into the nightmare.

Louisa.

She hummed as she descended, a soft, off-key tune that made his skin crawl. A tray balanced in one hand, her other lightly clutching the hem of her wrap dress, the fabric swaying with calculated ease.

She was smiling. Wide. Pleased. Predatory.

Rick sat up slowly, ignoring the way the chain at his throat tugged with the movement.

Louisa perched on the edge of the cot as she lifted a glass of juice, swirling the liquid with idle amusement before offering it to him. "Drink," she said sweetly, her tone deceptively light. "I made this just for you."

Rick's jaw tightened. Vanilla. His stomach turned. Every time he swallowed her juice, heat pooled in his veins, his body betrayed him, and he had been powerless to stop her.

His fingers twitched at his side. Just barely. A flicker of resistance. An instinctive reach toward something. Toward nothing.

Louisa saw it. Her smile faltered for a half-second before she recovered. Tilting her head, she watched him closely. "Ricky." The name slithered from her lips, soft and sickly sweet, like poison wrapped in honey.

Rick's stomach twisted. He hated that name. Hated the way she used it, like he was a child, something small and powerless. Like he belonged to her. His jaw locked, his breath coming sharp and uneven. "My name is Rick," he bit out, his voice low, raw.

Louisa smiled, tilting her head, her green eyes gleaming in the dim light. "No, Ricky," she murmured, dragging it out, savoring it. "You'll always be my Ricky."

Rick's hands curled into fists, nails biting into his palms. He would rather die than let her own him.

The taser crackled. Electricity snapped through the air like a warning shot. A promise. Louisa's fingers tapped against the glass, her smile as casual as ever. "Don't make me force you."

Rick stiffened. His breath hitched. That sound. That sickening, electric crack. Slowly, reluctantly, he took the glass. The liquid inside shimmered faintly, its color unnaturally vibrant. Poison. But not the kind that would kill him. That would have been a mercy. He lifted it to his lips, the weight of her gaze pressing down on him like a vise.

"That's it," Louisa purred. Her eyes gleamed as he swallowed. "Good boy."

Rick lowered the glass, his stomach churning. The thick sweetness clung to his throat like syrup. He wanted to gag.

Louisa sighed, stretching with the slow satisfaction of someone who had just completed a well-executed experiment.

Later, as she smoothed a hand down her dress and started picking up her tray, Rick glimpsed himself in the polished metal of the mini-fridge. He barely recognized the man staring back. Hollowed-out eyes. Bruises on his throat from the collar. The thin sheen of sweat on his skin. The way his hands trembled, despite his best efforts to stop them.

For a moment, he thought of Anne. Would she recognize him now?

Louisa's voice slithered in. "Do you want anything, Ricky?"

Rick didn't look at her. Didn't answer right away. Only stared at the ghost of himself in the reflection. "Freedom," he finally said.

She laughed. Delighted. "Try again."

Rick swallowed. "A Bible."

Something flickered across Louisa's face. Something unreadable. Then there was her trademark smirk. "I'll think about it." She turned. The lock clicked.

Rick sat in silence. His breath shallow. His body spent. His hands still shaking. He stared at his reflection. And for the first time since waking up in this nightmare, he wasn't sure if he was looking at himself anymore.

Chapter 8

> I know God hears me. I know He sees. But I don't understand why
> He's letting this happen. I keep praying for deliverance, but maybe
> I should be praying for endurance instead.
> – Rick's Journal

The Bible in Louisa's hands looked untouched. Pristine. Untainted. Everything he wasn't. Its leather cover gleamed under the dim cellar light, smooth and unbroken. Unlike him. Rick stared at it, his breath shallow, his body already tight with dread. He couldn't remember the last time he held a Bible. He wasn't even sure what day of the week it was anymore.

Louisa smiled, tilting her head as she studied him. "It's for you, Ricky," she murmured, her voice gentle, almost reverent.

His throat closed.

"Go on," she urged, extending it toward him. "Take it."

Rick's fingers twitched, but before he could reach for it, her fingers curled around his wrist, squeezing just enough to remind him who was in control. "No," she murmured, flipping the pages herself, her nails grazing the thin paper with slow, deliberate care.

She turned one page. Then another. A pause.

"This one," she decided, smiling as if the choice had been divine. "First Corinthians Thirteen. Read it aloud for me, Ricky."

Rick took a deep breath and began. "Love is patient and kind—"

Louisa's fingers trailed down his arm, featherlight, lingering.

"It does not envy or boast; it is not arrogant or rude—"

She laughed softly, shaking her head. "Not rude?" she mocked, her voice dipping into something softer, almost wounded. "But you're so cold to me, Ricky. You barely speak unless I make you." She sighed, trailing a finger down his forearm, her nails barely scraping the skin. "Where's the kindness?"

Rick's knuckles whitened on the pages. "It does not insist on its own way; it is not irritable or resentful—"

Louisa clicked her tongue, nails dragging lightly down his ribs. "But you *are* resentful, aren't you?" she purred, leaning in, her

41

breath brushing his jaw. "That's why you glare at me like a trapped little animal."

Rick's stomach clenched. "—Do I?" he whispered.

A flicker of something flashed across Louisa's face. Was it amusement? Perhaps annoyance?

She recovered quickly. "Oh, I'm sorry," Louisa smirked, tilting her head in mock innocence. "Do continue. Please."

Rick's fingers tightened on the Bible. "It does not rejoice at wrongdoing, but rejoices with the truth—"

Louisa tilted his chin up, her grip just firm enough to keep him from looking away. "The truth is, Ricky," she breathed, her voice a velvet trap, "you belong to me."

Rick's chest tightened. The words lodged in his throat. "Do I?"

This time, Louisa didn't laugh. A pause. A beat too long. Then—her smile widened. "Read it again," she whispered, her lips ghosting over his, hovering just close enough to make him flinch.

Later, after she had gone, Rick lay staring at the ceiling, his body cold, his mind running in loops he couldn't escape. The Bible sat beside him, untouched. For a long time, he didn't move. Then, almost against his will, a memory surfaced.

He could envision himself and his best friend Fitz Darcy sitting in their fifth-grade Sunday-School classroom at Croft Beach Community Church as if it were yesterday instead of over ten years ago. As often happened when the senior pastor's wife taught Sunday school, their minds had wandered, as was the case when she was droning on and reading 1 Corinthians 13 aloud.

Darcy, bored out of his mind, had leaned over and whispered, "Watch this."

Rick barely had time to process before Darcy rushed forward planting a fake plastic spider into the open pages of Mrs. Bertram's Bible as she took a second to answer a question from the hall monitor.

Rick had clamped a hand over his mouth, his eyes wide as Mrs. Bertram returned to her podium and turned the page—and screamed. The class erupted in chaos, kids shrieking, some laughing, while Mrs. Bertram threw her Bible into the air like it was possessed.

Darcy, straight-faced, had said, "I thought love is patient, ma'am."

Rick had lost it.

The rest of Sunday School was spent writing Bible verses as punishment. Fifty times each. Darcy had grumbled, muttering about cruel and unusual punishment, while Rick had just kept laughing under his breath. It was so stupid. So Darcy.

And yet—that moment came back to him as he stared down at the Scriptures. He would give anything to be back in that classroom writing lines for Mrs. Bertram instead of here in Louisa's domain as she held God's Word over his head like a weapon.

He didn't want to touch the Bible. Didn't want to read. Heck, he was sorely tempted to rip 1 Corinthians out of the Bible so Louisa couldn't use it against him again. But he wanted to believe that God still saw him and that patience, kindness, and truth still existed, even here.

Rick let out a slow, shuddering breath. The cellar was silent. But in his mind—he could still hear Mrs. Bertram screaming and Darcy's deadpan response. For the first time in weeks, a ghost of a smile flickered across Rick's lips. Just for a moment.

Then—it was gone.

Chapter 9

> God, I don't understand. If You see me, if You hear me—why am
> I still here? I know You don't abandon Your children, but I feel
> forsaken. I feel lost. Give me strength. Give me something to hold
> on to. Because I don't know how much longer I can do this.
> – Rick's Journal

The flickering light above him cast uneven shadows, bending the walls in ways that made the room feel even smaller and more confining. Rick sat hunched on the edge of the cot, his head bowed, his body curled inward, like it was trying to disappear. His fingers dug into his knees, nails pressing deep into bruised skin, grounding himself in the only pain he could control. The collar was a steady, suffocating weight, the chain cold where it draped against his bare chest.

The room stank of damp concrete, sweat, and something artificial. Her perfume had settled into the air, into his skin, into everything. He could taste it when he breathed. Thick. Cloying. There was no escaping it.

His mind wandered, desperate for something clean, something untouched. *Anne.* A memory crept in unbidden, bright and golden, slicing through the dark like something sacred. *Halloween.*

Anne had looped her arm through his, her touch light against his side, like she belonged there. The scent of cinnamon and vanilla had clung to her sweater that night, warmth against the crisp October air.

"I bet you won't guess what I am," she had teased, her nose scrunching slightly as she grinned up at him. The breeze had caught her hair, sending a strand across her cheek, and he had reached out instinctively, tucking it behind her ear.

"A detective?" he had guessed, smirking as she twirled in her long coat.

She had rolled her eyes dramatically. "No, Rick. A spy. A woman of mystery." She had leaned in then, close enough that he could smell cinnamon and vanilla on her breath. "Or maybe just someone keeping an eye on you."

A shadow moved on the stairs. His gaze lifted slowly, the past bleeding into the present. The memory ripped apart, vanishing like breath on glass.

The scent was wrong. Too sharp. Too artificial. Too much like Louisa. His stomach twisted. Not Anne. Never Anne.

Louisa smiled as she reached the bottom of the stairs, a bundle of neatly folded fabric in one hand, a glass of juice in the other. "Happy Halloween, Ricky," she sang, her voice too bright, masking something darker beneath it.

Rick stayed silent, his muscles stiff, his eyes tracking her every movement.

Louisa pouted. "Oh, don't be such a spoilsport. I've gone through so much trouble to make tonight special."

She unwrapped the bundle and held it up with a flourish— a black-and-white satin dress, lace trimmed, with thigh-high stockings and high heeled boots.

Rick's stomach turned. "You've got to be kidding me," he muttered, the words bitter in his throat.

Louisa beamed, her fingers smoothing over the lace, slow and deliberate, like she was savoring the moment. "Oh, I'm very serious," she said, holding the maid's outfit against her chest as if imagining him in it. "You've been begging for something to wear, haven't you? Isn't this just perfect? My good little houseguest deserves something—fitting."

Rick's fists clenched. "No."

Her smile didn't falter, but her eyes sharpened. She dropped the garment on the chair and moved toward the chest in the corner, unlocking it with deliberate slowness.

Rick's breath hitched as she pulled out the belt.

"Do you really want to make this difficult?" she asked softly, running her fingers over the length of leather. The threat hung in the air, suffocating.

His pulse pounded in his ears. His body remembered the last time. The sting. The welts. The shame. The pain that lingered for days. He swallowed hard, his hands shaking as he stood up and reached for the outfit.

Louisa's smile widened, victorious. "There's my good boy." She picked up the juice, swishing the liquid in the glass before holding it out to him. "But first let's not forget your treat."

Rick's jaw tightened.

"Don't make me force you." Her nails tapped against the glass—soft, rhythmic, menacing.

His fingers curled around the glass. He swallowed the juice in three quick gulps, his stomach twisting even before the warmth started spreading through his veins.

Louisa smirked, watching him closely. "Good boy."

The second he set the glass down, she tugged him closer with a pull of his chain. Rick staggered, his knees weaker than they should have been. He hated the way Louisa's eyes lit up, like she noticed.

Louisa's voice dipped into mock sympathy. "You poor thing. That's what happens when you don't take care of yourself."

She held up the dress, her smile widening as she watched realization dawn in his eyes. Rick's stomach turned. It was designed to be laced up the back—which meant she would have to touch him. His fists clenched, but he forced himself to move. The collar stayed tight against his throat, the chain rattling softly as he pulled his arms through the puffed sleeves.

"That's right, Ricky," Louisa cooed, stepping behind him. "Let's get you all laced up nice and snug." Her fingers slid along his spine, deliberately slow as she tightened the ribbons. Each tug cinched the fabric closer, molding it against his skin. "Perfect." Louisa's breath was warm at his ear, her hands lingering far too long. "My sweet little maid."

Rick's jaw locked, his breath shallow. The fabric scratched at his thighs, the lace at his collarbone itching like a noose. The chain was still there, heavy and unrelenting.

He hadn't gained an inch of freedom. Just a new humiliation.

Chapter 10

> Anne was supposed to be the mother of my children, and we were
> supposed to build a home filled with love, with light, and with
> everything I never had growing up. But now?
> – Rick's Journal

Louisa's fingers drifted to her stomach, brushing against the fabric in a slow, absent motion. Rick's breath stilled. She didn't realize she had done it.

Her expression flickered for a second into something soft and maternal, and then, like a snapped wire she tried to cover it. "Our little one is growing so quickly."

Rick's pulse stopped. The words slithered into his mind, wrong, impossible, unreal.

"You're going to be a father."

His stomach lurched. The floor beneath him tilted. "You're lying," he choked out, mentally begging her to deny it as a mad joke.

Louisa tilted her head, amusement flickering in her green eyes. "Am I?"

Rick's fists clenched, his knuckles going white. He shook his head, hard, rejecting it, rejecting her. "No. No, this—this isn't real. You're just saying this to—"

"To what, Ricky?" Louisa cooed, her voice syrupy with mock concern. "To keep you here? To make you mine?" Her smirk widened. "I didn't need a baby to do that. You already belong to me."

Rick yanked fiercely at the chain, fury and revulsion crashing over him in waves. "I don't belong to you!"

Louisa laughed, soft and knowing. "Oh, Ricky," she sighed, shaking her head. "Still so stubborn. But you'll see soon enough. Our little one—" she emphasized it, savoring his reaction "—is proof of how connected we are. Forever."

Rick's lungs felt too tight. His mind reeled, clawing for any escape from this reality. "Does Anne know?" he rasped, his voice barely more than a whisper.

Louisa's smile widened. "It's just you and me now, Ricky," she murmured, pressing closer. Her breath ghosted against his skin, warm and intimate. "Our little family. That's all that matters."

Rick's stomach twisted violently. He shut his eyes. *This can't be happening.* His breath came sharp, his heart hammering against his ribs. *Think, Rick. Find a way to cut through her madness.* He forced the words out. "What about your career?"

Louisa's fingers paused.

He pressed forward. "You're an engineer, Louisa. You always said you were highly sought after. You could work anywhere." He swallowed, grasping at straws. "Won't this—won't I—ruin that?"

For a split second, something flickered in her gaze. A crack in the perfect mask. Then, just as quickly, it was gone.

Louisa tilted her head, amusement curving her lips. "Oh, Ricky." She let out a breathy laugh. "Don't you get it yet?"

Rick's pulse thundered.

Her eyes gleamed, green and endless. "I chose this," she whispered. "I chose you." She let her fingers trail down his chest, savoring the way he flinched. "We have my trust fund, and honestly, careers come and go. Jobs are just—titles. But this?" Her nails pressed in, sharp against his skin. "This is real."

Rick fought the urge to vomit. She was insane. And worse—she believed everything she said.

Louisa's smile turned saccharine. "Isn't it funny? Walter always wanted Anne to give him a grandchild. A proper heir." She trailed a finger along her stomach. "Remember his disappointment when she refused to name her firstborn after our mother?"

Rick's entire body stiffened.

Louisa's smirk widened. "But don't worry, Ricky," she purred. "I'll make sure our baby has the name she didn't want to give a child."

His stomach twisted. *No. God, no.*

Anne had never wanted children in the next five years—had been so sure that marriage was enough, that she and Rick could be happy just the two of them. And now—

This was deliberate.

Louisa's nails grazed his collarbone, and he wrenched away, nausea rising fast and sharp. She giggled. "Oh, Ricky. You make this too easy."

The door slammed shut behind her.

Rick slumped forward, his breath ragged, his entire body trembling with a sickness that had nothing to do with the juice she always made him drink. The red light in the ceiling flickered, capturing the moment he fell apart for posterity.

Rick closed his eyes. "Give me strength, Lord."

Chapter 11

> Christmas is supposed to be about hope. About light in the
> darkness. But there's no light here. Just shadows. Just her. Still—I
> remember. I remember last year. I remember Anne. I remember
> laughter. And if I can remember that, maybe I haven't lost
> everything.
> – Rick's Journal

If Louisa was to be believed, today was Christmas Eve. A
day that was supposed to be one of joy, warmth, and hope. But
here, in this place, it was just another day of chains.

A sliver of winter sunlight filtered through the grime-
covered window far above him—a taunting whisper of the world
beyond. A world where Christmas still meant something. A
memory surfaced, bright and golden, slicing through the dark like
something sacred. Last Christmas.

Darcy's house had been a perfect, chaotic mess of pine
garlands, twinkling lights, and far too many scented candles. Anne
had laughed at the sheer number of them, rolling her eyes as Darcy
defended himself.

"A home should smell like the holidays," he'd declared,
waving a candle under Rick's nose.

"Cinnamon, fir, and something vaguely overpriced from
the mall," Rick had teased.

Darcy had smirked, unimpressed. "First of all, peasant, this
is holiday luxury. Second, if we don't commit fully to the festive
aesthetic, what do we have left? Subtlety? Taste? Please."

Anne had nearly choked on her cider, laughing. And
Rick—God, he'd laughed too. Easy. Free.

Anne had been so beautiful in the firelight, her eyes
crinkling at the corners as she shook her head at Darcy. "You're
impossible."

"I am," Darcy had agreed solemnly. "And yet, I am a
generous host. Mistletoe is over there, by the way, in case you two
feel the need to stop denying yourselves and just kiss already."

Rick had kissed her later that night. Not under mistletoe,
not with anyone watching. Just the two of them, alone beneath the
glow of the Christmas tree, love in every quiet breath.

The memory ripped apart, vanishing like breath on glass as Louisa's scent wafted down the stairs towards him. His stomach twisted. Not Anne. Never Anne.

"Merry almost Christmas, Ricky," she sang, her voice too bright, too sweet, a mockery of real joy. She held a small, wrapped box in her hands.

Rick didn't move. Her gifts were never gifts. They were just another way to prove he belonged to her.

"Aren't you curious?" she teased, setting the box down with a flourish. "Aren't you going to thank me?"

Rick's pulse hammered. Safer to play along. He forced himself to walk to the table. The wrapping paper was grotesquely cheerful—red and green with cartoon snowflakes, a parody of Christmas. His hands trembled as he tore through it. Inside was a leather-bound journal and a box of colored pencils. He stared, his mind stalling.

"I thought you could use something to occupy your time," Louisa said, feigning sweetness. "Write, draw—whatever your little heart desires. Consider it my way of showing appreciation."

Rick's lips twitched—the ghost of something bitter. Appreciation? For what? For surviving her? "Thanks," he muttered, the word brittle, robotic.

Louisa beamed. "There's more," she said, pulling a small envelope from her bag. She handed it to him.

His stomach coiled as he opened it. Black-and-white ultrasound pictures. His breath stopped.

Louisa smiled, pressing a hand against her stomach. "Our little girl."

Rick couldn't breathe. The world swayed. A girl. His throat was sandpaper. "A girl."

Louisa nodded, pleased. "I've been thinking about names." She stepped closer, brushing against him like they were co-conspirators instead of captor and captive. "What do you think of Lily?" she whispered, watching him carefully.

Lily. Rick's stomach clenched violently. Rick's hands curled into fists. "Lily's—a nice name," he said, hollow, knowing his opinion didn't matter.

Louisa smiled, triumphant. "I knew you'd agree," she said lightly. "You're finally starting to see things my way."

Rick shut his eyes. *God, help me.*

Louisa sighed dramatically and sprawled out on the cot, extending one foot toward him. "My feet are killing me."

Rick's stomach twisted, his hands trembling as he knelt before her. Obedience was safer.

Louisa sighed, content. "This is nice," she mused. "Just the two of us, planning our future. Our family."

Rick said nothing.

An hour later, he sat on the cot, the journal in his lap. A blank page. A choice. His fingers trembled as he picked up the pencil.

And then—he wrote.

Chapter 12

> There's no one left to look for me. No one left to wonder what happened to me. And Louisa knows it. She's winning. And I don't know how much longer I can hold on.
> - Rick's Journal

The sharp creak of the cellar door jolted Rick awake. His body tensed instinctively, muscles stiff from cold and disuse.

Louisa's boots clicked against the stone steps, each step deliberate, like she was savoring the fear she could smell off him. "Happy New Year, Ricky," she chimed, her voice ringing with false cheer. She carried a tray of food, a smirk sharp as glass.

Rick kept his eyes fixed on the floor. Silence was safer.

Louisa placed the tray down with exaggerated care, then perched on the edge of the cot, her fingers brushing his shoulder— a mockery of tenderness. "You're so quiet today."

Rick said nothing, his fingers curling into fists.

Louisa sighed, almost theatrically. "Don't you want to hear what's been happening upstairs?"

He didn't but she told him anyway.

"Father had a stroke."

Rick's head jerked up, his eyes widening. She said it like she was discussing the weather.

"Nearly ruined Christmas for the rest of us, of course."

Rick's throat clenched. Walter Elliot was a cruel man, cold and dismissive, but even he hadn't deserved to be discarded like this.

"Anne and I had to put him in a convalescent home. She fought it at first, of course—always the little martyr—but really, what choice did she have? He can't manage on his own anymore, and she's too busy in Boston."

Rick exhaled slowly, his hands trembling at the mention of Anne. He could picture it—her guilt, her sense of duty, the weight of it all pressing on her fragile shoulders. She would have wrestled with the decision, agonized over it, likely visited daily despite everything.

Louisa watched him closely, her lips curling. She had saved the worst for last. "Oh, Ricky. You're going to love this."

Rick went still. He knew that tone. It meant she was about to rip out something vital and watch him bleed.

"Anne brought someone home for Christmas."

His stomach turned.

"Peter," Louisa continued, watching him like a cat with a dying mouse. "He's a doctor. Handsome, charming, perfect. Tom and I even took them out on a double date over the holidays—can you imagine? Anne and Peter, laughing over dinner, sipping wine, looking so perfect together."

Rick's fists clenched. His breath burned in his chest as he forced out, "And what did they think of us?" His voice was sharp, edged with fury. "Of you playing the doting mother-to-be while shackling me down here?"

Louisa's smirk didn't falter. If anything, it deepened. She leaned in, her eyes gleaming. "Oh, Ricky," she purred, tilting her head, "do you really think they cared? I played my part beautifully. They see what I want them to see. A glowing mother, a woman moving forward. And Anne?" She sighed dramatically. "She was too busy being swept off her feet by Peter to ask any real questions."

Rick's stomach churned, his mind racing with fury. "And Tom Musgrove?" His voice was sharp, biting. "He just sat there, drinking his wine, perfectly fine with the fact that you're carrying another man's child?"

Louisa chuckled, shaking her head. "Oh, you are adorable when you get all possessive," she taunted. "Tom knows better than to ask too many questions. He assumes—like everyone else—that the father ran off and that I was left to handle things on my own. Poor, abandoned Louisa, carrying on so bravely." Her eyes flickered with something wicked. "Besides, what does it matter? I always get what I want. And Tom? He's hardly the type to dwell on morality."

Rick's stomach twisted violently. Every word out of her mouth was like a knife, cutting deeper, carving out what little hope he had left.

She leaned in, her lips grazing his ear, savoring his torment. "Face it, Ricky. She's not thinking about you anymore."

The words hit like a fist to the ribs. Rick's breath came shallow, uneven.

"Does it hurt?" Louisa whispered, leaning in, lips grazing his jaw. "They looked so happy together. Laughing, holding hands. He's going to propose soon, I just know it. Can't you just picture Anne as a doctor's wife?"

Rick's whole body locked up. A doctor's wife. Anne was gone. Truly, completely, gone. It shouldn't have hurt this much. She had made her choice. She had left.

But it felt like she was slipping away all over again, her image dissolving, her voice fading. And Louisa knew it. She saw the moment he broke.

Her hands gripped his shoulders, forcing him to meet her gaze. "You were saving yourself for her, weren't you?" she murmured, voice thick with mockery. Her fingers trailed down his chest, lower.

Rick's breath hitched.

"But she doesn't even remember you," Louisa whispered. Her nails bit into his skin. "And you—You're mine."

Rick shook violently, his whole body a cage of silent screams. His eyes burned, his fists clenched, his breath shattered. "Stop," he choked out, voice raw.

Louisa's smile widened. "Stop what?" she purred. "Stop telling you the truth? Or stop reminding you that you belong to me?"

Rick squeezed his eyes shut. "Please—just stop."

Louisa sighed, almost lovingly. "Oh, Ricky." Her laughter was soft. Cruel. "Beg all you want. It won't change a thing."

Tears spilled down Rick's cheeks, his sobs raw and guttural as she continued. He didn't know if he was begging her to stop taunting him with Anne's new life—or to stop what came after. He only knew he wanted it all to end.

When it was over, Louisa stood, smoothing her dress.

Rick lay curled on the cot, his body wrecked, his mind screaming, as Louisa brushed his hair back, her touch almost gentle. "You'll thank me one day," she murmured.

Rick felt sick.

Louisa retrieved a small metal file and clippers from her bag. Her smile tightened. "Let's take care of those nails, shall we?"

Rick froze. His hands curled instinctively into fists.

Louisa clicked her tongue. "Don't make this difficult, Ricky. I've noticed how often you dig your nails into your palms. It's bad for you."

She pried one hand open, her grip firm, unyielding. The final humiliation. The final act of ownership. Her movements were clinical but cruel, stripping him of another small autonomy. He couldn't even cut his own nails anymore. The realization hit like a floodgate breaking. His breath stuttered. His body shook. And then, Rick sobbed. Not the silent, shuddering cries he had learned to swallow. Not the muffled gasps of pain he had long since mastered. This was deeper. Raw. Helpless. A lifetime of grief. A lifetime of loss. All of it poured out of him, shaking his chest, cracking something inside him that could never be put back together.

Louisa didn't mock him this time. She just smiled. "There," she murmured, brushing a stray tear from his cheek. "Doesn't that feel better?"

Rick didn't answer. Didn't move. Didn't breathe. He just let her win.

At the base of the stairs, she turned back, smirk firmly in place. "Happy New Year, Ricky," she sang. "Here's to another wonderful year together."

The door slammed shut. Rick sat frozen.

Something inside him snapped. He clawed at the maid's costume Louisa had forced him to wear, ripping the lace and frills with shaking hands. Piece by piece, he destroyed it. The fabric tore easily, scattering across the floor like ashes as he tore at the laces of the boots, tossing them as far as possible against the wall. Rick slumped forward naked, his forehead pressing against the cold, unyielding stone.

This time, there were no prayers. No whispered pleas for deliverance. Only silence.

Chapter 13

> There's nothing left of the man I was. Nothing left to fight with. I
> don't pray for rescue anymore. I don't pray for strength. I just pray
> that whatever is left of me won't vanish completely.
> – Rick's Journal

The shredded remnants of the maid's outfit Louisa had
forced him to wear had never been replaced, leaving him
completely exposed to the cellar's relentless cold.

Nine months. Nine months of this nightmare. Rick traced
faint cracks in the ceiling with his eyes, wondering what Louisa
thought as she watched her security camera feed of him falling
apart in the cellar day after day.

It was Valentine's Day—or so Louisa had gleefully
informed him earlier. That morning, she had descended the stairs
with an almost childlike excitement, carrying a tray of food and
humming an off-key love song. Rick hadn't reacted, too cold and
numb to muster any response.

Now, as evening set in, the faint flicker of candlelight drew
his attention to the small table in the corner. Louisa had arranged
red and white candles there, their glow casting a cruel mockery of
warmth. It was a scene that might have once seemed romantic
when he had choices, back when he could have spent Valentine's
Day with Anne.

Anne. Her name brought a sharp, aching pang to his chest.
He thought of last Valentine's Day: a simple yet perfect evening
walking along the beach, sharing her favorite Italian takeout. Later,
Darcy had joined them, teasing Rick about his overly sentimental
streak. They had laughed until their sides hurt, the sound blending
seamlessly with the crash of ocean waves.

Darcy. If anyone would have looked for him, it would have
been Darcy. But nine months was long enough to accept the truth.
No one was looking. No one even knew where to look.

Anne was gone. Louisa had relished showing him a photo
of her with Peter, her new husband of just days. Walter was gone
too, locked away in a convalescent home, no longer an obstacle to
Louisa's desires. And Darcy had probably stopped searching
months ago. The world had moved on without him.

The sound of footsteps broke through his thoughts, dragging him back to the present. He didn't need to look up to know who it was. He could feel her presence. The weight of Louisa's existence was suffocating and inescapable.

"Happy Valentine's Day, Ricky," Louisa cooed as she descended the stairs, her voice syrupy and saccharine.

Rick kept his gaze fixed on the floor.

"Oh, don't be so cold," she teased, her laughter laced with malice. "I've gone to so much trouble to make tonight special for us." She gestured toward the table, her smile widening as she took in the flickering candlelight and the untouched plate of food she had placed there earlier. "Isn't it romantic?"

Rick finally lifted his head, his eyes narrowing. "What's there to celebrate?" he asked, his voice low and hollow.

Louisa tilted her head, her smile faltering for a moment before returning, sharper than before. "Our family," she said simply. "Our love. In a month, our little girl will be here. That's worth celebrating, isn't it?"

Rick's chest tightened. The baby. He hated that he felt anything for the child growing inside her. She was innocent in all of this, yet her existence was a constant reminder of everything Louisa had stolen from him.

Louisa moved closer, setting down a small basin and towel she had carried with her. She perched on the cot beside him, her hand resting possessively on his shoulder. "You're looking so— unkempt," she said lightly, brushing her fingers across his chest. "We'll fix that tonight."

Rick's stomach twisted as she pulled out a razor and shaving cream from her bag.

"No," he said sharply, his voice trembling. "You don't need to do that. I'll take care of it."

Louisa's laughter rang out, cold and mocking. "Oh, Ricky," she said, tilting her head. "You really think I'd trust you with a razor? No, no. This is my job."

Before Rick could protest further, Louisa shoved him back against the cot. She dipped a cloth into the basin and pressed it against his chest, the warmth of the water a jarring contrast to the icy air.

"You've always wanted to be a protector, haven't you?"
she murmured, tilting her head as if studying him. "A strong man.
A husband. A father."

The razor repeatedly glided over his skin, stripping away
the last physical markers of who he once was.

"But you don't look like a father now, do you?" she
mused, her fingers trailing over his freshly shaved chest before
reaching for his legs.

Rick shook violently, bile rising in his throat.

"You don't even look like a man anymore."

Louisa sighed contentedly, stroking his bare legs. "So
much better this way."

Rick turned his face away, his jaw tight as silent tears
spilled down his cheeks.

"Don't sulk," Louisa said, her tone sickeningly sweet.
"You should thank me. I've done you a favor." She stood,
adjusting her robe, then turned back to the table. "Oh," she said, as
if remembering something, and pulled out a small, carefully
wrapped package from the deep pocket. "I almost forgot your
Valentine's gift."

She set it on the cot beside him. Rick didn't move.

"Go on," she urged, eyes gleaming. "Open it."

Rick swallowed hard. His hands shook violently as he
unwrapped the paper. A tiny onesie looked up at him, its soft white
fabric unassuming except for the words scrawled across the front
in delicate pink cursive.

Daddy's Girl.

A small pink card was nestled inside the package as well.
Rick turned it over, his stomach twisting at the sight of Louisa's
neat handwriting.

'Love makes slaves of us all, Ricky. But isn't it beautiful?
Forever yours, Louisa.'

His hands trembled, his breath breaking apart in his throat.

Daddy's Girl.

The words blurred, twisting, taunting. The letters might as
well have been chains. His hands shook harder, his breath coming
in short gasps. *She's winning.* A choked sound scraped from his
chest—half a sob, half a laugh, brittle and broken. His hands
clenched the fabric as a memory surfaced.

"Rick, my man, you're about to witness romance in its purest form," Darcy had declared.

Rick had looked up from his coffee warily. "What did you do?"

Darcy had leaned back in the café booth, zero regrets written all over his smug face. "Oh, nothing too dramatic," he said airily. "I just might have sent Anne a love poem. From you, of course."

Rick had frozen. "You what?"

Darcy's grin widened. "Relax, it was Shakespeare."

"Darcy."

"Sonnet 18! You know the one. 'Shall I compare thee to a summer's day.' It's timeless."

Rick had nearly strangled him.

Then Anne had walked in, holding a piece of paper. "Hey," she'd said, smiling softly down at him.

Rick had panicked. Darcy, the absolute traitor, had immediately picked up his coffee and turned away like he had never seen Rick before in his life.

Anne had slid into the seat across from him, unfolding the note. "You know," she'd mused, "I didn't think you were the type to go full Shakespeare on me, but it's kind of sweet."

Rick had been seconds from confessing the truth when she'd leaned in, eyes teasing.

"Next time," she'd said, "just say it in person." Then she'd kissed his cheek.

And Darcy had fist-pumped in the background.

The memory shattered as he looked down at Louisa's version of a love note. The ink swirled elegantly, but it was wrong. Forced. This wasn't love. Rick curled into himself, his body shaking.

Louisa sighed contentedly, trailing her fingers over the curve of her stomach. "She's going to love you, Ricky," she whispered.

Rick couldn't move. Couldn't breathe. The lock snapped shut behind her. The candles flickered faintly in the corner. And Rick lay there, trapped in a nightmare wrapped in soft pink letters. His grip faltered, and the onesie slipped from his fingers, landing in a crumpled heap at his feet.

Chapter 14

> No matter what it takes, no matter how long it takes—I will get her
> out. God help me, I will get us both out.
> – Rick's Journal

The air felt charged, thick with something different. Rick was trying to put a finger on what it was when he heard the door. His body tensed before his mind even registered it, the instinct drilled into him over months of captivity. Footsteps echoed down the stairs—deliberate, unhurried. The scent of vanilla preceded her, cloying, suffocating. He forced himself not to recoil.

Louisa came into view, but this time, she wasn't alone. Rick's heart stuttered in his chest. She was cradling a bundle of pink fabric in her arms, holding it with an unfamiliar kind of delicacy.

At first, his brain refused to process it. It couldn't be. It was too soon, wasn't it? But then the fabric shifted, and a tiny face peeked out from the folds—a small, wrinkled thing, pink and fragile, eyes squeezed shut against the dim light.

A baby. *His* baby.

His legs nearly gave out beneath him as he stood.

Louisa smirked, watching his reaction like she was savoring a victory. "Well, Ricky," she crooned, shifting the bundle slightly, making the infant let out a faint, restless whimper, as she handed her over. "Aren't you going to say hello to your daughter?"

The words hit him like a fist to the gut. *Daughter.*

Rick lunged forward, his arms locking around the tiny body before she could fall. His breath hitched. She was so small. Too small. His grip tightened instinctively, shielding her from the cold, from Louisa, from everything.

Louisa scoffed. "I told Anne that I lost the baby."

Rick's stomach twisted violently. "What?" The word barely came out, breathless with horror.

Louisa rolled her eyes. "Oh, come on, Ricky. Do you really think I'd parade around town with this?" She gestured vaguely toward the baby, sneering. "Too small, too weak. If I'd known she'd turn out to be such a runt, I would've taken care of it months ago."

Rick stopped breathing. The world tilted, a violent, sickening lurch. *Taken care of it.* The words hit like a death blow, like something sacred being spat on and discarded. His arms tightened instinctively around Lily, his pulse a roaring drumbeat of fury. She stirred against his chest, so small, so fragile—so alive.

He looked at her, at the baby Louisa had wanted gone, and knew—deep in his soul—that no matter what happened, no matter what it cost him, he would never let her take Lily away again.

"I put together some supplies in this carrier bag, but be sure to use everything sparingly. You never know when or if I'll give you more." Louisa tilted her head, watching him absorb the words, watching the shift in him. Her smirk widened. "Oh, don't look so tragic," she said lightly. "I did give you that Valentine's Day gift, remember?"

Rick's heart pounded as his gaze flicked to the chair where he'd put the onesie—pink with soft embroidery. *Daddy's Girl.*

Louisa let out a soft, amused sigh, as if recalling something sentimental. "Funny enough, I went into labor right after leaving you that night," she mused, shaking her head with a smirk. "So, really, she is your Valentine. Poetic, isn't it?"

Something inside him broke. As he heard Louisa lock the cellar door above them, he looked down at Lily again, at her tiny, wriggling form, her fragile breaths puffing against his skin. She had no one else. But she had him.

Rick lifted his eyes to the dark ceiling where Louisa's camera watched his every move and upwards to the space beyond it where he knew—had to believe—God was still watching.

"I don't know how I'm going to do this, Lord. I don't know how I'll keep her safe in this hell. But You didn't let her die. You let her live. And that has to mean something. Please help me. Help me be the father she deserves. Help me survive long enough to save her."

For the first time in nine months, he had something to fight for. Louisa had taken everything from him. But she had given him Lily.

And Rick would never let her take that away.

Chapter 15

As long as she's breathing, I won't stop. I won't surrender. I'll give her more than this darkness. I'll give her the world.
– Rick's Journal

Rick cradled Lily against his chest, adjusting the thin blanket around her small body. She was too cold. The damp air seeped into the fabric, her tiny limbs trembling in his arms. He pressed her closer, trying to warm her with his own body heat, but it wasn't enough. Nothing was ever enough.

The cloth diapers Louisa had left were stiff with filth. Rick had scrubbed them as best he could, washing them in the rusted shower with a sliver of old soap, but the smell lingered. His fear of her getting sick clung to him, heavy and suffocating.

He shifted slightly, trying to ease the growing ache in his legs. The chain rattled softly, a constant, cruel reminder of its reach, of its weight, of how much control he had lost. Then, a memory surfaced. A different time, a different world.

The last time he had held a baby, he had been seventeen, volunteering in the church nursery with Darcy. It had only been because they had crushes on the two high school girls who actually knew what they were doing.

"You realize we have no idea what we're doing, right?" Darcy had muttered, staring at the wriggling infant in his arms like it was a live grenade.

Rick had stifled a laugh, rocking a fussy toddler back and forth. "Relax, man. Just hold the bottle at an angle."

Darcy had scowled, shifting the baby awkwardly before shoving the bottle into its mouth. "I feel like I'm bribing him for information."

Rick smirked. "Yeah? What's the ransom?"

Darcy had grinned, glancing over at the girls. "I don't know. Maybe Ashley's number."

Rick had rolled his eyes. "Right. Because nothing impresses a girl like barely keeping a baby alive for an hour."

Now, in the freezing darkness of the cellar, holding his own daughter, that memory felt like a cruel joke. Back then, it had been a game. A chance to impress a girl. Now, it was life or death.

The sharp creak of the cellar door jolted him back to reality. Rick's breath stilled, his arms instinctively tightening around Lily.

The click of heels against concrete echoed down the steps, deliberate and unhurried. She was in no rush. She was never in a rush.

Louisa stepped into view, a small bag swinging lazily from her fingers, her expression unreadable. But he knew her too well. Knew the pleasure she took in watching him suffer.

Her gaze flicked briefly to Lily, still asleep in his arms. Then she smiled. "Still alive, I see."

Rick forced himself to stay calm. He knew better than to let his emotions show, but anger churned in his chest, hot and poisonous. "She needs more," he said, his voice flat, controlled. "Her blanket is too thin. The diapers are filthy. We need more soap, more formula."

Louisa's smirk sharpened. "Oh, Ricky, always so needy." She sighed, mocking disappointment as she set the bag on the table. "What happened to that resourceful man? The one who thought he could take on the world?"

Rick bit back a retort. He couldn't afford to snap. Not with Lily at stake. He met her gaze instead. Steady. Unflinching. "She's your daughter too," he said.

For the briefest second, something flickered in her expression. Something vulnerable. Then, it was gone.

She shrugged, brushing the thought away like dust. "I told you before," she said airily, stepping closer, looming over him. "She's your problem now. I have better things to do than play house."

Rick's breath turned to ice. "Better things?" he asked, his voice low. "What about the house with the garden? The one you used to dream about? What about Lily running through the grass, laughing?"

Rick saw the hesitation in her face, the crack in her mask. But then, just as quickly, it hardened.

"Dreams change," Louisa said flatly, her voice devoid of the obsessive devotion that had once suffocated him. "I've moved on."

Rick's pulse stuttered. "Moved on?" His throat felt raw. "From her? From me?"

Her bitter smile twisted at the edges, something almost amused lurking beneath it. "From you, Ricky."

The words landed like a physical blow, sharper than the chain around his throat, more vicious than any of the wounds she had left on his body.

Louisa let out a soft, almost pitying laugh. "Do you know what I've realized, Ricky?" she mused. "It's time to think about the future. *My* future." She smoothed her dress, a satisfied smirk tugging at her lips. "Daddy's gone," she said, almost offhandedly. "Heart attack, just last week. He left me the house, of course. But now I have to be practical. I can't waste my time playing house with a man who will never be more than a broken toy."

Something cold coiled in Rick's stomach. She had spent months breaking and making him hers—destroying him, twisting him into whatever she needed. But now, with the fantasy in ruins, she was what? Moving on?

She leaned in slightly, voice lowering as if sharing a secret. "I've decided on someone, Ricky," she said, her eyes gleaming with something cruel. "Tom Musgrove."

Rick felt sick.

Louisa smiled, savoring his reaction. "He understands me, unlike you," she continued. "Tom is someone I can build a life with. Someone with power, with connections. And you?" She let out a soft, mocking laugh. "You're a liability."

Rick's stomach churned. He clenched his jaw. "What does Tom think about you keeping me locked in a basement?"

Louisa grinned, tapping a manicured finger against her chin. "Oh, Ricky," she purred. "Do you really think he'd believe you? That anyone would? You're already a ghost. Everyone thinks you ran off to some far-off island, heartbroken. Poor Anne has moved on. Peter is happily filling your place, and I—" she placed a hand over her stomach with a smirk "—I have my future."

The words rang in his ears, disorienting in a way that almost made him feel unsteady. Louisa had never once spoken about a future without him in it. And now, just like that he was disposable. Replaceable. Forgotten.

Rick held Lily tighter. She was trying to get in his head. Trying to break him. But this wasn't about him anymore. "You're abandoning her," he said, his voice low, fierce.

Louisa rolled her eyes. "Don't be dramatic." She flicked a glance at Lily, indifferent, dismissive. "I don't have time for a child who was never part of my plan."

Rick's stomach churned. She meant it. She was really going to leave Lily to him, completely. And he would have to keep her attention, or else they'd lose even the scraps she gave them.

Louisa smiled, sensing his realization. "Figure it out, Ricky," she said sweetly, before stepping toward the stairs.

Rick swallowed hard, calling after her. "If you won't do it for her, at least do it for yourself. Prove you're better than this."

She paused. Then she laughed. A cold, hollow sound. "Better than what? You?"

The door slammed shut.

Rick stared at Lily, her tiny breath against his chest. "We'll figure this out."

Chapter 16

> The den is still dark, but I hear a whisper in the silence.
> – Rick's Journal

One year. Rick had lost count of the days long ago, but Louisa hadn't. She marked the anniversary with a cruel smirk, a twisted celebration of his suffering. One year since she had stolen everything from him. One year since the world had forgotten he existed.

And yet he had refused to let her break him completely.

Lily, almost five months old, stirred in Rick's arms, her tiny fingers flexing against his chest, searching. She let out a hungry cry, her voice soft but sharp enough to cut through the silence.

Rick pressed a kiss to the crown of her head, rocking her gently. "I know, baby girl," he murmured, his voice hoarse. "I'm hungry too."

Her small whimpers settled, but the tension in Rick's chest didn't ease. His grip on her tightened as he exhaled a slow, uneven breath.

"You know what, Lily?" he whispered. "I think it's time for a bedtime story." He closed his eyes, searching through the vaults of his memory. Then, a faint smile tugged at the corner of his lips. "Once upon a time," he began, "there was a man named Daniel."

Lily let out a small sound, something between a sigh and a whimper, as he adjusted his hold.

"And Daniel? He was trapped too," Rick continued. "Thrown into a deep, dark place with lions all around him. Hungry lions." His voice dropped lower, soothing and steady, as if the words could hold back the cold and hunger. "But Daniel wasn't alone," he whispered. "God sent an angel to shut the lions' mouths. And when morning came, he walked out of that den without a single scratch."

Rick swallowed hard, his fingers brushing over Lily's soft curls.

"And do you know what, baby girl?" His voice trembled, but he kept going. "Those lions couldn't touch him because he belonged to Someone greater. Just like you do." He exhaled, his breath stirring the fine strands of her hair. "Just like I do."

The words settled in his chest, heavier than he expected. He hadn't just been telling her a story—he'd been telling himself.

The sound of footsteps shattered the fragile moment. Rick tensed as the cellar door groaned open, and Louisa appeared at the top of the stairs, her silhouette framed in the dim light. She descended slowly, heels clicking deliberately against the concrete. In her arms, she carried a large cardboard box.

"Happy anniversary, Ricky," she said, her voice light and dripping with satisfaction. She placed the box on the table with an exaggerated flourish.

Rick didn't respond. He just held Lily closer.

Louisa sighed. "Not in a festive mood?" She gestured toward the box. "I brought you something. A bed. Well—*her* bed."

Rick's stomach turned as he looked at it. The so-called "bed" was little more than a box lined with scraps of fabric. He clenched his jaw. "She deserves better."

Louisa smirked. "And yet this is what she gets." She stepped forward, closing the distance between them. "Now," she ordered, "put her in the box."

Rick flinched at the command in her voice.

Louisa's eyes darkened. "Ricky," she warned.

He hesitated.

She sighed as she clutched the chain around his neck and pulled hard. "You should be grateful, Ricky," she said sweetly. "Some men never get to know their children at all. And here you are, lucky enough to raise mine."

Rick's breath hitched. "You don't care about her," he rasped. "You never did."

Louisa tilted her head, considering. "No," she admitted, almost carelessly. "But you do. And that's all that matters."

The words landed like a stone in Rick's gut. Slowly, reluctantly, he forced himself to step toward the box. His hands trembled as he lowered Lily inside, her warmth leaving his chest like the last ember of a dying fire.

Lily whimpered softly, her fragile limbs curling in on themselves. She was still so small, her premature body fighting to catch up to where she should have been.

Rick swallowed hard, tucking the blanket around her. "I'm sorry, baby girl," he whispered. "This won't take long."

Louisa smiled, triumphant. "Good boy." She stepped toward him, reaching for the wrap of her dress—

Rick turned his face away, trying to rationalize his options. "I'll do whatever you need," he said suddenly. "Let me please you, Louisa."

Louisa froze. Her smirk faded for a second. Then, her lips curled. "Oh, Ricky," she murmured, pressing her lips against his. "Now, that's more like it." She stepped closer, letting her dress fall to the floor. "Maybe you're not completely useless after all."

The words burned. But Rick let them. Because as long as Louisa thought she was winning, she wouldn't see the fight still burning inside him, and hopefully she'd keep bringing the food and supplies Lily needed.

Later that evening, Rick sat in the dim light, his heart pounding in his chest. He wrote slowly, deliberately, making sure the words weren't too obvious in case Louisa should read his journal.

> *The lions are pacing, but they haven't devoured me yet. She thinks she has me, but she doesn't see it. The cracks are forming. The den is still dark, but I hear a whisper in the silence whispering, "morning is coming."*

He closed the journal, pressing his lips into a thin line. He wouldn't let her break him. Not completely. Rick glanced at Lily, asleep in the box beside him. One day, he would show her the ocean. The waves rolling in, the sand beneath her feet. She would see the vastness of it, the way it stretched beyond sight, the way it made a person feel small but free.

"One day, baby girl," he whispered. "I'll take you there." His voice was hoarse, but steady. "And we won't come back."

Chapter 17

> One child in the dark was already too much. But two? How will I
> keep them safe when I barely have the strength to stand?
> – Rick's Journal

The cellar door groaned open, slicing through the stale, suffocating air. Rick's body tensed before his mind fully caught up, his instincts sharpened by nearly two years of captivity. His arms reflexively pulled Lily close. She clung to him, her tiny fingers digging into his skin, her breath hitching as she buried her face against his chest.

At sixteen months old, she understood fear. Louisa delighted in the way her own daughter would flinch at the sight of her.

"Ricky!" Her sing-song voice echoed down the stairs, syrupy sweet, dripping with malice. She descended slowly, stretching out each step, savoring the moment.

But she wasn't alone.

Rick's pulse slammed against his ribs as he took in the bundle she carried—wrapped in a soft blue blanket, held with an unfamiliar kind of delicacy. His vision blurred at the edges, his brain rejecting what his eyes told him was real.

She stopped at the cellar floor, swaying slightly as she rocked the bundle. A smirk curled her lips. "Guess who's here to meet his daddy."

Rick's stomach twisted violently. No. No, this couldn't be real.

Louisa peeled back the blanket, revealing a tiny, sleeping newborn face—light wisps of hair, delicate features, a soft whimper escaping his barely parted lips.

Rick's breath caught in his throat.

"Meet Walter," Louisa cooed. "Strong. Healthy. Everything you should have given me the first time." Her voice hardened, sharp as glass. "But of course, you couldn't even get that right."

The words barely registered. Rick could only stare at the newborn, drowning in a flood of emotions he couldn't untangle. "Walter?" His voice cracked.

Louisa smirked, taking another slow step toward him, watching him unravel. "Yes, Ricky. Your son." She tilted her head, feigning sweetness. "Not that you deserve him any more than you deserve her." She flicked her gaze toward Lily who was still clutching him.

Rick swallowed hard. "Can I—?" He couldn't finish the sentence.

Louisa's smirk widened. "Of course," she said airily. Then, without warning, she shoved the baby into his arms.

Rick barely caught him in time. His body reacted on instinct, securing Walter against his chest. But the sudden shift jolted him, and then he realized—Lily. She had slipped. The moment his arms had adjusted to catch Walter, she had tumbled from where she'd curled up at his side, landing on the floor with a soft thump.

Panic surged through him.

Lily was already pushing herself up, rubbing at her sleepy eyes, confused but unharmed. Still, guilt crushed him.

Louisa let out a soft, mocking laugh. "Careful, Ricky. Dropping one child while fawning over another? Not a great look."

Rick ignored her, shifting Walter into one arm so he could scoop Lily back up. She latched onto him immediately, her tiny hands tightly clutching his chain and collar.

For the first time he held them both. Lily, his baby girl, was the one he had fought for every single day. Walter, his son, was so impossibly small, so new.

Louisa watched with amusement, tilting her head. "Quite the balancing act, isn't it?" she mused. "Two little ones. One useless father."

Rick tuned her out. He looked down at Walter, at the newborn's fluttering lashes and delicate fingers curled against his chest. Then at Lily, watching him curiously. Slowly, she reached out, brushing her tiny hand against Walter's arm.

"Baby," she whispered.

Rick's throat closed. "Yes, baby," he whispered back. "This is Walter."

Louisa scoffed. "Spare me the sentiment." She turned toward the table, dropping a bag of supplies with a thud. "Formula, diapers, baby food. Don't expect this generosity to last."

Rick lifted his head. "Lily needs clothes," he said, voice measured. "She's freezing."

Louisa's expression darkened. "Is she?" she murmured, feigning concern. She sighed dramatically. "Maybe you should have tried harder to give me the perfect family, Ricky. Then I wouldn't have to clean up your mess."

Rick clenched his jaw. "You're abandoning her."

Louisa rolled her eyes. "Oh, don't be dramatic."

He swallowed his rage, pivoting to another question that had burned in his mind since the moment she had arrived with Walter. "What does Tom think of this?" he asked, forcing his voice to stay even. "Of you having a baby that isn't his? Won't he ask about Walter? About where he is when you're with him?"

Something flickered in her eyes. Not quite anger—more like annoyance. "Tom understands his place," she said smoothly. "He knows not to ask too many questions."

Rick's stomach twisted. That meant Tom knew. At least in some way, he knew Louisa had hidden this baby from the world. And worse, he didn't care.

Rick's breath hitched. "You don't care about these children," he rasped. "You never did."

Louisa tilted her head, considering. "No," she admitted, almost carelessly. "But as I've said before, you do. And that's all that matters."

Rick tightened his grip on Walter. He couldn't afford to react. Couldn't afford to let her see how deep she had cut him.

She stepped toward the stairs, waving a dismissive hand. "Keep them alive. Keep me entertained." She paused at the door, turning back with a smirk. "Oh, and Ricky?"

He lifted his gaze.

She grinned. "Happy Father's Day."

The door slammed shut. The silence after her departure wasn't just silence—it was a chasm. Rick exhaled shakily.

He carefully laid Walter in the makeshift crib—the same cardboard box Lily had outgrown months ago. Then he turned to Lily, pulling her closer, pressing a kiss to her curls as she yawned. She nuzzled into him, her small body curling into the space beside his own, where she had always belonged.

Walter stirred in his sleep, a soft, breathy whimper escaping his lips. His children were his reason to fight and live.

Rick lifted his head, staring at the ceiling, where the shadows swallowed the corners of the room. Somewhere above, the world moved on without him. But here, beneath it, he was preparing for war. He reached for his journal, his fingers trembling as he pressed the pencil to the page.

> I don't know how to do this.
> One child in the dark was already too much. But two? Walter is so small. So light. It terrifies me. I thought I understood fear before, but I didn't—not like this. I have to be strong. For them.
> Lily touched his hand today. Called him baby. She doesn't understand what's happening, but she loves him anyway. That love is something pure, something Louisa can never take from her. From us.
> I can't let them die here. Lord, I know you're still there. Please show me the way out. Or give me the strength to carve one myself.

Chapter 18

> Hope is dangerous in a place like this. But I can't let it die—not
> when they need me to believe in something better.
> – Rick's Journal

Rick traced slow, deliberate circles on Lily's back, her small body curled against his chest, warm and trusting. Across the room, Walter shifted in his makeshift bassinet, his tiny fists clenching before he settled again.

The steady rhythm of their breathing was the only sound in the room, a fragile kind of peace that Rick had learned to cherish. But even in the quiet, his mind raced. He had no illusions. Peace never lasted long here.

Then came the creak of the cellar door. Rick's stomach clenched, his muscles coiling instinctively. The sharp click of Louisa's heels against the stairs sent his heart hammering, but he forced himself to remain still, to keep his expression neutral. Any sign of resistance, any trace of defiance, and she would make them all pay for it.

She descended slowly, deliberately. Her blonde hair was pinned back into an elegant twist, her fitted dress clinging to her like a second skin. A large tote bag dangled from one hand, a wine glass in the other. Her lips curled in amusement as she reached the bottom step.

"She's in a good mood," Rick muttered warily. That could mean anything.

"Evening, Ricky," she purred, swirling the wine in her glass as her gaze swept lazily around the room. She paused, looking him over like an owner inspecting a caged pet. "You look tired. Haven't been getting much sleep?"

Rick adjusted Lily in his lap, keeping his voice level. "It's been cold," he said simply. "The kids need warmer clothes."

Louisa scoffed, rolling her eyes. "And here I thought you'd be happy for me. But no, of course not. Always so selfish."

Rick's jaw clenched. *Here we go again.*

She set the wine glass on the table with a flourish, then turned to face him, her smirk widening. "Tom and I finalized the wedding plans."

The words hit harder than Rick expected. Not because he cared who Louisa married—he didn't. But because this was a shift. A sign that she was truly done with him, that she was no longer playing out the twisted fantasy of their "perfect" life together as a family.

"What plans?" he asked, keeping his tone carefully neutral.

"Paris honeymoon," she said dreamily. "Three weeks of pure bliss. Can you imagine?"

Rick forced his expression to remain blank, even as his mind reeled. *Three weeks*. Three weeks where she would be gone. Three weeks where anything could happen. His pulse quickened.

"What happens to us while you're gone?"

Louisa waved a dismissive hand. "Oh, I'll stock the fridge and bring you some extra formula." She smirked. "You'll manage. You always do."

His stomach twisted. She was reckless, but never this careless. Something about her nonchalance set off alarm bells in his head.

"And if something happens?" he pressed. "If the kids get sick or—"

"Figure it out," she cut him off, her tone sharp. "I'm not missing my honeymoon because of your incompetence."

Her words were like a slap, but Rick forced himself to stay calm. He couldn't risk angering her—not with Lily and Walter's lives depending on her whims. He adjusted Lily in his lap, her small hands clutching at his chest, and spoke carefully. "What changed?"

Louisa froze, her gaze narrowing as she studied him. She set the wine glass down on the table, her smile twisting into something cruel. "I broke you," she said coldly. "It was fun while it lasted, but let's face it, you're boring. Tom is too, but more importantly, Tom is what I need. He can offer me security and a name for my children."

Holding back the bile, he leaned forward slightly, his voice low and deliberate. "Then bring *me* upstairs. Make *me* your husband. Let me prove *I* can be your security and the father our children need."

Louisa stared at him, her lips curling into a sharp smile. "You?" she sneered, her voice dripping with disdain. "My husband? Ricky, you're here because I allow it. Nothing more."

"But you said you loved me," Rick pressed, ignoring the contempt in her tone. "You said you dreamt of us having a yard for the kids to run around in. Isn't that what all of this is about?"

Louisa's expression faltered, her gaze darkening. "Don't pretend to understand me," she said sharply. "You don't know what I need."

"Maybe I don't," Rick admitted, his voice soft but firm. "But I know the kids need stability. They need you to care."

Louisa's eyes flicked to the bassinet, her lips curling into a smirk. "Walter's just fine," she said lightly. "And Lily—well, she's your problem."

"She's your daughter," Rick said, his voice rising. "You can't just write her off."

Louisa's expression hardened. "Watch your tone," she warned. "You don't get to make demands."

Rick swallowed his anger, forcing himself to nod. He had to tread carefully. He needed to keep her engaged, to make her believe he was still worth her attention. "I just want what's best for them," he said quietly. "For all of us."

Louisa studied him for a moment, her gaze calculating. Then she chuckled, shaking her head. "You're pathetic," she said, turning toward the stairs. "But at least you're more entertaining when you plead."

"What does Tom think?" he asked, keeping his tone carefully measured.

Something flickered in Louisa's eyes. Not anger. Rather it was annoyance. "Why do you keep asking me that? I've told you. He knows better than to ask questions," she said smoothly.

Rick inhaled deeply and replied. "I know you said Tom doesn't ask questions. But he knows you had Walter. Where does he think he is?"

Louisa set the wine glass down, turning to him with a sharper smile. "Oh, that's the best part. He thinks my dear little son is tucked away with his Auntie Anne." Her lips curled, pleased with herself. "Tom likes solutions. Not problems."

Rick exhaled slowly. Tom wasn't just looking the other way. He was choosing to believe what suited him. And that made him just as,dangerous.

Louisa paused at the top of the stairs, her mocking smile cutting through the dim light. "Don't stay up too late," she said sweetly. "I expect you to be in top form next time I visit."

The door slammed shut, and the cellar descended into suffocating silence. Rick exhaled shakily, his hands trembling as he adjusted Lily in his lap. Walter stirred in the box, his soft whimper drawing Rick's attention.

Carefully, Rick lifted Walter into his arms, cradling him against his chest as Lily nuzzled closer to his shoulder. "It's okay," he whispered, his voice unsteady. "I've got you both."

He pressed a kiss to each of their foreheads, his tears slipping silently onto their soft skin. The words came quietly, raw and honest.

"Lord, give me the strength to endure. For them. For their future."

The cold darkness of the cellar remained unyielding, but Rick held onto the fragile spark of hope flickering deep within. For Lily and Walter, he would survive. He would play the game, endure the torment, and fight for the day they could be free.

One day.

Chapter 19

> A brother and a sister should never be separated. That's what I believe. That's what I know. I won't let her take him from us—not forever.
> – Rick's Journal

Rick had spent months memorizing the rhythm of his children's breathing. He knew the way Lily sighed in her sleep, the way Walter whimpered before fully waking. But that night, everything changed.

Walter wasn't in his bassinet. His soft coos, the ones Rick listened for in the dark to remind himself he wasn't alone, were gone. And Lily had noticed. She sat in his lap, shifting restlessly, her small hands gripping his bare chest as she twisted toward the empty bassinet. Her dark curls were damp against his skin, her body feverish from restless sleep and teething. She squirmed in his arms, letting out small, questioning whimpers, her mind slowly piecing together what her heart already understood. Her brother was gone.

The door at the top of the stairs groaned open, and Rick's entire body tensed. Footsteps. Louisa. His arms instinctively tightened around Lily as she let out a small squeal.

Louisa descended the stairs in slow, deliberate strides, her long dress brushing against the steps. Her makeup was flawless, her hair sleek—pristine, polished, a cruel contrast to Rick's half-starved, unshaven, and shirtless form. She looked untouchable. He looked like her prisoner.

Rick's throat locked as he took in the sight of her cradling his son in her arms as if she were a candidate for the mother of the year. His muscles coiled, every instinct screaming at him to lunge, to take back his son. But Louisa only smiled. That smile that made his stomach crawl.

"You're awake," she said, pleased.

Rick didn't answer. Lily did. Her tiny body jerked against his hold, her little arms stretching desperately toward Walter. "Bubba!" she babbled, her voice thick with need. "Bubba!"

Walter let out a soft coo in response, shifting against Louisa's chest.

Rick swallowed hard. "Louisa—"

She held up a hand. "Shh." She rocked Walter slowly as if she were some devoted mother. "You'll upset him."

Rick bit the inside of his cheek so hard he tasted blood.

Lily wasn't listening. She lunged forward, trying to wriggle out of Rick's grip, her whole body straining toward her brother.

Rick grunted as he adjusted his hold. "Lily, baby, no—"

"Bubba!" Lily cried again, louder this time, kicking her feet against Rick's stomach, using every bit of her strength to reach Walter. Her tiny fists grabbed onto Rick's hair, his shoulders, whatever she could use to push away from him.

Rick tightened his grip, but she was frantic now, twisting, thrashing, sobbing.

Louisa only sighed as she tilted her head at the scene. "Well, isn't that sweet?" she mused. "She doesn't want to let him go."

Rick gritted his teeth. "Then don't make her."

Louisa smirked. "Oh, Ricky." She rocked Walter slowly, deliberately, as if rubbing it in. "You're acting like I'm taking him away forever."

Rick's entire body went rigid. "Aren't you?"

"He belongs upstairs with Tom and me."

Rick's vision blurred with rage. "No," he said, his voice low, dangerous. "He belongs with me and his sister."

Rick's grip almost slipped. Lily squirmed harder, her cries turning desperate, her face reddening as she reached for Walter with everything she had.

Louisa sighed in mock pity. "You're making this worse, you know."

"Bubba!" Lily wailed, her body convulsing with sobs. She shoved at Rick's arms, clawing at his skin, trying to crawl away.

She didn't understand. She couldn't understand. Her little brother had been taken from her.

Rick couldn't hold her still. He lowered her to the ground, hoping—praying—she'd settle. She didn't.

Lily stumbled toward Louisa, her unsteady toddler legs working furiously to get to Walter. "Mama!" she shrieked, still too young to know what the word meant, still too innocent to understand Louisa wasn't a mother.

Louisa smirked down at her, unimpressed. Then, in one slow, deliberate step—she turned away.

Lily froze.

Rick watched it happen—the moment Lily understood. Her face crumpled. Then she screamed. Not a baby's cry. A real, raw, gut-wrenching scream.

Rick lunged forward, grabbing her before she could collapse onto the floor.

Louisa walked away. Up the stairs. Carrying Walter.

Lily screamed louder, writhing in Rick's arms, clawing toward the door as if sheer willpower could bring her brother back. Rick's own chest cracked open, but his arms locked around his daughter. He held her tighter, rocking her through the sobs, through the betrayal, through the loss she didn't know how to name.

He pressed his lips against her damp hair. "I know, baby," he whispered, his voice shaking. "I know."

The door slammed shut. The lock clicked. And Walter was gone.

Lily's cries echoed through the cellar, long after Louisa's footsteps had faded. Rick held her, rocking, whispering promises through his own silent tears. His lips brushed against her forehead, sealing his vow with the only thing he had left.

"I will bring him back to you," he swore, his voice raw, fierce, unbreakable.

Lily shuddered against him, her sobs slowly quieting into gasping hiccups.

Outside, Christmas lights were probably glowing in the windows of every home, families gathering for warmth, for love and yet down here, in the dark, a father and daughter clung to each other—two shadows left behind.

And Rick vowed, with everything he had left, that she would experience Christmas outside of the cellar.

Chapter 20

> A child should not know fear in her own home. A father should not beg for basic dignity. A man should not have to kneel before a monster. But here I am—on my knees, again.
> – Rick's Journal

Today was Lily's second birthday, and Rick refused to let darkness win. The small, misshapen cupcake sat between them on the table—a pitiful thing, but a labor of love. Rick had scrounged every scrap, crushed stale bread to mimic cake, used powdered formula to make something resembling frosting. A single candle flickered atop it, the tiny flame defiant against the suffocating cold.

Lily's wide brown eyes sparkled as she reached for the light.

"Not yet, Sweetheart," Rick whispered, gently pulling her tiny hand back. "You have to make a wish first."

Lily's nose scrunched in thought, her little fingers tapping her lips. Rick swallowed against the tightness in his throat. He didn't know what she might wish for, but he knew his own. Freedom. For Lily. For Walter. For all of them.

"Blow, Daddy!" Lily squealed, bouncing slightly in his lap.

"Go ahead, baby girl," Rick encouraged, forcing a smile.

Lily sucked in a deep breath and blew out the candle in one eager puff. Rick clapped, the sound bouncing off the stone walls like a challenge to the darkness.

Lily clapped too, her delighted giggles filling the air. "More, Daddy!" she declared, stuffing a crumbly handful of cupcake into her mouth.

Rick chuckled, brushing crumbs off her cheek with his thumb. "Slow down, Sweetheart. You're supposed to enjoy it, not inhale it."

Lily paused mid-chew, her little face scrunching in thought. Then, with a mischievous glint in her bright eyes, she grabbed a chunk of cupcake in her small, sticky hands and lifted it toward his face. Rick barely had time to react before she pressed it against his lips, missing his mouth entirely and smearing it across his cheek instead.

Lily gasped dramatically. "Oops!"

Rick let out a startled laugh, the unexpected joy bubbling up before he could stop it. "Oh, oops, huh?"

Lily giggled harder, her tiny shoulders shaking as she clapped her hands together. "I fix it!" she announced, leaning in with the clear intent to lick it off his face.

Rick yelped, laughing as he gently caught her before she could make contact. "Okay, okay! I think you've done enough damage, Picasso."

Lily squealed with delight, wriggling in his arms, her giggles filling every corner of the cellar. Rick's heart clenched—but this time, not from fear. For a moment it wasn't about the chains, or the cold, or the hopelessness pressing in. It was just this. Lily, bright and warm in his arms. Sticky fingers. Laughter. Joy. And for that fleeting second, he let himself believe that maybe he could hold onto this.

And then, the door creaked open, shattering all hopes. Rick's stomach clenched. Lily flinched in his lap.

Louisa descended the stairs slowly, deliberately, savoring the tension she created. Her hair was immaculate, her lipstick perfectly painted, her black dress form-fitting—she looked like a woman untouched by the filth she forced them to live in. A shopping bag hung from one wrist, a smirk playing at her lips.

"Well, isn't this just adorable," she cooed, stopping at the base of the stairs. Her gaze flicked over the remnants of the celebration, the candle's faint trail of smoke still curling in the air. "A party, Ricky? How quaint."

Rick didn't respond. Lily stiffened, pressing deeper into his chest.

Louisa set the bag on the table and pulled out a frilly pink dress, holding it up between her fingers like it was something precious. "A gift for the birthday girl," she announced.

Rick's gut twisted. What game was Louisa playing?

Louisa's smirk deepened. "Oh, you're welcome, Ricky," she said, saccharine-sweet. "I'm feeling generous today."

She ran a hand over her stomach absently—a motion so small she probably didn't even realize she had done it. But Rick had seen that before.

"I thought today was a good day to share some news."

Rick's stomach dropped.

She smiled, resting a hand on her stomach. Slow. Deliberate. Mocking. "I'm two months pregnant."

Rick stared at her, his entire body numb. "What?"

Louisa's eyes gleamed with vicious delight at his reaction. "You heard me," she said airily. "Another little one on the way. Let's hope they're as strong as Walter."

Rick's hands clenched around Lily. "Is it mine?" he demanded, his voice raw, shaking. "Or Tom's?"

Louisa tilted her head, feigning curiosity. "Does it matter?" she mused. "Either way, it's *mine*."

Rage surged up Rick's throat like bile. "You're married," he bit out. "Why do you still need me? Why can't you leave me and my children alone? Let us leave!"

Louisa's laughter was hollow. "Tom is practical," she said. "Respectable. But you, Ricky? You're entertainment."

The words sliced into him.

"I like it when you fight, Ricky." Louisa leaned in, her breath warm against his ear. "Happy Valentine's Day, baby."

Then she turned, ascended the stairs, and slammed the door behind her.

Rick collapsed to his knees, pulling Lily into his arms.

Her small fingers brushed against his face, wiping away a tear. "No cry, Daddy," she whispered.

Rick swallowed hard, pressing his lips against her curls. "No more crying, baby girl," he vowed. "I promise."

Chapter 21

> I once thought dignity was something no one could take from me.
> I was wrong. But for Lily, I'll give up even that. Just let me have
> this one thing, Lord—just let me be her father.
> – Rick's Journal

Rick sat cross-legged on the cot, his arms wrapped around Lily as she lay curled in his lap. The birthday candle had long since melted down, the crumbs from their meager celebration scattered on the table. Lily's breathing had slowed into the steady rhythm of sleep, but Rick couldn't rest. His mind wouldn't stop turning.

She was two now. No longer a baby—she was watching him, learning from him. And he had seen it in her eyes today. Confusion. Lily had noticed. She had looked at him differently. The moment had been brief—a flicker of something he couldn't fully name—but it had been there. Recognition. Awareness. And he felt shame. She was starting to understand. And that terrified him.

The sharp creak of the door sent a cold wave of dread down Rick's spine. He tightened his hold on Lily instinctively, his body bracing for whatever new cruelty Louisa was bringing this time.

Her heels clicked against the stairs, slow, deliberate. "Such a sweet little party," Louisa drawled as she reached the bottom step, surveying the remains of Lily's birthday celebration. Her eyes gleamed with amusement as she took in the single candle, the crumbs, the pink dress that still lay untouched where she'd dropped it earlier. Mockery was already curled on her lips.

Rick forced himself to stay calm. He had to do this right. Louisa thrived on control. He needed to make her believe she held the power, even as he was the one making the request. Taking a slow breath, he carefully shifted Lily off his lap, setting her down gently on the cot. She stirred but didn't wake, her tiny hand curling against the thin blanket. Rick stood.

The chain rattled slightly as he adjusted his stance, willing his voice to stay even. Controlled. "Louisa."

She raised an eyebrow.

Rick's fingers curled into fists, nails biting into his palms. He hated this. Every muscle in his body screamed against it. But

Lily had looked at him differently. And so, he forced himself to speak.

"I need clothes."

Louisa's smirk widened instantly, her eyes flashing with amusement. She toyed with the sleeve of her dress, feigning disinterest, even as she soaked in his humiliation. "Oh?" she mused. "Do you now?"

Rick swallowed hard, his throat tight. "Not for me," he said, forcing his voice to stay calm. "For Lily. She's old enough to—" He hesitated, then pushed forward. "She understands."

Louisa's smile sharpened.

"She looks at me differently," Rick continued, the words leaving a bitter taste in his mouth. "She's aware."

Louisa tilted her head, studying him. "Oh, poor Ricky," she purred. "Feeling a little—indecent?"

Rick gritted his teeth but held her gaze. "You said I was here to be useful," he said steadily. "I can't be useful like this. Just—just give me something. Anything. Please."

Louisa sighed theatrically, tapping a manicured nail against her lips. "I don't know," she mused. "You've lasted this long. Maybe I like you this way. Exposed. Helpless. Easily accessible."

Rick forced himself not to react. He would not give her the satisfaction. Slowly, deliberately, he lowered his gaze in a show of submission. "Please."

The word hung in the air, thick and suffocating.

Louisa smiled. She took a slow step forward, reaching out and trailing a single finger down his bare chest. Rick's muscles locked.

"Hmm," she murmured, as if considering. "Begging suits you, Ricky."

Rick squeezed his eyes shut. *Please, Lord, let her give me this.*

Louisa stepped back. She let the silence stretch, savoring her control over him. Then, finally, she shrugged. "I'll think about it."

Rick exhaled shakily. It wasn't a no. And for now, that was all he could get.

Louisa's gaze flicked toward the cot, where Lily was stirring, her small fingers curling against the blanket. "She really is getting so big," Louisa mused, her tone suddenly soft, almost—wistful.

Rick stiffened. That tone terrified him. He couldn't afford for her to decide to take Lily upstairs, leaving him here in the cellar alone. He wouldn't survive.

Rick forced his breathing to stay even. "She's a good girl," he said carefully. "She needs more clothes, too. She's already outgrown her outfit, and the dress you brought is too cold for down here."

Louisa sighed dramatically. "You're so demanding lately, Ricky," she drawled, flicking her hair over her shoulder. "But since it's her birthday I'll consider it."

Rick nodded. That was the best he could get.

Louisa smirked. "But don't think this means you can start asking for other things. You exist because I allow it. Remember that."

Rick forced himself to nod again.

"Be good, Ricky," she teased, her voice dripping with satisfaction. "And maybe I'll surprise you."

She lingered just a moment longer, her fingers grazing over his bare chest, nails scraping lightly against the bruises she'd left. Then, as if savoring her victory, she caught a tear slipping down his cheek and traced it with the tip of her tongue. A pleased hum vibrated from her throat.

"So sweet," she murmured, her eyes dark with triumph. "Your misery always tastes the best."

Rick stood frozen, his body rigid against the stone wall, willing himself not to recoil—because she liked that. Liked when he flinched, when he gave her that last shred of control. So, he forced himself still, locked his muscles into submission, and stared blankly at the flickering basement light until, at last, she turned away.

The sound of her retreating footsteps barely registered as he forced himself toward the far side of the cellar to the shower. He twisted the valve, and instantly, ice-cold water gushed down over him, piercing his skin like needles.

Rick braced himself against the wall, his hands splaying against the cold stone, his forehead pressing against his forearm as he let the freezing cascade hammer against his body. He scrubbed furiously—his chest, his arms, his thighs—raking his fingernails over every inch of skin she had touched. But no matter how hard he scrubbed, no matter how raw his skin became, he could still feel her. Still smell her. Still hear the soft, breathy sounds she made when she used him.

His stomach twisted violently, nausea curling deep in his gut. He clenched his jaw, swallowing hard, but it did nothing to stop the truth from clawing its way to the surface. His body had learned to respond to her. Louisa had taken him so many times over the last thirty-two months, twisted him into submission so thoroughly, that now, he didn't even need the drugs for his body to betray him.

Bile burned at the back of his throat, but he swallowed it down. Would she truly be the first and last woman he ever had sex with? The thought sent a fresh wave of revulsion through him. This couldn't be all there was for him. It couldn't be.

A shudder wracked his frame, and before he could stop it, a ragged sob tore from his throat. The water drowned out the sound, masking his broken gasps, his silent curses. His fingers dug into the wall as his chest heaved, his body shaking from more than just the cold.

He didn't know how long he stood there, letting the freezing water wash over him, trying and failing to scrub her from his skin, from his soul. Eventually, his legs gave out, and he turned off the spout with a shaky hand. He reached blindly for the towel Louisa had given them, drying himself off with quick, rough motions.

The cot creaked beneath him as he lowered himself onto the thin mattress. Lily lay curled on her side, her tiny fists clutching the thin blanket they shared, her breaths deep and even. He curled around her, cradling her against his chest, one arm wrapped securely around her small frame.

She was warm. She was real. She was the only proof that not all of him had been destroyed. Rick pressed his lips to her dark curls, breathing her in, grounding himself in the rhythmic rise and fall of her chest when a memory flickered, warm and golden, cutting through the cold.

Darcy's voice, full of laughter. The scent of fresh-cut grass. Summer heat pressing down on their backs as they sprawled out under the giant oak tree behind the church.

Rick wiped the sweat from his forehead, shooting a glare at his best friend. "You were supposed to help."

Darcy, lying flat on his back like he had no cares in the world, smirked without opening his eyes. "I was helping."

Rick snorted. "You spent the last hour charming the girls while I changed every diaper in the nursery."

Darcy cracked one eye open. "And who was it that suggested we volunteer for VBS nursery duty in the first place? Oh, right—you, because you wanted to impress Rachel Clarkson."

Rick groaned, running a hand through his hair. "It was a solid plan."

"Oh yeah. Real impressive. Girls love a guy covered in spit-up."

Rick threw a twig at him. "Rachel said she thought it was sweet."

Darcy sat up, looking entirely too pleased with himself. "You know what else she said? That I have a very 'mature' presence. That I'd make a great father someday." He flashed a grin. "Which I took to mean attractive and wise beyond my years."

Rick rolled his eyes. "More like lazy but good at talking his way out of work."

"Tomato, tomahto."

The memory faded. The warmth of the sun was gone. The laughter, the summer air—it all dissolved into the cold, stale reality of the cellar.

Rick exhaled slowly, tightening his grip around Lily.

One day. One day, he'd tell Darcy this story. One day, he'd be free enough to laugh about it. But for now, he held onto the memory like a lifeline.

Because hope—even in the form of an old, half-forgotten joke—was still hope.

Chapter 22

A father is supposed to shield his daughter from monsters. But
what happens when he is the one she needs saving from?
– Rick's Journal

Lily's small body curled against Rick's side as they sat
quietly on the cold cement floor. Her head rested on his shoulder,
her soft breaths warming his skin as her tiny fingers played with the
frayed hem of the blanket. He held her too tightly, unwilling to let
go, unwilling to acknowledge the presence across the room.

Louisa. She never gave him a moment to breathe. Instead,
she stood a few feet away, watching with a smirk of quiet
amusement, a bundle of fabric draped over her arm.

Rick's stomach twisted. He had known exactly what it was
before she even finished descending the stairs.

Louisa let the fabric slide through her fingers, tilting her
head as she studied his reaction. "Since you ruined your last dress,"
she said, mock disappointment lacing her tone, "I thought you'd
like something similar."

She lifted it higher, displaying it like a prize. Soft. Pastel.
Lace-trimmed. A dress.

Rick didn't move. Didn't look at it. Wouldn't.

Lily, oblivious to the tension in the room, giggled softly.
She lifted her head from Rick's shoulder, blinking sleepily.
"Dress?" she murmured.

Louisa's smirk widened. "Yes, Sweetheart," she cooed. "A
pretty dress for your pretty daddy."

Rick closed his eyes. No. Not in front of her. Lily,
innocent and trusting, was watching this. Witnessing this. She
would remember.

Louisa sighed dramatically. "I really should punish you for
your little tantrum. But—" She crouched in front of him, pressing
the dress against his chest. "I'm feeling generous today."

Rick flinched as the fabric brushed against his skin. Soft.
Light. Mocking.

Lily reached out, touching the fabric with small, curious
fingers. "Soft," she whispered.

Rick's throat closed.

Louisa's smirk deepened. She was making her part of this.

Rick held Lily closer, his body going rigid. *No. Not in front of her. Please.*

Louisa's fingers tightened in his hair, jerking his head back. "Rick."

His breath hitched. A broken sob fought its way up his throat. But he swallowed it down. Not in front of her. Not in front of his daughter.

Louisa watched him, savoring the moment. Then she leaned in, her lips brushing his ear. "If you make me ask again," she whispered, "I will make Lily help you."

Rick's entire body seized. No. No, she wouldn't—but of course, she would. Because she could. And because she knew what it would do to him.

Rick's hands moved before he could stop them. Shaking, trembling, they reached for the dress. The fabric was soft beneath his fingers. Delicate. Airy. Mocking.

Louisa leaned back, tilting her head in satisfaction. "That's my good girl."

Rick flinched. His vision blurred, his hands fumbling as he unzipped and stepped into the dress. The lace-trimmed sleeves slid over his arms, the skirt falling at his thighs in airy waves. Shorter than the last one. More delicate. The kind of thing a doll would wear. Or a pet.

Lily tilted her head, her small fingers brushing against the fabric. "Daddy?" she asked, confused.

Rick pressed a hand over his mouth, his body heaving with silent sobs.

Louisa sighed contently. "See?" she murmured. "That wasn't so hard."

Rick squeezed his eyes shut. She was wrong. It was. It was impossible. But so was saying no.

Chapter 23

> I failed Walter. I won't lose Sam too.
> – Rick's Journal

With his dress bunched around his thighs as he sat awkwardly on the floor, Rick wrapped his arms protectively around Lily. The damp air settled heavily around them, pressing against his skin like an unshakable weight.

Lily, thirty-one months old now, focused intently on a battered puzzle, her small fingers struggling to fit mismatched pieces together. She had found it weeks ago—discarded and incomplete—but she cherished it, the way she did anything that made her world feel bigger than this room.

Rick gently ran the comb Louisa had given them through her soft curls, savoring the moments they could share alone. "Almost, baby," he murmured. "That's it."

She beamed up at him, the pure joy in her eyes a sharp contrast to the dull, lifeless walls around them. Rick swallowed against the ache in his throat. She deserved more than this.

Then, the door creaked open. Rick's body tensed. His grip on Lily tightened instinctively. But there was something different. The usual crispness of Louisa's heels was missing. Instead, her steps were uneven, sloppy, her breath audible before she even reached the bottom. Rick's stomach dropped. She was drunk.

She emerged into view with a bundle in her arms, wrapped in a soft blue blanket. Her dress, usually pristine, hung slightly off her shoulder, her makeup smudged as though she hadn't bothered to fix it before coming down.

"Ricky," she slurred, swaying slightly, her eyes glassy but still gleaming with something sharp. "Meet your new little roommate."

Rick forced himself to stand, keeping Lily close. His pulse roared in his ears as Louisa took another unsteady step forward and thrust the bundle into his arms. The weight of the baby settled against his chest, fragile and warm. His breath caught. A baby. Another child. Another pawn.

"This," Louisa continued, her voice thick with liquor, "is another strong, healthy boy. Just like Walter."

Rick flinched at the name. Walter, who had been taken from him. The son who had been stolen and carried upstairs, away from his father and sister, never to return. His grip on the baby tightened.

"He's mine?" he whispered, his voice barely audible.

Louisa's smirk widened. "Yours," she confirmed. "And mine."

Rick adjusted his grip, his heart thundering in his chest. The baby stirred against him, a soft whimper escaping his tiny lips. "What about Tom?" he asked carefully, choosing his words slowly, as if speaking too fast would set her off.

Louisa's expression flickered, a shadow crossing her face. Then she snorted, rolling her eyes. "Tom and I are done," she muttered, waving a careless hand. "Turns out he's just like every other man—boring and predictable and can't keep it in his pants. Whatever. I got what I needed from him, and now I'm starting over."

Rick swallowed hard. "You used him."

Louisa's lips curled. "Oh, Ricky, don't act so righteous." She leaned in, her breath thick with alcohol, her voice dropping to a taunting whisper. "Didn't you hear me say that he cheated on me? But you wouldn't do that, would you?"

He didn't react. He wouldn't give her the satisfaction.

Louisa straightened, smoothing her dress—or at least trying to. "Now, take care of him," she said briskly. "It's about the only thing you're good for."

Rick's stomach churned as he looked down at the baby.

Louisa smirked, her voice light, almost mocking. "Oh, and his name is Sam."

Rick froze, his breath catching in his throat. Sam. Walter and Lily's brother.

Louisa turned toward the stairs, tossing a glance over her shoulder. "And teach Lily to share, will you? She's not the center of the universe anymore."

Rick barely had time to register the words before Lily let out a sharp, wounded cry. "No, Daddy," she whimpered, gripping Rick's dress. "No baby. Just Lily and Daddy."

Her tiny fingers twisted into the fabric, her entire body trembling against him. Her voice cracked, raw and breaking, like she was trying to hold onto something already slipping away.

Rick's breath caught as he knelt beside her, carefully settling Sam into the crude bassinet, made out of the box Louisa had first given them when Lily was a baby, before trying to pull Lily into his arms.

"Lily, this is Sam," he said, brushing his fingers through her hair. "He needs us, just like you needed me when you were little. We're a family."

Lily's face crumpled. "No!" she sobbed, burying her face against his chest. "Just Lily and Daddy!"

Rick held her close, feeling her little body tremble. "I love you, baby," he whispered. "That won't ever change."

Her cries softened, but the fear remained.

Then, Louisa swayed, her expression darkening. Without warning, her hand shot out. A sharp crack echoed through the cellar. Lily shrieked. Rick's stomach turned violently. Lily stumbled back, her hands clutching her backside, her breath hitching in ragged gasps.

Rick lunged forward, grabbing her before she fell. He pulled her against him, his pulse a roaring thunder in his ears. His body locked, screaming for action, for retaliation—but he didn't move. Couldn't move. Not if he wanted to protect them.

Louisa shook out her hand, flexing her fingers like she had just swatted a fly. "You do *not* get to be rude to my son," she said coldly.

Lily clung to Rick, sobbing. Rick's entire body coiled like a spring. He wanted to scream. To fight. But he forced himself to stay still.

Louisa sighed dramatically, as if the moment was exhausting for her. "Honestly, Ricky," she muttered, rubbing her temples. "Teach her some manners. Or next time, I'll do it again."

Rick couldn't breathe. His fury was suffocating.

Then Louisa stumbled toward the box. Rick's muscles tensed further as she reached down, picking up Sam's tiny hand in her own. She lifted it delicately to her lips, pressing a slow, deliberate kiss to his soft skin. The gesture was calculated. A reminder. A taunt. Sam was wanted and cherished. Rick felt Lily stiffen in his arms, her small sobs hiccupping against his chest.

Louisa smirked, her eyes gleaming as she turned and ascended the stairs. "Enjoy your little family, Ricky," she called, her voice coated in mockery. "While you still can."

The door slammed shut.

Lily let out a shattered wail, and Rick clutched her tighter, his lips pressing against her curls, his voice shaking as he whispered reassurances.

His own tears burned. His fury was suffocating. His fear was worse.

Rick shifted, carefully adjusting Sam in the box before gathering Lily close to him. Her sobs were quieter now, but her little fingers dug into his arm like she was afraid he would disappear too.

She lifted her tear-streaked face, whispering, "No take Sammy. Like Walter?"

Rick's breath caught. The memory of Walter's tiny hands reaching out as Louisa carried him away crushed him.

He pressed a trembling kiss to Lily's forehead. "No," he whispered. "Not like Walter."

Rick looked down at Sam, sleeping peacefully. His son. His responsibility. His chance not to fail. He exhaled shakily, his fingers tightening around Lily, his eyes burning with resolve.

I won't lose you too, my innocent son.

Chapter 24

> A father is meant to be a protector, a teacher, a shield. But how do
> I shield them when I'm the one who is bound?
> – Rick's Journal

Rick whispered to Lily again and again, the words empty before they left his lips. But promises in this place meant nothing. If he could carve them into the stone walls, etch them into something permanent, maybe then his promises would be true. Maybe then Lily wouldn't wake up screaming, reaching for a brother she would never see again.

A damp chill settled over his skin as he rocked Sam in his arms, the baby's soft whimpers filling the quiet. Beside him, Lily clung to his side, her small body curled against his for warmth. Her breaths came in uneven hiccups, the last remnants of the hours she had spent screaming, inconsolable in her fear that Sam would disappear just as Walter had.

Rick kissed the top of her head, her dark curls soft beneath his lips. "I won't let her take him," he whispered. Even if it killed him.

The cellar door creaked open. Rick stiffened at the sound of unsteady heels clacking against the stairs. The air shifted, thick with the heavy scent of alcohol. Louisa was drunk again.

Ever since her divorce, she loved nights like these, when the liquor loosened her grip on control just enough to let the sadism spill out unfiltered. Her movements were slower, but never clumsy. Even drunk, she was dangerous.

Rick placed Sam in his makeshift bassinet and pulled Lily closer, bracing himself.

Louisa's gaze swept over him, lingering on Sam before her lips curved upward, amusement flashing in her glassy eyes. "Ricky," she drawled, swaying slightly. "You've been busy."

His stomach twisted. "I need something for Lily," he said, forcing his voice to stay even, unaffected.

Louisa arched a brow. "Oh? A treat?"

Rick nodded once.

She stepped forward, letting the silence stretch, savoring his discomfort. Finally, she lowered herself onto the cot beside him with a smirk. "Then read to me," she purred.

Rick reached for the Bible, his fingers steady despite the disgust curling inside him. Before he could open it, Louisa snatched it from his grasp. She flipped through the pages with idle amusement, then pressed the book into his lap.

"Here," she said. "Read this. It's fitting."

His stomach sank when he saw the verse. "Train up a child in the way he should go; even when he is old he will not depart from it."

Louisa snorted, taking a slow sip from her tumbler. "Is that so, Ricky?" she murmured. "Is that why Lily is such a spoiled little brat?"

Rick's jaw tightened, but he didn't take the bait. He wouldn't give her the satisfaction.

She turned more pages, her fingers gliding over the worn paper until she found what she wanted. "Whoever spares the rod hates his son, but he who loves him is diligent to discipline him." Louisa's smirk sharpened. "Oh, I do like that one. Don't you, Ricky?"

Her hand shot out—fast, practiced. The slap snapped his head to the side, pain blooming hot across his cheek. His vision blurred for a second, his pulse hammering against the bruise already there.

Lily gasped, burying her face against his chest.

"Discipline, Ricky," Louisa cooed, brushing her fingers over the fresh welt. "You're such a failure of a father."

Rick clenched his teeth, breathing through the pain.

She turned another page, her smirk widening when she found what she was looking for. "One more for the night, Ricky."

"'Fathers, do not provoke your children to anger, but bring them up in the discipline and instruction of the Lord.'"

Louisa tipped her head back and laughed, the sound bouncing off the cold stone walls. "And yet," she mused, wiping at an invisible tear, "look at your daughter. Always whining. Always begging. I think you've failed at that too."

The tumbler shattered against the floor. Rick flinched, instinctively shielding Lily as Louisa's face twisted with something raw, something vicious.

"You dare sit there," she hissed, "and act like you're some godly, righteous father when you're the reason they're in this hellhole?"

Rick's breath stilled.

"You think you're a good father?" Louisa snarled. "You're not a father at all. You're a prisoner. You're mine. And your kids? They only exist because I allow it."

He lowered the Bible. A mistake. Louisa lunged. Her hand wrapped around his throat above where the collar marked him as her property, shoving him back against the cot, pressing down just enough to send panic shooting through him.

Lily screamed, her tiny hands clawing at Louisa's dress. "Stop!" she sobbed. "No hurt Daddy!"

Louisa shoved her off. Lily hit the ground hard, a sharp cry bursting from her lips. Rick didn't think. Didn't breathe. One second, Louisa was standing over Lily. The next, his body surged forward, tearing free, arms reaching—

Louisa stumbled back, breathing heavily, her chest rising and falling.

Rick clutched Lily tightly, her little body trembling as she buried her face against his shoulder. His own breathing was uneven, but he forced his voice to stay calm. "It's okay, Sweetheart," he murmured. "Daddy's here. I've got you."

Louisa wiped at the liquor splattered on her dress, glaring at the mess she had created. With a breathless laugh, she ran a hand through her hair, shaking her head as if amused by herself. "Oh, Ricky," she sighed. "You make everything so difficult."

The door slammed shut. The lock clicked into place. Only then did Rick let himself breathe.

His fingers trembled as he brushed Lily's damp cheeks, pressing a kiss to her forehead. "Shhh, Sweetheart," he murmured. "It's over."

Lily's sobs slowed into exhausted whimpers. Rick exhaled shakily, holding her close. His gaze shifted to Sam, still sleeping peacefully in his makeshift crib. And finally Rick allowed himself a moment of quiet. A moment to pray.

"Lord, let me survive one more day. Let me be strong enough. For them."

Chapter 25

> Monsters don't always have fangs or claws—sometimes, they wear
> perfume and whisper lies in the dark.
> – Rick's Journal

Rick dreamt of warmth. It wrapped around him, sinking
into his bones, dissolving the ache of cold that had become his
constant companion. The scent of lilies filled the air—soft, floral,
familiar.

When he opened his eyes, she was there. Anne. She knelt
beside him, her touch featherlight as her fingers brushed over his
cheek.

"Rick," she whispered, her voice filled with so much love
it made his chest tighten. "I found you."

His breath hitched. His hands trembled as he reached for
her. "Anne?"

She smiled, her eyes brimming with unshed tears. "It's
me."

A sob caught in his throat. He cupped her face,
memorizing every curve, every freckle, every breath. She was real.
She had come back for him. "You're here," he whispered in awe.
"You came back."

She leaned into his touch, her warm breath ghosting over
his lips. "I could never leave you, Ricky. Not really."

Something shifted. Anne's breath was too warm. The scent
of lilies sharpened—sickly sweet, suffocating. The soft fingers on
his cheek pressed too hard, nails grazing skin. A distant cry.

"Daddy?"

Rick stiffened. The warmth soured, twisting in his gut.
Anne's touch became wrong. The floral scent turned cloying,
choking. Beneath it—vanilla and alcohol. The sound came again,
muffled but desperate.

"Daddy?"

His eyes snapped open. The world around him fractured.
Anne's face blurred—no, shifted—her soft eyes darkening into
cruelty. Her hands, once gentle, tightened in his hair. And the
warmth—it wasn't warmth at all. It was heat. Stifling. Suffocating.
Trapping. His chest caved in, his breath hitching. The heat pressing

against him wasn't comfort. No, it was weight. His stomach lurched, a violent tremor wracking through him.

No. *No, no, no.* He wasn't dreaming anymore. It wasn't Anne's breath against his lips. It wasn't Anne's body pressed against his. It was Louisa. Bile rose in his throat. His entire body recoiled.

"Good morning, Ricky," she purred, amusement thick in her voice.

Rick gagged. He tried to move, to shove her away, but his limbs felt heavy, useless. Louisa wasn't just on top of him—she had invaded his dream, twisted it, stolen from him. He choked out a sound—half a sob, half a plea.

Louisa only smirked, her breath reeking of whiskey as she leaned in. "What's wrong?" she cooed. "You were so eager just a moment ago. Told me you loved me and everything."

Rick's body shook violently. "Get off," he rasped, panic clawing at his throat. "Get—off—"

She tsked, pressing a single finger against his lips. "You know I like when you read to me," she whispered. "But this—." Her nails dragged down his chest, the sensation making his stomach lurch. "This is better."

Rick squeezed his eyes shut, his mind screaming for a way out. *Lily!* Her cries cut through his panic like a knife. Rick's eyes snapped open. Where was she? His breath came fast, his head jerking toward the sound as his blood turned to ice. Lily was across the room, tied to the radiator.

Thick metal handcuffs dug into her small wrists, her arms straining as she hiccupped through sobs. Her tiny body trembled, her chest rising and falling in shallow gasps, terror leaking from every part of her. Rick lurched forward, his entire body thrashing, but Louisa pressed him back down effortlessly.

"Shhh," she murmured, lips brushing his jaw. "You'll wake the baby."

His entire body convulsed, muscles screaming with rage. Louisa only laughed, delighted. She had planned this. She had moved Lily while he was asleep. Chained her up. Left her helpless, terrified, watching. And now she wanted Rick to break. She wanted him to scream. To beg. To give her everything she fed off of.

Rick's voice broke. "Please."

Louisa hummed, tracing a lazy circle on his chest. "Please what?"

His voice cracked. "Let Lily go. You can do whatever you want to me, just—just let her go."

Louisa tilted her head, pretending to consider it. "Hmm. Tempting. But no."

Rick nearly lost it. He thrashed harder, the chain around his neck cutting into his skin as he fought against her.

Louisa only sighed, bored, and sat up. She adjusted her dress as if nothing had happened, then smirked down at him. "You really should be thanking me, Ricky."

His breathing was ragged, his body shaking with fury, shame, and disgust.

Louisa sighed dramatically, rolling her eyes. "At least tell me you love me first," she said, mocking his dream.

Rick wanted to tear her apart. But he had to think of his children so he did the only thing he could. He whispered, "I love you."

Louisa grinned, satisfied. "I knew you did."

Then, as if to drive the knife even deeper, she reached into her pocket and pulled out a small silver key.

Rick's stomach twisted. "The cuffs?" he asked, his voice barely above a whisper.

Louisa dangled the key in front of him, her smirk widening. "Mmm, I don't know," she mused. "What's in it for me?"

Rick clenched his fists, his nails biting into his palms. "Louisa."

She leaned down, her breath warm against his lips. "Kiss me like you mean it."

His stomach lurched.

"Do it," she whispered, her fingers twisting into his hair. "Or maybe I'll just leave Lily there for a while."

Rick swallowed the bile in his throat. Then, slowly, he did as he was told. Her lips tasted of alcohol and bile, her tongue pushing into his mouth felt like a violation. The scent of her perfume—vanilla and decay—clung to his skin as she sighed contentedly against him.

When she finally pulled away, she licked her lips, smug. "See? That wasn't so hard."

She pressed the key into his hand before standing, smoothing out her dress as she turned toward Sam's bassinet. With calculated slowness, she picked up Sam and cradled him against her chest. She kissed his tiny hand. A final, cruel snub. Then she turned toward the stairs, pausing by the single chair in the room, where a teddy bear sat.

"See you soon, Sweetheart. Enjoy the treat." The door slammed shut.

Rick rushed across the room to Lily, his hands shaking as he fumbled with the key. The cuffs fell away. Lily sobbed, her arms immediately wrapping around his neck. Rick held her, his own body trembling.

He had to survive. He would survive. Not for himself. For them.

Chapter 26

> Even in the lion's den, God was there—so I have to believe that
> He's here too.
> – Rick's Journal

Rick knelt by the small electric hot plate, carefully stirring the thin porridge in a chipped bowl. The air in the cellar was stale, thick with the absence of Sam. The box where Sam had once slept sat empty. Rick hadn't moved it. Couldn't. It gaped at him, a wound in the room, a reminder of Louisa's cruelty that no amount of prayer could erase.

But Lily was still here. And as long as she was here, Rick had to keep moving forward.

Lily sat on the cot, her legs swinging as she watched him with quiet curiosity. "What's for breakfast, Daddy?"

Rick forced a smile, though his stomach clenched at the small portions. "Something special," he said. "Oatmeal and the last banana."

Her brown eyes widened. "The last one?"

Rick nodded, peeling it carefully and breaking it into three small pieces. He placed two on a plate in front of her, keeping the last for himself. He felt her eyes on him, studying the portion he had taken.

"Daddy," she said softly, holding out her piece. "You have more."

Rick shook his head. "No, Sweetheart. You need it more than I do."

Lily hesitated, her small fingers tightening around the fruit. "You need to be big and strong."

Rick smiled, reaching over to tuck a loose curl behind her ear. "And you need to grow healthy." He nudged the plate closer. "Eat, baby. Please."

She bit her lip but obeyed, nibbling at the fruit as Rick stirred the watery oatmeal. "Daddy?"

"Yeah, Sweetheart?"

"Tell me about Daniel."

Rick stilled, the spoon pausing in the bowl. Daniel was her favorite story. She always asked for it when she needed comfort, so he sat beside her, wrapping an arm around her shoulders. "A long time ago, there was a man named Daniel. He was very brave, and he loved God more than anything."

Lily grinned. "Like you?"

Rick's throat tightened, but he forced a smile. "Maybe a little," he said. "Daniel was strong," he continued, "but he didn't fight with his fists. He fought with his faith."

Lily blinked up at him, listening intently.

"The king made a law," Rick said. "No one was allowed to pray to God. But Daniel knew what was right. He prayed anyway."

Lily gasped softly. "Then the bad men came."

Rick nodded. "They threw him into the lions' den. It was dark and scary, and the lions were hungry."

Lily clutched his dress. "Did he cry?"

Rick thought about that for a moment. "Maybe," he admitted. "But he didn't run. He knelt down and prayed, even when it felt like no one was listening."

Lily exhaled slowly. "Then the angel came."

Rick smiled faintly. "Yes, baby. The angel came. He shut the lions' mouths and stayed with Daniel all night."

Lily chewed on her oatmeal thoughtfully. "We don't have an angel."

Rick kissed the top of her head. "Maybe we do," he whispered. "Maybe we just can't see them."

As she ate her oatmeal, Rick subtly tipped his own spoon into her bowl, making sure she got more. She was too focused on his voice to notice, eagerly scooping up another bite between sentences.

"You pray, Daddy?"

Rick nodded. "Every day, baby."

Lily's brow furrowed. "Even though God didn't stop Mama from hurting you last night?"

Rick's hand trembled slightly as he scooped another spoonful into her bowl. He forced himself to meet her eyes, to offer the answer she needed, not just the one that made sense in his own pain. "Yes," he said softly. "Even then."

Lily looked down at her bowl, quiet for a long moment. Then she reached over and took his hand, squeezing it. Rick's breath caught, but he squeezed back.

"Bad men didn't win," Lily whispered.

Rick's smile wobbled. "No, Sweetheart. They didn't."

She chewed thoughtfully, then nodded with quiet certainty. "God's gonna send us an angel, Daddy."

Rick swallowed against the lump in his throat. "Yes, Sweetheart," he whispered. "One day."

The bowl of oatmeal sat untouched beside him. He no longer felt hungry.

Lily sighed contently as she finished her oatmeal and climbed onto his lap, wrapping her arms around his neck.

Rick exhaled slowly, pressing his lips to her curls. "We'll make it," he murmured. He didn't know if he was speaking to her, to himself, or to God.

But he had to believe it.

Chapter 27

> I traded my soul for books, but was it enough to save hers?
> – Rick's Journal

"Daddy," Lily said, holding up her picture with pride. "Look! It's our home."

She was nearly five now, her curiosity burning as brightly as ever—a fragile but unbreakable light in their suffocating world. Her drawing was full of color, bringing to life a sun, a house, and four stick figures holding hands, just like the picture Rick had drawn for her months ago.

Rick forced a smile, brushing a stray curl from her face. "It's beautiful, Picasso," he murmured, his chest tightening. "Just like you."

She beamed. "This is you, and this is me," she explained, pointing to the stick figures. "And here's Walter and Sam."

Rick swallowed hard. Walter and Sam. He hadn't seen Walter in over three years, hadn't held Sam since the night Louisa took him away almost two years ago. The absence was a wound that never closed.

But he buried it, forcing himself to nod. "I love it," he said. "Maybe one day, we'll have a house just like this."

Lily nodded eagerly, her curls bouncing. "And we'll all be together again."

Rick's throat constricted. *I don't know how to make that happen, baby girl.* But he couldn't say that. Instead, he kissed her forehead. "That's right," he whispered. "We will."

But stories weren't enough anymore. She needed more than dreams. She needed to learn. That night, after Lily had fallen asleep curled up beside him, Rick lay in the darkness, his stomach twisting. He had traded himself for food before, for medicine. But this wasn't for survival. This was for something more. Something bigger. Something that would outlast him. But asking Louisa for anything meant paying a price.

The next morning, the cellar door creaked open. Rick tensed as Louisa descended the stairs, her heels clicking against the concrete. He stood, positioning himself between her and Lily, who was still rubbing sleep from her eyes.

Louisa smirked, crossing her arms. "What now, Ricky? I'm not in the mood for your whining today."

Rick clenched his fists. He hated this. Hated needing her. "Lily needs books," he said. "She's almost five. She needs to learn."

Louisa arched a brow, her smirk widening. "Books?" she repeated, amused. "And why would I waste my time on that?"

"Please." The word burned his throat, but he forced it out. "I'll do whatever you want."

Her smile deepened, her eyes gleaming with triumph. She stepped closer, trailing a finger down his chest. Rick forced himself to stay still, though every instinct screamed at him to pull away. The air between them thickened, suffocating. He knew that look. Knew that smile. The request was coming, but he didn't know if he was ready to hear it.

"Whatever I want?" Louisa purred.

Rick nodded once. His hands curled into fists at his sides.

Louisa leaned in, her breath warm against his ear. "I was going to do this anyway, Ricky," she whispered, her voice thick with mock sweetness. "But you just made it so much more fun."

His stomach dropped.

She laughed, running a hand through her hair as if discussing something mundane. "You know, Ricky, I was thinking—it's been a while since Sam was born. Don't you think it's time for another baby?"

Rick's body turned to ice, nausea clawing up his throat. His skin burned, his stomach churned, but he forced his mouth to move. Forced the word out like poison.

"Fine."

Louisa tilted her head, feigning curiosity. "That's it? No fight? No begging?"

Rick's jaw tightened. "Books," he gritted out. "And a chalkboard."

Louisa let out a delighted laugh, running her fingers lightly over his cheek before slapping him playfully. "Oh, Ricky. You really do know how to work a bargain."

She turned toward the stairs, waving a dismissive hand. "Fine. You'll have your little schoolhouse, and I expect you to be a happy, active participant in our love-making."

The next day, she returned, carrying a small stack of books and a child-sized chalkboard easel. She dumped them onto the floor with a theatrical sigh.

"Aren't I just the picture of generosity?" she cooed.

Rick didn't acknowledge her. He knelt beside the books, running his fingers over the spines. Most were defaced by crayon marks and battered, some missing pages, but they were treasures in a place where there were no other books but the Bible.

Lily rushed over to him, her wide eyes full of wonder. "Daddy, what are these?" she asked breathlessly.

"Books, Sweetheart," Rick murmured, his voice shaking. "I'm going to teach you how to read."

Lily clapped her hands, bouncing on her heels, her whole face alight with joy. "Really? I can read?"

Her excitement was pure, untainted. She had no idea what it had cost.

She dropped to her knees, carefully picking up a book from the pile. As she flipped through the worn pages, something made her pause. A bright yellow dog with long ears smiled up at her from the cover. She frowned, pointing at it. "What's that, Daddy?"

Rick's throat tightened. She didn't know. She didn't even know what a dog looked like. He forced his voice steady, his heart twisting as he smoothed a hand over her curls. "That's a doggy, Sweetheart."

Lily's brow furrowed, considering this. "A doggy," she echoed, testing the word.

Rick swallowed hard and nodded. She studied the book for a moment longer, then nodded in quiet acceptance before flipping the page. Rick watched her, his chest aching with a grief too deep for words.

Louisa watched with amusement. "Enjoy your little school," she said with a smirk. "But don't forget. I'll be back tonight, Ricky, for your end of the bargain."

The door slammed behind her.

Rick let out a slow breath and turned to Lily, who was flipping through a book, her small hands carefully tracing the illustrations.

"Come here," he said softly, sitting beside her. "We'll start with this one."

That evening, they practiced letters until her eyelids grew heavy. Rick tucked her into a blanket on the floor of the shower cubicle, brushing her curls back as her tiny fingers clung to his hand.

"Thank you, Daddy," she murmured. "I love you."

Rick's breath hitched. Did she know? Did she somehow understand what he had traded? He forced his voice steady. "I love you too, Lily. Always."

As she drifted off, Rick closed the shower curtain around her and sat on the cot, staring at the books neatly stacked in the corner. The weight of what he had done pressed against his chest like iron. The cost of Louisa's attention was suffocating, but Lily's smile made it worth it.

His hands trembled as he folded them together. "Lord, I don't know if You still hear me. But if You do—don't let her become cold and cruel like Louisa. Please keep her innocent and sweet."

The cold walls of the cellar loomed around him, but Lily's joy was a fragile beacon of light in the darkness. And for that, Rick would endure anything.

Chapter 28

> Faith isn't about seeing the way out—it's about walking forward anyway.
> – Rick's Journal

Lily's laughter bubbled through the cellar like sunlight breaking through storm clouds. She sat cross-legged on the cot, rocking side to side in excitement, the chalkboard standing ready before her. A scrap of cloth she'd turned into a rag dangled from her tiny fingers, evidence of her impatience as she waited for Rick to begin the lesson.

Rick stretched, rubbing the exhaustion from his eyes before reaching for the chalk. His muscles ached from another restless night spent serving Louisa, but the sight of Lily's eager smile forced a small one from him in return.

She was nearly five now, her dark curls tumbling around her face, her eyes bright and filled with something Louisa hadn't managed to take from her—wonder. As Rick studied her, the warmth in his chest tinged with gratitude. She looked like him. She had his dark curls, his dark brown eyes. He didn't have to wake up every day and see Louisa or even Anne staring back at him. In a world where everything had been taken from him, that small mercy meant more than he could explain.

"What story should we start with today?" he asked, kneeling beside the cot.

Lily barely hesitated before bouncing on the mattress. "Daniel and the lions!" she declared, squeezing her stuffed bear tight.

Rick chuckled, shaking his head. "Of course."

He moved to the chalkboard and, with slow, deliberate strokes, wrote Daniel in large letters at the top. Lily leaned forward, watching every movement with rapt attention.

"Do you remember why Daniel ended up in the lions' den?" Rick asked, tapping the board lightly.

Lily nodded, her small fingers curling around the bear's worn fur. "Because he prayed to God, and the bad men didn't like it."

Rick's chest tightened with pride. "That's right," he said. "Daniel loved God so much that he prayed every day, even when a law was made saying he couldn't. Some jealous men tricked the king into making that law just so Daniel would get in trouble."

Lily's eyes widened. "But Daniel prayed!"

Rick nodded. "He did because Daniel knew that God was more important than any rule made by men." He paused, kneeling beside her. "The king didn't want to punish Daniel, but the law said he had to, so the king threw Daniel into a den full of lions."

Lily gasped, her little hands covering her mouth. "Did he think the lions would eat him?"

Rick shook his head. "No, Sweetheart. Daniel trusted God to protect him. And do you know what happened?"

Her voice dropped to a whisper, as if the moment deserved reverence. "God sent an angel to save him."

"That's right," Rick confirmed, his voice steady but filled with quiet conviction. "The lions didn't hurt Daniel at all. And when the king came to check on him the next morning, he saw that Daniel's God was real and powerful. Therefore, the king made a new law that everyone should worship Daniel's God."

Lily's face lit up with wonder. She clapped her hands, sending a small cloud of chalk dust into the air. "God saved Daniel! Daniel trusted Him!"

Rick chuckled as he reached over, gently brushing the dust off her nose. Lily wrinkled her face at the touch, giggling.

"That's right," he said, pulling her into a quick hug. "God is always with us, even when things seem scary or impossible. We just have to trust Him, like Daniel did."

Lily turned her wide eyes up at him. "Like us?"

Rick's breath caught. She didn't know how much their lives mirrored Daniel's. She didn't realize that every morning, Rick woke up in a lion's den of his own, hoping today wouldn't be the day the beast finally struck. But she didn't need to know that. Not yet.

"Like us," he whispered, pressing a kiss to the top of her head.

Lily beamed, bouncing on the cot. "Can we write lions next, Daddy?"

Rick exhaled a quiet breath, gathering himself before standing again. "Of course."

He carefully wrote lions beneath Daniel, pronouncing each letter as he wrote. "L-I-O-N-S. Lions."

Lily mimicked his movements, pointing at each letter. "Lions!" she cheered. "Daniel and lions!"

Rick smiled as he stepped back, watching the way her eyes sparkled. "You're amazing, Lily."

Her pride was infectious. "Can we draw lions too?"

Rick let out a soft chuckle. "Of course we can."

He handed her a piece of chalk, and together, they filled the board with wobbly lions and small stick figures. Lily laughed as she added whiskers to one of the lions, her giggles lighting up the room in a way that made Rick's heart ache with something almost like hope.

By the time they finished their lesson, the board was covered in scribbles—evidence of a morning well spent. Rick helped Lily clean up, her laughter still ringing softly in the cellar as they wiped the board, preparing it for tomorrow's lesson.

That night, after tucking Lily into their cot, Rick sat on the edge, his gaze lingering on the now-clean chalkboard. The faint outline of the words Daniel and lions remained, a quiet echo of today's lesson.

He folded his hands, bowing his head. "Lord," he murmured, "thank You for giving me moments like these. For her joy, her curiosity. Please protect her. Help me keep going, to be the father she needs. And—help us find a way out."

Lily's breathing was soft and even, the sound grounding him as exhaustion pulled at his limbs. The walls of the cellar remained as unforgiving as ever, but tonight, they felt a little less suffocating. For now, Lily's light was enough to keep him moving forward. She was a reminder of God's love.

And Rick clung to it with everything he had.

Chapter 29

> I used to think there was a limit to how much someone could take before breaking. Now I know—there is no limit. You just keep surviving, even when every piece of you is shattered.
> – Rick's Journal

The air in the cellar was thick with dampness, the kind that clung to skin and settled into bones. But it wasn't the cold that made Rick's body tense—it was the weight of Lily's silence. She sat on the cot, her arms crossed, her legs kicking restlessly, her stuffed bear abandoned beside her. Her glare had barely wavered since Louisa left, and Rick knew this was more than just jealousy.

She was waiting for him to say something, anything, to make it better. But nothing could make this better.

The pink bundle in his arms shifted, a small whimper escaping Ellie's tiny lips. Rick adjusted her carefully, his fingers tracing the curve of her delicate head. Another child, another innocent life dragged into this nightmare.

Lily let out a sharp huff. "I don't like her."

Rick sighed, already expecting the defiance but still feeling the sting of it. "Lily—"

"I don't want her here!" The words came out as a shout, her little fists balling in her lap. "She's noisy, and she smells bad, and she takes you away from me!"

Rick's chest ached. "That's not true, Sweetheart—"

"You always say we're a family," Lily interrupted, voice cracking. "But Walter's gone! Sam's gone! And now she's here!"

Rick exhaled slowly, forcing his own emotions down. "I know it's hard—"

"YOU DON'T KNOW!"

The cellar door creaked open. Lily's head snapped up. Rick's arms tightened around Ellie.

Louisa took her time coming down, her lips curling into something close to amusement. She took in the scene—Lily curled tight with anger, Rick holding the baby protectively—and her smirk deepened. "Well, isn't that sad?"

Rick's stomach clenched.

Louisa crouched in front of Lily, her eyes gleaming with something cruel. "Poor little Lily. Not Daddy's princess anymore, are you?"

Lily flinched, but her glare didn't waver.

Louisa's tone turned mockingly sweet. "You had a good run, but babies take a lot of attention. Poor Ricky is going to be so busy."

Rick saw the slight tremble in Lily's hands, the way she pressed her lips together to keep them from quivering. And Louisa saw it too.

Rick moved to stand, but Louisa's hand shot out, gripping Lily's chin between her fingers. Lily whimpered.

Rick's body went rigid. "Let her go."

Louisa ignored him. "You know," she murmured, tilting Lily's face side to side, "I used to think you were cute. But looking at you now—you're just a little nuisance, aren't you?"

Lily's lower lip wobbled, but she stayed silent.

Rick forced himself to keep his voice steady. "Louisa, stop."

Louisa hummed, turning her gaze back to him. "What's it worth to you?"

Rick's heart pounded. "What do you want?"

She smiled. "Tell me you love me."

Rick's stomach twisted.

"Say it like you mean it," Louisa taunted, pressing her fingers into Lily's cheeks.

Rick swallowed back bile. "I love you, Louisa."

She tilted her head. "Try again."

Rick clenched his jaw. "I love you, Louisa."

Louisa's smirk widened. "That's more like it."

She released Lily suddenly, making her stumble backward. Rick lunged, catching her against his chest. Lily buried her face in his hated dress, her tiny body trembling.

Louisa turned her attention to Ellie. Slowly, she reached down and traced a single finger down the baby's cheek, her nail barely pressing into the fragile skin. Rick's body locked up.

Louisa smiled. "So small. So helpless." Her voice was soft, almost a whisper. "And she belongs to me."

Rick saw Lily's wide, terrified eyes watching the exchange. She understood.

Louisa straightened, dusting off her hands. "I think I'll come back later. You'll be grateful, won't you, Ricky?"

Rick's nails dug into his palm. "Get out."

Louisa laughed. The door slammed shut. The lock clicked into place.

Rick collapsed onto the cot, pulling Lily against him, shielding Ellie between them.

Lily let out a choked sob. "I don't want her to take Ellie like she took Walter."

Rick pressed his lips to her curls, whispering, "I won't let her."

But as he held both of his daughters close, Rick knew—he had to find a way out.

Before it was too late.

Chapter 30

> I always told Lily that lions only hurt when God allows them to.
> But maybe some lions just enjoy the suffering. Maybe some were
> never meant to be tamed.
> – Rick's Journal

Rick's arms trembled as he cradled Ellie against his chest, her tiny body warm and fragile. Across the room, Lily sat huddled by the furnace, the heavy chain locked around her ankle glinting in the dim light. The clinking of metal echoed through the cellar every time she shifted, a sharp, cruel reminder of Louisa's punishment.

She hadn't spoken in an hour. Rick's pulse pounded with guilt and fury, his throat raw from screaming until his voice gave out.

Louisa had barely reacted. She had taken her time, unspooling the chain from the locked chest in the corner where she kept her so-called toys, handling it with the care of a carefully chosen gift. Her expression remained eerily calm as she wrapped the cold metal around Lily's ankle and clicked the lock into place.

"You want to act like a wild animal?" she had murmured, brushing Lily's curls from her face. "Fine. Let's see how you like being treated like one."

Rick had lunged so hard his chain yanked him back, bruising his throat. His body hadn't even registered the pain—just the sound of Lily's sobs.

Now, hours later, she was still curled into herself, her stuffed bear clutched against her chest, her sobs broken by hiccups.

Rick adjusted Ellie in his arms, pressing a gentle kiss to her forehead as he set the empty bottle down on the floor. She stirred but didn't wake. He could feel Lily's eyes watching them as he moved about the small room to clean the bottle. She shifted slightly, the chain clinking again. A fresh tear slipped down her cheek.

"Daddy," Her voice was barely a whisper, "I'm scared."

Rick reached towards her as far as his chain would allow, his fingertips just barely brushing hers. "I'm here, Lily, and you have God and you have Bear Bear," he whispered. "You're not alone."

Her shoulders trembled. She wiped at her tears with the beloved Bear Bear's worn fur. "What did I do wrong?" she whispered. "Why does she hate me?"

Rick's heart twisted so violently it nearly took his breath. "You didn't do anything wrong," he said firmly. "Lily, you made a mistake. Shaking Ellie's box wasn't okay because it could have hurt her. But mistakes don't make you bad. They don't mean you deserve this."

Her small hands curled into fists, pressing against her tear-streaked face. "I was mad," she whispered. "I didn't mean to."

Rick swallowed hard. "I know, baby. I know you didn't."

She rocked back and forth, voice small, breaking. "I was bad. I was bad."

Rick forced himself to keep his voice steady. "No. You weren't bad." He reached out again, fingers brushing hers. "You're good, Lily. You're my brave, smart, amazing girl. Don't ever think you have to change who you are for her."

Lily's breath hitched. For a long moment, she said nothing. "Then why doesn't God stop her?"

The words gutted Rick. His throat tightened. He forced himself to take a slow breath. "You remember your favorite Bible story?" he murmured. "Daniel in the lions' den?"

Lily hesitated, then gave a small nod. "He was brave because God was with him," she whispered.

Rick swallowed against the lump in his throat. "That's right. And God is with us too. Even here. Even now. He's always watching over us."

Lily's lips trembled. "Daniel was saved."

Rick closed his eyes for half a second. "We just have to trust Him, like Daniel did. God will show us the way."

Lily's tiny fingers pressed into his palm. They both knew the truth. They were still waiting for their rescue.

Rick exhaled, forcing a soft smile. "Let's pray together."

Lily nodded. She closed her eyes, bear still tight against her chest.

Rick bowed his head. He couldn't break. Not in front of her. So, he whispered, "Lord, please give us strength. Protect Lily. Protect Ellie. Show us the way."

The chains remained. The cellar walls still loomed. But Lily squeezed his fingertips.

Rick exhaled slowly, brushing a curl from her face. "For you," he murmured, voice raw. "For both of you, I'll keep going." *No matter what it takes*, he silently vowed.

Chapter 31

> I gave her everything I could tonight—my food, my warmth, my
> promises. But it wasn't enough. It's never enough.
> – Rick's Journal

Rick stood at the table, sorting through the meager pantry supplies Louisa had just delivered. Dented cans, their labels faded and peeling, stared back at him, most of them well past their expiration dates. Still, it was food. They would eat comfortably for the next week, and for that, he was grateful.

He pulled out a can of chicken noodle soup, setting it aside, when something at the back of the box caught his eye. A can of peaches in syrup. It wasn't much. Certainly, it was not a Thanksgiving feast, not like the ones he remembered from years ago. However, for his girls, it was something sweet, something special.

Behind him, eight-year-old Lily sat cross-legged on the cot she shared with her little sister, Bear Bear resting in her lap. Almost-two-year-old Ellie clung to her older sister, her tiny fingers fisting the hem of Lily's dress.

"Daddy," Lily called, her voice bright with curiosity. "What's that?"

Rick turned, lifting the can like a magician revealing a prize. "This," he said, rolling it in his palm, "is our Thanksgiving dessert."

Lily's face lit up. "Peaches?"

"Peaches," Rick confirmed with a soft chuckle. "They're really sweet and juicy."

Ellie, nestled close to Lily, clapped her hands clumsily. "Peech!" she babbled.

Rick leaned down, ruffling Lily's curls and pressing a kiss to the top of Ellie's head. "Want to help me make dinner?"

Lily nodded eagerly, and Ellie copied her, bouncing on her unsteady legs.

As Rick warmed the soup, Lily and Ellie helped put the cans and supplies into the cupboard. Rather, Lily put things away while Ellie proudly pulled them back out, giggling as if it were a game.

Rick caught Lily's exasperated look and winked at her. "She's helping in her own way."

Lily huffed but didn't argue. "Tell us a story, Daddy," she said suddenly, glancing toward him. "A good one."

Rick smiled. "What about the fiery furnace?"

Lily gasped in delight. "Yes! That's a good one."

As the watery soup simmered, Rick wove the tale of Shadrach, Meshach, and Abednego, his voice steady and warm. Lily hung on every word, her eyes wide, while Ellie clutched Bear Bear, fascinated but too little to fully understand.

When the story ended, Lily's expression grew thoughtful. "Do you think God will save us, Daddy?" she asked softly.

Rick hesitated but forced himself to nod. "I think He's with us, Lily. Just like He was with them."

She nodded slowly, pressing closer to Ellie. "I hope so," she whispered. Lily wrapped her hands around the warm bowl, inhaling deeply as steam curled into the air. "It smells good, Daddy," she said, her voice filled with that soft, unwavering trust that made Rick's chest ache.

"It's just chicken noodle soup, Sweetheart," he murmured, stirring his own with his spoon. "But I'm glad you like it."

Ellie, perched beside Lily, picked up her spoon in her fist, stabbing at the bowl with a delighted squeal before managing to scoop some up. Half of it dribbled down her chin, but she smacked her lips together in approval. "Yum!" she announced, her words still soft and babyish.

Rick chuckled. "I'm glad, Little Love."

It wasn't a feast. It wasn't turkey or mashed potatoes, stuffing or pumpkin pie. But it was warm, it was food, and for now, it was enough. He exhaled softly, setting his spoon down. "Since it's Thanksgiving, why don't we say what we're thankful for?"

Lily perked up, always eager for a game, but Ellie, who had lost interest in her soup, was already bouncing in place. "Bear Bear!" she squealed, hugging the threadbare stuffed animal to her chest. "Bear Bear best!"

Rick chuckled. "Of course, Bear Bear."

Lily grinned, shaking her head at her little sister before turning to Rick, her expression softening. "I'm thankful for you, Daddy."

Rick froze.

Lily beamed at him, completely unaware of the way her words knocked the air from his lungs. "You take care of us. You're my hero."

Rick's throat tightened, emotion clawing at his chest. He forced himself to swallow the lump rising there, to keep the smile on his face for them—for her. "My Lily," he murmured, brushing his knuckles lightly over her cheek. "I'm thankful for you, too."

Lily giggled before looking up at him expectantly. "And Ellie."

Ellie, still cradling Bear Bear, blinked up at them. "Ellie, too," she echoed, as if just realizing she was part of the conversation.

Rick laughed softly, pulling both girls closer, holding them tight against his sides. "I'm thankful for both of you," he amended, pressing a kiss to the top of Lily's head, then to Ellie's soft curls. "More than anything in the world."

Lily hummed contentedly, leaning into his side. "One day," she mused, twirling a lock of her hair between her fingers, "when we have a real Thanksgiving, we should have turkey. And stuffing. And pie. Just like the Thanksgivings you told me about."

Ellie gasped, her little hands flying up. "Pie!" she repeated, her toddler lisp making it sound closer to "Pye!"

Rick let out a low chuckle, rubbing his hand up and down Lily's back. "One day," he promised softly.

The moment was fragile but real. Then the door creaked open. Rick's stomach dropped. Lily's head snapped up as she grabbed onto Ellie.

Louisa descended the stairs with her usual air of cruel amusement. Her gaze flicked over the three of them, her lips curling. "Well, well," she drawled. "Isn't this domestic?"

Rick forced himself to remain still, shielding Lily and Ellie with his body as best he could. "What do you want?"

Louisa smirked, stepping closer. "I'll be taking Ellie upstairs now."

Rick's blood ran cold. "No," he said immediately, rising to his feet. His chain rattled as he stepped forward, his voice shaking. "Louisa, please. Leave her here."

Louisa arched a brow, her amusement only growing. "Are you giving me orders now, Ricky?"

Ellie whimpered, sensing the tension.

Lily clutched her sister tighter. "No! She stays with me!"

Louisa sighed, stepped forward and yanked Ellie from Lily's arms. The toddler let out a shriek, her tiny hands dropping Bear Bear as she grabbed desperately for her sister.

Lily wailed. "Ellie! No! Don't take her!"

Rick dropped to his knees, reaching toward Louisa in desperation. "Please," he begged, his voice raw. "You can do anything you want to me—just don't take her."

Louisa tilted her head, considering. "Anything?"

Rick swallowed hard, his jaw clenching. "Anything."

Louisa smirked, then leaned down, her lips brushing his ear. "I like when you beg," she murmured. Then she turned, carrying Ellie away.

Lily collapsed onto the cot, her small frame trembling, the chain around her ankle rattling as she curled into herself. "Why, Daddy?" she whispered between hiccupped sobs. "Why does she always take them away?"

Rick gathered her into his arms, pressing a kiss to her hair as he rocked her gently. "I don't know, Sweetheart," he whispered, his own voice breaking. "I don't know."

The can of peaches sat forgotten on the counter, its promise of sweetness now nothing but a cruel reminder of all they had lost.

Rick closed his eyes, holding Lily tighter, his prayer whispered into the darkness. "Please, Lord—bring her back to us."

But the only answer was silence.

Chapter 32

She is nine today. The number feels too big for a girl still trapped
in chains. Too big for the world I've given her.
– Rick's Journal

Today was Lily's ninth birthday. It was a bittersweet
milestone that Rick was determined to make special. She had
woken up humming, her small hands twisting the frayed edges of
the blanket she kept on her cot, a quiet joy in her face despite the
bleakness of their world.

"Almost ready, Sweetheart," Rick said warmly as he stirred
the contents of a small, dented saucepan on the electric hot plate.
The scent of canned peaches filled the air, mixing with the faint
trace of burnt sugar. It wasn't cake, but it was something sweet.
Something special.

Lily tilted her head, watching him with wide, curious eyes.
"Is it a cake?" she asked hopefully.

Rick chuckled. "Not quite, but close enough."

Her smile made it worth it. For a moment, Rick allowed
himself to believe that today was different. That Lily was just a little
girl celebrating her birthday, not a prisoner with a chain around her
ankle. That he was just a father making dessert, not a man
desperate to keep hope alive. Then the cellar door creaked open,
and the warmth vanished in an instant.

Louisa's heels clicked sharply against the concrete as she
descended, her movements slow and deliberate. In her hand, she
carried a neatly folded bundle wrapped in clear plastic. A smirk
played at her lips, self-satisfaction radiating from every step.

Rick's grip on the spoon tightened, but he forced himself
to stay still.

"Happy birthday, Lily," Louisa cooed, her tone dripping
with mock sweetness. She set the bundle on the cot, her gaze
shifting to Rick with something smug and knowing. "A little gift
from your generous mother."

Lily's eyes flicked to Rick, uncertain, before slowly
reaching for the package. Her fingers trembled slightly as she
peeled away the plastic, revealing a light blue dress with white trim.
It was brand new with the price tag still attached.

Rick barely had time to process the look on his daughter's face before Louisa spoke again. "Well?" she prompted. "Aren't you going to thank me, Lily?"

Lily's hands smoothed the fabric, her wide eyes filled with an innocence that made Rick's chest ache. "Thank you, Mama," she whispered, her voice breathless with awe. "It's so pretty."

Louisa's smirk deepened. "Much better than those rags your father makes you wear, don't you think?"

Rick forced himself to swallow the bitterness rising in his throat. He could feel it—the shift. The way Lily's attention had turned away from the humble bowls of peaches he had worked so hard to make special. The way Louisa had effortlessly inserted herself into the moment, taking it from him like she always did.

Lily's fingers ran reverently over the smooth, unfrayed seams, her voice soft with wonder. "Do you think Daddy can get a new dress too?"

The words slammed into Rick like a punch. His breath caught, his body going rigid, but Lily was oblivious. She wasn't mocking him. She wasn't like Louisa. She just didn't know. She had only ever seen him in a dress since she was two years old. Her innocent question was simply that—innocence. Louisa, on the other hand, was delighted.

"Oh, Lily," she laughed, her voice rich with amusement. "What a wonderful idea. Daddy really should have something new to wear, shouldn't he?"

Rick's stomach twisted. He willed himself not to react, not to give her the satisfaction of seeing how deeply those words cut.

Lily turned to him, her dark eyes bright with excitement. "You've had the same dress forever, Daddy," she pointed out, brushing a hand against the faded, worn fabric covering his knee. "If I get a new one, shouldn't you?"

Louisa sighed dramatically. "You poor thing," she said, shaking her head with mock pity. "It's true, Ricky. You've been such a good little girl for me all these years. Maybe I should reward you with something fresh, just like Lily."

Rick clenched his jaw so hard it hurt. Lily had no idea. She had no idea what Louisa was doing, no idea what her words meant. She only saw a new dress in her hands, something soft and clean, something better than the threadbare, ill-fitting things Rick had no choice but to wear. She didn't know that it wasn't the same. She didn't know that he hadn't chosen this.

Rick forced himself to smile. "I don't think so, Sweetheart," he said gently, keeping his voice even.

Lily frowned. "But why not?"

He opened his mouth, scrambling for an answer, but Louisa was quicker. "Oh, don't worry, Lily," she purred, placing a hand on Rick's shoulder. Her fingers dug in just enough to remind him that she could dress him however she pleased. "Daddy will get what's coming to him soon enough."

Rick's stomach twisted. He willed himself to stay still, to not react.

Lily, satisfied with that answer, turned her attention back to the dress, holding it up against herself with a delighted smile. "I love it," she said, her excitement untouched.

Louisa beamed. "I thought you might."

And just like that, she had won. Rick sat frozen as Louisa straightened and smoothed her dress, the smirk never leaving her face. She had taken something from him—his meager attempt at making today about Lily. He had wanted to give his daughter something that was his, something that wasn't tainted by Louisa's control. But Louisa had stolen the moment, twisting it into her version of a birthday celebration. Like always.

"Enjoy your special day, darling," Louisa said sweetly before turning toward the stairs. As she reached the bottom step, she shot Rick a look that made his skin crawl. "And Ricky, if you ever want to match your daughter, all you have to do is ask."

Rick stared at the floor, his hands clenching into fists. The door slammed behind her.

For a long moment, the cellar was silent except for Lily's soft, contented sigh as she held her dress close. She had already forgotten about the peaches, about the quiet dinner Rick had tried to make special. And he couldn't blame her. A dress was something real. A dress was something tangible Lily could hold onto. A bowl of canned peaches couldn't compare.

Rick swallowed hard and reached out, pulling Lily into a gentle hug. "I love you, Sweetheart," he whispered against her curls, forcing his voice to stay steady.

Lily hugged him back, warm and soft and still blissfully unaware of what had just happened. "I love you too, Daddy," she murmured.

Rick sighed as he held his beloved daughter in his arms. His eyes flickered to the corner of the room, where the small red light of the security camera glowed, unblinking. It had been there for years, a silent reminder that Louisa was always watching. Every movement, every whispered word, every moment of comfort he tried to give Lily—nothing was truly theirs.

Lily followed his gaze, her small brow furrowing. "Daddy," she whispered, "is Mama watching?"

Rick forced a smile, stroking her hair. "Maybe not right now, Sweetheart," he murmured. "It's just us."

Chapter 33

> Her breaths were shallow, her small body burning with fever, and
> yet she whispered that I was her hero. I don't deserve the title—but
> I'll die trying to earn it.
> – Rick's Journal

The stench of mildew and despair clung to every surface of the cellar, an unrelenting reminder of their prison. Rick sat on Lily's cot, cradling her fragile body in his lap. She felt too small for nine, her thin frame burning up against him. He adjusted his own blanket around her, tucking it close, his hands trembling as he brushed her dark curls from her forehead. They were damp with sweat, her skin alarmingly hot beneath his touch.

"Hold on, Sweetheart," he whispered, his voice cracking under the weight of his desperation. "Daddy's here. Just hold on."

Her small fingers toyed weakly with the frayed edge of her blanket, her grip barely strong enough to hold onto the thread. Then, in a voice so faint he almost missed it, she murmured, "Daddy—do you think—when we get out of here—we can have Pluto come live with us?"

Rick stilled, his heart squeezing painfully at the fragile hope in her voice. He forced a small chuckle, pressing a kiss to her overheated forehead. "Don't you think his pals might miss him?"

Lily gave a weak giggle, a faint, airy sound—one that made Rick desperate to hold onto it, to keep it from slipping away. "I guess," she whispered. She swallowed, her throat working against the fever. "Can we visit him at the park you told me about?"

Rick closed his eyes for a second. It was such an innocent dream, one that should have been so simple for any other child. But for Lily, amusement parks were as make-believe as Pluto himself—best reserved for bedtime stories. And yet, she believed in it. She believed there was an "out."

Rick swallowed past the lump in his throat and forced a smile. "That would be awesome, my Lily," he whispered. "I think that can be arranged."

Lily hummed, half-drifting into sleep, but then, after a long pause, she whispered, "Pluto got off his chain."

Rick's chest went tight. Her eyes stayed closed, her body relaxed against him, but her fingers found the cold, rusted chain around her ankle and tugged at it absently. "He got to run—be free—" she murmured, her voice growing softer with exhaustion.

Rick exhaled sharply through his nose, his arms tightening around her. She hardly remembered life without it. A part of him shattered.

Lily let out a soft sigh, her breathing slowing. "I wanna be like Pluto," she mumbled, slipping further toward sleep.

Rick pressed his lips to her temple, rocking her slightly, trying to keep the tears from falling. "You will be, baby," he whispered. "You will be."

Lily's fingers went slack against the chain as she finally drifted off to sleep.

Rick held her even closer, whispering a promise into the darkness. "We'll go to a theme park. We'll get a dog. We'll be free."

The scent of soup hit him a second before the familiar creak of floorboards. His stomach twisted. The lock on the steel door clicked open. Rick's body tensed, instinctively shielding Lily as much as his own chain allowed. Louisa.

Her heels marked her approach deliberately on the steps, and Rick didn't need to look up to know she was smirking. She balanced a tray in her hands, steam rising from the bowl of soup beside a small bottle of medicine. She set it down with theatrical slowness, letting the moment stretch, letting her power seep into every corner of the room.

"Ricky," she cooed, her tone syrupy sweet. "How's my little angel today?"

"She needs a doctor," he said, his voice low but edged with raw desperation. "If you don't help her, she'll—"

Louisa sighed, a mockery of exasperation. "We've been through this," she interrupted, her tone sharpening. "You know I can't risk questions. Do you want the police sniffing around, Ricky? Is that what you want?"

Fury boiled beneath Rick's helplessness. "She's dying," he said, his voice trembling with restrained rage. "If you care about her—if you care about me—please."

Louisa stepped closer, crossing her arms. "What? You'll do anything?" she asked softly.

Rick's stomach twisted. He knew what she wanted. He always knew. "Yes," he whispered, the word barely audible.

Louisa's lips curled in triumph. She reached out, brushing her fingers over his cheek, a mockery of tenderness. Rick fought the urge to flinch.

"Good," she murmured. She turned toward the stairs, pausing before glancing back. "See that she eats," she said flippantly, gesturing to the tray. "We wouldn't want her getting weaker now, would we?"

The steel door slammed shut. Rick sat frozen, arms trembling as he held Lily tighter. For a moment, the scent of soup sent his mind spiraling somewhere else—another time, another life.

Darcy's cramped college apartment.

Rick was laid out on the couch, feverish and miserable, while Darcy hovered over him with a bowl of soup. "You look like you got run over by a semi," Darcy had said, deadpan, as he plopped onto the chair beside him.

Rick groaned. "Thanks for the sympathy."

Darcy smirked, dunking a spoon into the soup and holding it out. "Come on, princess. Open up."

Rick swatted his hand away, groaning again. "I can feed myself, you idiot."

Darcy leaned back, shrugging. "Fine, but if you die of starvation, I'm putting 'Too Stubborn to Accept Help' on your tombstone."

Rick had snorted, then regretted it as a fresh wave of congestion took hold.

The memory felt like another lifetime. How simple it was to be sick when you were free. When help didn't come with a price. Rick blinked back into the present.

Lily stirred in his arms, whimpering, and he reached for the medicine. He lifted the spoon to her lips. "Just a little, Sweetheart," he murmured. "Come on."

Lily's lashes fluttered as she struggled to wake. Her fever-bright eyes met his, and for a split second, Rick saw himself reflected back—weak, exhausted, but still fighting. She parted her lips slightly, accepting the spoon.

"That's my girl," Rick whispered.

Lily swallowed, her breath shaky. "Tastes funny," she mumbled.

Rick glanced at the medicine bottle Louisa had left, his stomach churning. He didn't trust it. Didn't trust her. But what

128

choice did he have? He set the bottle aside, focusing instead on what he could control. For now, it was the warmth of the soup. The feel of Lily in his arms. The quiet promise that he would get her out of here.

Rick held her a little tighter. "Hold on, baby," he murmured. "We're going to make it. I promise."

And somewhere, deep in his heart, he let himself believe it.

Chapter 34

> Her small hand in mine is the only anchor I have left; I won't let
> go, no matter how deep the darkness.
> – Rick's Journal

Rick Wentworth had learned to survive the cold, the hunger, the suffocating darkness. He had endured a decade of chains, of nights spent in restless agony while the weight of captivity pressed against his ribs. But nothing had prepared him for this.

Lily was slipping through his fingers.

She lay in his lap, her frail body wrapped in every blanket he had, but she still shivered violently. Sweat dampened her curls, her face pale beneath the fever's flush. Every breath she took rattled in her tiny chest, and each exhale was a battle.

Rick rocked her gently, whispering against her curls, "Stay with me, Sweetheart. Just hold on."

She barely stirred. His throat burned. He tilted his head up toward the security camera, its small red light glowing like an unblinking eye in the darkness. He knew she was watching. He *had* to make her listen.

"Louisa," he said, his voice hoarse but firm. "She's dying." His grip on Lily tightened. "You want me broken? You won. I'm broken. But please don't let her die."

Silence.

Rick's breath turned ragged. His patience snapped. "Damn it, Louisa!" His voice cracked, raw with desperation. "She's just a little girl! You want to punish me? Fine. But don't let her die down here!"

For a moment, nothing. Then the lock clicked. Rick stiffened as the steel door groaned open.

Louisa's sharp heels echoed against the stairs as she descended, her expression one of mild annoyance, like he had inconvenienced her. "What's all this noise, Ricky?" she asked coolly. "You're disturbing my evening."

Rick stood carefully, Lily limp in his arms. He forced himself to stay calm. He couldn't afford to make her angry—not now. "She needs a doctor," he said, his voice steel despite the tremble underneath. "She won't last the night without help."

Louisa sighed, rolling her eyes as if he were being dramatic. She examined Lily's frail form, tapping a manicured nail against her lip. Finally, she let out an exaggerated sigh. "Fine," she said, waving a dismissive hand. "I'll call someone. But don't think for a second that you can play the hero and escape."

Rick exhaled, his knees nearly buckling with relief. "Thank you," he choked out.

Hours passed before the lock turned again. This time, Louisa wasn't alone. A man followed behind her—older, graying hair, glasses perched on a lined face. His hands shook slightly as he clutched a worn black bag.

"This is Doctor Carter," Louisa said with syrupy sweetness. "He's here to help. Don't embarrass me, Ricky."

Rick ignored her. All of his focus was on the doctor.

Doctor Carter took one look at Lily's limp frame and the chain around her ankle that slithered out from under the blanket, and his expression shifted from wariness to horror. He moved quickly, kneeling beside the cot and pulling out a stethoscope. His hands were steady, but his brow furrowed deeply.

Rick barely breathed as the man worked—checking her pulse, listening to her chest, pressing a hand against her burning forehead. When Doctor Carter finally spoke, his voice was grave. "It's most likely pneumonia."

Rick felt his heart crack wide open.

Doctor Carter glanced at Louisa, his mouth tightening. "She's critically ill. She needs oxygen, IV antibiotics— hospitalization."

Rick latched onto the word like a lifeline. "Then take her," he pleaded, his voice breaking. "Please. Take her to the hospital. Save her."

Louisa's lips curled into something cruel. "She stays here."

Doctor Carter hesitated. "Ms. Elliot, if she doesn't get proper care, she—"

Louisa turned sharply, her gaze slicing through him. "You know what's at stake."

The doctor visibly stiffened. Something flickered in his expression—guilt, fear, something heavy. Rick's stomach twisted. Louisa was controlling him, too.

After a long silence, Doctor Carter let out a resigned sigh and reached into his bag. He handed her a bottle of antibiotics and a list of instructions. He turned to Rick, his voice a whisper. "I'm sorry."

Rick's world tilted.

Doctor Carter left, his shoulders hunched beneath invisible chains as he climbed the stairs. The steel door slammed shut behind him.

Louisa lingered. She smirked, watching Rick with a sick sort of satisfaction. "Make sure she takes the medicine," she taunted. Then, with a final glance at Lily, she waltzed out of the cellar.

The door locked behind her.

Rick knelt beside the cot, carefully measuring out the first dose. "Come on, Sweetheart," he murmured, coaxing Lily to swallow. "Just a little bit."

Her lips trembled, but she obeyed. Her fever-bright eyes fluttered open. "Daddy—do dogs like wearing leashes?"

Rick blinked. "What?"

She shifted weakly, barely lifting her hand from the cot. "Dogs. Do they like it? Being on a leash?"

His chest tightened. He wanted to lie. He wanted to say yes, that they loved it, that it made them feel safe. But he couldn't. Instead, he brushed damp curls from her forehead. "I think it depends," he said quietly. "Some dogs like it because it means they get to go outside. Run. See new things. But some—" His throat closed, but he forced himself to finish. "Some just want to be free."

Lily's small fingers curled around her ankle shackle. "I want to be free," she whispered.

Rick swallowed the lump in his throat and kissed her cheek. "You will be, Sweetheart."

But time was not on their side. And suddenly, he was back—years ago—with Darcy at his side. Rick, arms crossed, standing outside his wreck of a car after it had broken down at midnight.

Darcy, leaning against his own car, smirked. "I told you not to trust that mechanic."

Rick let out a frustrated breath. "You could just say 'I'll give you a ride' instead of 'I told you so.'"

Darcy grinned, tossing his keys in the air. "Where's the fun in that?"

Rick sighed. "You're insufferable."

Darcy shrugged. "And yet, you know I'd never leave you stranded."

Rick had rolled his eyes. But deep down, he had known—Darcy was the one person who would always show up. Now, feeling the strain of time as Lily's life seemed to be fading in front of him, the memory burned. Because if Darcy knew—if he had any idea where Rick was—he wouldn't have left him behind.

And Rick wasn't leaving Lily behind, either. He would never allow his daughter to die on his watch.

Chapter 35

> I used to think surviving was enough. But survival is nothing
> without freedom.
> – Rick's Journal

The weight of Lily's fevered body pressed against Rick's chest, her shallow breaths barely disturbing the air. He stroked her damp curls, whispering to her even though he wasn't sure she could still hear him. "Hold on, Sweetheart," he murmured, voice raw. "Daddy's here. You're not alone."

The words felt like a lie. He had never felt more alone in his life. Above them, floorboards creaked. Rick stiffened. A second later, the lock slid open.

He wrapped his arms protectively around Lily as Louisa's heels announced her arrival as she came down the concrete steps, slow and deliberate. She carried a small bag in one hand, and the smirk she wore made Rick's stomach churn.

"How's my little drama queen today?" she asked, tilting her head toward Lily on the cot as she set the bag down with an audible thud. "Still making you beg for scraps, Ricky?"

Rick rose to his feet, fists trembling at his sides. "She's dying," he said instead, voice stripped down to its most desperate, most broken. "She needs a hospital—real medicine, real care."

Louisa's expression flickered, just for a moment. A breath. A heartbeat. Then, the smirk returned, sharper than before. "She's always been weak," she said dismissively, shrugging. "Not my problem."

Something inside Rick snapped. For ten years, he had endured. Every slap, every insult, every violation. He had taken it. For Lily. For Walter. For Sam. For Ellie. But Lily was dying, and Louisa didn't care.

"SHE'S YOUR DAUGHTER," he roared, stepping forward, fists clenched. "YOUR RESPONSIBILITY TOO!"

Louisa didn't flinch. She only smiled. A slow, taunting, venomous smile. "What are you going to do, Ricky?" she purred. "Hit me?"

Rick's breath came in sharp, ragged bursts. He wanted to. More than he had ever wanted anything in his life. Then he saw it.

Her phone. It peeked out from her skirt's pocket, the screen briefly flashing before going dark. His pulse thundered.

He lunged, not for her—but for the phone.

Louisa's shriek echoed through the cellar. "You bastard!"

She clawed at him, but Rick was faster. His fingers closed around the device just as her nails raked across his arm.

With shaking hands, he swiped at the screen. Locked. His heart pounded. No dial pad. No way to call out. Then he saw it! A flash of red. The emergency call button. Rick pressed it.

A heartbeat. A pause.

Then— "911, what's your emergency?"

Rick's breath stalled. For a moment, he couldn't speak. *This is real.*

The line crackled. "Hello? Are you there?"

Rick swallowed the terror in his throat and forced the words out. "This is Rick Wentworth," he said, his voice shaking but determined. "I've been held captive for ten years. My daughter is dying—she's feverish, barely breathing. We're chained in a cellar at the Elliot house. Please, send help."

A pause. The operator's voice stayed steady, but there was urgency beneath it. "Sir, can you tell me your location?"

Rick turned. Louisa wasn't smirking anymore. Her face had gone stark white, her mouth slightly open, her chest rising and falling in rapid breaths. For the first time in a decade, she actually was afraid.

"The Elliot estate in Camden," Rick said quickly. "The cellar. Please, hurry. She's dangerous—she'll try to stop you."

The second the words left his mouth, Louisa lunged. Rick barely had time to brace before her body slammed into him. The phone went flying.

Rick hit the ground hard, Louisa's weight crushing him as she clawed at his face, his arms, his throat. "You think you can take this from me?!" she shrieked, nails raking across his cheek.

Rick gritted his teeth against the pain and wrenched her wrist, forcing her off him. For a single, terrifying moment, he thought the call had disconnected.

Then— "Sir? Are you still there?"

Rick's head snapped toward the phone, where it had landed a few feet away. Louisa lunged. Rick was faster. He scrambled forward on hands and knees, fingers closing around the phone just as Louisa's nails sank into his back.

"Sir, if you can hear me, police are on their way."

Rick went still. Louisa did too.

There was a beat of silence before Louisa screamed. It was a shriek of pure, animalistic rage.

Rick rolled onto his back, panting, as she staggered upright. Her hair was tangled, her lipstick smudged, her chest heaving, and when she turned to him, her eyes were wild.

"You don't have to do this," she whispered suddenly. "Ricky, listen to me. Just—just let me go. I'll disappear. I won't come back."

Rick didn't answer. He knew she could see it in his face. It was over. With a final, desperate sob, Louisa turned and bolted.

Rick didn't chase her. Lily was all that mattered.

He crawled to her, his hands shaking as he brushed damp curls from her burning forehead. "Stay with me, baby," he whispered, his breath trembling. "Hold on. Please."

The sirens grew louder.

Footsteps thundered upstairs.

A voice bellowed, "POLICE! DON'T MOVE!"

Then—chaos. Boots slammed against the floor. Shouts. Screams. A gun cocked.

Rick curled over Lily, shielding her as flashlights cut through the darkness.

"Holy—" An officer's voice caught as he took in the scene.

Rick looked up. A uniformed officer stood at the base of the stairs, gun lowered. His face, previously tense and focused, shifted into something Rick couldn't quite place. Shock. Horror. Recognition.

Then he spoke to someone over his shoulder. "Get the medics down here. Now."

Hands touched Rick's shoulders, his arms. Voices murmured reassurances, but none of it felt real. Rick looked down at Lily, brushed a kiss against her fevered forehead.

She stirred. Her tiny fingers curled around Bear Bear. A weak, barely-there whisper. "Daddy?"

Rick let out a ragged sob. "We made it, baby," he whispered, his breath trembling. "You're safe."

A pause. A hesitation. Then—Lily's weak fingers squeezed his hand. "Promise?"

Rick's chest shattered. He cupped her cheek, kissed her temple, and closed his eyes. "I promise."

Part II. Half Hope

She took everything from me—
my freedom, my dignity, my name.
But she couldn't take my hope.
Not forever.
- Rick's Journal

> I used to dream about freedom. I never thought it would be the thing that scared me most.
> – Rick's Journal

The cold air of the cellar gave way to something almost blinding. Flashlights sliced through the darkness, exposing every scar, every horror, every hidden truth that had been buried for ten years. The space that had once been his entire world felt small now, fragile under the weight of the outside pressing in.

Rick's arms tightened around Lily's frail body, shielding her from the chaos. Her fever-warmed skin burned through the fabric of his dress as she whimpered softly, fingers weakly clutching at his collar. Every breath she took was a whisper of life he refused to let slip away.

"Sir, we're here to help," an officer said, kneeling in front of Rick. His voice was steady, practiced, but his eyes carried the horror of what he saw. The chains. The bruises. The hollow shell of a man and his dying daughter.

Rick's voice felt like gravel in his throat. "She's sick," he rasped. "She needs a hospital. Now."

A woman stepped forward—a paramedic. She had a glowing tan, which made him and Lily look even more pasty white in comparison, sleek black hair pulled into a low ponytail, and almond-shaped eyes that held something Rick hadn't seen in a long time. Kindness.

"I'm Marianne," she said, kneeling beside Lily. "We're going to take care of her, okay?"

Rick wanted to believe her. He couldn't. Not yet.

The bolt cutters came next. "Hold still," an officer instructed.

Rick barely had time to brace before the sharp snap of metal filled the room. The chain around Lily's ankle broke, falling to the floor with a lifeless clatter. Rick stared at it in shocked amazement. It was gone.

Then, the collar. The moment the metal snapped, he gasped. A shallow, shaky breath that felt foreign in his own lungs escaped his lips. His hand shot to his throat, fingers brushing over bruised, raw skin where the weight had once pressed down. Ten years. And now, in seconds, it was gone.

"You're free," the officer said softly.

Rick didn't know what to do with the words. His legs nearly gave out, but he caught himself. Lily. Her weight in his arms anchored him. He held her tighter, pressing his lips against her sweat-damp curls. "I'll carry her," he said because letting her go wasn't an option.

A firm hand landed on his arm—one of the firefighters, steady, strong. "Easy," the man said. "We've got you."

Rick barely registered the words, his focus locked on the little girl in his arms. His legs trembled, his body weak from starvation and years of confinement, but he gritted his teeth. "I've got her," he insisted, adjusting his grip. "I'm not letting go."

The firefighter didn't argue. Instead, he slipped an arm under Lily, helping to bear some of her weight without taking her away. At the same time, a police officer positioned himself behind Rick, steadying him as his legs wobbled beneath him.

The stairs felt too long and too short at the same time. Too long because every step dragged him further away from the only world he had known for nearly a decade. Too short because, suddenly, he was in the house after 9 years, 7 months and 23 days.

Rick stumbled. The chandelier overhead cast a golden glow over white marble floors, expensive paintings, crystal vases untouched by dust. This place had been a palace while he and Lily had been kept in its dungeon. The scent of luxury was suffocating. The walls stretched too high, the air smelled too clean. Everything felt too bright, too wrong.

And then he heard them. Children's voices. His breath caught. The air left his lungs in a single, desperate whisper. "My children—they're upstairs."

An officer turned to him. "We'll find them."

Rick gripped Lily tighter as he felt the firefighter's reassuring hands on his waist. He wanted to believe it.

The night air hit like a punch. The lights, the movement, the voices were all too much. He barely noticed the flashing red and blue, the people swarming around him. All he could see was Lily. He climbed into the ambulance, his hands still trembling as paramedics lifted her onto a stretcher. She looked so small. So fragile.

Marianne worked quickly, placing an oxygen mask over Lily's mouth as her partner silently placed a blood pressure cuff on Rick's arm. "She's going to be okay," Marianne reassured him, but she was watching him too thoughtful.

Then, for the first time, Rick saw himself reflected in the ambulance's glass door. The filthy, tattered dress clung to his body, the fabric worn thin, the hem frayed and stiff with years of dirt. A grotesque mockery of the man he once was. He felt the paramedics' gazes linger. He tensed, waiting for the reaction, for the judgment—

But the man simply removed the cuff, jotted down some numbers on his pad and started cleaning a scrape on Rick's hand with antiseptic as Marianne adjusted the blanket around Lily, as if she hadn't noticed. Or maybe she had, and simply chose not to react.

"Do you need me to call someone for you?" she asked gently. "A family member? A friend?"

Rick's throat tightened. The first name that formed in his mind—the name that had lived in the deepest corners of his soul for ten years—Anne. He almost said it. He could feel it on his tongue. But she wasn't his to call. She had a family now in Boston.

His hands clenched into fists, his chest a battlefield of old wounds reopening. He forced another name. The one person who had never failed him. "Fitz," he rasped. "Fitz Darcy of Croft Beach. It's in Southern California."

Marianne's brow furrowed slightly, a flicker of recognition in her expression as if the name was familiar. Without hesitation, she pulled out her phone, her fingers flying over the screen. Rick barely processed it before she pressed the speakerphone button and held the phone between them.

It rang twice before an accented woman's voice answered. "Marianne?" A note of surprise in the feminine voice. "Hey, what's going on?"

Rick's breath stalled. He knew that voice. He hadn't met many Nigerian-American women with that sexy accent.

"Caroline," Marianne said, urgency in her tone, "I need to talk to Darcy—now."

A pause. Then Caroline's voice sharpened. "Wait, what? Why? What's happening?"

Marianne exhaled. "Just—Caroline, trust me, it's important."

Rick stared at the phone, dazed. Ten years had passed, and somehow, in the world beyond his prison, Caroline Bingley was close enough to Darcy to be answering his phone? And how in the world did this paramedic in Camden know people he assumed still lived in Croft Beach? Before he could process it, there was a soft shift in the silence—a transfer.

Then—a new voice. Low. Controlled. Familiar.

"Babe?"

Rick's chest tightened.

Marianne spoke before he could. "Is this Fitz Darcy?"

A brief pause. Then a sharp intake of breath. "Yes. Who is this?"

Marianne glanced at Rick, her voice steady. "I have someone here who needs you."

Another pause, this one stretching longer, heavier. Then Darcy's voice shifted. Sharpened. "Who?"

Rick swallowed past the lump in his throat. His name had probably been erased from Darcy's world years ago. But he had to say something. "Darcy?"

Silence.

Then a single word spoken so quietly, it almost wasn't real. "Rick?"

A ragged breath left Rick's lips. His hands clenched. He closed his eyes. He had survived the cellar.

Now, he had to survive this.

Chapter 37

> Freedom wasn't supposed to feel this loud.
> – Rick's Journal

Rick barely registered the cold as he stumbled through the automatic doors of the emergency room, the sudden burst of fluorescent light nearly blinding after years of dimness. Lily was limp in his arms, feverish against his chest, her breath shallow. His knees buckled.

A firm grip caught him before he could collapse. "I've got you," the male paramedic said, his strong arm sliding around Rick's waist to hold him up. "You're doing good, man. Just a little further."

Rick barely processed the words. His focus remained on Lily, on the too-pale skin and fragile body against him.

"Come on," Marianne urged, stepping in beside them, her voice steady. Together, she and the paramedic guided Rick toward the waiting stretcher.

As soon as Lily was laid down, nurses surrounded her, their hands moving with trained urgency. A blood pressure cuff wrapped around her frail arm, oxygen had already been fitted over her mouth, and one nurse called out her vitals.

Rick swayed. His arms, empty now, felt weightless and foreign. His body trembled with exhaustion, muscles locking in protest.

The paramedic stayed close, adjusting his grip on Rick. "Easy. You need to sit down."

Rick shook his head, still watching Lily. "I'm fine."

But then her small hand slipped from his, disappearing under the flurry of medical attention. His breath hitched. His legs gave out. The paramedic was already prepared. With practiced ease, he and a nurse aide pushed a wheelchair up behind Rick just as his knees buckled, easing him into the seat before he could hit the floor.

"No shame in needing help," the paramedic said, giving Rick's shoulder a firm pat.

Rick barely heard him, his chest rising and falling too fast. He tried to stand, to move toward Lily, but the paramedic kept a steady hand on his shoulder.

"She's in good hands," Marianne murmured beside him, crouching to his level. "They're going to take care of her. Let us take care of you, too."

Rick swallowed hard, every muscle in his body aching from too many years of pushing forward alone. He didn't know how to let go, but right now, he didn't have a choice.

Rick barely noticed when Marianne passed Lily's chart to a nurse. "She's been running a fever for at least two weeks," she reported. "Severely dehydrated, oxygen levels were at 86 in the ambulance, respiratory distress—possible pneumonia."

"Got it," a doctor confirmed. "Let's get a full workup—"

Then a voice. A name.

"Carter, we need you over here."

Rick's body locked up. And then he saw him. Doctor Carter walked to the foot of the stretcher, flipping through Lily's chart, his face calm. Too calm.

Rick's pulse thundered. The noise in the room vanished. His breath came too fast, his vision tunneling to the man who had looked at Lily suffering in that cellar and walked away.

Rage snapped through him, hot and raw. His voice roared through the emergency room. "GET AWAY FROM MY DAUGHTER! YOU LEFT HER TO DIE!"

The room froze.

Doctor Carter's head snapped up, eyes going wide.

Rick surged forward, his body moving on pure instinct out of the wheelchair, grabbing for him—

A pair of police officers cut in, one stepping between them, the other grabbing Rick's arm before he could reach Carter.

"Sir, back up!" one barked, holding him firm.

Carter took a full step back, his hands raising. "I—I don't know what he's talking about." His voice wavered. "I've never seen him before in my life."

Rick lunged again, his entire body shaking. "LIAR!" His voice cracked with fury. "You were in that cellar! You saw her! I begged you to take her to the hospital, and you did nothing!"

Carter blanched. "I—" He darted a quick glance toward the officers. "He's confused; he's been through trauma—"

The nearest cop turned on him, disgust flashing across his face. "You saw that child dying in a cellar," he said, his voice sharp, deadly calm. "And you walked away?"

Carter stiffened. "I—I had no choice—"

"You had a choice." The cop's voice was like a blade. "You just made the wrong one."

"Enough," another voice cut through the tension.

Doctor Thompson, a senior physician, had arrived on the scene. His sharp gaze flicked between Doctor Carter and Rick before landing on the officers. "Carter is off this case," he said firmly.

One officer grabbed Carter by the arm. The other looked at Rick. "We'll be questioning him further. If he did something wrong, don't worry. We'll get to the bottom of it. Right now, your priority is your daughter."

Rick's breath heaved, his pulse pounding in his ears as the paramedic gently pushed him back into the wheelchair and wheeled him closer to Lily. Her small body was so still. Tubes, wires, oxygen, and monitors everywhere. But she was here. Alive.

A caseworker approached, clipboard in hand. "Mr. Wentworth, I know this is a lot, but I need to confirm a few things for Lily's intake," she said, flipping to the first page of her paperwork. "For the record, today is February 28. Your daughter was admitted at 9:42 p.m."

Rick barely heard her as she continued rattling on.

February 28. Two weeks. Two weeks since Lily's ninth birthday. Since she had collapsed in his arms, burning with fever. She should have been eating cake. Laughing. Opening presents. Instead, she had almost died in that cellar.

Doctor Thompson flipped through the chart Doctor Carter had left, his brow furrowing as he scanned the notes. "She's severely malnourished and immunocompromised. Her lungs are weak, and pneumonia at this stage is serious. We've started her on treatment, but she's going to need weeks of monitoring and recovery before she's stable enough to leave."

Rick's stomach churned. Weeks. His voice came out hoarse. "I don't care about me. Do what you must; just don't separate us. We've never been apart in nine years. She needs me."

Doctor Thompson studied him for a long moment before nodding. "You'll be admitted as well."

Rick exhaled, tension easing slightly.

The doctor flipped to another page in the chart. "We need to start slow. Both of you will be put on a carefully monitored nutrition plan—small portions, high-calorie intake, but introduced gradually so your systems can adjust. It's going to take time."

Rick nodded stiffly, guilt pressing heavy on his chest.

Doctor Thompson continued, "You'll also be starting physical therapy. Your muscles have atrophied after years in confinement. Pushing too hard could cause injury, and we're going to make sure neither of you overdo it."

Rick swallowed, his body aching even as he sat there. He'd powered through for Lily. But what happened when he had nothing left to push through for?

Doctor Thompson's voice gentled. "And psychiatry. We'll have specialists assigned to both of you. We need to help Lily process everything she's been through. And you too, Mr. Wentworth."

Rick flinched at the last part, instinctively rejecting it. He didn't need therapy. He wanted to argue. But then he glanced at the hospital bed, where she lay small and fragile under a thick blanket covered in wires and cords and tubing, her tiny chest rising and falling with effort.

Doctor Thompson set the chart aside. "We'll find you both a room on the children's ward so you can stay together. That's non-negotiable. I promise."

Then another realization hit Rick, sharp and cold. His voice came out rough, almost embarrassed. "I doubt I have insurance anymore."

Doctor Thompson didn't hesitate. "You let us worry about that." Rick frowned, ready to argue, but Doctor Thompson shook his head firmly. "The priority is getting you and Lily healthy. Everything else can be sorted out later." His tone left no room for debate.

Rick swallowed hard. For the first time in years, someone was telling him he didn't have to fight alone.

The doctor signaled to a nearby nurse, a bubbly young man with rainbow colored hair, bright turquoise earrings, and scrubs decorated with tiny stars. The nurse approached with a mega-watt smile.

"This is Adrian," Doctor Thompson said. "He'll help get you settled."

Adrian beamed. "Hey there! Wow, Mr. Wentworth, I have to say—you must be a true angel watching over your daughter like that. It's an absolute honor to help you today."

Rick blinked, unprepared for the sheer brightness of him.

Adrian clapped his hands together. "Okay! Let's get you off your feet before you completely collapse, yeah?" He motioned to an orderly pushing a gurney toward them.

Rick instinctively resisted. "I can walk."

Doctor Thompson didn't bother arguing. He just gave a knowing look and said, "And yet, you won't. I need to do a full exam, so do as Nurse Adrian tells you, please."

Adrian winked. "Yeah, doc's got a point. And trust me, there is no shame in a dramatic hospital entrance. Let me do my job, Angel."

Before Rick could protest further, Adrian and the orderly moved seamlessly. One supported Rick from behind, and the other kept a careful hand at his side, guiding him onto the gurney without stripping him of his dignity.

Rick barely had time to catch his breath before Adrian gently placed a warm blanket over him and placed a blood pressure cuff on his arm. "See? Not so bad. And hey, silver lining—you get to stay with your little warrior."

Rick turned his head toward Lily, watching as the medical team continued monitoring her.

Together. They would stay together.

Rick exhaled, exhaustion overtaking him as the hospital lights blurred overhead.

Marianne reappeared and hesitated for half a second beside his gurney before handing over a Camden EMS sweatshirt. "God bless you," she said softly.

Rick met her eyes, too raw to find words, but he nodded.

She squeezed his arm once, then stepped back. "Take care of her."

Then she was gone.

Chapter 38

> Freedom is supposed to feel like air after drowning. But I've
> surfaced, and I still can't breathe.
> – Rick's Journal

Rick's body felt heavy, and his limbs ached as the
wheelchair rolled down the quiet hallway of the children's ward
well past midnight. Beside him, Lily lay on a hospital bed, her small
frame dwarfed by the crisp white sheets. She was groggy, and
fever-flushed, but awake. Her fingers gripped the blanket as she
tried to take in the world around her.

Adrian, the bright and cheerful nurse from the emergency
room, wheeled Rick forward with an easy, confident rhythm.
Another nurse, a woman called Misty from the children's ward with
soft red curls, guided Lily's bed, keeping one eye on the monitors
attached to her.

"You're officially VIP guests now," Adrian said cheerfully,
maneuvering Rick's chair through the doorway to their room.
"Welcome to your palace."

Rick blinked as they entered the room. It was bright, open
and perfect. Large windows let in slivers of moonlight. A colorful
mural stretched across one side—cartoon sea creatures playing in
waves, their smiling faces adding a touch of playfulness to the
otherwise sterile space. Two beds sat side by side, already
positioned close together, blankets neatly folded at the foot.

Lily's head lifted slightly, her eyes still heavy with
exhaustion, but curiosity flickered in them. She turned to Rick, her
small voice uncertain. "Is this a bedroom?"

Adrian grinned. "Pretty much! A super fancy one with lots
of cool gadgets."

Lily looked around again, her gaze catching on the flat
screen TV mounted to the wall. Her brows furrowed. "What's
that?"

Rick followed her gaze, his own mind sluggish. His heart
twisted. Of course, she had never seen one. His grip tightened
slightly on the armrest of his wheelchair.

Adrian, as if sensing the moment, crouched slightly to be
eye-level with her. "That's a TV, Sweetheart. You can watch
movies, cartoons—whatever you want."

Lily blinked, like she wasn't sure she had heard right. "Watch?"

The female nurse chuckled softly, adjusting Lily's blankets. "Yep. Just press this button, and boom! Magic pictures on the wall."

Lily's gaze flickered to Rick for confirmation. He swallowed past the lump in his throat, forcing a smile. "You're gonna love it, Baby."

Adrian wheeled Rick toward the bed, then turned to the female nurse. "All right, let's get this VIP settled."

Together, they helped ease Rick onto his own hospital bed, the weight of his body sinking gratefully into the mattress. His muscles ached, protesting every movement, his limbs heavy with exhaustion. He had been walking in the cellar unaided for years, but that space had been a fraction of the world beyond it—confined, controlled. Out here, distances stretched farther, rooms felt larger, and his body was feeling every step of it. His strength hadn't caught up to his freedom yet, and he hated to admit his body demanded rest.

Before Rick could dwell on the frustration gnawing at him, Adrian and Misty carefully transferred Lily to her hospital bed. Once she was settled, Adrian engaged the brakes and gently pushed her bed closer to Rick's, ensuring their beds were touching.

"There," Adrian said with a grin. "Now you two are officially ready to have a slumber party."

Lily reached out immediately, her tiny fingers searching for Rick's hand. He squeezed them, feeling the warmth of her skin beneath his own.

The female nurse, Misty, adjusted an IV line before stepping back. "We've got you both set up here. You'll be staying together while you recover. And don't worry—we'll take good care of you."

Lily turned to Rick, her brows furrowing. "You'll sleep here?"

Rick swallowed hard. "Yeah, baby. Right here."

Satisfied, Lily sighed, her body relaxing as she nestled into her pillows.

Adrian gave them both a final nod. "All right, you two. Rest up. The real adventure starts tomorrow—movies, pancakes, physical therapy, and, if you're feeling up for it, a tour of the ward's fish tank. Trust me, the fish are very dramatic."

"What's a fish?"

Adrian's eyes widened in playful shock at Lily's question before he grinned, dramatically flipping a section of his rainbow-colored hair. "Oh, Sweetheart, you are in for a treat. Fish are like tiny, slippery, water-dancing divas. They wiggle around all day, never blink, and some of them are as bright and fabulous as my hair—though, let's be honest, nothing beats this level of style."

He struck a playful pose before leaning in conspiratorially.

"And the ones in our tank? Total drama queens. I swear, they spend half their time throwing silent tantrums and side-eyeing each other. It's like reality TV, but with fins." His grin softened. "You'll get to see them soon. But until then, check out the mural on your wall—your fishy neighbors are already here to keep you company."

Rick drifted off to sleep with a quiet chuckle. The last thing he saw was Lily's wide-eyed, open-mouthed expression—her face frozen in pure astonishment, resembling a fish herself.

After the most refreshing nap he had enjoyed in ten years on the comfiest bed, Rick woke to find Lily fiddling with the remote control watching a cartoon with wonder in her eyes and open-mouthed fascination.

"Daddy," she whispered, her voice raspier than usual from the oxygen tubing in her nose, "it's like a book, but it moves! Nurse Misty set me up with orange juice, and she said I won't have to worry about running out! Can you imagine?"

Rick swallowed hard, forcing down the tightness in his throat. There was so much newness that it was as if they had been transported to a different world. He smiled, smoothing a hand over her curls. "Pretty awesome, huh?"

Lily's fingers toyed with Bear Bear. "Can we find the puppy on the tv?" she asked, hope flickering in her tired eyes.

Rick hesitated, fiddled for the remote on the side of his bed and flipped through the channels. There were cartoons but nothing familiar to him, and certainly nothing with a dog wearing a green collar. He clenched his jaw, frustration bubbling beneath his ribs. She had spent so much of her life with nothing—he just wanted to give her this.

A soft knock at the door made him glance up. Marianne stepped inside, fresh off her overnight shift, with a bouquet of bright pink lilies. "I was worried you guys would be asleep," She smiled as she noticed Lily's captivated stare at the television. "Well, someone's a fan of TV," she said warmly.

Lily turned her head slightly, still staring at the screen. "It's magic," she whispered in awe.

Marianne's smile widened. "Yeah, it kinda is, isn't it?"

Rick sighed, running a hand through his long hair. "I'm trying to find her a cartoon with Pluto. I don't even know if they still make those."

Marianne tilted her head, thoughtful, before her face lit up. "Hold on," she said, reaching into her pocket and pulling out her phone. "I think I can help."

With a few swipes, she tapped on a familiar streaming app and scrolled through options. A few seconds later, a yellow dog filled the screen.

Lily gasped.

Rick barely had time to react before his daughter was reaching for the phone, her fingers trembling with excitement.

Marianne chuckled, setting the phone on the tray table in front of her so she could see better. "There you go, Sweetheart."

Lily's eyes widened as she watched colorful cartoon characters bound onto the screen full of cheerful greetings.

A breathless giggle burst from Lily's lips. "It's really him," she whispered in wonder, her whole body leaning forward despite her exhaustion.

Rick felt something inside him crack wide open. She had so little for so long. And yet, here she was filled with joy over something as simple as a cartoon dog.

Marianne glanced at Rick, her expression soft, as she sat down on the edge of Lily's bed. "You okay?"

Rick swallowed, nodding. "Yeah," he said, voice thick. "Thanks."

Marianne nudged his arm gently. "Anytime."

Lily turned to him, her face glowing despite the fever. "Daddy, look! He's chasing a ball!"

Rick followed her gaze to the cartoon dog on Marianne's phone, bounding happily across the screen. His little girl's excitement at something so simple tugged at something deep in his chest.

Marianne smiled at Lily's delight, but Rick's mind was still buzzing. There was something he hadn't asked yet. Something he should have asked earlier back in the ambulance, but he'd been too overwhelmed to think straight.

He turned to Marianne. "How do you know Darcy?" Rick frowned, shaking his head. "I mean, I know he was the one I asked for. But I don't remember how you got involved."

Marianne tucked a stray strand of hair behind her ear. "Caroline Bingley is one of my closest friends. She's actually the one who called Darcy for you."

Rick stared. "Wait." He held up a hand. "Back up. You're friends with Caroline Bingley?"

Marianne laughed at the sheer disbelief in his voice. "Yeah. Why does that sound so impossible?"

Rick let out a breath, rubbing his temple. "Because the last I remember, Caroline Bingley was a nightmare. She hated Lizzie and Anne. She treated me like I was nothing. And now, you're telling me she's the one who got Darcy on the phone earlier?"

Marianne grinned. "Well, yeah. She's changed."

Rick gave her a skeptical look. "Changed how?"

Marianne tilted her head, considering. "She's been a born-again Christian for two years now."

Rick blinked. "You're kidding."

Marianne shook her head. "Nope. She actually gave her life to Christ, and honestly? She's a completely different person now."

Rick sat back, still trying to process it. "And she and Darcy are together?"

That made Marianne laugh outright. "Oh, definitely."

Rick squinted, as if trying to make sense of a completely upside-down world. "Caroline Bingley? The same woman who used to try and break Darcy up with Lizzie Bennet?"

Marianne grinned. "The very one."

Rick exhaled. "I must still be drugged."

Marianne nudged him playfully. "You're not. I promise."

Rick shook his head, still baffled. "So, wait—if you and Caroline are friends, does that mean you've known Darcy for a while too?"

Marianne nodded. "A couple of years. But it wasn't until after I had brought you and Lily in that I realized you were the Rick Wentworth Darcy always talked about."

Rick ran a hand down his face. "This is insane."

Marianne smiled, her voice softer now. "You'll get used to it."

Rick wasn't sure about that. But as Lily, giggling at the cartoon dog, snuggled up against him, he figured there were stranger things to adjust to. And if Caroline Bingley could change? Maybe—just maybe—there was hope for him too.

Not much later, Rick had just started on his breakfast platter when the door swung open. Rick stiffened instinctively; his body still wired for survival. However, it was not the nurse as he'd expected. Instead, the scent hit first—clean, expensive cologne and crisp linen.

And then the deep familiar voice. "Rick?"

Rick's stomach twisted. His pulse lurched. He had known this moment would come. Had braced himself for it. However, nothing could have prepared him for the way it felt to see Darcy coming around the curtain.

Darcy looked exactly the same—sharp cheekbones, dark curls, an air of effortless control—but there was something else now. A weight behind his eyes that hadn't been there before.

His best friend. His brother in all but blood.

Rick barely had time to sit up in bed before Darcy moved.

A firm grip on his shoulders. A rough exhale. And then— Darcy hugged him. The contact sent a jolt through Rick's system. It had been years since anyone except Lily and his children had touched him like this—without cruelty, without expectation.

Rick's body locked up. His throat closed.

Then, a weak little voice broke through. "Don't hurt Daddy!"

Darcy froze. Rick turned his head sharply.

Lily was watching, her eyes hazy with fever, her fingers clenched around her stuffed animal. Her small body trembled slightly as she stared at the unfamiliar man gripping her father.

Rick felt the tension in her little frame, the way she curled into herself, cautious, assessing.

Darcy stepped back immediately. "I won't, Sweetheart," he said, his voice gentler now.

Lily studied him for a long moment. Her gaze flickered to the suit, the polished shoes and the careful way he looked at Rick.

Rick shifted slightly as he offered a small smile. "Lily, this is my best friend," he said softly. "This is Darcy."

Lily blinked slowly, her fingers reaching over and grasping Rick's hand.

Darcy, still keeping his distance, crouched slightly—close enough to be eye level but far enough to not scare her. He smiled, easy and warm. "Hey there, kiddo."

Lily swallowed. "You—you're Daddy's best friend?"

"That's right," Darcy said. "Your dad and I have been best friends since we were five years old."

Lily hesitated, then looked at Rick. "Like how I'm your best friend?"

Rick's throat tightened. He brushed a hand gently through her curls. "Yeah, Picasso. Like that."

Lily considered this, her little brows furrowing in thought. "What do I call him?"

Darcy's grin widened. "You can call me Uncle Darcy, if you want."

Lily's lips parted slightly. "Uncle?" She blinked. "What's an uncle?"

Rick and Darcy exchanged a glance. Darcy chuckled. "An uncle is like—a really fun grown-up who's not your dad but still gets to love you a whole lot."

Rick smirked. "And spoil you rotten."

Darcy nodded solemnly. "Oh, definitely. That's the main job."

Lily stared at him, processing. Then, very softly, she whispered, "I never had one before."

Something in Rick's chest ached.

Darcy's playful grin softened. "Well, Sweetheart, you've got one now."

Rick felt her body relax next to him ever so slightly as she looked at Darcy like someone who might be safe.

She blinked slowly. "Did you bring Daddy a clean dress?"

And just like that, Rick's stomach plummeted.

Darcy's expression shattered. His gaze snapped back to Rick, and this time, he really took an inventory of his appearance.

The scrubs, the long hair down to his waist, the exhaustion carved into his face and the way his body looked too thin, too battered, too far from the man he had once been even covered by the blankets. There was also the wheelchair in the corner waiting to transport Rick around the hospital.

Darcy's jaw tightened. His hands curled into fists.

Rick's pulse pounded. This was it. The moment everything changed.

Darcy inhaled sharply.

Rick flinched.

Darcy glanced at Lily, then back at Rick. His expression was tight, controlled, but his voice softened as he spoke. "Come talk to me while I grab some breakfast. I drove straight through after I got the call last night. You know what a beast that drive is up from Orange County."

Rick's body locked up.

Leaving Lily—even for a second—sent panic crawling under his skin. His mind screamed at him to stay put, to keep her within reach, to never let her out of his sight again.

But Darcy wasn't budging. "She'll be fine," Darcy assured him. "There are nurses everywhere."

Rick swallowed, glancing at Lily. She had returned to devouring her breakfast platter as she watched a morning cartoon on the television.

She was safe. For the first time in years, she was safe. But walking away from her, even for a moment, felt impossible.

Darcy stepped closer, lowering his voice. "Rick, I get it." His eyes softened, understanding in every line of his face. "But I need you to come with me."

Rick's shoulders sagged. His body felt like lead, every muscle screaming in protest, exhaustion anchoring him to the bed. He shifted slightly, trying to push himself up, but the weakness hit hard.

Darcy saw it. Without hesitation, he stepped forward, crouching beside the bed. "Here," he murmured, steady hands reaching out. "Let me help."

Rick stiffened instinctively. Years of surviving on his own, of not being touched unless it was to hurt him, made his breath hitch. But Darcy wasn't rushing him, wasn't forcing anything.

"Easy," Darcy said gently, positioning himself to take most of Rick's weight. His grip was firm but careful, supporting rather than controlling. "I've got you."

Rick swallowed hard, the frustration clawing at his chest. He had walked in the cellar. He had moved within his small, controlled space, pacing the same few feet day after day with the weight of his chain grounding him. But that had been different. The real world was bigger, demanding more from his body than it had in years.

His pride hated this—hated how quickly exhaustion overtook him, how weak he felt just trying to stay upright. Darcy must have sensed it because he said quietly, steady as ever, "This isn't weakness, man. It's just getting back on your feet."

Rick clenched his jaw but gave a small nod as he shifted forward as Darcy eased him into the wheelchair. His legs trembled, and for a second, his balance wavered.

"I've got you," Darcy repeated, steadying him as he sank into the chair.

Rick exhaled sharply, gripping the armrests of his wheelchair as he tried to steady his breath. His body ached, his muscles weak and unsteady, but he was upright. That was something.

He turned to Lily, who lay curled up in her hospital bed, her small fingers clutching Bear Bear. Even though she was still pale, the fever had lessened, and she looked more alert than she had the night before.

"Picasso, Daddy is going to go get some breakfast with Uncle Darcy for a few minutes, okay?" Rick asked gently, bracing himself for her reaction.

Lily's little brows knit together, her fingers tightening around her stuffed animal. "You're leaving?"

Rick's stomach twisted. He hated the way she said it—like it was something permanent, like it was something to be afraid of.

But before he could say anything, the morning nurse, Natasha, stepped into the room, her bright smile and cheerful energy breaking the moment. "Good morning, Sweetheart," she said warmly, carrying a juice cup and a blood pressure cuff. "I thought you might like another orange juice, and I need to check your numbers."

Lily hesitated, torn between her worry over Rick and the distraction of the nurse's attention.

Natasha crouched beside the bed, winking. "And guess what? After we finish, we can take a stroll with your walker to see all the pretty fish."

That did it. Lily's face lit up. "Real fishies?"

Misty grinned. "Absolutely. What do you think?".

Rick felt the tension in Lily's small shoulders start to ease as she slowly nodded.

"I'll be back soon," he promised softly, reaching out to squeeze her tiny hand. "I'm just going to make sure Uncle Darcy eats something so he won't pass out. You'll be okay with Nurse Natasha, won't you?"

Lily looked up at him, searching his face, then back at the nurse.

Natasha gave a playful gasp. "Wait a second—am I not good company?" she teased lightly. "Because I was pretty sure we were best buddies."

Lily giggled just a little, still clutching Bear Bear, and finally nodded. "Okay."

Rick swallowed past the lump in his throat, squeezing her fingers one last time before Darcy moved behind his chair and gently pushed him toward the door. As they rolled into the hallway, Rick exhaled. He hadn't realized how much he needed that reassurance too.

The hallway was quiet, as all the nurses were busy delivering breakfasts and morning medication. Darcy kept moving until they'd wound their way to the elevator. As soon as the sliding doors closed, Darcy turned and crouched slightly to be eye-level with Rick.

Then Rick saw it. The full weight of emotion in Darcy's face. Raw. Furious. Heartbroken. The look in his best friend's eyes made him want to run.

Chapter 39

> I used to think the hardest part of surviving was the pain. The hunger. The chains. But I was wrong. The hardest part is sitting face to face with the man who remembers me as I was, while I no longer recognize myself.
> – Rick's Journal

The hospital cafeteria smelled like French toast and extra strong coffee. Trays clattered, voices murmured, and somewhere near the entrance, a child giggled between spoonfuls of cereal. The world buzzed around Rick—too bright, too loud, too much.

Rick sat at a table near the window, his wheelchair positioned slightly away from the morning crowd. A paper cup of coffee sat untouched in front of him. He had eaten something high protein for breakfast earlier just prior to Darcy's arrival, but he couldn't even remember what it was with everything he'd been through. Overnight, he had spent what felt like hours answering questions from police, child services and doctors. He'd told the same story over and over again, signed forms, nodded when necessary, and agreed to things he barely registered.

Now, the fluorescent lights of the cafeteria felt like knives behind his eyes. He slipped on a pair of dark shades a nurse had given him earlier, hoping to dull the assault of artificial brightness. His body ached, weak from malnutrition and years of forced stillness.

Darcy sat across from him, a tray in front of him piled with eggs, toast, and a large cup of black coffee. He wasn't eating, though. He was watching Rick. Studying him.

Rick ignored the weight of the stare, fingers drumming absently against the table. His gaze stayed fixed on the window, watching the early morning city stir to life.

Darcy sighed, finally breaking the silence. "I heard some things on the news while I drove up." His voice was measured, careful. "But I need to hear it from you."

Rick tightened his grip around the coffee cup. He didn't lift it, didn't drink. Just sat there, still as stone.

Darcy didn't push. He let the quiet stretch, waiting.

Rick's voice was hoarse when he finally spoke. "I don't know what you want me to say."

Darcy's jaw ticked. "I don't either."

Rick huffed a bitter breath that might have been mistaken as a laugh in another life.

Darcy leaned back in his chair, his gaze still locked on Rick. "Lily talked about you wearing dresses like it was normal. Like it was all she's ever known."

Rick swallowed, his throat dry. "Yeah." He still couldn't look at Darcy. "She doesn't know any different."

Darcy's expression darkened. His gaze flickered to the bruising around Rick's throat, the raw skin where the collar had sat. Slowly, he leaned forward, lowering his voice. "What happened to you?"

Rick's fingers clenched tighter around the cup. His stomach twisted. "What happened?" he echoed, the words bitter and empty. His voice felt foreign, like it belonged to someone else. "I was buried alive for ten freaking years. And no one dug me out."

Darcy inhaled sharply. He didn't speak, didn't try to fix it.

Rick finally turned his head, meeting his best friend's eyes through the dark lenses of his shades. "I didn't have a choice," he said, voice flat. Emotionless.

Darcy didn't look away. "I know."

Rick scoffed, a harsh sound in the quiet space between them. "Do you?"

Darcy's jaw tightened. "I do now."

Rick wanted to call it a lie. He wanted to scream that Darcy didn't know a damn thing about it. But there was something in his voice—low, sure, steady—that made Rick pause.

Rick exhaled, shaking his head. "I don't even know how to be me anymore."

Darcy's answer was immediate. "You don't have to figure it out alone."

Rick clenched his jaw, his hands shaking as he lifted the cup to his lips.

Darcy's hand hovered for a second before gripping his shoulder, firm and steady. "You're not alone, man."

Rick exhaled, his hands clenching and unclenching on the coffee cup.

Darcy just stayed. And suddenly, Rick's hand wasn't my his anymore. It was shaking, moving forward, grasping Darcy's before he could stop it.

Chapter 40

> I never expected kindness to feel foreign. But it does. And maybe that's the hardest part.
> – Rick's Journal

Rick's body ached from exhaustion, but the weight of Lily's fevered hand in his own kept him grounded. The hospital bed was comfortable, far more than what he had known for the past decade, but it didn't stop the discomfort that ran deeper than his muscles. His world had been a single room for so long, a single set of expectations, and now everything was shifting too fast.

A knock at the door broke through the rhythmic beeping of the monitors. Rick turned his head as Darcy stepped inside, carrying a large suitcase. His best friend looked sharp as ever. He wasn't alone.

A tall woman followed, her deep brown skin radiant even under the fluorescent lighting. She carried herself with an air of quiet confidence, her eyes sharp and assessing as they swept the room. When they landed on Rick, her expression softened.

Darcy set the suitcase at the foot of Rick's bed, then came forward into the room without hesitation. His grip landed firm on Rick's shoulder, grounding, solid. Before Rick could react, Darcy's hand moved to Lily, brushing over her small fingers resting on the blanket.

Lily stirred. Her fevered eyes fluttered open, heavy with exhaustion. "Uncle Darcy," her voice rasped through the oxygen tubing. "I had physical therapy today."

Darcy's breath hitched, his grip tightening slightly before he knelt beside the bed. "Hey, Sweetheart," he said softly. "How did it go?"

Lily shifted, her fingers twitching against Bear Bear's fur. "The lady said I did really good and will be running soon." Her gaze flickered to the woman beside him.

The woman's voice was warm, smooth, but carried an underlying steel. "Hi, Lily. I'm your Aunt Caroline. Since Marianne called me yesterday, we've been praying for you and your daddy."

Rick's breath stilled. Caroline was praying? He blinked, eyes darting to Darcy. This wasn't the same woman he had known in college. The sharp-tongued, manipulative socialite who had tried to sabotage Darcy's life. That woman wouldn't have been caught dead saying a prayer for anyone.

Rick swallowed. Marianne had been telling the truth. Caroline Bingley had changed. The realization settled uneasily in his chest. He had spent years believing that people didn't change—not really. He had lived it, survived it, seen firsthand how power twisted people into something unrecognizable. But now, standing in front of him, was proof that maybe—just maybe—transformation was possible.

And if Caroline Bingley could change, what did that mean for him?

Lily's murmured, "you speak so pretty," caught his attention and drew Rick back into the moment.

Caroline's lips curled into a warm smile. "Thank you, Darling." She crouched beside Lily's bed, keeping her movements careful. "I hope we'll be good friends."

Darcy cleared his throat and unzipped the suitcase. "We figured you'd want something nice to wear when you leave this place," he said, flipping it open to reveal neatly folded clothes.

Lily's breath caught. Despite her exhaustion, her eyes lit up. "Are those for us?"

"Absolutely." Darcy nodded. "They're all for you and your daddy."

Rick's hands clenched against the sheets. The world had been small for so long. Clothes had been dictated for him. What he ate, where he stood, how he moved—everything had been decided for him. Now, in front of him, lay something simple, something normal. And yet, his hands wouldn't move.

Darcy didn't push. He just waited.

Rick reached out, hesitating, fingers brushing over the soft fabric. A hoodie. Solid. Masculine.

Then small hands touched the jeans.

Rick flinched.

Lily ran her fingers over the fabric, her brows furrowed. Then she looked up. "Did you get Daddy a dress too, Uncle Darcy?"

Rick's chest tightened. For a second, something dark flickered behind Darcy's eyes. A rage Rick recognized. The kind that could burn everything down if he let it.

Rick forced his voice steady. "No, baby," he said. "No dress."

Lily frowned. "But—these are different."

Rick exhaled, gripping the denim in his hands. "Yeah," he whispered. "They are."

Lily studied him for a long moment. Then, after a pause, she nodded. "They're soft."

A breathless, broken laugh escaped Rick.

Darcy's fists clenched at his sides. The tension radiated from him in waves. Finally, he spoke. "I didn't think it was real," he said, his voice low, tight. "Even when I heard her say it yesterday. I didn't want to believe it."

Rick locked his arms around the clothes in his lap, feeling something protective, something raw course through him.

Darcy's gaze flickered to the bruising on Rick's throat where the collar had sat. His hand lifted, hesitating for just a second before brushing over the damaged skin. His voice dropped lower, careful now. "What did she do to you?"

Rick let out a bitter breath, eyes drifting down to the hoodie.

Caroline's voice was firm as she placed a hand on Darcy's shoulder. "Rick."

He turned.

Her gaze was steady, unwavering. "You don't have to wear anything you don't want to. Ever again."

Her words settled over him like an anchor in the storm.

Lily turned to Rick, her voice small. "Do you like these clothes?"

Rick let out a shuddering breath. His fingers curled tighter around the fabric. "Yeah, Picasso," he murmured. "I do."

Lily's face brightened. "Then I like them too."

Rick pulled her into his arms, holding her tight, as he watched Caroline reach out, squeezing Darcy's hand briefly.

After a few minutes, Darcy shifted, breaking the silence. "You had physical therapy today, yeah?"

Rick blinked, still disoriented from everything. "Yeah," he murmured.

Darcy nodded, thoughtful. Then, a little too casually, he added, "Think you're up for another bit of fresh air?"

Rick frowned. "Now?"

Darcy shrugged. "Sure. Let's take your wheelchair for a spin in the hallway."

Rick hesitated, glancing at Lily.

She yawned, eyes fluttering. "Go, Daddy. I'll talk to Aunt Caroline."

Rick's heart clenched, but when she offered him a sleepy, trusting smile, he knew this was okay.

Caroline adjusted the blanket around Lily. "I'll stay with her."

Rick swallowed hard, then met Darcy's gaze. "All right," he said, pushing back the nerves. "Let's do it."

Darcy's answering grin was full of quiet encouragement.

Rick put his dark shades on as Darcy got Rick safely settled into his wheelchair. Once Rick was in his chair, Darcy stepped behind him and slowly started to push the wheelchair into the hallway. Darcy gave a thumbs up at a nurse who blushed.

"Still the Casanova?" Rick asked in amusement.

"I'm a one-woman man now." Darcy laughed as he kept pushing the chair towards the bank of elevators.

Rick exhaled through his nose and squeezed his eyes closed as the elevator doors closed and the whir of machinery surrounded him.

Darcy watched him quietly before taking Rick's hand in his own. Rick didn't need words as he allowed the comforting pressure of his best friend's hand to ground him.

"So," Darcy said after they'd made their way to the outside courtyard, casual but pointed. "What's next?"

Rick frowned slightly, curling his hands around the wheels of his chair. "What do you mean?"

"I mean, what's next for you? You're free, Rick." Darcy glanced at him, his expression unreadable. "Have you thought about what you're going to do now?"

Rick focused on the tile ahead of him. "I have to take care of my kids."

Darcy nodded. "Yeah. But that's not what I asked."

Rick's grip tightened. His breath came out heavier. "I don't have an answer."

"All right." Darcy accepted it easily, but he wasn't done. "So, let's start smaller. When are you gonna cut your hair?"

Rick blinked. "What?"

Darcy smirked. "I mean, unless you're going for some wise guru aesthetic, in which case, I fully support it."

Rick rolled his eyes. "I haven't really thought about it."

"Well, I have," Darcy said dryly. "And you've officially reached hermit status. Why didn't Louisa let you cut it?"

Rick's eyes dropped at the mention of her.

Darcy caught it immediately. "I'm sorry. Forget I asked."

They passed a waiting area, the hum of the hospital continuing around them.

After a stretch of silence, Darcy spoke again. This time, his voice was quieter. "You do get that you're allowed to want things and make decisions for yourself, right?"

Rick kept his gaze focused ahead. "I want to be a good father."

"I know. But that's not all you are."

Rick exhaled slowly as he pushed up from his chair. Darcy's hand shot out just in case, but he didn't touch him. Rick steadied himself as he took a couple steps forward.

His jaw clenched. "It's all I can focus on right now." He took another step, his voice steady despite the uncertainty settling deep in his chest. "Do you think you can help me get custody of them? I mean, I don't want to scare them by seeing me like this. But once I'm out of here, once I have a place I can call home, I want all my children together."

Darcy nodded, no hesitation. "Okay. We'll start there."

Rick's shoulders eased slightly, though the weight of everything still loomed. The police had told him that the kids were staying at the house with Anne and her husband, but that wasn't permanent. It couldn't be. They were his children, no matter how much Anne cared about them. And Rick—he had already lost ten years. He wasn't going to lose more.

Chapter 41

> Daniel wasn't saved from the lions' den. He was saved in it. Maybe that's how God works—not by pulling us out of the darkness, but by holding us through it.
> – Rick's Journal

The steady beeping of the heart monitor filled the hospital room, a quiet rhythm that had become strangely comforting. Rick sat in his hospital bed, glancing over at Lily, who was coloring carefully between the lines of her latest drawing. Her crayons, a gift from Darcy, were scattered across her blanket.

Bear Bear was tucked under her arm as always, but for the last week, he had company. Leo the Lion, the plush toy Darcy had given her, sat propped up in the crook of Lily's other elbow. She occasionally reached over to straighten his mane, smoothing the golden tufts between her fingers.

Rick stretched his aching leg, the movement limited by the brace stabilizing his knee. The morning's physical therapy session had left him exhausted, but he knew it was the only way he'd regain his strength. Lily, too, had started using a cane to help her walk short distances, but for longer stretches, they both still relied on wheelchairs and rollator walkers. Progress was slow, but it was happening.

"Daddy," Lily said suddenly, holding up her drawing. "Do you think Daniel was scared when the lions were growling at him?"

Rick leaned in, taking in the image she had sketched— Daniel, the towering lions, and a beam of light shining down from above.

"Maybe a little," he admitted. "But he trusted God, even when things were really scary."

Lily nodded thoughtfully, her small fingers trailing over Leo's fur. "And God saved him," she whispered, glancing at Rick with wide, knowing eyes. "Just like He saved us from our den."

Rick's breath caught. His throat tightened as he reached over, brushing a curl from her forehead. "Yeah, Sweetheart," he murmured. "Just like that."

The door opened later that morning, and Caroline Bingley stepped inside. Her usual sharp elegance was softened by something gentler as she met Lily's eyes.

"Aunt Caroline!" Lily rasped, her voice scratchy but filled with excitement.

Caroline's lips curled into a warm smile that stretched from ear to ear. "I come bearing gifts," she announced, holding up a small velvet pouch.

Lily's eyes widened as she sat up a little straighter, her fingers gripping her stuffed animals tightly. "For me?"

Caroline arched an eyebrow. "Who else would it be for? Your father has more than enough presents from me—his stunning new wardrobe being one of them."

Rick huffed a quiet laugh, shaking his head.

Caroline sat on the edge of Lily's bed and opened the pouch. A delicate silver anklet slipped into her palm, dainty but sturdy, adorned with a tiny, shimmering heart charm. It was small—appropriate for a child of nine—but beautiful.

Lily gasped, her hands covering her mouth. "It's so pretty!" she whispered.

Caroline smiled, but there was something deeper in her eyes as she reached for Lily's ankle. "May I?"

Lily nodded quickly, barely containing her excitement. Caroline carefully fastened the anklet around her thin ankle, the silver chain resting just above the small indent where another chain had once been. Then, she leaned down and kissed Lily's scar.

Rick's breath caught. He could have sworn he saw a tear drop onto Lily's ankle. His fingers curled into the fabric of the hospital blanket.

Lily wiggled her foot, watching the charm catch the light. "I love it," she whispered. Then, quieter, "It's better than the old one."

Rick closed his eyes briefly, the weight of her words pressing deep.

Caroline stroked Lily's cheek gently. "I thought you deserved something prettier," she murmured. "Something yours."

Lily reached out, throwing her small arms around Caroline's neck, surprising them both. "Thank you," she said, her voice muffled against Caroline's side. "It makes me feel—like a princess."

Caroline hesitated for only a second before hugging her back. "Well, obviously. I only shop for princesses."

Rick swallowed the lump in his throat. Lily wasn't shackled anymore. She was free. And now, she had something beautiful where the weight of a chain had once been.

As Lily was admiring her anklet, the door opened again, and Darcy strode in with a purposeful energy. His gaze flicked briefly to Rick before landing on Lily in Caroline's arms. He carried a small duffel bag and, in his other hand, a neatly wrapped gift.

"Uncle Darcy!" Lily grinned, coughing lightly as she sat up straighter. "Did you see my present from Aunt Caroline?"

Darcy whistled appreciatively before handing a wrapped box to her. "Not as fancy as that bauble, but that's for you, Picasso."

Lily tore through the paper, revealing a thick storybook about brave historical women. Her gasp of delight was instant. "Oh, thank you, Uncle Darcy! I can't wait to read it."

Rick met Darcy's gaze, his chest tightening. He didn't need to say thank you. Darcy just nodded, already knowing.

Then, from the duffel bag, Darcy pulled out something small and wrapped in cloth. He hesitated for just a second before setting it on the table beside Rick.

Rick frowned slightly, his gaze flicking from the bundle to Darcy. "What is this?"

Darcy just nodded at it. "Open it."

Rick unwrapped the cloth, his breath catching the second his fingers brushed against smooth glass. It was a small bottle, filled with sand and bits of sea glass in different shades of blue and green. The colors of the ocean. The colors of freedom. His throat tightened.

"I stopped by The Beach Shack before driving back up here," Darcy said quietly. "Figured it's been a while since you've seen the ocean."

Rick swallowed hard, unable to tear his eyes away from the bottle. He could almost hear the waves, the distant cry of seagulls. He could almost feel the salty air against his skin. A life waiting for him to return.

"It's—from Croft Beach?" he asked, his voice barely above a whisper.

Darcy nodded. "A little something from home."

Rick curled his fingers around the bottle. A gift that said everything Darcy didn't need to put into words. A reminder. A promise.

Rick's hands tightened around the glass, his voice rough with emotion. "Thank you."

Darcy clapped him on the shoulder, his smirk gentler this time. "Just don't get sand all over the hospital floor. I don't want security throwing me out."

For the first time, Rick let himself believe that he'd see the ocean again.

Darcy's expression shifted. "I have an update on Louisa."

Rick stiffened but grabbed his cane and followed Darcy into the hallway where Lily couldn't overhear them.

"Her lawyers filed an insanity plea. They're spinning the story that she believed she was protecting you."

Rick scoffed. "Protecting me?" He ran a hand through his hair. "She wasn't protecting anyone. She was living out some twisted fantasy."

He exhaled, slow and steady, and let his gaze drift back to Lily's hospital room. "She's my future," he said quietly. "Her, Walter, Sam, Ellie. That's what matters now."

Darcy nodded. "And you're not alone in this. As of this morning, the judge granted me temporary guardianship."

Rick's pulse stuttered. "What?"

Darcy held his stare, unwavering. "They'll be staying with me, Rick, when I go back to Croft Beach on Sunday night. And when you're released, so are you."

Rick exhaled sharply. "Darcy, you don't have to—"

Darcy scoffed. "You'd rather they move back east with your ex-fiancée and her doctor husband? You want them growing up in a house where no one will even say your name?"

Rick's stomach twisted.

Darcy crossed his arms. "Not happening. The kids are moving to my house in Croft Beach. And when you're out, you're coming home."

Rick let out something close to a laugh, shaking his head. "I hate you."

Darcy grinned. "You love me."

Rick sighed, rubbing a hand over his face. "You always do this. Make decisions before I even realize I need them."

Darcy shrugged, then hesitated. "Speaking of things you may or may not be ready for—" He reached into his jacket pocket, pulling out a crisp envelope. "Anne wrote you a letter."

Rick's breath caught. His body tensed at the sight of his ex-fiancée's familiar handwriting.

Darcy held it out but didn't push. "I wasn't sure if you wanted it now or—"

Rick stared at it for a long moment, his chest tightening. Then, slowly, he shook his head. "Hold onto it," he murmured. "I'll ask for it when I'm ready."

Darcy studied him, then gave a small nod, tucking the envelope back into his pocket. "Whenever you are."

Rick swallowed hard. The past still loomed, waiting, but for the first time in years, he wasn't facing it alone.

Chapter 42

> I used to dream about the ocean. But dreams never smelled like salt
> or felt like freedom.
> – Rick's Journal

The hallway buzzed with quiet morning activity as nurses passed by with charts and carts, soft conversations threading through the air. But inside the hospital room, everything slowed.

Rick adjusted the surgical mask over his face, shifting uncomfortably in the wheelchair as he glared at Doctor Thompson. "This is ridiculous."

The doctor sighed, unimpressed. "It's protocol. You're being discharged after weeks of hospitalization and extensive physical therapy. Humor me."

Rick scowled but didn't argue further. His muscles were still weak, his stamina nowhere near what it had been before Louisa locked him away, but he had been walking. Slowly, painfully—but walking. This unfortunately felt like another reminder that he wasn't fully free yet.

Across the room, Lily sat in her own wheelchair, Leo the Lion in her lap. She handed Bear Bear reverently to Nurse Misty as she hugged her tight. "You'll make sure Amy from therapy gets him?"

"You have my word," Misty promised as she hugged Lily.

Darcy stood near the window, his arms crossed, amusement flickering in his eyes. "Just enjoy the ride, Wentworth."

Rick shot him a glare before turning back to Doctor Thompson. "You're letting me walk to the car."

Doctor Thompson didn't blink. "We'll see."

A knock at the door interrupted them before Adrian strode in, his rainbow-colored hair now transformed to a bright turquoise that matched his turquoise earrings. Those earrings glittered as he grinned at them. "All right, my favorite VIPs, time for your grand exit."

Another nurse who had cared for them both during their month-long stay wheeled in a cart stacked with bags. "We couldn't let you leave empty-handed."

Rick frowned as Adrian pulled out a few neatly packed gift bags and handed them to Darcy.

Doctor Thompson clapped a hand on Rick's shoulder. "We've set you both up with continued physical therapy in Croft Beach. And don't worry about insurance—we've worked it out with social services."

Rick exhaled, tension easing from his shoulders. "Thank you," he said, voice thick. "For everything."

Adrian's eyes twinkled. "Just doing our jobs." He nudged Rick's knee. "And hey—some of us might have placed bets on when you'd be swimming in the ocean again. Don't let me down, Wentworth."

Rick chuckled softly, gripping the wheels of the chair, but before he could attempt to prove a point, Adrian placed a firm hand on the handles behind him.

"Ah-ah, I got this."

Across from them, Misty knelt beside Lily. "You ready, Sweetheart?"

Lily nodded eagerly, slipping her arms into the sleeves of her jacket. "I can't wait to get my puppy dog!"

Overhearing her, Doctor Thompson knelt beside Lily's wheelchair, his voice gentle but firm. "I know you're excited about the idea of a puppy, Miss Lily, but right now, your body is still getting stronger. Your immune system needs more time to rebuild before you can safely be around animals. Once you're home and we see how you're doing—maybe in a few months—we can talk about it again. But for now, let's focus on getting you well first, okay?"

A moan of disappointment escaped Lily's lips, but she nodded and kissed Doctor Thompson on his cheek before he helped her put her face mask on.

As they rolled into the hallway, applause rippled down the corridor. Doctors, nurses, and hospital staff lined the hall, clapping and cheering them on.

Lily's eyes widened in surprise. "They are clapping for us!"

Rick reached out and squeezed her hand. "Yeah, baby girl. They are."

She giggled behind her mask, waving like a queen in a parade.

Darcy smirked as he pushed her toward the exit. "Told you, kid. You're famous."

Rick let himself sink back into the chair as Adrian pushed him toward the exit. His body was weak, but his heart had never been stronger.

The sunlight hit differently than he remembered. Rick had stepped outside the hospital multiple times in the last few weeks for regular short walks with his physical therapist and Darcy, but this time was different. This time, he wasn't going back inside.

Darcy loaded their bags into the trunk as Rick stood from the wheelchair, bracing himself against the car door. The cane felt steady beneath his grip, even as his legs trembled from the exertion.

"See?" Rick muttered, eyeing Doctor Thompson, who stood to the side watching. "Told you I'd walk to the car."

The doctor smirked. "Enjoy your victory lap, Wentworth."

Rick slid into the passenger seat, exhaling as he adjusted. Lily climbed into her brand-new booster seat in the back, her mask still firm in place as she took in the new surroundings.

As Darcy pulled onto the freeway, the world stretched open in a way that made Rick's chest ache.

Lily shifted behind him, kicking her feet slightly. "Uncle Darcy?"

Darcy glanced at her in the rearview mirror. "Yeah, princess?"

She hesitated. "Can Daddy get a haircut today?"

Rick blinked, startled by the suggestion.

Darcy grinned. "Oh, absolutely."

Rick groaned, but Lily's eager expression softened any protest he might have had.

So, they drove to the barbershop.

The bell above the door jingled as they stepped inside. The shop smelled of aftershave and warm shaving cream, the low hum of clippers buzzing in the background. The scent wasn't familiar, but it wasn't unpleasant. Just another piece of the world he was learning again.

The barber, an older man with silver hair and kind eyes, waved them over. His gaze lingered on Rick for a half-second longer than necessary before he casually reached up and switched off the overhead television, which had been playing the news.

Rick swallowed.

Darcy smirked. "Breathe, Wentworth. It's just a haircut."

Rick rolled his eyes, but Lily tightened her fingers around his. "It smells funny in here," she whispered.

Darcy grinned. "That's the smell of freedom, kid."

Rick huffed a quiet laugh despite himself.

The barber leaned against the counter, eyeing Rick with an easygoing smile. "All right, son. What are we thinking?"

Rick hesitated, staring at his reflection in the large mirror across the room. His hair hung past his shoulders in uneven waves, too thick, too everything—one of the last remnants of Louisa's control. It had been one of her acts of control not letting him use scissors or a razor. And now, with every snip, he'd be taking another piece of himself back. Still, his fingers twitched against his sides, too used to inaction.

Darcy clapped a hand on his shoulder. "Short. Clean. Something that doesn't make people wonder if he's been living in a cellar for ten years."

Rick shot him a glare. "Thanks for the support."

"Anytime."

The barber chuckled as Rick lowered himself into the chair while Darcy sat Lily down on the vacant chair next to Rick's and leaned the two canes against the wall. A cape settled around his shoulders, and the first snip of the scissors sent a shiver down his spine. With every cut, strands of hair tumbled to the floor, taking pieces of the past with them.

"Daddy—"

Rick turned slightly, meeting Lily's wide, solemn eyes. She was watching the falling hair with a deep frown, her little hands clasped together.

"I'm gonna miss your hair." Her voice was soft, almost sad.

Rick's chest ached. For her, it wasn't a reminder of pain and control. It was just another thing, like the hated dress, that she associated with her daddy.

He reached out, gently squeezing her small hand. "I know, baby," he murmured. "But it's time for something new."

Lily studied him for a long moment, then nodded. "Okay. But you'll still look like my daddy, right?"

Rick's throat tightened. He managed a small smile. "Yeah, Sweetheart. Still me."

The moment stretched—quiet, tender—before Darcy cleared his throat dramatically. "Yeah, yeah, this is all very touching, but let's hurry it up before he starts looking too handsome and steals my spotlight."

Rick groaned. Lily giggled.

By the time the barber finished, Rick barely recognized himself. His face was sharper, his eyes brighter, the weight of the past—at least physically—gone.

Darcy gave an approving nod. "Now that is a man who doesn't wear dresses."

Rick rolled his eyes, but he couldn't stop the small, real smile tugging at his lips. Because for the first time in a long, long time—he felt like himself again.

"Can I have a haircut too?"

Rick's breath caught as he turned to look at his daughter. He hadn't even thought about it, but Lily had never had a real haircut either. She was ready to make her own choices now.

The barber's smile softened. He glanced at Lily, at the faint shadows beneath her wide, eager eyes. He looked at her like she could have been his granddaughter, like he understood exactly what this meant. Then, carefully, he knelt beside her chair, looking her straight in the eyes. "Sweetheart," he said gently, "I'd be honored."

Lily's face lit up, and she kicked her feet joyfully as the barber secured the cape around her.

"What are we thinking?" he asked kindly.

Lily frowned in deep concentration. "Not too short," she decided. "But maybe a little like Daddy's?"

Rick let out a quiet, choked laugh as Darcy leaned in, smirking. "So, business casual for the little lady?"

Lily giggled. "Nooo. Just pretty."

The barber chuckled. "I can do pretty."

Rick watched, emotion thick in his throat, as Lily experienced something normal. Something that should have happened years ago. Her eyes were wide with wonder as the scissors snipped, locks of hair falling to the floor. It was such a simple thing. And yet, for both of them, it meant everything.

When the barber finished, Lily beamed at her reflection. Her hair was still long but lighter, neater, brushing just below her shoulders. She turned to Rick, grinning. "Do I look pretty?"

Rick's heart broke in the best way. He pushed off the barber chair and reached out, brushing a hand over her soft, freshly trimmed hair. "You look perfect, baby."

She giggled, then let out a small cough behind her mask before turning to Darcy, expectant. Darcy arched an eyebrow, feigning deep contemplation. "Hmm. I don't know—"

Lily pouted. "Uncle Darcy!"

He smirked. "Fine, fine. You stole my spotlight now."

Lily giggled harder, clapping her hands in delight.

Rick shook his head as the barber brushed loose hairs off Lily's cape. And then—Darcy pulled out his phone. "All right, we need a picture. Lily's first haircut? That's a milestone."

Lily beamed as Darcy motioned for the barber to join them in the frame. The older man hesitated for a moment before stepping beside them, standing tall with quiet pride.

Darcy took a few shots, then grinned. "Perfect. Croft Beach's newest residents are looking sharp."

Rick smirked, shaking his head. But his chest felt light. As he helped Lily with her cane and then grabbed his own, the barber clapped Rick on the shoulder. "This one's on the house."

Rick blinked. "Wait, what?"

The man simply nodded toward Lily, who was still admiring her reflection. "I don't take payment for first haircuts." His gaze flicked back to Rick. "And yours—well, let's just say it's long overdue."

Rick swallowed past the lump in his throat. "Thank you."

The barber just gave him a knowing smile. Laughter from the barbershop still echoed in Rick's ears as they stepped outside, the crisp afternoon air wrapping around them.

Darcy unlocked his sleek SUV and turned with a knowing smirk already in place. "Ready for the next chapter?" Darcy asked, swinging the car door open for Lily to climb into the back.

Rick exhaled, adjusting his grip on Lily's hand. "Ready as we'll ever be," Rick murmured.

Lily bounced on the balls of her feet, her voice raspy but bubbling with excitement as she handed Darcy her cane to be stowed in the backseat. "Uncle Darcy, are we really going to see the ocean?"

Darcy crouched to her level, his smirk softening into something more genuine as he picked her up and settled her in her pink booster seat. "We sure are, kiddo. And trust me—you're gonna love it."

The drive down the coast to Orange County was thrilling, filled with Lily's chatter as she flipped through the new picture book Uncle Darcy had given her that morning—about a princess in a tower. She traced the colorful illustrations with her small fingers, occasionally pausing to cough into her elbow.

"Why didn't she just climb down herself?" she asked at one point, frowning at the page.

Rick's throat tightened. "Sometimes," he murmured, his voice rough, "you need someone to catch you at the bottom."

Darcy flicked him a glance but said nothing.

Lily hummed thoughtfully, turning the page. "I think she's brave."

Rick exhaled. His fingers curled against his knee. "Yeah, baby girl. She is."

And then Darcy lowered the car windows and he was hit by the scent of—salt. Then came the sound. Waves. Rolling. Rising. Crashing. Not metal chains. Not footsteps on cellar stairs. But water meeting earth, endless and free. Rick's breath hitched. His chest tightened, his fingers flexing restlessly against his jeans.

Darcy's voice was softer than usual. "We're here." He pulled into a small lot near the dunes, rolling up the windows before shutting off the engine and grabbed a blanket and slung Lily's backpack over his shoulder. "Let's make this a moment to remember."

Rick turned to Lily. Her wide eyes shimmered with wonder, and her small fingers clutched her seatbelt as she looked out the window.

"It's so big," she whispered.

Rick swallowed past the lump in his throat, pushing open his door. His legs felt extra stiff as he stood after hours in the car but he was steady as he opened Lily's door.

Lily reached for her mask, hesitating. "Daddy, do I need this?"

Rick started to nod automatically, but Darcy's hand touched his arm lightly. "She'll be okay, man. We're outside. Fresh air, hardly anyone around."

Rick looked down at Lily's eager face, at the way she was already slipping off her sandals, ready to sink her toes into the sand. Slowly, he nodded.

"It's okay, Sweetheart," he said. "Go on."

Her tiny fingers pulled the mask down, tucking it into her pocket as she gripped her cane and carefully hopped out of the car. The moment her foot touched the sand, she gasped. She wiggled her toes, the warm grains shifting around her feet. A giggle burst from her lips. "It's soft!"

Rick chuckled, tightening his hold on his own cane as he tossed his own sandals beside the car and stepped beside her. He had forgotten this feeling—the way the sand adjusted under his weight, the way the breeze carried the salty tang of the ocean.

Lily squealed and took an eager step forward—too fast. Her cane wobbled in the uneven ground, and before Rick could steady her, she stumbled. She braced herself, her hands sinking into the warm sand. Her chest rose and fell too quickly.

Rick's heart clenched.

Darcy had already moved, pulled out the inhaler from Lily's backpack. "Easy, princess," he murmured, kneeling beside her. "Deep breaths. You know the drill."

Rick crouched beside her, rubbing circles on her back as she took the inhaler from Darcy with shaking fingers. She pressed it to her lips, inhaling deeply. One. Two. Rick watched her closely, waiting for the tightness in her chest to ease.

After a moment, Lily let out a slow, relieved breath and lowered the inhaler. "I'm okay," she rasped.

Rick brushed a curl from her forehead, scanning her face. "You sure, baby?"

Lily nodded, determination flaring in her big brown eyes. "I just got to go slow. Doctor Clarkson told me, but I got excited."

Rick swallowed against the wave of emotion tightening his chest.

Darcy rocked back on his heels. "Yeah, yeah. No Olympics trials yet. Let's keep things simple."

Lily nodded, gripping her cane more firmly this time. Her steps were smaller, more careful as they made their way down toward the water.

The tide rolled in, the foamy edges licking at the sand. The sky stretched wide above them, painted in soft pastels, the horizon endless.

Lily's fingers curled into Rick's free hand. "Can we build a castle?" she asked.

Rick's throat tightened. For nine years, every structure she had known had been a prison. Now, she wanted to build something of her own. His voice was hoarse when he spoke. "Of course, baby girl."

They spent the next hour creating something only love could build. Rick helped Lily dig moats and shape lopsided towers, their hands covered in sand, their laughter carried away by the wind. Darcy played the role of reluctant assistant, tasked with fetching seashells while loudly complaining that manual labor was not part of his daily routine. Rick sat back, shaking his head as Lily meticulously placed the final seashell on the tallest turret.

"Perfect," she declared proudly.

Rick chuckled. "Yeah, baby. Perfect."

Then—he heard it. A click. His head snapped toward Darcy, who stood a few feet away, phone raised. Rick tensed. "Darcy—"

Darcy smirked. "Relax, Rick. You're not escaping this one."

He turned the phone toward Rick, revealing the screen. The photo that stared back at him was of himself, crouched beside Lily, their castle between them, and her laughter caught mid-giggle.

Rick exhaled, something loosening in his chest as Darcy snapped another. Then another. He lowered the phone with a grin. "I wanted you to have proof."

Rick swallowed hard. Proof. That this wasn't a dream. That they had made it.

As the sun was setting, Lily stood at the shoreline, toes curled into the wet sand. The tide lapped at her ankles, swirling foam dancing around her feet. She gasped and giggled. "Daddy, it's cold!"

Rick gripped his cane and took a few slow steps forward, his feet sinking into the sand. He reached for Lily's hand, ready to guide her further into the water just as she wobbled slightly, exhaustion etched in her small face.

Darcy clicked his tongue as he secured the straps of Lily's sandals, brushing sand from her toes. "All right, fun's over. Time to get back to the car."

Rick shook his head. "No."

"Rick—" Darcy folded his arms. "You've both been out here for over an hour, and you are both barely standing."

Rick's jaw tightened. He looked at Lily. Yes, she was tired, but she was also full of wonder. She deserved this moment. Heck, he deserved hundreds of moments.

Rick bent down, his legs trembling with effort as he set his cane aside and lifted Lily into his arms. She curled against him immediately, her head resting on his shoulder, her fingers tucked against his chest.

Darcy sighed dramatically. "If you collapse, I'm not carrying both of you back."

Rick smirked. "You'd try."

Darcy rolled his eyes but didn't argue.

Rick waded in deeper, the cool water swirling around his ankles. The tide pulled gently, but he stood firm, holding Lily close. For the first time in years, water touched his skin without drowning him.

Lily pressed her forehead to his cheek, sighing. "Daddy, this is the best day ever."

Rick kissed the top of her head, his own eyes burning. "It's only the beginning, Sweetheart."

The sun melted into the horizon, setting the world on fire in gold and pink. Lily nestled closer, yawning. "It looks like a painting," she murmured sleepily.

Rick stared at the sky's shifting hues, the way the water reflected every impossible color. "It does, baby girl," he whispered. "But this time, it's real."

Lily's fingers curled around his neck. "Can we come back?"

Rick's voice was thick. He could barely push the words out. "As often as you want."

Behind them, Darcy stretched with an exaggerated groan. "All right, time to head home."

Rick chuckled, grateful for Darcy who handed him the canes and then took Lily into his own sturdy arms. She had already begun to doze, her breath steady against Darcy's chest.

Rick buckled her in, placed Leo the Lion into her arms, and brushed a stray curl from her forehead. She barely stirred, her lips parting on a sleepy sigh.

He turned back toward the shore—one last look. There was the endless blue. Stretching forever before him or so it seemed was the horizon that had no walls.

For ten years, he had been buried in darkness. For ten years, he had dreamed of the sky and the sea. And now it was real.

Darcy's voice cut through his thoughts. "This one's for the scrapbook."

Rick turned. Darcy raised his phone again, showing off a final picture he'd captured a couple minutes ago—Rick, standing at the edge of the world, the ocean stretching before him, holding his daughter close.

Chapter 43

> Survival was easy. Hope is harder.
> – Rick's Journal

The drive to Croft Beach was quiet, the streetlights casting long, golden shadows over the road. Lily slept soundly in the booster seat Darcy had bought her, her small fingers still gripping Leo the Lion.

Rick exhaled slowly, his heart pounding as they passed through the gate and turned onto a tree-lined street he had visited hundreds of times since he and Darcy had met in kindergarten at Austen Academy.

Darcy pulled into the driveway of a beautiful two-story home he had inherited from his parents while Rick was locked up. The porch light illuminated the doorway, where Caroline stood waiting with a welcoming smile on her lips.

Rick swallowed hard. This wasn't just any stop. This was their new temporary home.

Caroline stepped forward, her voice warm. "Love the haircuts, you two. Welcome to civilization."

Rick snorted as he gingerly stepped out of the car, his legs feeling the strain from his earlier activities at the ocean. He turned to reach for Lily but ruefully shook his head seeing he'd been too slow as Darcy already had unbuckled Lily and lifted her against his chest.

As they made their way inside Darcy's house, Rick froze. Three small faces were turned toward them. Walter. Sam. Ellie.

Walter, the eldest at seven, stood in front, his sharp green eyes locked on Rick, cautious but full of something deeper— something aching. Sam, six, peeked from behind him, his own green eyes flicking nervously to Lily who slept in Darcy's arms. Ellie, sat cross-legged on the floor, clutching a floppy-eared bunny and surveying them with brown eyes, so like Rick's, bright with curiosity.

Lily stirred in Darcy's arms, a soft, sleepy sound escaping her lips. Her small fingers curled into his shirt as her lashes fluttered, adjusting to the dim light of the entryway. She hadn't said anything yet, but she was aware—watching, taking in the moment unfolding before her.

Rick barely had time to brace himself before Ellie barreled into him with all the energy her little body could muster. His already aching muscles protested as he staggered back and plopped down on the entryway tile, but he didn't care. Ellie's arms wrapped tight around his neck, her warmth pressing into him as she clung with everything she had.

"You came back, Daddy!" Her voice was muffled against his chest, her tiny hands patting at his face as if she had to be sure he was real.

Rick's throat tightened, his vision blurring as he pressed a kiss to the crown of her head. "I'm here, Little Love," he whispered. "And I'm never leaving again."

A movement caught his eye. Just behind Ellie, Walter and Sam stood frozen in place, watching. Their expressions were hesitant, unsure, and yet there was something else there too. Recognition. Curiosity. A longing neither seemed ready to voice.

For two weeks, they had heard stories. They had seen photos that Uncle Darcy had dug out. They knew who he was. They had been told that he was their father. But knowing and believing were two very different things.

Walter shifted first, glancing at Darcy, then back at Rick. His brow furrowed as if working through something; his small hands clenched at his sides. And then, Walter took a cautious step forward. Then another.

Rick didn't move, didn't push. He just waited.

And finally, Walter closed the distance in a rush, crashing into Rick with enough force that would have sent them both to the floor if Rick wasn't already sitting there with Ellie. A choked breath escaped him as his arms automatically opened wider, wrapping Walter into the embrace. The boy pressed his face into Rick's shoulder, his body trembling slightly, but he didn't pull away. No words, no questions. Just this.

A second later, Sam was there too, smaller, more hesitant, but just as real. Rick barely had time to shift before his youngest son pressed against his side, fitting into the space that had been waiting for him all along. Rick pulled him in, his heart breaking and healing in the same moment.

Darcy shifted nearby, adjusting Lily against his chest. She was fully awake now, though still quiet, her eyes locked onto the scene unfolding in front of her. Rick met her gaze, his breath catching as he saw the way she was taking everything in as if trying to understand what it all meant. There was something unreadable in her expression, something cautious.

Then, slowly, her grip on Darcy's shirt loosened. Her fingers flexed as if preparing for something. And then, with a small breath, she reached out.

Rick barely had time to process before Darcy carefully lowered her into his arms. She settled against him with a soft sigh, the weight of her instantly familiar. Her small fingers clutched at his sweater's collar as she pressed her face into his neck.

Rick closed his eyes, pressing his lips to her hair as he held all four of his children close. His arms trembled, not just from exhaustion, but from the sheer weight of this moment—of everything they carried between them. The fear, the hurt, the years of separation. He tightened his grip, unwilling to let go, unwilling to let this be anything less than real.

Finally, Rick let out something close to a breathless laugh, though his eyes were still burning. He turned slightly, looking at his best friend. "Thank you," he whispered.

Darcy just nodded. "Anytime."

Chapter 44

> I can't get back the years that were stolen. I can't rewrite the childhoods I missed. But today, I got to be his dad. And maybe— just maybe—that's enough.
> – Rick's Journal

Rick leaned his cane against the log beside him, shifting carefully to find a comfortable position. His muscles still ached from physical therapy last night, and his body was making sure he remembered every movement he'd made. The morning air was crisp, laced with the scent of lake water and damp earth, the sunlight glinting off the rippling surface. A dragonfly hovered lazily nearby, its iridescent wings shimmering in the light before darting to just above the water.

Picking up the fishing pole, he rolled his shoulders and cast his line. The soft whir of the reel broke the stillness, followed by the quiet plunk of the lure disappearing beneath the water. Beside him, Walter sat cross-legged on the bank, his small hands steady on his own fishing rod. The kid was focused, serious, his brow furrowed in concentration.

Rick swallowed the tightness in his throat. *God, I've missed so much.* "Any luck yet?" he asked, keeping his voice low.

Walter didn't answer right away. He kept his eyes on the water, brow furrowed in concentration. "Not yet," he finally said. "Do you think they're asleep?"

Rick chuckled. "Could be," he mused. "Or maybe they're just playing hard to get."

Walter considered this, then glanced sideways at him. "How long do we wait?"

Rick pretended to think about it. "Could be five minutes. Could be an hour. Sometimes they make you work for it."

Walter's lips quirked into a tiny smirk. "I can wait."

Rick's chest tightened. *Yeah, kid. You can.*

For a while, they sat in companionable silence, the gentle sounds of nature wrapping around them. The distant chirp of birds, the rustling of leaves in the morning breeze, the faint lap of water against the shore.

Then, without warning—Walter's pole jerked. "Whoa!" Walter yelped, gripping the handle tighter as the line pulled.

Rick's heart leapt. "You got one, Buddy! Reel it in slow—steady—"

Walter fumbled with the reel, his excitement getting the better of him. The fishing rod bent as the fish fought back. "I think it's huge!" Walter gasped.

Rick reached over; his hands steady over Walter's. "Not too fast, or you'll lose it—"

And then—snap! Walter's line went slack.

Walter stared at the water, his mouth slightly open. "Did I—did I just lose my first fish?"

Rick pressed his lips together to keep from laughing. "Well, technically, yes," he admitted. "But hey—you got it to bite, which is more than I can say for myself."

For a brief second Rick thought his son was going to burst into tears but then his lips twitched. "I guess I scared it away with my mad skills," he said, trying to sound nonchalant.

Rick burst out laughing, ruffling his son's blond hair. "That's exactly what happened."

The laughter faded into an easy silence. Rick watched Walter out of the corner of his eye, taking in the way the morning light caught the golden strands of his hair—the same shade as Louisa's. But his green eyes weren't cold like hers. There was something steadier about him, something cautious but open.

God, he looks so much like her. But he's his own person.

"Did we ever do this before?" Walter asked suddenly, not looking up.

Rick's breath hitched. His grip on the fishing pole tightened. "No," he admitted, his voice quieter. "We never got the chance. But I thought about it. A lot." His throat tightened. "I used to dream about taking you fishing, showing you how to cast a line, teaching you all the tricks I was taught as a kid."

Walter was silent for a moment, his fingers restlessly playing with his rod before he finally asked a question Rick had been bracing for all week since they'd all moved in together. "Mom said you didn't like doing stuff like this," Walter said, his voice careful. "She said you didn't want to be my dad."

Rick inhaled sharply. He forced himself to keep his posture loose, to meet Walter's eyes without flinching. "I think your mom and I had very different ideas about what I wanted," he said evenly.

Walter turned his head slightly, his green eyes studying Rick. "So, she lied?"

Rick let out a slow breath. "I think sometimes people tell stories the way they need to believe them," he said carefully. "But I don't want you to believe me just because I say so. You'll get to decide for yourself what's true."

Walter mulled over this. His fingers tightened briefly on the handle of his fishing rod. Then he smiled. Small, but real. "I'm glad we're doing this," he admitted.

Rick's breath caught. "Me too, Buddy," he murmured.

A mischievous glint flickered in Walter's eyes. "But you still haven't caught anything yet."

Rick scoffed. "Oh, you're gonna bring that up now?"

Walter shrugged. "I mean—I'm just saying."

Rick feigned deep offense. "Well, then. I guess it's time to show you how it's really done."

Walter grinned. "Bet I'll catch one before you do."

Rick raised an eyebrow. "Oh, it's on now."

They cast their lines back into the water, a playful competition brewing between them. But as Rick was holding his pole, his fingers trembled slightly, a sharp ache shooting through his shoulder. His body was still adjusting, still recovering. He sighed and put down his rod so to reach for his cane, shifting carefully to ease the strain on his muscles. As much as he hated to admit it, he needed to slow down.

Admitting defeat, he sat back down on the log. "Walter, can you grab my pain meds and water from the backpack?" he asked.

Walter immediately set his fishing rod down and hopped up, hurrying over to where Rick had left his bag. He rummaged through it and pulled out the bottle and water, bringing them over with careful hands. "Here," he said, watching as Rick twisted off the cap and shook out a pill.

"Thanks, Buddy," Rick murmured, taking a sip of water to swallow it down.

"When's Uncle Darcy picking us up?"

Rick refused to be offended that his son was already thinking about the end of their outing as he checked his watch. "We have about an hour left. Afraid I'll beat you to catching a fish?"

"Nah." Walter laughed. "Are you sure you're okay though, Dad? Your medicine helping?"

Rick stilled, caught off guard by the quiet sincerity in Walter's voice. He had assumed his son was tired and wanted to go home. But now, hearing the concern in Walter's question, guilt pricked at him. This boy wasn't counting down the minutes to be done with their time together. He wasn't eager to get away. He was worried about him.

Rick cleared his throat, offering a small, reassuring smile. "Yeah, Buddy. It's helping. Thanks for getting it for me."

Walter nodded, watching him for another second before turning his attention back to his fishing rod. The challenge in his eyes from earlier was still there, but now, there was something else too—something solid, something trusting.

Rick exhaled, stretching his aching legs in front of him. Maybe he wasn't the man he used to be. Maybe he was still figuring things out, still learning how to be a father outside of survival mode. But sitting here, feeling the warmth of the sun on his skin, his son by his side, he knew one thing for certain. This moment—this bond—was real.

And he wasn't going to waste a second of it.

Chapter 45

> Persuasion isn't always loud. Sometimes it whispers over and over
> until your soul starts to believe the lie. For ten years, she rewrote
> who I was. But every time I held my children, every time I
> remembered pure love—I rewrote it back.
> – Rick's Journal

The low hum of conversation and clinking silverware filled the steakhouse, a comfortable sort of noise that still felt foreign to Rick after years of silence. Across from him, Darcy leaned back in his chair, swirling the last bit of his drink with a smirk that had lawyer mode written all over it.

"You look like you're expecting an ambush," Darcy remarked.

Rick huffed, shifting in his seat. "Still not used to this. People. Choices. Noise." His fingers drummed against the table before he stopped himself. "I used to have to ask permission just to—" He exhaled sharply, shaking his head. "Never mind."

Darcy's smirk faded slightly. "Yeah. Ten years of that will do a number on any guy."

Rick stayed quiet, watching the ice in his glass melt.

Darcy let the silence settle before cutting to the chase. "So, Pastor Eddie's expecting you next week."

Rick glanced up. "Already?"

Darcy tilted his head. "Yeah, Rick. I figured once you were sleeping under my roof, eating my food, and letting Caroline babysit your kids, it was time to get you professional help."

Rick rolled his eyes. "Subtle."

"Look, man, you need this." Darcy leaned forward, elbows on the table. "You spent ten years being brainwashed into thinking you had no choice. That she was the only voice that mattered. That she owned you."

Rick stiffened but said nothing.

Darcy studied him, then softened his tone. "She tried to persuade you, Rick. For ten years." He let that hang in the air for a second before adding, "But she didn't win."

Rick swallowed, his throat tight. "Didn't she?"

Darcy's jaw clenched. "You're sitting here. She's not. That's a win in my book."

Rick let out a bitter breath, shaking his head. "You weren't there. You don't know how deep she got into my head. She broke me down until there was nothing left of the man I used to be. She took everything. My body, my dignity, my will. And the worst part?"

His voice dropped, raw and low, barely more than a whisper.

"She trained me to want it. She conditioned me to respond like I had no say, like my body belonged to her." His fingers curled into fists on the table, his knuckles white. "I was a virgin. I had saved myself for my wife, for love, for something real—and instead, I was a freaking sex slave for a decade."

His breath came out uneven, his voice thick with disgust.

"At first, she had to use drugs. Slipped things into my juice, forced pills down my throat, made sure I had no way to fight back. But after a couple years?"

His stomach twisted, the shame curdling deep inside him.

"She didn't even need them anymore. My body had learned to respond to her like I was some animal trained to perform. It didn't matter that I hated her, that I wanted to rip my own skin off just to get rid of her touch. My own damn body betrayed me!"

His jaw clenched as he forced out the words, his voice shaking with rage.

"Do you have any idea what it's like to be trapped in yourself like that? To feel your own flesh turn against you?"

Darcy exhaled sharply, his own expression darkening with something unreadable—anger, grief, maybe both. But there was no pity in his eyes, only unwavering conviction. "Of course you did."

Rick blinked. "What?"

"That's how this works." Darcy shrugged. "Doesn't matter how strong you are. If someone tells you something long enough, forces it on you, your brain starts making room for it. It's a survival mechanism. But here's the thing." He set his drink down. "She didn't finish the job. You still got out."

Rick let that sit for a second, staring at the grain of the wooden table.

"Besides, persuasion's a two-way street, my friend. You can argue she had you convinced, but I seem to remember a certain marine biologist who always fought back."

"Not in the cellar." Rick exhaled, shaking his head. "Not always."

"You fought back every time you told her no. Every time you thought about escaping. Every time you held onto Lily and the others instead of giving up. And now, you're free. Tell me—who persuaded who?"

Rick stared at Darcy, something twisting deep in his gut.

Darcy grinned. "Exactly."

Rick let out a breath.

Darcy picked up his drink again. "You know, I had this client once. A cop."

"What happened to him?" Rick frowned.

Darcy leaned back, rolling his glass between his fingers. "His wife used to drug him and beat him up each night. Then she'd—" He waved vaguely, letting Rick fill in the blanks. "He never told anyone because, well, who's gonna believe a big burly six-foot-four man in uniform, right?"

Rick swallowed hard.

Darcy's expression turned serious. "By the time he came to me, she'd nearly killed him. Still, first thing he asked was whether the court would call him weak for letting it happen."

Rick shook his head. "That's insane."

"Yeah," Darcy agreed. "But you know what I told him?"

Rick raised a brow.

Darcy leaned forward, his smirk fading into something quieter, weightier. "I told him that if being a victim made him weak, then I guess Jesus was weak too—for letting them crucify Him." Darcy took a sip of his drink before adding, "Told him survival's not weakness—it's proof of strength." He lifted his glass in a salute. "Same applies to you, Rick. You made it out. That means you win."

Rick exhaled slowly.

Darcy grinned. "But hey, if you wanna sit around and let Louisa live in your head rent-free, be my guest. Just let me know when she starts charging."

Rick snorted. "You're an idiot."

"An idiot who just bought you steak," Darcy countered.

Rick shook his head, but the weight on his chest felt just a little lighter as he reached for his cane. Maybe persuasion was a two-way street after all.

As they left the restaurant, the cool night air hit Rick like a shock to the system.

Darcy jingled his keys, glancing over at him. "You did good in there."

Rick raised an eyebrow. "What, eating?"

Darcy smirked. "Eating. Sitting in a crowded place. Talking. Not punching anyone." He shot him a sideways look. "That's progress, Wentworth."

Rick scoffed, shoving his hands into his jacket pockets.

Darcy let a beat pass before continuing. "So, since you survived this, how about leveling up?"

Rick glanced at him warily. "What does 'leveling up' entail?"

Darcy clicked the SUV open. "Church. Sunday. Biblical counseling."

Rick hesitated, shifting his weight.

Darcy sighed. "Look, man. Nobody's judging you for missing last week. Lily was sick. You had your hands full."

Rick exhaled sharply. "She was nervous."

"She was sick." Darcy shot him a knowing look. "But yeah, nerves probably didn't help."

Rick frowned at the pavement.

Darcy shrugged. "So, you missed one week. Big deal. But Eddie's expecting you this Sunday."

Rick met his gaze.

Darcy continued, his tone lighter now. "He's solid. You'll like him. He's not the fire-and-brimstone type. More sit-down-and-actually-listen type. Which, given your stubborn streak, is probably a necessary skill."

Rick scoffed. "You sure you're not his PR rep?"

"Just giving you fair warning." Darcy stepped off the curb, opening the car door. "You survived ten years with Louisa, Rick. I think you can handle a one-hour service."

Rick sighed, shaking his head. "Yeah. We'll see."

But as he climbed into the car, something about the idea didn't feel so impossible anymore.

Chapter 46

> A father isn't measured by the years he's there but by the moments
> he refuses to miss.
> – Rick's Journal

Rick leaned heavily on his cane, watching Sam weave through the grass, dribbling the soccer ball with fierce concentration. April sunlight danced across the field, the air thick with the scent of fresh-cut grass and sizzling hot dogs from a nearby cart. Laughter from the playground carried on the breeze, but Rick only heard one voice.

"Watch me, Daddy," Sam called, his little legs moving fast as he maneuvered the ball with precision. He attempted a dramatic spin, nearly losing his balance before recovering with a laugh.

Rick grinned. "That was impressive, Buddy. Where'd you learn that?"

Sam puffed out his chest proudly. "I watched the big kids at recess. Walter helped me practice, but I'm better at it now."

Rick shifted his weight, adjusting his grip on the cane. He wasn't ready to be running around, but when Caroline had offered to watch the other kids so Darcy could take him and Sam out to the park, he'd jumped at the opportunity. "I can tell. You've got some serious skills. Show me another move."

Sam beamed, rolling the ball back with his foot before attempting to flick it up with his toe. The ball barely left the ground before wobbling off to the side, but his enthusiasm didn't waver. "Did you see that?"

Rick nodded. "Sure did. That was awesome. I think you're a natural."

Sam giggled, running after the ball. "Do you know how to play soccer, Daddy?"

Rick chuckled, shifting his weight around. "Not really, but I'd love for you to teach me."

Sam's eyes widened at the thrill of being in charge. "Really? I can teach you?"

"Absolutely," Rick said, grinning. "Start with the basics. I'm a total beginner."

Sam placed the ball in front of Rick's feet, suddenly all business. "Okay, you gotta kick it like this," he said, demonstrating small, precise taps. "But don't let it go too far, or it'll get away."

Rick lifted his foot carefully, using his cane for balance as he mimicked Sam's movements. His touches were far clumsier, the ball rolling further than intended, but Sam just laughed and darted after it. "No, Daddy!" He giggled. "You're supposed to keep it close!"

Rick raised his hands in mock surrender. "Okay, okay! Show me again. I'll get it this time."

For the next half hour, they passed the ball back and forth, Rick moving cautiously but determined. When he couldn't maneuver well enough to keep up, he adapted—practicing trapping the ball with his cane or tapping it gently to Sam. Every stumble was met with Sam's bright laughter, every small success with his enthusiastic cheers.

"You're getting better, Daddy," Sam declared after Rick managed to stop the ball without letting it roll away. "But you still need more practice."

Rick chuckled, ruffling Sam's hair. "I'll take all the practice I can get. You're a great coach, you know that?"

Sam's grin stretched ear to ear as he plopped down on the grass, his small legs sprawled out in front of him. "This is fun," he said, his voice quieter now, like a secret meant just for them.

Rick lowered himself onto the grass beside him, groaning in relief to be off his legs as he stretched out, leaning back on his palms. "I like playing soccer with you too, Sam," he said, his voice steady but warm. "I missed out on a lot of time with you, but I want to make up for it. I want to be there for all the things you love."

Sam tilted his head, thoughtful, tracing patterns in the dirt with his finger. "I think I like it better now," he said after a moment. "'Cause now you're here for real."

Rick's throat tightened. He wrapped an arm around Sam's small shoulders, pulling him close. "I'm here, Buddy. And I'm not going anywhere."

Sam leaned into him, silent for a beat, then added, "Mom had other guys around sometimes, but I didn't like them." His nose wrinkled in distaste. "They weren't fun. They didn't listen or play with me like you do."

Rick swallowed hard. He had spent so many years wondering what kind of life his boys had upstairs, if they had been safe, if they had been loved. And now hearing this, it struck deep. He pressed a gentle kiss to Sam's head. "Well, I'm really glad we get to have this time together now," he said, his voice steady despite the lump in his throat.

Sam nodded, content. "Me too," he said simply. "Can we do this again next Saturday?"

Rick smiled, his heart swelling. "Absolutely, Buddy. We'll make it our thing."

Sam leaned closer, his little body radiating warmth and trust. "Do you think I'll be as good as the big kids someday?"

Rick didn't hesitate. "I think you're going to be even better," he said. "Because you've got something special—heart."

Sam giggled, suddenly reinvigorated. He scrambled up, holding the ball with determination. "Okay, Daddy, your turn! Let's see if you can kick it past me."

Rick laughed, shaking his head as he carefully pushed himself back up, using his cane to steady himself. His body ached, but for Sam, he'd keep trying. "All right, Coach," he said, rolling the ball into place. "Let's see if I've still got it."

Sam darted into position, his arms spread wide like a goalie. Rick took a second to just look at him—the light in his green eyes, the way his blond hair stuck to his forehead from running, the way his small body vibrated with energy and confidence.

Rick took a deep breath, a quiet smile tugging at his lips. The road ahead wouldn't be easy. He couldn't change the years he lost. But right here, right now, with Sam's laughter ringing out, he realized something. He didn't have to fix the past.

He just had to show up, every day, for the future.

Chapter 47

> As I watched my kids walk through the Sunday School doors, hand in hand, I realized something. Faith isn't just about the past. It's about what comes next. And maybe, just maybe, we're ready for that.
> — Rick's Journal

Rick gripped his cane tightly as he stepped into the bustling church he had attended before his captivity. Lily's small hand wrapped tightly around Leo the Lion as she dragged at his side as Ellie skipped alongside them happily chatting away. The familiar blend of musicians warming up and quiet conversations surrounded him, a stark contrast to the suffocating silence of the past decade. His steps were careful, each one measured, but it wasn't just his body that was uncertain—it was the weight of returning to a place that had once been home.

Darcy walked ahead with Walter and Sam, shaking hands and exchanging greetings with familiar faces. The boys had already started to settle into this life, meeting people, making friends. Rick swallowed hard. The last time he had set foot in this church, he had been a free man. A different man. He had attended here for years—through childhood, teenage years, and even into college, sitting beside Darcy in the pews. But that was ten years ago.

Some faces had moved on, but others, like the reliable children's ministry leader, Pastor Fanny, remained. She approached with a warm smile, her hand already lifted in a wave.

Lily hesitated beside him, tugging at his sleeve. "Daddy," she whispered, her voice muffled slightly behind her mask. "Do we have to go inside?"

Rick stopped, crouching to her level with a wince, steadying himself against his cane. "It's okay, Sweetheart," he said gently, brushing a curl from her face. "You remember Pastor Fanny from when she visited? She'll be there. And you've got Walter, Sam, and Ellie with you."

Lily shifted uncomfortably, her fingers tightening around the handle of her own small cane. She hated using it, hated how it made her different. Because of the embarrassment of her cane and her mask, she had avoided eye contact with anyone since they arrived. Her knuckles turned white where she gripped the fabric of his sleeve.

"What if—" she swallowed, her voice barely above a whisper, "what if you're not here when I come back?"

Rick's heart twisted painfully. He placed both hands on her small shoulders, anchoring her. "Hey," he said softly, leaning in. "I promise you, when you come out, I'll be standing right here. And you know what? We'll go get cookies together. Just you and me."

She still didn't look convinced. Her eyes darted toward the sanctuary, to the unfamiliar faces beyond.

A warm voice cut through the moment. "Lily, I'm so happy to see you again."

Pastor Fanny knelt to Lily's level, her kind expression steadying. "We've got a wonderful class today—songs, a fun Bible story, and a craft. I even saved a seat right next to me."

Lily shifted again, hugging Leo the Lion closer to her chest.

Walter stepped forward, his voice strong but gentle. "I'll go with you, Lily," he promised. "We can sit together, and I won't leave your side unless you want me to."

Sam beamed. "And I'll sit next to you too! You'll be safe. Promise."

Ellie nodded enthusiastically. "Me too! Sissy, we get snack time, too."

Lily's fingers clenched the stuffed animal, hesitation still lingering. "You promise?"

"I promise," Walter said firmly, his gaze unwavering. "And Dad's going to be right here waiting for us when we're done."

Lily studied her brother's face for a long moment before giving a small nod. "Okay," she whispered.

Rick kissed her forehead, his heart full of pride. "You're so brave, Sweetheart. Go have fun, okay?"

She nodded again, following Pastor Fanny toward the children's wing, her cane tapping softly against the floor as she walked away with Walter, Sam and Ellie. Rick exhaled.

"She's doing great," Caroline said from beside him, her voice full of quiet encouragement. He hadn't even seen her arrive at church. "And Walter is pretty incredible."

Rick nodded, emotion thick in his throat. "Yes. They all are."

A tall figure approached just as Rick turned back toward the sanctuary. He was lean, broad-shouldered, and carried himself with an easy confidence that spoke of both discipline and approachability. Dark brown hair flecked with the beginnings of gray framed his face, and sharp blue eyes held warmth, intelligence, and an almost unsettling ability to see through walls people thought they had carefully constructed.

Rick recognized him immediately from Darcy's description. Pastor Eddie Ferrars.

His smile was genuine, his handshake firm. "Rick Wentworth," he greeted, his voice smooth, confident, but with a gentle undercurrent of excitement. "Man, it's good to finally meet you in person."

Rick felt the weight of Eddie's gaze, assessing him—not in judgment, but in understanding. "Darcy's been talking me up, huh?" Rick asked, shifting slightly under the scrutiny.

Eddie chuckled. "Oh, nonstop. Between him and Pastors Ned and Fanny, I think I've got half your life story already." His tone was light, teasing, but Rick didn't miss the sincerity beneath it.

Rick nodded, glancing toward the sanctuary doors. "Guess that means you know what you're getting yourself into tomorrow."

Eddie crossed his arms, leaning slightly against the doorway. "I know when I see a man who's carrying more than he should," he said simply. "And I know that God didn't bring you this far just to leave you drowning in it."

Rick swallowed hard. Something about Eddie's certainty rattled him.

"You're coming tomorrow afternoon?" Eddie asked, his voice casual but expectant.

Rick hesitated. Then, to his own surprise, he nodded.

Eddie grinned, clapping him on the shoulder. "Good. I'll see you then."

Rick exhaled as the pastor stepped away, heading into the sanctuary.

Darcy nudged him. "See? That wasn't so bad."

Rick huffed. "You're enjoying this too much."

"Absolutely," Darcy admitted, grinning. "And now that you survived the restaurant on Friday night and met Eddie, I say you're ready for the full church experience."

Rick scoffed but didn't argue as they stepped inside.

The service flew by, the weight of the sermon settling deep in Rick's chest. By the time it ended, he was already making his way to the Sunday school room, eager to see the kids.

The door swung open before he could reach for it. "Daddy!"

Lily ran straight into his arms, nearly knocking him back. He braced himself with his cane, steadying them both. In her free hand, she clutched a brightly colored lion mask.

Rick bent down hugging her close. "Wow, Picasso," he murmured, warmth spreading through him. "You made this?"

She nodded. "We talked about Daniel again! And Walter stayed with me the whole time."

Rick's eyes flicked to Walter, his oldest son standing just behind her, proud and protective. "Thank you, Buddy," Rick said, voice thick with emotion. "I'm so proud of you."

Walter shrugged, but his smile gave him away. "She's my sister."

Sam piped up beside him, waving his own craft. "And I made a lion too! But mine's a superhero lion."

Rick chuckled, ruffling his son's hair. "Of course he is."

"Up, Daddy," Ellie demanded, her big brown eyes shining with determination. "Carry me!"

Rick huffed out a quiet laugh, shaking his head. "Little Love, Daddy's still using his cane."

Ellie was undeterred. "Pleeeease?" she whined, bouncing on her toes. "Just for a little bit?"

Rick sighed, already knowing he was about to give in. With a bit of effort, he shifted his cane to his other hand and carefully hoisted her up onto his hip. She immediately snuggled in, her tiny arms wrapping around his neck as if she had no intention of letting go.

"Happy now?" he murmured, adjusting his stance to compensate for the extra weight.

Ellie grinned against his shoulder. "Mmmhmm."

Rick took a few steps, his muscles protesting but holding. Six weeks of physical therapy had done wonders, but carrying a wiggly toddler while relying on a cane was still a challenge. He wasn't about to risk both of them ending up on the ground in an undignified pile.

After a few more steps, he exhaled and pressed a kiss to Ellie's curls. "Okay, Little Love. Time to use those legs again." Ellie pouted as he set her back down, but before she could argue, he pointed toward the coffee station where Caroline stood chatting with a group of women. "Hey, why don't you run over and say hi to Aunt Caroline?" he suggested, tapping the tip of her nose.

Ellie considered it for a moment, then nodded, immediately scampering off.

Rick straightened, rolling his shoulder to ease the ache as he adjusted his grip on the cane. He caught Darcy watching him knowingly.

"You just got played," Darcy commented, amusement dancing in his voice.

Rick scoffed, shaking his head. "I know."

Darcy clapped him on the shoulder. "She gets it from you, you know."

Rick sighed, watching Ellie barrel into Caroline's legs with uncontainable enthusiasm as Lily approached at a more cautious and relaxed pace. "Yeah," he admitted, a soft smile tugging at his lips. "I know and I wouldn't have her any other way."

Caroline's smile widened as she saw the men and boys approaching. "Rick, come meet my friend Marianne."

Rick's chest tightened as the woman turned. Their eyes met, and for the first time in weeks, a connection hit him like a jolt.

"You're—" he started, voice trailing off.

The Asian woman extended her hand, her smile warm. "Marianne Dashwood," she said. "We've met before, though under very different circumstances."

Rick hesitated, then took her hand. "You—you were the paramedic," he said, the realization striking fully. "You helped Lily."

Marianne nodded. "She was so brave that day. And so were you."

Rick met her gaze, something unfamiliar settling in his chest.

Chapter 48

> I used to think chains were only made of metal—until I learned the
> heaviest ones are the lies we tell ourselves.
> – Rick's Journal

"Amen." Pastor Eddie Ferrars' voice carried through the small counseling room, steady and grounding.

Rick exhaled slowly, trying to ease the tension tightening in his chest.

Across the table, Darcy shifted in his seat, rubbing a hand over his jaw. "So, uh—just want to say upfront, I know I don't need to be here. Probably should've just dropped them off." He glanced between Pastor Eddie and Pastor Fanny Bertram, offering a small, self-aware smirk.

"But I asked you to be here, Uncle Darcy," Lily interrupted, climbing into his lap and clutching Leo the Lion close to her chest. "You are family."

Darcy's smirk softened into something warmer. "And I'm here, kiddo."

"That's completely fine, Darcy," Eddie assured him. "This is a safe space, and if the kids want you here, then we're happy to have you."

Rick exhaled again, his gaze shifting to his four children beside him—Walter, Sam, Lily, and Ellie. His family. His heartbeat.

Eddie leaned forward slightly, folding his hands on the table. "Before we begin, let's talk about what biblical counseling is. A lot of people think of it like therapy, but really, it's about discipleship. Pastor Fanny and I are here to help you learn how to trust God and find joy, even when things feel hard or confusing. God wants your family to have peace and love, and we're here to help you understand how He can heal hearts and bring you closer together."

Pastor Fanny smiled warmly. "And part of that healing comes from learning. The Bible is filled with people just like us—people who struggled, who messed up, who went through pain, and who grew because of it." She looked at the kids. "So, I want to ask each of you—who's your favorite person in the Bible? Can you name someone you admire and want to learn from?"

Lily straightened immediately, her brown eyes lighting up. "Daniel!"

Rick smiled at her immediate answer.

"Why Daniel?" Eddie asked, interest warm in his expression.

"Because he was brave," Lily said, gripping Leo a little tighter. "Even when the lions were right there, he wasn't scared. He trusted God—just like Daddy did in the cellar."

Rick swallowed hard and reached over to squeeze her hand.

Fanny nodded. "That's a wonderful choice, Sweetheart."

Eddie turned to the boys. "Walter, what about you?"

Walter hesitated. "I don't know," he admitted. "Mom never really talked about the Bible, and we didn't go to church before moving in with Uncle Darcy. So—I didn't really know the stories until Pastor Fanny started telling them."

Fanny's smile was kind. "And is there one you've liked the most so far?"

Walter thought for a moment. "David and Goliath, I guess," he said slowly. "David was small, but he still won. He wasn't afraid to fight, even though Goliath was huge."

Eddie nodded. "That's a great one. David trusted God, and that's what gave him strength."

Sam, sitting beside his brother, fidgeted slightly. "I like Jonah."

Rick tilted his head in confusion. "Jonah?"

Sam nodded quickly. "Yeah. 'Cause Jonah didn't help at first. He ran away when God told him to help the bad people." He shifted uncomfortably, lowering his voice. "But then he did help them. He changed. I wanna be like Jonah."

Pastor Fanny sat forward and asked, "What do you mean, Sam?"

Sam's fingers twisted in his lap. "Jonah didn't help the bad people at first, but then he did, and just like him," He swallowed, "I didn't help Daddy. Or Lily. Not at first."

Walter lowered his gaze, silent but clearly feeling the same.

Rick's heart ached.

Eddie leaned in, his voice soft but firm. "You boys didn't know. You were just kids."

"But we should've known," Walter said, frustration creeping into his tone. "We should've done something."

The weight of guilt hung thick in the air.

Pastor Fanny reached for her Bible, flipping through the pages until she found what she was looking for. "I want to share something with you," she said gently. "Romans 8:1. 'There is therefore now no condemnation for those who are in Christ Jesus.'"

Walter swallowed hard.

Fanny continued, her voice steady. "You didn't do anything wrong, Sweetheart. And feeling guilty over something that wasn't your fault? That's not from God. That's the enemy trying to keep you trapped in a lie."

Eddie nodded. "And when we do mess up—when we do have guilt that belongs to us? That's where repentance and grace come in. We don't live in guilt. We bring it to God, and He washes it away."

Sam glanced at Walter. Slowly, cautiously, some of the tension drained from their little shoulders.

Rick reached for both of them, squeezing their hands. "You didn't fail me," he murmured. "You didn't fail Lily. And I never want you carrying that weight. It doesn't belong to you."

Silence stretched between them.

And then Ellie, small and soft in Rick's lap, broke the heaviness of the moment with a whisper. "I just wanna be a good sister and daughter."

Walter smiled. "You are."

Ellie beamed, clearly pleased with that answer.

Eddie let the quiet settle before speaking again. "So, if this setup works for everyone, here's what we'll do. Rick and I will meet once a week, and at the same time, Pastor Fanny will meet with you kids. We'll talk about things like today—guilt, forgiveness, healing—but we'll also learn more about the Bible, and ask big questions. And at the end of the hour, we'll come together to pray and debrief. Does that sound good?"

The kids exchanged glances, then nodded. Rick swallowed thickly, nodding along with them.

Eddie smiled. "All right. Then before we wrap up, does anyone have any last questions?"

"Is Mama going to hell for what she did to Daddy and Lily?"

Silence.

Eddie took a slow breath, his blue eyes steady but kind. "That's a big question, Walter," he admitted. "And I won't pretend I have all the answers. But here's what we do know—God is just. He sees everything, and He will hold her accountable for what she's done. But we also know something else—no one is beyond saving."

Walter hesitated before whispering, "But—what about me?" His voice was small, unsure. "I never asked Jesus to save me—does that mean I won't go to heaven?"

Rick's heart clenched.

Eddie's expression softened. "That's a really important question, Walter," he said. "Would you like to ask Jesus to be your Savior?"

Walter nodded slowly. "I think I do."

Eddie's smile widened. "Then let's do it."

They all bowed their heads as Eddie led Walter in prayer. When they looked up, Walter's face was glowing.

Rick pulled him into a tight hug, pressing a grateful kiss to the top of his head. "I'm so proud of you, Buddy."

Sam suddenly sat up straight, grinning. "I did it, too! Did Jesus hear me, too?"

Pastor Eddie's face lit up. "Of course He did, Sam."

Lily burst into tears and threw her arms around them. "You're really going to be in Heaven with me?"

Sam nodded. "Yep!"

"Forever!" Walter yelled in excitement.

Ellie, not wanting to be left out, jumped in, wrapping her tiny arms around all of them. "Group hug!"

Rick let the moment sink in, his chest full, his heart lighter than it had been in years. Healing wasn't just possible. It was happening—right in front of him.

Pastor Eddie smiled, his voice gentle but firm. "Lily's right," he said. "This is forever. Nothing can separate you from God's love now."

His boys had made the biggest decision of their lives. And his daughter—the little girl who had spent nearly a decade in darkness—had been the first to grasp the eternal weight of it.

Pastor Fanny wiped her own damp eyes before saying, "Sounds like today's a day to remember."

Darcy, never one to let a moment stay too serious, clapped his hands together. "All right, now we definitely need pizza. And extra toppings since this is a major celebration."

After saying their farewells, Rick stood in the church parking lot, his hands gripping the railing of the sidewalk ramp leading to the car. His breath came unsteady, like his body was trying to catch up to what had just happened.

His kids had prayed. His boys had asked Jesus into their hearts. They were going to be in Heaven together.

A sound broke from him—half-laugh, half-sob—and he ran a shaking hand through his hair. His chest felt too full, too tight, like something was pressing down on him, demanding to be let out.

Footsteps behind him. A familiar presence. Darcy leaned against the railing beside him, hands in his pockets. For a moment, neither of them spoke.

Darcy finally huffed out a small laugh, shaking his head. "Well. That happened."

Rick let out a breathless chuckle, one hand still gripping the railing like a lifeline. "Yeah." His voice was rough, unsteady.

Darcy smirked, nudging him lightly with his elbow. "So. How's it feel knowing your boys just secured their VIP passes upstairs?"

Rick swallowed hard, staring at the pavement. "It feels like—" He trailed off, his throat thick, the words sticking like tar.

Darcy waited.

Rick exhaled, voice barely above a whisper. "I don't deserve this."

Darcy's smirk vanished.

Rick shook his head, his grip tightening on the railing. "I lost so many years with them. I couldn't protect them. I let them—" His voice cracked. "I should've been the one teaching them about God. Not—not playing catch-up."

Darcy let out a breath, watching him closely. Then he pushed off the railing slightly, turning toward Rick, his voice quieter but firm. "You remember what Eddie and Fanny said in there? About Satan keeping you trapped in guilt? About the lies that make you feel unworthy?" He arched a brow. "Because that's what this is."

Rick frowned. "It's not the same."

"It's exactly the same." Darcy turned fully to him, his voice lower now, insistent. "You're still listening to her voice. Still believing the lie that you failed them. But Rick, you didn't."

Rick clenched his jaw, looking away.

Darcy didn't let up. "They could've asked that question about salvation at any time. At school. At church. To someone else. But they didn't." He paused, letting it sink in. "They wanted you to be involved. They wanted to know the truth with you because you are their father."

Rick swallowed hard.

Darcy exhaled, his voice gentler now. "That woman spent ten years persuading you that you were nothing. That you didn't matter." He shook his head. "But today? Today was proof that she was wrong."

Rick let out a shaky breath.

Darcy watched him carefully, the weight of his words settling between them. Then, softer, more personal, he added, "You won, man."

Rick's chest ached. He turned to Darcy, really looking at him, this brother in all but blood, and felt the truth of it. He won. His hands finally loosened from the railing, the tension draining from his shoulders. Rick swallowed hard. "Thank you."

Darcy gave a lopsided smirk, clapping him on the back. "Anytime, Wentworth. Now, let's go eat some celebratory pizza."

Rick huffed a laugh, rolling his eyes. And as they walked toward the car—toward his kids, toward his future—he let himself believe it.

Maybe, just maybe, God had given him this moment to remind him. He wasn't late. He was right on time.

Chapter 49

> The hardest part isn't the nightmares. It's waking up and
> remembering they weren't just dreams.
> – Rick's Journal

The darkness was absolute. The air was thick, heavy with the scent of damp earth and something rotten beneath it. The walls pressed in around him, swallowing him whole. He was there. Again. The chain around his neck dug into raw skin. The dress clung to his body, lace scratching against his throat, a suffocating reminder of what he wasn't allowed to be.

Louisa's voice curled around him, sweet and poisonous. "You belong to me, Ricky. Say it."

He shook his head, throat tight, but the words came anyway. They always did. "I belong to you."

Then her hands were all over his body. Cold. Rough. Unyielding. Pain.

He was screaming and fighting. But there was nowhere to go. There was never anywhere to go.

The world around him shattered—and suddenly—light. A hand gripping his shoulders—shaking, steady, real.

"Rick!" The sound was sharp, urgent. "Wake up, man!"

Rick gasped, jerking awake, his entire body drenched in sweat. His chest heaved, his hands fisting the sheets like they were the only thing tethering him to reality. His vision swam, blurring between then and now. The darkness of the cellar still clung to him, pressing in, choking him—

"Rick."

The voice was calmer now. Familiar. Steady. His mind clawed through the haze, searching—Darcy.

Rick blinked hard, his breathing ragged. The dim glow of the bedside lamp cast flickering shadows, nothing like the suffocating pitch black of there.

Not there. Not anymore.

Darcy stood beside the bed, his grip still firm but not forceful. His brow was furrowed, his expression unreadable, but there was something solid in the way he looked at him. Rick swallowed, his throat raw. He tried to speak, but no words came.

Darcy exhaled, running a hand through his curls. "You were screaming," he said quietly. "Woke up the whole house."

Rick let out a shaky breath, dragging a trembling hand down his face. Of course he had. He felt sick. "The kids okay?"

Darcy nodded but didn't move, just studied him carefully. Then—after a long silence—he sighed. "Was it—" He hesitated, then cleared his throat. "The dresses?"

Rick flinched. His stomach turned.

Darcy cursed under his breath, dragging his hands down his face. "I hate that I even have to ask that."

Rick didn't answer. Couldn't. The silence stretched, thick and suffocating.

Then Darcy shifted, sitting on the edge of the bed with a sigh. "Look, man," he muttered, rubbing the back of his neck. "You want to talk about it?"

Rick shook his head.

Darcy nodded like he expected that. "You want me to sit here anyway?"

Rick swallowed hard. His hands were still shaking. He clenched them into fists, trying to steady himself. Then, after a long moment he gave a small, barely-there nod.

Darcy didn't say anything else. Just leaned back against the headboard. He didn't push. Didn't pry. Didn't fill the silence with empty words. He just stayed.

Rick was still shaking. Not as violently as before, but enough that his hands curled into the sheets, gripping the fabric like it might hold him together. His breathing was uneven, the raw edge of panic still clawing at his throat.

Darcy exhaled beside him, shifting his weight against the headboard. "You're still in it, huh?"

Rick didn't answer. Didn't know how to answer.

Darcy sighed. "All right. Guess I'll just talk until your brain catches up."

Rick huffed something that might have been a laugh if he weren't still struggling to breathe.

Darcy took that as permission. He flopped back onto the pillows, stretching out beside Rick like this was completely normal—like they weren't two grown men lying in the same bed because one of them had screamed himself awake. "So, get this,"

Darcy started, voice deliberately casual. "I read somewhere that octopuses can dream."

Rick blinked at the ceiling. "What?" His voice was rough, hoarse from the screaming.

"Yeah." Darcy turned his head toward him. "Apparently, they change colors while they're sleeping. Scientists think they might be dreaming, like dogs twitching in their sleep." He paused, then added, "Or maybe they're just showing off, who knows."

Rick swallowed. The tightness in his chest eased—just a little. "You made that up."

Darcy scoffed. "I did not. It's a real thing. Google it."

Rick didn't move. Didn't need to. Because for the first time since waking up, his mind wasn't spiraling back there.

Darcy shifted again, folding his arms behind his head. "Okay, fine. If you don't like octopi facts, how about this—did you know I once got banned from a casino before I was even old enough to gamble?"

Rick turned his head slightly, giving him a wary look. "How?"

Darcy smirked. "Well, it's a tragic tale of misunderstanding, really." He sighed dramatically. "I was innocently observing a poker table, purely for educational purposes, when apparently, some security guy thought I looked 'too interested' in the game."

Rick stared at him. "You were cheating."

Darcy grinned. "I was winning."

Rick shook his head, a breathless chuckle escaping before he could stop it.

Darcy's smirk softened into something quieter. Something intentional. "See?" he murmured. "Still here, Wentworth."

Rick let out a long, slow breath. The nightmare wasn't gone—not completely. But it wasn't suffocating him anymore. Darcy—without saying it, without making it a thing—had pulled him out.

Rick swallowed, turning his palm upward. His fingers twitched. Darcy didn't hesitate. He clasped Rick's hand in his own, grounding, steady. A silent promise. Rick exhaled.

As Darcy shifted to get comfortable, he gave Rick's hand one last squeeze before saying, "You know, Wentworth, I never thought I'd end up being your emotional support animal."

Rick huffed, exhaustion still heavy in his voice. "Trust me; you're the least cuddly emotional support animal I could've gotten."

Darcy gasped in mock offense. "Excuse you. I am an excellent stand-in for a Golden Retriever."

Rick groaned but didn't pull his hand away. "Just go to sleep."

Rick woke to the soft sounds of shuffling feet and the faintest whisper of giggles. He barely had time to process before two small figures climbed up onto the bed—Lily, wide-eyed and grinning as she placed her cane down on the bed beside her, and Walter, looking equally suspicious and amused.

Rick blinked.

Beside him, Darcy groaned, rubbing his face. "It is too early for this."

Lily ignored him, turning her full attention to Rick. "Daddy, did Uncle Darcy have a bad dream too?"

Rick's face burned.

Darcy, now fully awake, smirked. "Nah, Sweetheart. Your dad just didn't want to sleep alone."

Rick kicked him.

"Ow!" Darcy grunted but still grinned. "Okay, okay. Guess he woke up screaming, so I stayed. You know, for emotional support."

Lily tilted her head. "Like a teddy bear?"

Rick groaned. "Lily."

Darcy beamed. "Exactly like a teddy bear."

Walter giggled. "Daddy, do you need a teddy bear?"

Rick glared at Darcy, who was thoroughly enjoying this. "I need sleep."

Darcy stretched, looking annoyingly pleased with himself. "And you got some, didn't you?"

Rick sighed. Lily giggled. Walter giggled. Darcy? Darcy just laughed. Rick wanted to die.

Chapter 50

> How can I ever repay Darcy for all he's done? His generosity
> mirrors the boundless grace and gifts from God, reminding me
> daily that some debts are met only with gratitude, not repayment.
> – Rick's Journal

Rick ran a hand over his face, the remnants of the nightmare still clinging to his skin like sweat. He hadn't slept much after the kids had barged into his room at dawn, but at least the laughter had drowned out the echoes of his past.

Now, standing in the kitchen with a fresh cup of coffee, he watched as his children bustled around, their chatter filling the space.

Tuesday morning. Lily's first day of school. She sat at the table, fully dressed in her new uniform—navy polo, khaki skirt, clean white sneakers. Her backpack was slung over the chair next to her cane. But instead of eating the toast on her plate, she picked at the crusts, her little fingers worrying the edges.

Rick's chest tightened. He knew that look. Walter and Sam, already dressed and ready, noticed it too.

"You okay, Lily?" Walter asked, nudging her lightly with his elbow.

She hesitated, glancing at Rick before lowering her gaze. "What if I get lost?" she whispered.

Sam, ever the problem solver, perked up. "You won't! I know where everything is. The playground, the lunch tables—oh! And I can show you where the bathroom is so you don't have to ask a teacher."

Lily wrinkled her nose. "I know how to ask a teacher, Sam."

Sam shrugged. "Yeah, but now you don't have to."

Walter leaned in, more serious. "You'll be okay, Lil. We'll be with you. You won't be alone."

Lily bit her lip. "You promise?"

Walter nodded. "Promise."

Sam grinned. "And if anyone is mean to you, I'll just tell Uncle Darcy. He's a lawyer. He'll sue them."

Rick huffed a quiet laugh, rubbing a hand over his face. "No one's suing anyone, Sam."

Darcy strolled into the kitchen at that exact moment, coffee cup in hand, smirking. "Depends on how mean they are."

Lily giggled, some of her nerves easing.

Rick crouched beside her, tucking a curl behind her ear. "You're going to do great, Sweetheart. And if you need me, I'm just a phone call away."

Lily looked at him, wide-eyed. "You have a phone?"

Rick opened his mouth—then shut it.

Darcy cleared his throat, setting his coffee down on the counter. "Which reminds me—" He reached into his pocket and pulled out a set of keys. "Here."

Rick frowned, taking them automatically. "What's this?"

Darcy smirked. "Your car."

Rick blinked. "My what?"

Darcy jerked his head toward the driveway. "Figured it was about time you had one. It's parked out front."

Rick's stomach dropped. "Darce—"

"Nope." Darcy cut him off immediately, shaking his head. "Before you even try, don't. This isn't charity. This is practicality. You're a dad of four, Rick. You need a car."

Rick's grip tightened around the keys. "But—"

"It's done," Darcy said simply, taking a long sip of coffee. "If it makes you feel better, I spoke with your physical therapists, and they said as long as you stay off the freeway and within a ten-mile radius, you should be perfectly fine driving."

Rick exhaled sharply, glancing out the window toward the driveway. Sure enough, a sleek, dark blue SUV sat parked outside, gleaming under the morning sun.

He swallowed hard. He had nothing. No savings. No income. Everything he had right now—the roof over his head, the food on the table, even the car keys in his hand—was because of Darcy.

Darcy, sensing his hesitation, clapped him on the shoulder. "You're my best friend. You think I'm going to let you haul four kids around in Uber rides forever?"

Rick let out a breathless chuckle, shaking his head. "You're impossible."

Darcy grinned. "I prefer 'exceptionally generous and devilishly handsome.'"

Lily giggled, and Rick pocketed the keys. He didn't have the words to thank Darcy, not really. But Darcy didn't need them. He just raised his coffee cup in a mock toast.

"Now, go be a responsible parent and drop your kids off at school. And have fun with Ellie today."

Ellie, who had been swinging her legs happily from the kitchen chair, perked up. "Ducks!" she declared excitedly.

Rick smiled. "Yes, Little Love. We're going to see the ducks." She beamed, bouncing in her seat. Rick turned back to Lily, running a gentle hand over her curls. "You ready, Sweetheart?"

Lily took a deep breath, then nodded. "Yeah. I think so."

Walter patted her shoulder. "Come on. Let's go."

With that, they all filed toward the door, the morning sun casting long shadows across the driveway. Ellie babbled happily about ducks as he settled her into her car seat at the back of the SUV.

A new day. A new start.

After seeing the older three children off to school, Rick strolled with Ellie through the park, the bright morning filled with birdsong and the distant laughter of children. The warmth of her small hand pressed into his, the way she clung to him instinctively was still overwhelming. Some days, he still feared waking up to find it had all been a dream.

Ellie's curls bounced as she pointed excitedly toward the pond. "Look, Daddy! Ducks!"

Rick chuckled, following her gaze as he sank down onto a low bench near the water. "Do you want to feed them?"

Ellie nodded enthusiastically, but when Rick pulled a small container of frozen peas from his bag, she frowned. "Peas?" She wrinkled her nose. "Ducks don't eat peas, Daddy! They eat bread."

Rick laughed as he pulled her into a hug. "Actually, Little Love, peas are better for them. Bread can make them sick."

Ellie gasped, clutching Bella, her beloved stuffed bunny, to her chest. "We don't want sick ducks!"

Rick laughed softly, pouring some peas into her tiny hands. "No, we don't. So, let's give them something healthy."

She toddled closer to the water's edge, throwing the peas into the pond with exaggerated gusto. The ducks swam over eagerly, quacking and bobbing their heads as they gobbled up the offering. "They like it!" Ellie giggled, bouncing on her toes. "I'm a duck doctor!"

Rick grinned, his heart swelling at her pure joy. "You're the best duck doctor I've ever met."

Ellie beamed up at him, but then her little brows furrowed. "Daddy, did we feed ducks before? When I was a baby?"

Rick's breath hitched. His throat tightened at the innocent question. Their Thanksgiving together had been spent eating soup in a damp cellar. Their bedtime stories had been whispered in the dark, their celebrations reduced to whatever small moments of joy he could carve out of their nightmare.

He crouched beside her, brushing a curl from her cheek. "No, Little Love. We didn't get to do this before. But I used to tell you stories about ducks and all kinds of animals. And I dreamed about bringing you to a park like this someday."

Ellie's lips pursed, her fingers playing with Bella's ears. "I think I 'member your stories," she said thoughtfully. "But it's fuzzy."

Rick's chest ached. He pulled her into another hug, pressing a kiss to her soft curls. "That's okay, Ellie. What matters is we're together now. And we can make all the memories we want."

Ellie wrapped her arms around his neck, squeezing tight. "I like being with you, Daddy."

Rick swallowed hard, holding her just a little closer. "I like being with you too, Little Love."

Chapter 51

> As I watched my children play, laughter ringing clear, I praise God
> for the second chance to be the father I always hoped to become.
> – Rick's Journal

Several hours later, Austen Academy's doors swung open, and a flood of kids spilled out. Rick's heart clenched slightly at the sight of Walter, Sam, and Lily among them—his children, walking freely in the afternoon sun, backpacks slung over their shoulders, laughing with their classmates. They looked so—normal.

Lily spotted him first. Her brown eyes lit up, and her cane clattered to the ground in her excitement as her arms joyfully came around him. "Daddy!" she called, her voice high and full of joy.

Rick barely had time to adjust his hold on his own cane when she barreled into him. He let out a breathless laugh, wrapping his free arm around her. "Hey, Sweetheart. Good first day?"

Lily pulled back, her face glowing. "It was the best day ever!"

Sam and Walter arrived a beat later, more controlled but still smiling. "You survived," Walter teased, ruffling Lily's hair.

"I did more than survive," Lily declared proudly. "I made friends! I sat with a girl named Sophia at lunch, and she let me try her fruit snacks, and she likes lions too!"

Rick grinned, his heart swelling. "That's amazing, Baby."

Lily nodded enthusiastically. "And I wasn't even scared! Well, I was a little scared at first, but then Sam showed me the bathroom, and Walter walked me to class, and then it was okay!"

Sam puffed out his chest. "Told you I'd help."

Lily beamed at him. "You did! And guess what? My teacher said I'm really smart, and she let me read a book to the class during story time!"

Walter grinned. "Not surprised. You read all the time."

Rick squeezed her shoulder, pride swelling in his chest. "I'm so proud of you, Lily. You were really brave today."

Lily's cheeks flushed with happiness. "I was, huh?"

Ellie, who had been listening with wide eyes, suddenly clapped her hands together. "Lily, Lily! We saw ducks today!"

Lily turned to her little sister, her excitement doubling. "You did?"

Ellie nodded eagerly, lifting her stuffed duck Rick had bought her at the souvenir shop. "Look! This is Quackers. He's my new friend."

Sam snorted. "Quackers?"

Ellie nodded solemnly. "He quacks."

Rick bit back a chuckle. "She's got a point."

Lily giggled, reaching out to pat the stuffed duck's head. "I like him."

Rick glanced between his kids, his chest tight with something he still wasn't used to—happiness.

"So," he said, taking the kids' hands as they crossed to where he'd luckily parked the SUV in the nearest handicapped parking space. "I was thinking we should celebrate Lily's first day of school with some ice cream. What do you guys think?"

Ellie gasped dramatically. "Sherbert!"

Rick laughed, adjusting her on his hip. "Sure. Sherbert for the princess."

Walter grinned. "I'm in."

Sam whooped, pumping his fist in the air. "Yes! Ice cream!"

Lily bounced on her toes. "Can I get chocolate and strawberry together?"

Rick smirked. "Kid, after today, you can have whatever you want."

Lily's face lit up. "Best. Day. Ever."

Rick ruffled her hair, warmth filling every inch of his being. Together, they piled into the SUV, laughter ringing through the air as they set off down the road.

For the first time in a long time, Rick didn't feel like a prisoner of his past. He felt like a father. A real one. And it was the sweetest feeling in the world.

That evening, after baths and bedtime prayers, Ellie curled into Rick's lap, her head nestled against his chest. Her little fingers absently stroked Quackers as she blinked sleepily. Across the room, Lily sat cross-legged on her bed, hugging Leo the Lion.

"Daddy," Ellie murmured, voice thick with exhaustion. "Can you tell me a story?"

Rick smiled as he brushed her curls until they shone. "How about we let Lily tell it tonight?" he suggested gently. "She used to be the best storyteller in the cellar. Right, Lily?"

Lily perked up, eyes shining with quiet pride. "I can tell one," she said, sitting up straighter. "Do you want to hear about Joseph and his colorful coat?"

Ellie's eyes widened as she clutched Quackers closer. "A coat? Like mine?"

Lily giggled. "Kind of! His coat was really special—his dad gave it to him because he loved him so much. It had lots of bright colors, and it was super fancy."

Ellie gasped. "I like colors! Was he happy?"

"At first," Lily nodded, "but his brothers didn't like that he got something special. They got jealous and did something really mean."

Ellie's small fingers toyed with her stuffed animal. "What did they do?"

"They threw him in a pit," Lily said seriously. "And then they sold him as a slave to Egypt."

Ellie gasped. "No!"

"Yep." Lily hugged Leo a little tighter. "But you know what? Even though Joseph had to go far away, even though his brothers hurt him, God was still with him. He helped Joseph in Egypt and made him important."

At that moment, Walter and Sam peeked into the room, their curiosity drawing them in. "What are you guys talking about?" Walter asked, stepping inside.

"Lily's telling us about Joseph and his colorful coat!" Ellie announced excitedly.

Sam climbed onto the bed beside Lily, his forehead creased in thought. "I think I heard that one in Sunday school," he said. "Didn't he have dreams?"

Lily nodded eagerly. "He did! Before his brothers got jealous, Joseph had dreams about being a ruler one day. His dreams came from God, and even though bad things happened, God never left him."

Walter crossed his arms. "But his own brothers sold him. That's pretty messed up."

Rick listened silently, watching the way his children's minds worked through the story.

"Yeah," Lily admitted, "but later, when Joseph became really important, there was a big famine, and his brothers had to come to him for help."

Ellie frowned. "Did he help them?"

"He did," Lily said softly. "Even though they were mean to him, he forgave them. He told them that even though they had meant to hurt him, God had a plan to use it for good."

Sam's fingers curled into the blanket. "So, God used something bad and made it good?"

Lily nodded. "That's what Daddy always says. That God never leaves us, even when things are really hard."

Walter was quiet for a moment, his green eyes thoughtful. "Do you think God had a plan for us?"

Rick's breath caught, but Lily didn't hesitate. "I think so," she said firmly. "Daddy always told me that God was with us, even in the cellar. Even when we didn't understand why it was happening."

Sam's voice was smaller now. "So—does that mean we should forgive Mom? Like Joseph forgave his brothers?"

Rick finally found his voice, steady and warm. "Forgiveness doesn't mean what happened was okay. It just means we trust God to handle it instead of carrying the hurt ourselves."

Sam nodded slowly. "Joseph didn't forget what they did," he said. "But he didn't let it make him bitter."

"Exactly," Rick murmured.

Ellie yawned, rubbing her eyes. "I like Joseph," she murmured sleepily. "He had big dreams."

Lily's voice was soft but certain. "You can have big dreams too, Ellie. Just like Joseph."

After the boys returned to their room, Rick gently tucked Ellie into bed. Lily lingered by her own, hugging Leo tightly. Rick pressed a kiss to her forehead, whispering, "You told that story beautifully, Sweetheart." Rick noticed her hesitation. "Everything okay?"

Lily nodded but glanced at Ellie's bed. "Can I—sleep next to her tonight?" she asked softly.

Rick's heart swelled. "Of course you can."

With careful movements, Lily climbed into bed beside her sister, wrapping an arm around her. Ellie stirred, her sleepy eyes fluttering open. "Night, Lily," she murmured, her voice barely above a whisper. "Love you."

Lily squeezed her gently. "Love you too."

Rick lingered in the doorway, watching his daughters curled up together, their bond unbreakable. The sight nearly undid him. They had lost so much. But they still had each other.

"Goodnight, my girls," Rick whispered into the stillness, his heart full.

Tonight, they were safe. They were loved. And they were free.

Chapter 52

> Seeing faces from days long gone stirs a quiet dread within me, a fear of judgment and falling short, as I grapple with the shadows of my agony and wonder how I might measure up in the eyes of those who knew me before.
> — Rick's Journal

Saturday morning dawned with soft golden light filtering through the kitchen windows, casting a warm glow over the countertops. The scent of fresh coffee mingled with the hum of children's chatter, but Rick barely noticed anything as he stood by the sink, gripping his mug tightly. His sleep had been restless again, haunted by memories he couldn't shake. The kind that clung to him even after waking.

Across the room, Lily and Ellie sat at the table, chattering between bites of cereal, Ellie swinging her legs as she drowsily hugged her stuffed animal. At the other end of the table, Walter and Sam were mid-debate over whether soccer or baseball was the superior sport, their voices full of easy energy. Rick envied them— the way they could throw themselves into something so simple.

Then, in typical Darcy fashion, his best friend strolled in, already dressed, already looking far too awake for a Saturday. He clapped a hand on Rick's shoulder, smirking. "Men's breakfast at church. Free pancakes. You're coming."

Rick groaned, rubbing a hand over his face. "Do I have to?"

Darcy's smirk widened. "Unless you plan on explaining to Lily why you're skipping a church event, yeah, you do."

Rick glanced over. Sure enough, Lily was watching him expectantly, her brown eyes wide. "Uncle Darcy says you should go," she announced between spoonfuls of cereal.

"But what about the kids? We can't just leave them here," he countered.

"Already taken care of." Darcy looked entirely too pleased with himself. "Caroline's coming over to do some grading while they play in the backyard. You're out of excuses, Wentworth."

Rick sighed. He wasn't winning this one.

The fellowship hall was filled with the comforting scent of bacon, syrup, and fresh coffee. The room buzzed with conversation—deep voices carrying over the clatter of silverware and the occasional burst of laughter. It was loud, unfamiliar, overwhelming.

Rick adjusted his grip on his cane, shifting uneasily as they stepped inside. As he scanned the room, he recognized faces. Older now, with grayer hair or softer edges, but familiar all the same. These were the men who had been part of his life before everything fell apart—mentors, coaches, church members who had once greeted him with the same easy warmth he saw now.

It should have been comforting. Instead, it made his skin itch.

Darcy nudged his elbow. "Relax, man. It's pancakes, not a firing squad."

Rick shot him a glare. "Easy for you to say."

"Yeah, well, if you pass out in the syrup, I'm not carrying you out of here," Darcy muttered with a smirk.

Rick rolled his eyes but barely had time to process the jab before a deep, familiar voice cut through the room. "Rick Wentworth!"

His breath caught. He turned, heart hammering, and found himself staring into the warm, knowing gaze of Pastor Ned Bertram—the man who had baptized him in this very church twenty years ago.

Ned's face had aged, his once dark hair now mostly silver, the lines around his eyes a little deeper. But his presence was the same—solid, steady, a weight that anchored Rick to something long forgotten. The older man studied him for only a second before stepping forward, pulling Rick into a firm embrace.

Rick froze, breath hitching, before his body finally responded. He gripped Ned's back, holding on for a moment longer than he probably should have. The familiar scent of worn flannel and aftershave grounded him, sent him reeling into memories of a past that felt too distant to be real.

When Ned pulled back, his throat worked like he was holding something back. "Son," he said, voice thick, "I prayed for this day for a long time."

Rick swallowed hard, forcing out words. "I—" His voice wavered. He cleared his throat, blinking rapidly. "I didn't see you Sunday."

Ned chuckled, squeezing his shoulder. "I've been out of town visiting my sister's family for the past month. But I told Eddie I wasn't about to miss this." His gaze swept over Rick, something both knowing and deeply proud in his expression. "You look good, son. Different, but good."

Rick huffed a quiet laugh. "Not sure about that."

"I am," Ned countered simply. His eyes softened, and he gave Rick's shoulder another firm squeeze. "Fanny told me you brought four little blessings with you."

Rick's chest tightened—not painfully, but in a way that made him feel unsteady. "Yeah," he said, voice rough. "They're my everything."

Ned nodded, the corners of his lips twitching. "I'd love to meet them properly."

"They're—" Rick hesitated, emotions pressing hard against his ribs. "They're great kids."

"I have no doubt," Ned said, his tone warm with certainty. Then, after a brief pause, his voice softened. "Would you mind if I came to your biblical counseling session on Monday? I'd like to walk this road with you, if you'll have me."

Rick barely managed to nod. "Yeah," he rasped. "I'd—I'd like that."

The older man's smile widened, his throat visibly working. "Good," he said. "Then I'll see you Monday."

Rick exhaled, feeling steadier than he had in weeks.

"Now," Ned added, a teasing glint in his eye, "let's get you some pancakes before Darcy eats the whole stack."

Darcy, overhearing, gasped dramatically. "I am deeply offended by this slander."

Rick snorted.

Several hours later, the lake stretched before Rick and his son Walter as the last light of evening succeeded in casting rippling gold and amber streaks over the water. The quiet hum of crickets filled the air, the occasional splash breaking the surface as fish moved beneath them in the water.

Rick sat on the wooden dock, holding his fishing rod while Walter knelt at the edge, his feet dangling as he tossed small pebbles into the water. Their second fishing trip in as many weeks, and already, Walter seemed more at ease.

Rick exhaled slowly, taking in the moment—the peace, the simplicity of it all.

Walter hesitated, glancing at him. "Dad?"

Rick turned his head. "Yeah, bud?"

The boy hesitated, rubbing at a knot in the wood. "Why is my last name Musgrove and not Wentworth?"

Rick's grip tightened around his rod. He should have expected this question. But somehow, it still blindsided him. He set the rod aside, turning to give Walter his full attention. "I never got a choice in what you were named," he admitted, his voice careful but honest.

Walter frowned. "What do you mean?"

Rick took a slow breath. "Your mother never asked me. She controlled everything, and honestly, it would've been dangerous for her to give you my name. Someone might've asked questions. People like your Uncle Darcy and Aunt Anne didn't know where I was. If she'd named you after me, someone might have figured it out."

Walter absorbed this, his brows furrowed. He kicked his legs slightly, processing. "So—you didn't get to pick any of our names?"

Rick shook his head. "No."

"That's not fair," Walter muttered.

"You're right," Rick agreed.

Walter thought on it for a long moment, then, with determination flickering across his face, he asked, "Can we change it?"

Rick blinked.

Walter met his gaze, jaw set. "I want to be a Wentworth. I *am* a Wentworth."

Rick's chest ached with pride. His son wanted his name. "Then we'll look into it." He exhaled, his voice steady. "I'll talk to Darcy, see what we need to do to make it official."

Walter's face softened with relief. "Lily, Sam, and Ellie too?"

Rick nodded. "Lily officially became a Wentworth while we were in the hospital. As for Sam and Ellie, we'll talk to them and see what they want. If they want to change their names, we'll make it happen. It might take some time, but we'll get there."

Walter smiled slightly, looking back at the water. "Good."
Suddenly there was a sudden tug on his fishing rod. "Whoa!"
Walter yelped, gripping the handle tight. "I got one!"

Rick steadied Walter's hands, guiding him through the reel.
His son's grin widened as he pulled the fish in. Rick moved in,
steadying his son's grip. "Nice and slow, Buddy. Let him fight, but
don't let him win."

Walter gritted his teeth, focused as he worked the reel,
muscles straining in his small arms. A flash of silver broke the
surface, droplets scattering like tiny sparks in the fading sunlight.
With one final pull, Walter lifted the fish from the water, his chest
rising with triumph.

Rick grinned. "You did it."

Walter held the fish carefully, studying its sleek body as it
twisted in his hands. For a moment, he looked proud and then
suddenly thoughtful. "Here," he said softly, kneeling at the dock's
edge. "Go back home." He released the fish, watching as it darted
beneath the surface.

Rick raised an eyebrow. "Didn't you want to bring it back
and show off your catch?"

Walter shook his head. "He's just a baby." He watched the
water for a long second, voice quiet but sure. "His dad would miss
him too much."

Rick felt his throat tighten, the weight of those words
settling deep. He swallowed against the sudden burn in his chest,
reaching out to ruffle Walter's hair. "That was a good choice,
Walter."

Walter beamed up at him. Rick exhaled, watching the last
of the sunset fade behind the lake. His son's words echoed in his
mind, the weight of everything they had been through pressing
against his ribs.

A father missing his child. A child missing his father. After
all these years, they were finding their way back to each other.

Chapter 53

> Though I never anticipated where I would end up, I trust that I am exactly where I am meant to be, guided by a hand greater than my own.
> – Rick's Journal

Rick sat on the couch, an open parenting book resting in his lap, though he hadn't turned a page in at least ten minutes. The house was quiet now, the kids all tucked into bed after another full day. Ellie had fallen asleep mid-sentence, curled up between Bella the Bunny and Quackers the Duck. Lily had whispered her prayers, gripping Leo the Lion, while Walter and Sam had talked in hushed voices about Walter's idea to officially become a Wentworth before finally drifting off.

Rick exhaled, sinking deeper into the cushions, the weight of the past few weeks settling in his chest. The house wasn't just full of children now—it was full of *his* children. Lily Wentworth was legally recognized as his daughter, and now the boys wanted to be recognized as his sons too. That thought alone left him breathless.

Lily's process had moved faster than anyone expected. While she had been in the hospital, social services and law enforcement had worked quickly to correct what Louisa had stolen from her—establishing her birth records, issuing her social security number, and confirming Rick as her legal father in every official way.

He hoped it would be just as easy for the boys.

The front door creaked open, and Rick looked up just as Darcy stepped inside, tossing his keys onto the entryway table. He looked far too pleased with himself, his jacket slung over one shoulder, a satisfied smirk playing on his lips.

Rick raised a brow. "Good date?"

Darcy grinned, dropping onto the armchair across from him. "Caroline picked the restaurant this time. Steak, jazz music, and a crème brûlée that I'm pretty sure could convert an atheist." He leaned back, stretching his legs out on the coffee table. "You should get out more, Wentworth. There's a world outside of bedtime stories and fish hooks."

Rick snorted, closing the book. "I'll take bedtime stories over crème brûlée any day."

Darcy smirked, but his expression softened. "Yeah, well, if anyone deserves that, it's you."

Rick hesitated, watching him for a moment before shaking his head. "I still can't believe it sometimes."

Darcy arched a brow. "What, that you're free?"

Rick exhaled. "That, too. But I meant you and Caroline. You used to hate her."

Darcy chuckled, rubbing his jaw. "Hate is a strong word. She was—determined."

Rick shot him a dry look. "She did everything short of bribing professors to break you and Lizzie up."

Darcy winced, but his grin didn't fade. "Yeah, well. People change." He tilted his head, thoughtful. "Lizzie nearly dropped her drink when she saw us together at a wedding last year."

Rick smirked. "I can imagine."

Darcy shrugged. "God's plans are better than ours. I thought Lizzie was the one for me, but turns out, God had other ideas." He looked over at Rick, his expression turning more serious. "Sometimes we don't end up where we thought we would, but that doesn't mean we're in the wrong place."

Rick glanced down at the book in his lap, then closed it completely. "Speaking of God's plans—I wanted to talk to you about something."

Darcy lifted a brow, gesturing for him to continue.

Rick ran a hand over his face. "Lily's officially a Wentworth now. Everything's been corrected—her birth certificate, her social security, everything." He hesitated. "But the others—"

Darcy nodded, already ahead of him. "They still have the names Musgrove and Elliot."

Rick's jaw tightened. "Yeah." He met Darcy's gaze. "I never got a choice in what they were named. Louisa had all the power. And I get why she didn't give them my last name. She might have been found out faster. But now—" He exhaled. "Now they have a choice."

Darcy was quiet for a moment, then nodded. "You thinking about getting their names changed officially?"

Rick hesitated. "I'd never force it. But Walter already asked me about it today at the lake, and Sam is on board with the idea. Ellie is happy to do anything the others do."

Darcy let out a low whistle. "That's big."

"Yeah." Rick nodded. "I want to make it happen."

Darcy studied him for a moment, his smirk fading slightly. "You know there's going to be some legal hurdles."

Rick's stomach tightened. "Like what?"

Darcy leaned forward. "Lily's process was expedited because she technically didn't exist in the system. The courts corrected that. But the boys? Legally, I'm still their guardian, not you."

Rick inhaled sharply.

"You're their father," Darcy continued quickly. "And we're working on restoring full parental rights to you. But since Louisa's case is still ongoing, the courts haven't officially terminated her parental rights yet. Until that happens, we can't finalize custody or name changes without her explicit agreement."

Rick clenched his jaw. "So, what do we do?"

Darcy exhaled, his lawyer tone taking over. "We keep pushing. Your case is solid—social services, public opinion, and law enforcement are all backing your claim. Once Louisa's rights are terminated, we file to transfer full custody to you. The name change petition will be easy once that's finalized."

Rick swallowed hard, the weight of it settling on his shoulders. He had his kids, he was raising them, but on paper, they still belonged to someone else. "I hate that she still has a say," he muttered.

Darcy's expression darkened. "She won't for long."

Rick exhaled slowly, nodding. "And the kids? Do we tell them?"

Darcy considered that, then shrugged. "They don't need to know every legal technicality. They already see you as their dad. The paperwork will catch up eventually."

Rick ran a hand through his hair, then looked over at Darcy. "Think you can make sure it catches up fast?"

Darcy smirked. "Oh, I guarantee it."

Rick let out a breath, shaking his head. He still couldn't believe he was having this conversation about legal battles and custody hearings. But this time, he wasn't powerless. And soon, no document in the world would deny that these were his kids.

Chapter 54

> On this Palm Sunday, I am reminded of the enduring strength of hope, which guides us through our trials and heralds the victory of renewal in our lives.
> – Rick's Journal

The drive to church was filled with excitement, mostly from the back seat. Lily bounced lightly in her booster seat, her hands gripping Leo the Lion while her feet kicked against the seat in front of her.

"I can't believe it's almost Easter!" she said, grinning up at Rick.

Sam, sitting behind her, huffed. "You act like you've never heard of Easter before."

"I have," Lily shot back, unbothered. "But this is my first Easter in the real world. Daddy told me all the stories. Now I get to see everything myself."

Rick's grip tightened slightly on the door handle. He had told her the stories about Palm Sunday, Good Friday, and about the empty tomb, but he had never been able to take her to experience any of it until now.

Ellie, strapped into her car seat, squirmed impatiently. "I wanna see the donkeys!"

Walter snorted. "There's no donkeys, Ellie."

"But there was a donkey!" Lily piped up in defense of her younger sister. "Jesus rode one into the city, and the people put their cloaks and palm branches down to welcome Him. They shouted 'Hosanna!'"

"Right," Sam muttered, eyeing the church as they pulled into the parking lot. "And then a week later, they killed Him."

Darcy's grip on the steering wheel tightened. "Yeah. People can say one thing and do another. Some only care about what they can get from you." His jaw twitched, his voice laced with something harder, something unspoken.

Rick exhaled, keeping his own voice steady. "But Jesus knew they would. And He still loved them anyway."

Walter frowned, rolling that over in his mind. "That's kinda hard to understand."

Rick unbuckled his seatbelt. "Yeah. It is."

Darcy sighed, running a hand through his curls as he stepped out of the car to open the rear door for the kids. "Come on, let's get inside before Ellie starts preaching from the backseat."

Ellie, still buckled into her car seat, giggled as Rick reached inside to lift her down. "I wave my palm now?" she asked, holding up her tiny fists in anticipation.

"Not yet, Sweetheart," Rick said with a smile, setting her on her feet. "There will be branches when we get inside."

Inside the church lobby, the kids were immediately greeted by a cheerful volunteer handing out palm branches. Lily's eyes went wide as she took hers, gripping it reverently in her hand. "My very own," she whispered. "Just like Daddy told me."

Rick's chest ached as he rested a hand on her shoulder. "That's right, baby girl. Just like the stories."

Walter and Sam, slightly less reverent, were already sizing up their branches. Sam gave an experimental wave, only for Walter to swat at his with his own.

"Guys," Rick warned, leveling them with a look.

Sam sighed. "No palm fights in church."

Walter huffed. "Even though they're perfect for it."

Lily ignored them, her focus still locked on her palm branch. "Jesus rode a donkey through town, and everyone bowed their branches down for Him," she recited softly.

Pastor Fanny who was standing nearby, overheard and beamed down at Lily. "That's exactly right, Sweetheart." She gave Rick a smile before turning her attention to Ellie, who had yet to receive her palm. "And what about you, Ellie? Would you like one too?"

Ellie's entire face lit up. "Yes, please!"

Rick knelt down, helping her hold it properly as she clutched the long leaf with both hands, treating it like a sacred treasure.

As the group made their way deeper into the lobby, the boys suddenly perked up. "It's Marianne!" Walter blurted out, spotting her near the coffee station.

Rick's gaze snapped to where Marianne Dashwood stood, deep in conversation with a group that included Caroline. She was dressed in a casual but elegant spring outfit, her long dark hair shining under the overhead lights. As if sensing their presence, she turned and her almond-shaped eyes lit up as she spotted them.

Before Rick could say a word, all four kids surged ahead. "Miss Marianne!" Lily squealed, waving her palm branch wildly.

Marianne barely had time to brace herself before Ellie crashed into her legs, clinging with all the enthusiasm only a toddler could manage.

"You're here!" Sam grinned.

Marianne laughed, crouching to pick up Ellie before ruffling Sam's hair. "Of course, I'm here." She stood with Ellie on her hip and turned to Rick, her expression warm. "Good morning."

Rick nodded, amazed at the way his heart thudded at the sight of his baby girl curled up against this woman. "Morning."

Caroline, tall and effortlessly elegant in a pastel spring pant suit that complemented her striking dark complexion, kissed Darcy before turning back to Marianne. "Have you told them the good news?"

Marianne smiled. "I found a condo."

The boys cheered. Ellie clapped. Lily gasped, gripping her branch as she stared up at Marianne with tears in her young eyes.

"You're staying?" Lily asked, between sobs.

Marianne nodded in alarm as she lowered Ellie to the ground and wiped away Lily's tears. "I'm officially a Croft Beach resident. Hopefully that's a good thing?"

Lily looked to Rick, her expression practically glowing as she chocked over her sobs of joy. "Daddy! She's not leaving!"

Rick felt his heart tighten at the joy Marianne brought his children, shifting slightly on his feet. "I see that."

Caroline smirked. "And she's joining us for Easter dinner."

Marianne shot her a look. "You could've at least pretended to invite me."

Caroline grinned. "Where's the fun in that?"

Darcy, who had finally caught up with them, clapped a hand on Rick's shoulder. "Well, well, Wentworth. Guess you'll have to start getting used to seeing her around."

Rick shot him a dry look. "Guess so."

Marianne rolled her eyes at Darcy before turning back to the kids. "Are you all excited about the palm parade?"

Lily bounced on the balls of her feet. "Yes! It's my first in the real world!"

Marianne's smile softened. "Then we better find a good spot."

Sam grinned. "Sit with us!"

Walter nodded eagerly. "Yeah, you should!"

Marianne hesitated for only a second before nodding. "I'd love to."

Rick watched as the kids practically surrounded her, excitedly chattering about their branches and what they'd learned. He wasn't sure when this woman had become so intertwined in their world, but standing there, watching them all together, he couldn't bring himself to mind.

Darcy nudged him with an elbow. "You're staring, Wentworth."

Rick didn't take his eyes off the scene before him. "Shut up, Darcy."

Darcy smirked but wisely said nothing.

As the sanctuary doors opened, the kids rushed ahead, palms in hand, laughter ringing through the church.

Chapter 55

> I am profoundly grateful for the second chances we've been given and the blossoming hope that renews our spirits, just as spring breathes new life into the world around us.
> – Rick's Journal

The house was alive with energy and the scent of roasted ham, Jollof rice, and green bean casserole. The dining table was set beautifully with fresh spring flowers, and soft, golden light spilled through the windows. The kids had been buzzing between the kitchen and dining room, riding the sugar rush from their Easter baskets, their excitement palpable.

Rick stood at the counter, carving the ham, though his mind was only half on the task. Every now and then, his gaze flicked to the dining table where his children currently sat, all four of them, chattering away. He could hardly wrap his head around the fact that he was here, free, carving a luxurious ham for his kids, in a home filled with laughter instead of being grateful to Louisa for two eggs for his meal with the girls last Easter in a cold cellar filled with fear and hunger.

Darcy leaned against the counter beside him, swirling a drink in one hand. Caroline, radiant in a yellow dress that complemented perfectly her complexion, smirked at Darcy from across the table. "Have you told Rick the good news?"

Rick shot a wary look at his best friend. "Should I be concerned?"

Darcy clapped a hand on his shoulder. "Relax, Wentworth. It's just a job."

Rick stiffened. "What?"

Caroline grinned. "Darcy got you a part-time job at his law firm."

Rick turned to Darcy, his brows raised. "You got me a job?"

"Answering phones. A few hours in the mornings while the kids are at school," Darcy said with a shrug, like it was the most natural thing in the world. "Gotta ease you back into the working world somehow."

Rick exhaled, rubbing a hand over his face. The thought of working again—of stepping into an office, of being around normal people—made his stomach tighten. But it wasn't just about him anymore. It was about the kids, about proving to them that they were safe now, that life could be normal.

"What about my physical therapy appointments?"

"We'll work around them," Darcy shrugged.

"I don't even own a suit," he muttered.

Caroline waved him off. "You don't need a suit to answer phones."

Lily perked up from her plate. "What about Ellie?"

Caroline smiled. "She'll be at the firm's daycare, making lots of new friends. Uncle Darcy has already arranged everything."

Ellie gasped dramatically. "I get friends?"

Caroline laughed. "Lots of them."

Ellie clapped her hands. "Yay! I'm going to tell Quackers!" She snatched up her stuffed duck and whispered something excitedly in his ear.

Rick shook his head in disbelief. "You really took care of everything, didn't you?"

Darcy smirked. "That's what I do."

Caroline raised an eyebrow. "That's what you do when you love someone."

Marianne, who had been listening with amusement, glanced at Rick. "Was Darcy always so generous?"

Rick snorted. "Yeah right. He gave me a wedgie on the first day of kindergarten."

Marianne's eyes widened in surprise as Darcy smirked unapologetically. "In my defense, you were the new kid in town, and I had to test your resilience."

Rick shot him a look. "Pretty sure you just wanted to see if I could dangle from a coat hook."

Darcy grinned. "And now I get him jobs. See? Character growth."

Laughter rippled through the table, lightening the weight in Rick's chest.

As the meal wound down and the kids darted off to inspect their candy stashes, Rick hesitated, his fingers drumming lightly against the table. His heart pounded as he cleared his throat. "Uh, Marianne?"

She turned toward him, her dark almond-shaped eyes warm. "Yes?"

He shifted slightly in his chair. "We're going bowling next week for my birthday." He rubbed the back of his neck, his voice awkward but sincere. "Would you like to join us?"

A small smile played at her lips. "You're having a birthday celebration?"

Rick exhaled, nodding. "First one in over ten years."

Before Marianne could respond, a sharp gasp cut through the room. Rick turned, startled, just as Lily's eyes filled with tears. She stood frozen, her small hands trembling at her sides, her Easter basket on the floor forgotten, her little face crumbling with realization. "Daddy," she whispered, her voice cracking. "I never knew your birthday."

Rick's chest clenched, the air thick with unspoken grief. Lily launched herself into his lap, wrapping her arms around his neck. He held her tight, stroking her hair as she trembled against him.

"I never felt much like celebrating in the cellar," he murmured, pressing a kiss to her curls. "It's okay."

Lily sniffled, her tiny hands clutching his shirt. "But I should have known."

Rick pulled back slightly, looking into her watery brown eyes. "Sweetheart," he said gently, brushing a tear from her cheek. "None of that matters now. What matters is that we get to celebrate together this year."

She sniffled again, nodding. "Okay."

Walter, Sam, and Ellie crowded around, each offering a hug of their own, their little voices a mix of reassurances and excitement for their dad's birthday.

Marianne watched, something soft and unreadable in her expression. Then, finally, she smiled. "I'd love to come."

Rick let out a breath, warmth filling his chest.

Darcy clapped a hand on his back. "Look at you making birthday plans, getting a job, and a going on a date. You're officially a functioning member of society again."

Rick groaned. "It's not a date."

Darcy smirked. "Sure, sure. You keep telling yourself that."

Marianne just laughed.

Chapter 56

> My children teach me daily the importance of hope in second
> chances. For them, I hope and pray.
> – Rick's Journal

The hum of quiet conversation filled Pastor Eddie's office as Rick sat across from him and Pastor Ned, a cup of coffee in hand. The warmth of the mug seeped into his fingers, grounding him, though his nerves hadn't quite settled from the morning.

His first day of work had been strange. Not bad, really. It was more just unfamiliar. He'd been given a desk, a phone, and a routine that didn't involve just survival. And now, here he was sitting with a man who had watched him grow up in this very church, discussing second chances, his upcoming birthday, and the fact that—somehow—he had managed to invite Marianne to join his family for bowling.

Pastor Ned leaned back in his chair, a knowing look in his eyes. "So, you survived your first day at the law firm?"

Rick huffed a small laugh. "Barely. I forgot how fast people talk on the phone. I had to ask a guy to repeat himself three times before I realized he was just giving me a case number."

The younger pastor chuckled. "At least you're easing back in. A few hours answering phones is a good start."

Rick nodded, taking a sip of his coffee. "It's—different. Feels like I am stepping into someone else's life." He set the cup down, rolling his shoulders. "But it's a step forward."

Ned smiled, his voice gentle but firm. "And that's what matters. The past is real, Rick. It shaped you. But it doesn't get to define you."

Rick exhaled, nodding. "I know."

Eddie leaned forward, resting his forearms on his desk. "And then there's the other big news. I hear you have birthday plans."

Rick smirked, shaking his head. "Word travels fast."

Ned chuckled. "You're an interesting case, son. Ten years missing, and suddenly, you're back, throwing birthday parties and taking a lady bowling."

Rick scoffed. "Not a date."

Eddie raised an eyebrow. "You sure?"

Rick hesitated just a second too long. "She's coming for the kids."

Ned's lips twitched. "Uh-huh."

Rick groaned. "Not you too."

Eddie laughed, then reached for his Bible, flipping through the pages before settling on a passage. "You ever think about second chances, Rick?"

Rick glanced at him, brow furrowed. "All the time."

Eddie nodded, tapping a finger against the worn page. "Isaiah 43 says, 'Remember not the former things, nor consider the things of old. Behold, I am doing a new thing; now it springs forth, do you not perceive it? I will make a way in the wilderness and rivers in the desert.'"

Rick swallowed, his fingers tightening around his mug.

Ned's voice was quiet but firm. "God didn't just rescue you from Louisa's hands. He's restoring you, Rick. There's a difference."

Rick's jaw tensed. "Still doesn't feel like I deserve it."

Eddie leaned forward. "None of us do. That's the point."

Rick let Eddie's words sink in, feeling their weight and their truth. Before he could respond, the door burst open, and a wave of excited energy flooded the room.

"Daddy!" Ellie charged toward him, Quackers clutched tightly in one hand, her curls bouncing. Behind her, Walter, Sam, and Lily followed, their faces lit with excitement.

Pastor Fanny trailed after them, laughing. "I tried to keep them from running, but I think they were too excited to share what we talked about."

Rick barely had time to react before Ellie launched herself into his lap, beaming up at him. "We talked 'bout camels, Daddy!"

Rick blinked. "Camels?"

Lily nodded, her brown eyes bright. "And rich people and heaven and how God gives second chances!"

Walter flopped onto the chair beside Rick, looking thoughtful. "Pastor Fanny told us about the man who asked Jesus how to get into heaven. Jesus told him to give away all his stuff." He frowned. "Jesus said it's easier for a camel to go through the eye of a needle than for a rich man to go to heaven."

Ned smiled, glancing at his wife. "You guys really went for the deep stuff today."

Fanny chuckled. "They asked big questions, so we had a big discussion."

Sam scooted forward, gripping the edge of the chair. "But his buddies were confused since they thought rich people were God's favorites. If they couldn't go to heaven, then who could?"

Eddie nodded at the young boy. "And what did Jesus say?"

Lily sat up straighter, gripping Leo the Lion tightly. "He said, nothing is impossible with God."

Rick inhaled sharply, glancing at Eddie and Ned, who both looked pleased. He turned back to his kids. "That's a really important lesson."

Ellie, not wanting to be left out, piped up, "Jesus gives second chances!"

Rick's chest tightened. Second chances.

Walter's voice was quieter now, hesitant. "Pastor Fanny said it's not about being rich or poor. It's about who we trust."

Sam frowned. "The man wanted his stuff more than Jesus." He twisted his fingers in his lap. "But Jesus still loved him. Even when he walked away."

Rick glanced at Fanny, who nodded and said, "That's right. Jesus wasn't angry at the man. The Bible says He looked at him and loved him. Even when people reject Him, His love doesn't change."

Rick swallowed hard, nodding.

Lily tilted her head, studying him. "Do you think that means Mama has a second chance?"

The room stilled. Rick's throat tightened. He felt the weight of the question settle over everyone.

Ned spoke first, his voice gentle but firm. "Yes, Sweetheart. As long as someone has breath, they have the chance to turn to God."

Lily considered that, her fingers tracing over Leo's fur. "Even after everything she did?"

Eddie leaned forward, his expression serious but kind. "Even after everything." He flipped open his Bible, glancing at Rick before reading, "'For I am sure that neither death nor life, nor angels nor rulers, nor things present nor things to come, nor powers, nor height nor depth, nor anything else in all creation, will be able to separate us from the love of God in Christ Jesus our Lord.'"

Lily's forehead creased. "So—God still loves her?"

Rick exhaled, rubbing a hand over his face before resting it on her back. "Yes, Lily. He does."

She nodded slowly, gripping Leo tighter. "That is hard to picture."

Rick pressed a kiss to the top of her head. "I completely agree."

Sam leaned forward. "Do you think she'll ever ask for a second chance?"

Rick met his son's green eyes, his chest aching. "I don't know, Buddy. That's between her and God."

Fanny's voice was steady. "But what we do know is that we're responsible for our own choices. We can't make anyone else choose Jesus, but we can choose Him for ourselves."

Walter sat back, nodding slowly. "That makes sense."

Ellie yawned, rubbing her eyes. "I wanna tell Jesus I love Him."

Rick smiled, pressing a hand over her back. "You already do, Sweetheart."

Ned clapped his hands together. "Well, I'd say that was a discussion worth having."

Fanny nodded. "Your kids ask the best questions, Rick."

Rick glanced at them, warmth spreading through his chest. "Yeah. They do."

"They remind me of a certain young boy I had in Sunday school some twenty years ago."

Rick sighed and smiled as he hugged Pastor Fanny.

After closing in prayer, Pastor Eddie stretched. "Same time next week?"

The kids all nodded enthusiastically.

As he left the office, walking hand in hand with his children, Rick felt the truth settle deep inside him. Second chances weren't just possible.

They were happening. Right here, right now.

Chapter 57

> Growing up I never thought much of what clothes said about a
> person and then I spent years in dresses.
> – Rick's Journal

Rick climbed into Darcy's SUV, shifting uncomfortably as he shoved his cane into the back and settled into the passenger seat.

He glanced at the list Darcy had handed him of essentials for work and sighed. "You really don't have to do this," Rick muttered as Darcy started the engine. "The clothes you gave me in the hospital are fine."

Darcy shot him a look. "Rick, you've been rotating the same three outfits for weeks. You need variety. And no offense, but clients will take you more seriously if you look the part."

Rick exhaled sharply, his fingers tightening around the seatbelt. "Still feels strange wearing anything at all," he admitted. "After ten years of practically nothing."

Darcy's grip on the wheel tightened. His knuckles turned white, his jaw tense. Rick caught the reaction from the corner of his eye. He knew what Darcy was thinking—that the idea of ten years without basic dignity was unbearable. That he wouldn't have survived it. But Rick didn't need to hear that.

He let out an awkward chuckle, rubbing the back of his neck. "I mean, for the last seven years, I wore nothing but dresses. Louisa said it made things—easier. Gave her better access to my 'hot body.'" He forced a laugh, the words tasting like ash, but old habits die hard. *Deflect*, he thought. *Make it sound less horrific than it was.* "Real thoughtful of her, huh?"

Darcy's knuckles were still white against the steering wheel. With his jaw locked, the muscle in his cheek ticked dangerously. "Damn it, Rick," Darcy bit out, his voice rough with barely restrained fury. "That's not funny."

Rick's smirk faltered. He glanced out the window, his stomach twisting. "Yeah," he murmured. "I know."

Darcy's breath came out harsh and uneven. He didn't speak right away, and when Rick glanced at him, his best friend's face was tight with controlled fury.

Rick forced out a humorless chuckle. "At least it was an improvement after two years of being naked. Did I ever tell you what I had to wear before that? A maid's dress like you see in the Halloween stores."

Darcy's head snapped toward him, eyes flashing. "A maid's dress?" His voice was low, sharp. Dangerous.

Rick shrugged, keeping his gaze on the road ahead. "Yeah. I looked really sexy."

Darcy swore under his breath. "Rick—" His grip on the steering wheel flexed again before he forced himself to take a breath, his nostrils flaring. "I knew she was sick," Darcy said finally, his voice thick with restrained rage. "I knew what she did to you was evil. But hearing that?" He shook his head, exhaling sharply. "I don't have words."

Rick glanced at him. "That's a first."

Darcy huffed, shaking his head again. "You joke, but I swear, if she wasn't already in that psych hospital—" He let the thought hang in the air, unfinished but clear.

Rick didn't answer. The reality was, Louisa being in custody didn't undo anything.

Darcy swallowed, then shifted in his seat. "Okay," he muttered, his voice hoarse but steady. "That's it. You're getting new clothes today. Clothes made for you."

Rick's throat tightened, but he nodded.

The menswear store smelled faintly of cedar and fabric softener, the polished displays gleaming under bright lights. Darcy moved through the aisles like he owned the place, plucking shirts, ties, and slacks with the efficiency of someone who had done this a hundred times before. Rick trailed behind, feeling like he was in a foreign world.

Darcy held up a navy dress shirt. "Try this," he said, adding it to Rick's growing pile. "And this tie—it'll bring out your eyes."

Rick snorted. "I'm just answering phones and filing papers, Darcy. Nobody's looking at my eyes."

Darcy smirked. "Doesn't matter. Presentation counts."

Rick hesitated, then took the items, retreating to the dressing room. The moment he buttoned up the shirt, something in him shifted. It wasn't just about looking decent—it was about reclaiming something.

When he stepped out, Darcy grinned, giving him a once-over. "Now that looks like Rick Wentworth."

Rick tugged at the collar. "Feels like it's choking me."

Darcy laughed. "You'll get used to it." As they continued to browse the racks, Darcy's tone shifted. "Rick, I've got a favor to ask."

Rick raised an eyebrow. "What kind of favor?"

Darcy grinned. "Help me pick out a ring for Caroline."

Rick blinked. "Wait! What are you saying? You're proposing?"

Darcy nodded, his expression softening. "Yeah. It's time."

A couple hours later, Rick leaned against a display, still processing. "I still can't stop thinking about how back in college you called her—what was it? The thorn in your side?"

Darcy smirked. "I believe I once referred to her as the bane of my existence."

Rick huffed a laugh. "Sounds about right. She did try to break you and Lizzie up."

Darcy laughed despite himself. "Repeatedly."

Rick shook his head. "And now you're buying her a ring."

Darcy shrugged. "Turns out God had better plans than I did. She's changed. And so have I."

Rick's gaze drifted toward the engagement rings, thoughtful. "She's good with Ellie," he said. "Really good. She'll make a great mom someday."

Darcy's grin widened. "I know. That's why I want this to be perfect."

After several failed searches, Rick's eyes landed on an emerald ring, the deep blue-green stone set in a delicate yet intricate gold band. "That one," Rick said. "It's elegant but strong. Feels like her."

Darcy picked up the ring, turning it over in his hand. The emerald caught the light, its color deep and vibrant. He let out a small breath, then muttered, almost to himself, "It's even more perfect because green's on the Nigerian flag."

Rick glanced at him, raising a brow.

Darcy met his gaze and shrugged. "Caroline's parents immigrated from Nigeria. Feels right, doesn't it? A piece of where she comes from, her strength, wrapped in gold. Like if they were still here, they'd give their blessing."

241

Rick took a slow breath, studying the ring again. It did feel right. More than that—it felt like it was made for her. "You're sure?" Rick asked, watching Darcy's face carefully.

Darcy didn't hesitate. "Yeah," he said, his voice sure. "This is it."

As they stepped out of the store, Rick felt confused and torn about the slew of emotions colliding inside him.

Darcy glanced over as they climbed into the car. "Thanks for coming with me."

Rick shrugged. "It's what friends do."

"And here I thought you were just in it for the free shopping trip."

Rick rolled his eyes, shaking his head.

As they drove, Darcy glanced over. "You ready for bowling night?"

Rick let out a small breath. "Sure, should be fun. Lily can't stop talking about it. She's been watching YouTube videos of bowling so she can get a strike."

"That's my girl. I called ahead and they said they have an actual bowling ball ramp you guys can use to not put too much strain on your arms and legs. How rad is that?" Darcy grinned.

"Seriously?" Rick looked at Darcy in amazement. "I can't believe how much effort you've put into everything."

"Your first birthday celebration in over a decade is going to be one to remember."

Rick frowned. "It is just a birthday, man."

"You're allowed to have good things, Rick."

Rick stayed quiet.

Darcy nudged him. "And don't think I didn't notice you asking Marianne."

Rick sighed, pinching the bridge of his nose. "It's not a date."

Darcy chuckled. "Sure, sure. But for the record? She didn't hesitate to say yes."

Rick exhaled, shaking his head, but deep down, something warm and unfamiliar settled in his chest.

Chapter 58

> What did I do to deserve my beautiful children? Their love reminds me of God's goodness every moment I look at them.
> – Rick's Journal

The ocean had become a sacred place for Rick and Lily. A retreat. Their own quiet world. Every visit carried a weight of healing, an unspoken promise between them. But today, Rick sensed Lily's nerves as they arrived, her grip on his hand unusually tight.

The vast expanse of blue stretched before them, waves rolling in a rhythmic dance against the shore. A salty breeze played with Lily's hair, her small face pinched with thought. "Do you think the waves remember us, Daddy?" she asked softly, her voice barely audible over the distant crash of water.

The depth of her question catching him off guard. Taking a steading breath, Rick took her cane and set it down on the blanket with his own before he crouched beside her. "I think they do, Sweetheart," he murmured, squeezing her hand. "The ocean is always moving forward, no matter what it's been through. Just like us."

Her lips curled into a small, thoughtful smile. "Let's go say hi, then."

Hand in hand, they walked toward the water, the sand cool beneath their feet. The first wave kissed their toes, and Lily gasped before giggling. "It's colder than last time!"

Rick chuckled. "That's just the ocean reminding us it's still here."

Lily tilted her head, considering that, before taking a step deeper, the water reaching her ankles. "Do you think I'm brave, Daddy?"

Rick smiled, brushing a damp curl from her cheek. "Lily, you're the bravest person I know." His voice was steady, sure. "The ocean is strong, but it doesn't choose to be—it just is. You, though? You choose to be brave every single day."

Her smile widened, confidence settling into her little shoulders. "Can we look for shells?"

"Of course."

For the next half hour, they scoured the shoreline, collecting treasures buried beneath the sand. Every discovery was a victory—Lily's delighted squeals ringing out as she uncovered shiny, smooth, and uniquely shaped shells.

"This one's my favorite," she announced, holding up an iridescent fragment that glowed in the sunlight. "It's like a rainbow."

Rick turned it over in his hand, nodding. "It's beautiful. Just like you."

Lily blushed, slipping the shell into her pocket. "I'm keeping it forever so I never forget our trips here."

"You don't need a shell for that," Rick told her, his voice warm. "This is our place, Lily. It'll always be here for us."

Exhausted from the combination of physical therapy earlier in the day and the exercise of walking around the shore, the father and daughter sat on a blanket as they shared a simple picnic Darcy's housekeeper had packed. Between bites of her sandwich, Lily planned their next visit. "Next time, we'll build the biggest sandcastle ever! We can put all our shells on it."

Rick smiled. "That sounds perfect."

As the sun dipped lower, painting the sky in shades of gold and pink, they walked along the shore, their footprints marking the sand. Lily looked up at Rick, her small hand warm in his. "Do you think God made the ocean for us?"

Rick glanced at the endless horizon, his heart swelling at her innocent question. "I think He made it to remind us of His love," he said. "It's big and endless, just like His care for us. And even when we don't feel it, it's always there."

Lily's eyes brightened. "I like that," she said, nodding. "I think God knew we needed a place like this."

Rick wrapped an arm around her. "Maybe He did." He pressed a kiss to her temple. "And maybe He brought us here to show us how strong we can be—together."

Lily hesitated, her fingers brushing over the shell in her pocket. Then, with a small, shy smile, she whispered, "I love you, Daddy. Happy birthday."

Rick swallowed past the tightness in his throat, emotion swelling in his chest. He hadn't celebrated his birthday in ten years, but somehow, hearing Lily say it made it feel real.

"I love you too, Sweetheart," he murmured, squeezing her close.

As they walked back to the car, Lily clutched her box of seashells like rare treasure, her earlier nerves replaced by peace. She hummed softly, a melody she made up on the spot, and Rick smiled.

"Did you have fun today?"

She nodded, running her fingers over the smooth surface of her favorite shell. "I can't wait to show my shell to everyone."

As soon as they got home, Lily held up her prized shell. "Look what I found!" she said excitedly. "We went to the ocean."

Walter came to greet them, curiosity sparking in his green eyes. "That's cool! Can I see?"

Lily handed it over without hesitation. "Next time, you can come, too."

Rick's chest tightened with pride. Their moment at the ocean had been deeply personal, but Lily was willing to share it with her brothers.

"Thanks, Lily," Walter said, turning the shell over before passing it to Sam. "It's really smooth."

"Yeah, it's awesome," Sam agreed. "Did you find more?"

Lily nodded eagerly. "A whole bunch! We'll have to bring a bucket to put them all in next time."

The warmth in the house wrapped around Rick as the kids chattered excitedly about their next ocean trip. Their voices overlapped—talk of waves, shells, and plans for the biggest sandcastle ever.

Then the back door creaked open. "So, who's ready for some mad bowling?" Darcy called as he stepped into the living room with Caroline.

The lively hum of the bowling alley filled the air as soon as Rick stepped inside. There was the crash of pins, the buzz of overlapping conversation, and classic rock playing overhead. It was the perfect setting for Rick's first birthday celebration in ten years. No shadows. No cellar. Just life, laughter, and the people who mattered most.

Marianne, who had arrived just ahead of their group to the bowling alley, was greeted immediately by the kids. Rick still couldn't decide when or why they had practically adopted her into the family. Even Ellie, usually shy around new people, had grabbed her hand as soon as they walked in, leading her toward the lanes like she belonged there.

Marianne, dressed in capri jeans and a fitted t-shirt, sat beside Ellie as the older kids eagerly picked out their bowling balls.

"Okay, Team Wentworth," Darcy declared, rolling his shoulders dramatically. "Who's ready to witness my unparalleled bowling skills?"

Sam snorted. "You mean your gutter balls?"

Caroline smirked, adjusting her elegant spring blouse. "Oh, don't let him fool you, kids. Uncle Darcy will pull some ridiculous trick shot at the end and act like he planned it all along."

Darcy gasped in mock outrage. "How dare you expose my strategy?"

Marianne chuckled, nudging Rick. "Was he always this highly competitive?"

Rick huffed a small laugh. "He takes everything seriously when there's a chance of bragging rights."

"All right," Lily announced, hands on her hips. "Who's first?"

"Me!" Ellie piped up, bouncing on her toes.

The problem? The smallest bowling ball still looked comically oversized in her tiny hands.

Marianne knelt beside her. "Tell you what. How about we do this together?"

Ellie's face lit up instantly. "Really?"

"Really," Marianne promised, taking the ball and helping Ellie position her fingers. "Okay, now we hold it just like this—" She guided Ellie's hands, crouching beside her. "Now, on three, we roll it. Ready?"

Ellie nodded excitedly.

"One, two—three!"

Together, they rolled the ball down the lane at a painfully slow pace, but that didn't matter. The ball teetered toward the pins before one finally wobbled and toppled over.

Ellie shrieked with delight, jumping up and down. "We got one!"

Marianne clapped her hands. "Nice job, Ellie! You're officially a bowler."

Ellie turned to Rick, her eyes wide with joy. "Daddy, did you see? Marianne helped me!"

Rick smiled, warmth spreading through his chest. "I saw, Little Love. That was amazing."

Marianne's eyes met his, holding something soft, something unspoken, and suddenly, Rick wasn't thinking about anything else but this moment as unspoken words drifted between them.

As the game went on, the group settled into an easy rhythm of playful taunts and cheers. Lily was determined to beat Darcy, who continued to tease her for "cheating" with her bowling ball ramp that everyone else seemed to want to use as well. Sam and Walter argued over who had the most power behind their throws, while Ellie cheered wildly for everyone.

When it was Rick's turn, he took a breath, lifting the ball and stepping up to the lane. His last birthday outside the cellar had been a lifetime ago. He couldn't even remember what Darcy and Anne had done to celebrate the moment. This moment, however, being surrounded by his kids, Marianne, Caroline, and his best friend felt real and he had a feeling he would never forget it.

He rolled the ball forward, watching as it knocked over all the pins. The kids erupted in cheers, while Darcy groaned dramatically.

"Beginner's luck," Darcy muttered, shaking his head.

Rick turned, smirking. "I'd like to thank my coach," he said, nodding toward Ellie, who giggled with pride.

Marianne laughed beside him. "I think you might have a hidden talent, Mr. Wentworth."

Rick shrugged. "Just trying to keep up with these guys."

Later, as they moved to the party area, pizza and cake appeared like magic—courtesy of Darcy, who had ordered enough food to feed twice as many people.

Caroline, ever the documentarian, snapped a picture of Rick cutting his cake, narrating, "Historic moment: Rick Wentworth's first birthday celebration in a decade. He looks overwhelmed."

Rick shook his head, laughing, but there was truth in her words. Because he *was* overwhelmed. With gratitude. With this life he had been given back.

The kids chatted happily, their voices blending into the background of bowling alley noise. Lily excitedly recounted their ocean trip from that afternoon day, pulling Marianne into the conversation as if she had been there, too.

Then, Darcy slid a small wrapped box across the table. "One last thing before we call it a night."

Rick eyed it warily. "You already did too much."

"Shut up and open it."

Rick sighed but peeled back the wrapping to reveal a leather-bound journal. His fingers traced the smooth cover, the weight of it settling in his palms. For a moment, he couldn't breathe.

Nine Christmases ago, in the cellar, Louisa had given him a journal. She hadn't given it out of kindness. It was just another way to keep him trapped in her control. He had filled its pages anyway, as it was the only escape he had. His words had been his method of rebellion, his prayers scribbled between the lines.

Now, Darcy had placed a brand-new one in front of him. No tainted memories. No cellar. Just blank pages waiting for him to fill them. Rick swallowed hard.

"It's for writing your story," Darcy said, his voice quieter than usual. "Because the world needs to hear it."

Rick ran a hand over the smooth cover, something tight unraveling in his chest.

For the first time in years, he wasn't trapped in writing his agony. Now, he could finally write his hopes.

As the evening wound down, Marianne lingered beside Rick while the kids gathered their things. "You have a pretty amazing family," she said softly. "You're doing a great job, Rick. They're lucky to have you."

Rick's gaze drifted to his kids, who were now laughing near an arcade game with Caroline and Darcy. His throat tightened. "I'm the lucky one," he said. "They're my whole world. And—I don't think I've said this enough, but thank you for everything you did for Lily and me. You gave us our lives back. She could have died if it weren't for you."

Marianne's expression softened, a quiet warmth in her gaze. "You've built something beautiful out of everything you've been through, Rick. That takes strength."

Before he could reply, Ellie bounded over, clutching Bella the Bunny. "Marianne, can you help Bella?" she asked, holding out the tiny bunny sweater with hopeful eyes.

Marianne knelt beside her, deftly dressing the stuffed bunny. "Of course. Bella needs to stay warm, too."

Ellie nodded solemnly. "She gets cold."

Marianne finished and tucked Ellie's flimsy scarf snugly around her neck. "There, now you both are all set."

Ellie hesitated before throwing her arms around Marianne's neck in a quick, shy hug. "Thank you," she whispered.

Rick watched, something deep and unspoken tightening in his chest. Ellie didn't warm up to other people this fast.

Later, as Rick and Darcy returned their bowling shoes, Sam sidled up beside Rick, his voice quiet. "Dad?"

Rick turned, sensing the seriousness in his son's tone. "What's up, Buddy?"

Sam glanced back toward the table, where Marianne was helping Lily with her sweaters. "She's really nice," he said simply. "Like—Mom nice."

Rick's breath caught. "Sam—"

"I mean it," Sam continued, his voice firm. "She's like someone who could—you know, be family."

Rick looked at his son, his throat thick with emotion.

As he returned to the table, Lily tugged on Rick's hand. "Daddy, is Marianne coming home with us?"

Rick's heart ached at the hope in her voice. "No, Sweetheart," he said gently. "Not tonight."

"But maybe someday?" Lily pressed.

Rick glanced toward Marianne, who was chatting with Caroline, and, for the first time, he let himself imagine what "someday" could look like. "Maybe," he said softly. "Maybe someday."

Chapter 59

> How I wish that I could turn back the hands of time.
> —Rick's Journal

The evening had settled into a comfortable rhythm. The hum of the dishwasher, the flickering glow of a lamp in the living room, and the soft murmurs of the kids winding down for the night created a peaceful backdrop until it was shattered by a sudden, piercing scream.

"DON'T HURT UNCLE DARCY!"

Rick's stomach dropped. His chair scraped against the floor as he bolted from the kitchen. By the time he reached the living room, Lily had already thrown herself into the middle of the scene. Her small body slammed into Caroline with surprising force, pushing her off Darcy with everything she had.

"Get off him!" Lily sobbed, planting herself between Caroline and Darcy, her fists clenched. "Don't hurt him!"

Caroline, startled, half-tumbled to the side, bracing herself against the couch. Darcy, mid-laugh only seconds ago, froze, his breath caught as the reality of what had just happened sank in.

Walter and Sam ran in from the hallway, their eyes darting between Lily and the adults, confusion written across their faces.

Ellie, clutching Quackers, toddled in, rubbing her sleepy eyes. "Lily?" Ellie asked, her little brow furrowed. "What's wrong?"

Lily ignored them, her entire body trembling as she turned on Caroline, her voice breaking through her sobs. "That's what she did to Daddy! She kissed him, and he didn't want it!"

Rick sucked in a sharp breath. The air in the room shifted, the weight of Lily's words pressing down on everyone.

Caroline paled, her hands still raised in surrender, her expression stricken. Darcy's head snapped toward Rick, his face etched with something between horror and heartbreak.

Rick's chest ached. His brave, fierce Lily had seen something playful and innocent and, in her panic, had equated it with Louisa's cruelty. She had lumped Caroline in with Louisa.

Darcy inhaled shakily, sitting up straighter. "Sweetheart," he started carefully, his voice softer now. "Caroline wasn't hurting me."

Lily shook her head wildly, her eyes darting back to him. "She was on top of you! You were trying to push her off! That's what she used to do to Daddy!"

Caroline pressed a hand to her mouth. Darcy exhaled slowly, running a hand through his hair.

Rick moved first, kneeling beside Lily, keeping his hands gentle but firm on her shoulders. "Lily, Sweetheart, look at me," he murmured.

Her breathing was fast, erratic little gasps that Rick knew too well—panic, terror, the past blurring into the present.

Darcy swallowed hard, keeping his voice careful. "Lily, I promise, Caroline wasn't hurting me."

Lily's lip trembled. "But she kissed you," she whispered. "You didn't want her to. You were saying no and pushing her away."

Caroline sucked in a breath, but Rick saw her hold herself perfectly still, not wanting to startle Lily further.

Darcy sighed, his voice steady but kind. "Lily, listen to me. We were playing a game. Has anyone ever tickled you before and you yell, 'Merc, mercy,' but you're giggling because you're having so much fun?"

Lily looked so lost and confused.

Rick tried again. "There's a difference between good touches and bad touches."

Lily's brow furrowed, her body still rigid.

Rick squeezed her hands, keeping his voice warm, reassuring. "A bad touch is when someone does something to you that makes you feel scared or trapped. That's what your mama did to me. And that was wrong."

Lily's wide eyes flickered to him, still seeking reassurance.

Rick nodded. "But what Uncle Darcy and Caroline were doing? That was different. Uncle Darcy wanted those kisses."

Lily blinked rapidly, looking at Darcy. "You did?"

Darcy nodded. "Yeah, Sweetheart. Caroline is my girlfriend, and I love her. Sometimes when people love each other, they kiss and play around. But only when both people want to."

Caroline finally found her voice, soft and full of understanding. "Lily, no one should ever force someone to kiss or touch them," she said gently. "That's wrong. But Darcy and I? We were both okay with it. I know it looked like he was fighting me off, but it was a silly game, which is why we were laughing. He wasn't upset. I would never do anything to him that he didn't want."

Lily hesitated, her small hands twisting the fabric of her shirt.

Walter shifted uncomfortably, scratching the back of his head. "I don't get it," he admitted, looking at Rick. "How's she supposed to know the difference?"

Rick exhaled, his fingers tightening around Lily's shoulders. "You know that feeling in your stomach when something doesn't feel right? That's your body's way of telling you it's wrong. But when two people love and trust each other, there's no fear."

Lily's lower lip wobbled. "But she was on top of him."

Rick cupped her cheek, brushing away a tear. "I know, Sweetheart. And you were trying to protect him. That was very brave."

Lily's hands gripped his sleeves. "I just don't want anyone to hurt you or Uncle Darcy ever again."

Rick pulled her into his arms, holding her tight. "No one will," he whispered. "I promise."

Ellie, still holding Quackers, shuffled forward and tugged on Lily's sleeve. "Caroline loves Uncle Darcy," she declared, her tiny voice serious. "Daddy loves us. Love is good."

Lily's breath hitched, but she looked at Ellie, considering her words.

Caroline, who had been holding herself perfectly still, finally spoke again. "Lily, I would never hurt Uncle Darcy. And I would never hurt you."

Lily hesitated, then finally looked at Caroline—not as an enemy, not as a threat, but as someone she had misread. Caroline opened her arms slightly, giving her the choice. Slowly, hesitantly, Lily stepped forward and wrapped her arms around Caroline's waist. Caroline exhaled, hugging her back, whispering soft reassurances into her hair.

Rick met Darcy's gaze over Lily's head. Something deep, raw, and unspoken passed between them.

Lily pulled back, rubbing her nose on her sleeve. "Okay," she said in a small voice. "I think I get it now."

Rick kissed the top of her head. "That's my girl."

Darcy let out a slow breath, shaking his head. "Well," he muttered, rubbing his jaw, "that was a wake-up call."

Caroline nudged him. "No more tickle fights in front of Lily."

Darcy smirked, ruffling Lily's hair. "Noted."

Lily still clung to Rick's sleeve, but the trembling had stopped.

Rick glanced toward the hallway, where Sam and Walter lingered, still absorbing everything. "Boys, you good?"

Sam nodded, glancing at Lily. "I get why she got scared," he said honestly.

Walter crossed his arms. "I'm still confused, but I think I understand."

Ellie clutched Quackers tighter. "Caroline is nice," she said, as if this was all the logic needed.

Rick huffed a laugh, shaking his head.

Lily looked up at Caroline again, her voice smaller now. "I'm sorry I pushed you."

"Thank you for that." Caroline brushed a curl from Lily's face. "I know why you did, Sweetheart. And I'm not mad."

Darcy exhaled, rubbing his hands over his face. "Okay. Well. That was enough emotional processing for one night. Who wants ice cream?"

Lily sniffled, her lip trembling. "Can I have extra sprinkles?"

Darcy grinned, scooping her up onto his shoulders. "Sweetheart, you can have all the sprinkles in the world."

The tension in the room finally cracked, giving way to relieved chuckles and nodding heads. As the kids rushed toward the kitchen with their Uncle Darcy, Lily glanced back at Caroline before giving her a shy smile.

Rick met Caroline's eyes, gratitude shining in his. Tonight had been a setback, but it had also been a step forward.

As the evening settled, ice cream was scooped, sprinkles were piled high, and laughter filled the kitchen, easing the lingering weight of Lily's panic.

Healing took time. And tonight, love had won another small battle.

Chapter 60

> In the circle of their embrace, I find the strength to face any darkness, for together, we are unyielding and bound by love that transcends all fears.
> - Rick's Journal

The soft glow of morning sunlight filtered through the curtains as Rick poured himself a cup of coffee, the rich aroma filling the kitchen. From the living room, the sound of cartoons and children's laughter drifted in.

Walter and Sam were sprawled across the couch, deep in an animated debate over which superhero would win in a fight. On the floor, Lily sat cross-legged, clutching Leo the Lion, her fingers absently running over his fur. In the armchair, Ellie perched with Quackers the Duck tucked firmly under her arm, humming softly to herself as she rocked slightly.

Rick leaned against the counter, savoring the moment. Two months ago, mornings like this had been impossible to imagine. Now, these simple, chaotic weekend mornings filled his chest with something warm—something that felt like home.

A knock at the door broke through the moment.

"Good morning," Caroline called cheerfully from the porch. "I come bearing gifts—specifically, breakfast."

Rick opened the door to find her standing there, holding a tray of warm cinnamon rolls, their golden-brown edges glistening. The sweet scent immediately wafted inside.

"Caroline, you're going to spoil us," he said with a grin, stepping aside to let her in.

"Well, it's a special morning," she replied, a knowing smile playing on her lips. "And I happen to know this crew loves cinnamon rolls."

Sam, already mid-leap from the couch, whooped in excitement. "Cinnamon rolls!"

Walter followed, less dramatic but just as eager, while Ellie clambered off the armchair, her tiny hands reaching up toward Rick expectantly.

Rick chuckled, setting his coffee on the island counter as he hoisted Ellie up onto his hip. "You just had cereal and already have room for cinnamon rolls?"

Ellie nodded solemnly, Quackers tucked firmly in the crook of her arm. "Quackers wants one too."

Caroline laughed, setting the tray down. "Well, lucky for Quackers, I made extra."

As the kids swarmed around the counter, the back door creaked open, and Darcy strolled in, hair damp from an early swim, a towel slung casually over his shoulder. "Ah," he said, grabbing a plate without hesitation. "Caroline's outdone herself again."

Rick smirked, watching his best friend unabashedly steal one of the biggest rolls. "Darcy, she's putting you to shame. You better step up your game."

Darcy winked at Ellie, who was now perched on Rick's lap, happily swinging her legs as she nibbled her treat. "It's hard to compete with Caroline's cinnamon rolls," he said. "But at least I managed to show up on time for the announcement."

Rick raised an eyebrow. "Announcement?"

Caroline shot Darcy a look, her cheeks tinged pink but her smile radiant. "We have some news," she said warmly. "Uncle Darcy and I are engaged."

The room froze for a beat, then erupted with excitement.

"Engaged?" Walter gaped.

Sam's eyes widened. "Like, getting married?"

Darcy grinned, slipping an arm around Caroline. "That's right. Caroline's going to be part of our family."

Sam blinked once, then grinned. "Does that mean more cinnamon rolls?"

Caroline burst into laughter as Darcy groaned. "That's your takeaway from this?"

Lily, who had been quietly absorbing the moment, looked up from Leo with furrowed brows. "Mama used to say only weak people get tied down in marriage," she murmured hesitantly. "She said Daddy was silly for waiting to get married before——." Frustration colored her voice as she sought for the words she wanted. "Well, I can't remember what she said but she said something."

The room fell silent, the weight of her words pressing down like a held breath.

Rick set Ellie down gently before kneeling beside Lily, placing a steady hand on her shoulder. "Lily," he said softly, his voice strong, "Your mom said a lot of things. Not all of them were

255

true. Real love—the kind that's patient and kind, like we read about in the Bible—isn't weak. It's one of the strongest things someone can choose."

Lily's small fingers tightened around Leo. "But she said your waiting was silly."

Rick met her gaze, his tone gentle but firm. "She was wrong about that, too. Saving something special for someone you love isn't silly—it's a way of showing respect, trust, and love the way God intended."

Walter stepped forward, his voice steady. "Dad, we know you're not weak. You've done everything to take care of us. That's what matters."

Sam nodded, his small face serious. "Yeah, we're a family now. Mom didn't decide that. We did."

Ellie toddled closer, her little voice piping up. "Quackers loves Leo." She held out her free hand to Lily. "And I love you."

Lily's eyes shimmered, and she pulled Ellie into a tight hug. "I love you guys, too," she whispered, her voice thick with emotion.

Rick swallowed hard, blinking back the sting behind his eyes, and pulled all his children into his arms. "I love you all so much. And we're a family. No matter what."

Darcy stepped forward, resting a supportive hand on Rick's shoulder. "And you've got Caroline and me too. Always."

Caroline, watching the exchange with glistening eyes, took a deep breath and clapped her hands. "Now," she said brightly, "how about we eat those cinnamon rolls before they get cold?"

The tension in the room melted as the kids bolted for the counter where their abandoned rolls sat, their laughter chasing away the shadows of the past conversation. Rick stood for a moment, watching them with a quiet ache in his chest.

They were healing.

Chapter 61

> Even all these miles away, she still spins a web and tries to poison
> our new beginnings.
> – Rick's Journal

The diner buzzed with the sounds of clinking dishes, bursts of laughter from a nearby table, and the steady hum of conversation. The air smelled of sizzling burgers and golden fries, and for the first time in a long while, Rick allowed himself to relax.

June 20th. Walter's eighth birthday. Three months ago, they had been strangers under the same roof, adjusting, healing, learning how to be a family. And now? Now they were here together—celebrating with Darcy, Caroline, Marianne, eating their way through gigantic burgers, towering milkshakes, and extra-crispy fries.

Ellie was happily dipping her fries into her milkshake, unconcerned about the sticky mess covering her fingers. Lily sat beside her, carefully removing all the pickles from her burger, her movements slow, thoughtful. Across the table, Walter and Sam had been joking, their energy high from the sugar rush, until suddenly, Walter went quiet.

Rick caught the shift instantly. The way Walter's fingers slowed as he pushed his fries around the plate. The unmistakable tension settling into his shoulders.

Then, without preamble, Walter dropped a bomb. "She called us, you know."

Rick's stomach tightened. He set his coffee cup down slowly. "Who?"

Sam scoffed, folding his arms. "Who do you think?"

Rick's fingers curled around the ceramic, a slow dread unfurling in his chest.

Walter lifted his gaze, his expression unreadable. "Mom. She called the house. Talked to me and Sam when you and Uncle Darcy were out."

The conversation at the table stilled.

Rick felt Caroline shift beside him. Marianne, who had been laughing at something Lily had said just moments ago, had gone rigid. Across from them, Darcy's jaw tightened slightly.

Rick forced himself to keep his voice steady. "When?"

Walter shrugged, but there was something almost defiant in the movement. "A few days ago, when we were home with Mrs. Reynolds."

"My housekeeper?" Darcy asked incredulous.

"Yeah, she gave us the phone. It was Mom." Sam muttered, barely above a whisper. "She said she misses us."

Rick inhaled sharply, his chest constricting. "What else did she say?"

Walter hesitated, his fingers tapping lightly against the edge of his plate. "She wants to see us." He swallowed. "She said she's been trying to reach us for months, but you wouldn't let her."

Rick clenched his jaw, his breath coming slow and deliberate. "That's not true."

Walter's gaze sharpened. "Then why didn't she call before?"

Darcy exhaled, finally speaking, his voice low and controlled. "If you are going to blame anyone, blame me. As your legal guardian, I told the psychiatric hospital not to allow her to contact you. And I see now I should have told Mrs. Reynolds not to put through any calls from there."

Walter's scowl deepened. "What's wrong with her talking to us?"

Rick's stomach churned. He had known this moment would come—the moment they started questioning, the moment they wanted to hear her side of the story.

Sam spoke up, his voice quieter but laced with frustration. "She said you wouldn't let us visit."

Before Rick could answer, Lily's voice cut through the conversation, sharp and trembling. "Why do you even want to see her?"

Walter turned to her, frowning. "Lily—"

"She doesn't love you! She never did!" Lily's hands clenched into fists on the table, her entire body shaking. "She chained me up, too! She kidnapped Daddy! She didn't care about us! Not ever!"

Heads turned. Conversations paused around them. The weight of eyes on them pressed in. Rick heard the murmurs.

"That's him, isn't it?"

"The guy from the news—"

"Those poor kids."

A cold sweat prickled at his skin. His chest tightened, his breathing hitched. The diner suddenly felt too small.

Walter's brows furrowed. "She's still our mom."

Lily stood up and slammed her tiny hands onto the table, rattling the plates. "NO, SHE'S NOT!"

Ellie, startled by Lily's outburst, clutched Quackers the Duck tightly to her chest. "Lily mad?" she asked in a small voice.

Lily wiped at her eyes furiously, her breath coming in uneven gasps. "She doesn't miss you. She's lying. That's what she does."

Rick's throat felt tight, but he reached over and gently touched Lily's hand. "Sweetheart, I know this is hard," he said softly.

Lily shook her head, tears glistening in her eyes as she looked at him with wide, pleading desperation. "She hurt you, Daddy. Why do they want to see her?"

Rick exhaled, forcing himself to speak past the lump in his throat. "Because she's still their mom."

Walter and Sam sat stiffly, not meeting her gaze.

"If it means that much to you both, I will drive you up next Saturday," Darcy cut in.

Lily's expression crumbled, and she turned her face away, her fingers tightening around Leo the Lion.

Marianne leaned in, her voice gentle. "Lily, you don't have to see her. No one is making you."

Lily sniffled but didn't respond.

Walter shifted uncomfortably. "I just—I just want to know why she did it," he admitted quietly. "That's all."

Rick hesitated, then nodded. "I get that," he said. "I really do."

Walter's lips pressed together. "Then why aren't you coming?"

Rick swallowed hard, the room spinning around him. His hand clenched against the table. Then, slowly, he reached up and tugged down the collar of his shirt.

The air in the diner shifted. The boys froze.

The deep, raw scar wrapping around his throat like a noose was visible beneath the warm glow of the diner's lights. The permanent reminder of the chain Louisa had kept around his neck for ten years.

Walter's mouth parted slightly. Sam turned pale. Marianne and Caroline couldn't hold back the gasps of horror, despite having seen the scars before.

Rick's voice was quiet but unshakable. "She did this to me."

No one said anything until finally Darcy spoke. "That's why he's not going."

Rick barely heard the rest. The voices in the diner were getting louder. The stares, the whispers. His vision blurred at the edges. His chest felt like it was caving in.

"Time to go," Darcy said abruptly, pulling his wallet out and tossing a few bills onto the table despite the protests of the owner who looked at them all with sympathy and pity.

Marianne was already moving. "I got him," she said before Rick even realized she was at his side.

The fresh air hit his face as they stepped outside. He sucked in a sharp breath, unsteady, his fingers gripping her shoulders to steady himself.

Marianne didn't let go. "Breathe, Rick. I'm right here."

His pulse hammered in his ears. He squeezed his eyes shut, focusing on the warmth of her hand against his back, the steady rise and fall of her breath. Slowly, his own breath began to match hers as he inhaled her intoxicating rose-scented fragrance.

She shifted slightly, her arms wrapping around him in a firm, grounding embrace. Rick stiffened for half a second—but then, before he could stop himself, he leaned into her. His forehead brushed her shoulder, his body sagging slightly against hers.

Marianne held him, steady and sure. "You're okay," she murmured. "You're safe."

Rick's fingers curled against the fabric of her jacket. He didn't let go. When he looked up, he saw Darcy watching them, his arms crossed. Seeing the smirk that tugged at his best friend's lips, Rick rolled his eyes and turned back towards Marianne.

By the time they got home, Caroline offered to usher the kids upstairs for baths and bedtime before heading out for the night as Darcy helped Rick up the stairs, steadying him when his body threatened to give out.

When they finally collapsed onto Rick's bed, Darcy sprawled out beside him, exhaling dramatically. "You know,

Wentworth," he mused, stretching his arms behind his head, "if you wanted to get Marianne to hold you, there were easier ways than a full-blown panic attack."

Rick groaned, throwing an arm over his eyes. "Shut up."

Darcy snickered, propping himself up on one elbow. "Not that I blame you. That hug lasted at least a minute longer than necessary."

Rick let out a breathless laugh, shaking his head. "You keeping track now?"

"Absolutely," Darcy said smugly before kicking off his shoes as he settled back against the pillows. "I'm crashing here, by the way."

Rick huffed a quiet laugh. "Figures."

Darcy sighed dramatically. "You know, I'm starting to think you just fake these episodes to get me into bed."

Rick snorted, too tired to fight the smirk pulling at his own lips. "Yeah, you got me. All part of my grand master plan."

Darcy gave his hand a squeeze. "I knew it. Manipulative bastard."

Rick chuckled. "You love me."

"Can't argue with that." Darcy exhaled. "I've loved you since we were five."

Neither of them moved. The weight of the night still lingered, but it wasn't unbearable anymore.

Chapter 62

> My heart clenched with anxiety, haunted by the fear that Louisa's dark influence might yet claim them from me, as I waited for them to return home.
> – Rick's Journal

The clock on the wall ticked too loudly. The hum of the dishwasher had long since faded into the background. Rick sat on the couch, his hands loosely clasped, his knee bouncing in restless agitation.

It was late. Too late. They should have been home hours ago.

Beside him, Lily curled into a tight ball, clutching Leo the Lion in a white-knuckled grip. Sleep had no chance of claiming her. "They should be home by now," she murmured, her eyes locked on the door.

"I know, Sweetheart." His voice came out low, rougher than he intended.

He hated this—hated not knowing, hated that he'd sent his boys into that place, into her presence.

Then, at last, the unmistakable rumble of Darcy's SUV rolled into the driveway, sending a jolt through Rick's chest.

Lily shot upright. "They're here!"

Rick was already on his feet by the time the front door swung open.

Darcy stepped in first, his expression grim, one hand resting lightly on Walter's shoulder. The boy's face was pale, his green eyes red-rimmed. Behind them, Sam walked in silently, arms wrapped around himself. He didn't look at anyone.

Rick's gut twisted. "Hey," he started. "How was—?"

Walter broke. Tears spilled down his cheeks as he lunged forward, throwing his arms around Rick's waist. His small body shook as he clung to him, pressing his face against Rick's chest. "I'm sorry," Walter choked out. "I'm so sorry, Dad."

Rick exhaled sharply, wrapping his son in a firm embrace. "Shh, it's okay," he murmured, pressing a kiss to Walter's hair. "You don't have to be sorry."

Walter shook his head fiercely. "I—I believed her. Even after everything, I wanted to believe she was different." His voice wavered. "But she wasn't. She looked at us like we were nothing. And then she said you lied. That you—" His voice cracked, a fresh sob tearing through him. "She said we were fools for loving you."

Rick closed his eyes, pressing his cheek against Walter's hair, gripping him tighter. "She's wrong," he said firmly. "You're not a fool."

Walter pulled back slightly, looking up at him with glassy eyes. "I should've never doubted you."

Rick cupped his son's face, his own voice rough with emotion. "You're a kid, Walter. It's okay to have questions. It's okay to want to believe she's someone she's not. But listen to me— nothing she says changes who you are to me. You are my son. And I love you. Always."

Walter let out a shaky breath and buried his face back into Rick's chest.

Lily hovered nearby, her small hands curling into fists. "She's a liar," she muttered, gripping Walter's fingers. "She lied to all of us."

Walter squeezed her hand but didn't answer.

Rick's gaze lifted to Sam, who stood near the stairs, staring at the floor. He hadn't said a word since walking in. "Sam?" Rick called softly.

Sam stiffened, then shook his head. "I'm tired," he mumbled and started up the stairs without another glance.

Rick's heart clenched as he watched his middle son disappear.

Darcy sighed, rubbing a hand over his face as he shut the door behind them. "That went about as well as you'd expect," he muttered.

Rick exhaled, rubbing a hand over Walter's back before gently steering him toward the couch. "Go sit with your sister, Buddy. I'll get you some juice."

Walter nodded tiredly and sank onto the cushions. Lily followed, sitting close enough that their shoulders touched.

Rick made his way into the kitchen. Darcy, already there, leaned against the counter, his arms crossed. "She tore them apart," Darcy said quietly.

Rick gritted his teeth as he grabbed the pitcher of juice from the fridge. "I didn't think it would be that bad."

Darcy's expression darkened. "She told them you were a liar. That everything you did—every hug, every 'I love you'—was just an act. That you only wanted them now because you had no one else. That you let her keep you locked up, not because you had no choice, but because you were too weak to leave. Too spineless to be a real man, let alone a real father. And if they couldn't see that, then they were just as blind and gullible as you always hoped they'd be."

Rick's fingers clenched around the pitcher.

Darcy let out a slow breath. "She barely even looked at them, Rick. Acted like she was doing them a favor by acknowledging them."

Rick closed his eyes for a brief moment, forcing the fury down. "I should've gone," he muttered, gripping the counter.

"No," Darcy said, sharp and firm. "You shouldn't have. You know exactly what she would've done if you had been there. She wanted a reaction. She wanted control. And you didn't give it to her."

Rick swallowed hard, staring at the juice swirling in the pitcher. "Sam won't talk about it."

Darcy sighed. "He shut down as soon as we left. Didn't say a word on the drive home. Just stared out the window. I've never seen that son of yours sit still for seven hours."

Rick let out a slow breath. "I'll talk to him tomorrow."

Darcy nodded, but his expression remained troubled. "He's hurting."

Rick met his best friend's gaze. "So am I."

Darcy was quiet for a long moment before finally shaking his head. "I hate her, you know that?" His voice was low, edged with something dark. "I hated her before. But seeing those boys walk out of that place looking broken—" He exhaled sharply, his hands flexing at his sides. "It took everything in me not to tell her exactly what I think of her."

Rick set the pitcher down, rubbing a hand over his face. "You didn't need to. She already knows."

Darcy let out a short, humorless snort. "Yeah. But I still wanted to."

For a while, they stood there in silence. Rick finally leaned against the counter beside him. "Thanks for taking them."

Darcy gave him a pointed look. "You don't need to thank me, man."

Rick huffed a quiet laugh. "I do."

Darcy shook his head. "They needed to see for themselves. Now they know who she really is. And they know exactly who you are, too."

Rick glanced toward the living room where Walter and Lily sat huddled together, the TV playing softly in the background.

"They love you, Rick," Darcy said quietly. "Nothing she said changed that."

Rick swallowed past the lump in his throat. "I just hope Sam knows that, too."

Darcy clapped a hand on his shoulder. "He does. Give him time."

Rick nodded, exhaling slowly as he arranged the pitcher and a couple of glasses on a tray. He walked into the living room, the weight in his chest easing slightly at the sight of his children safe, here, with him.

For now, that was all that mattered.

Chapter 63

> Under the brilliant burst of Fourth of July fireworks, we celebrated
> our freedom together, embracing the joy and laughter that now
> define our lives, far from the shadows that once held us captive.
> – Rick's Journal

The summer air buzzed with excitement as they stepped
through the grand entrance of the theme park, the scent of
popcorn and something sugary filling the air. Fourth of July
fireworks were still hours away, but the sky was already painted in
hues of pink and gold, the perfect backdrop for their long-awaited
day of fun.

Rick adjusted Ellie's sunhat and took in the sheer joy on
his daughters' faces. This was a first for them both. The first time
they'd stood in a place built for magic, where castles rose high and
music played from unseen speakers, wrapping around them like
something out of a dream.

"All right, troops," Darcy announced, unfolding a park
map with an exaggerated flourish. "We have one mission today:
fun. Just rides, ridiculous amounts of food, and…" He turned to
Lily with a wink. "Finding a certain dog you've been waiting to
meet."

Lily gasped, gripping Rick's hand. "Really?" she asked, her
voice barely containing her excitement.

"As promised," Rick said, squeezing her hand.

She practically vibrated with excitement, and even Sam,
who had been withdrawn since the visit to Louisa, let out a small
smirk at her enthusiasm.

"We'll find him," Darcy assured her. "And while we are
here, I intend to prove that I am the undefeated champion of roller
coasters. Who's brave enough to challenge me?"

Walter and Sam immediately straightened.

"You're going down," Walter said.

Sam didn't speak, but there was a gleam in his eye that
Rick hadn't seen in a while.

As their party moved into the thick of the crowd, Rick
walked at an easy pace, his one hand holding tightly to Lily while
the other pushed Ellie's stroller. She sat comfortably, her small
hands gripping Quackers, the stuffed duck he'd bought her on their

first daddy-daughter date, tucked securely against her chest. Her wide eyes darted around, taking in the sights and sounds with fascination. Every so often, she kicked her feet excitedly, looking up at him with a bright grin, as if to make sure he was seeing everything too.

Ellie's eyes went wide with wonder not at the gorgeous castle that rose in all its grandeur above them but at the pond below. "Daddy! Ducks!" she gasped, pointing toward the water.

Rick smiled as he parked the stroller by the pond and lifted Ellie out of her stroller so they could step closer to the railing while Caroline led the rest of the party to stand in line to get a photo in front of the castle. A small group of ducks floated lazily along the water's edge, some preening their feathers, others dipping their heads beneath the surface.

Ellie squeezed Quackers, her fingers brushing over the stuffed animal's worn beak. "Look, Quackers! Your friends!"

Rick chuckled. "Think they know you brought their cousin along today?"

Ellie giggled, then leaned forward, eyes full of awe. "They swim so good, Daddy."

"They do," Rick agreed, watching as one duck flapped its wings, sending small ripples across the water. "One day I'll teach you how to swim, just like them."

She gasped dramatically. "Me and you? And Quackers too?"

Rick grinned. "Of course. Quackers wouldn't miss it."

Ellie beamed, content, then rested her head against his shoulder as she watched the ducks glide across the water. "Love you, Daddy."

Just as Rick let himself settle into the quiet moment, Darcy's voice cut through the peace. "Well, isn't this adorable?" he teased, stepping up beside them. "Look at you, Wentworth. Soft dad moment, castle backdrop, perfect lighting. If I didn't know better, I'd say you're trying to get on the next park commercial."

Rick rolled his eyes, shifting Ellie in his arms. "Yeah, that's the dream, Darcy. Me and Quackers, starring in a primetime ad."

Darcy smirked. "Hey, I'd watch it. Probably cry a little." Then he clapped Rick's shoulder. "Now, come on, Daddy of the Year, it's almost our turn for the big family castle pic. I know how much you love standing awkwardly in front of a crowd while a stranger tells you to say cheese."

Rick huffed but reluctantly followed Darcy who was steering the stroller through the crowd as Ellie giggled, still holding tight to Quackers.

The first few hours of the day were a whirlwind of rides, laughter, and snack breaks. But as the midday heat settled in, Darcy took the younger girls and Caroline to a ride full of brightly colored sea creatures and a singing princess, grumbling about enduring a musical number for the sake of his honorary nieces.

That left Rick with his boys, and they needed no time to decide exactly what ride they wanted to explore with their dad as they rushed him to a land of superheroes.

Once strapped into their ride vehicle, the boys were focused, determined to win, while Rick was just hoping to keep up.

"You ready for this?" he asked, glancing at Walter.

Walter smirked. "Are you?"

The moment the ride launched into action, they were thrown into chaos and adventure, reacting on instinct and working together toward a common goal.

Rick found himself laughing more freely than he had in years, losing himself in the game, in the rush of competition, in the simple joy of being with his sons.

When they finally stumbled off the ride, breathless and grinning, Walter rolled his shoulders dramatically, as if he'd just survived a life-or-death battle.

"You're getting old, Dad," he teased. "You barely kept up."

Rick scoffed, still catching his breath. "Barely? I got the best score of our team!"

Sam, who had been mostly quiet since their visit to Louisa, finally smirked. "Dad—that wasn't your score. That was mine."

Rick froze, brow furrowing. "Excuse me?"

Walter pulled out his phone, grinning smugly as he brought up a photo he had taken of the scoreboard right before they stepped off the ride. "See for yourself, Dad. Sam smoked all of us."

Rick squinted at the screen. "Nah. That's gotta be wrong."

Sam folded his arms. "It's literally a photo, Dad."

"Photos can be doctored," Rick countered, straight-faced.

Walter snorted. "Oh yeah? You think I had time to Photoshop the score while we were still strapped in?"

As the boys howled with laughter, Rick sighed dramatically. "Wow. Betrayed by my own sons."

Just then, Darcy strolled up, hands in his pockets, grinning like a man who knew exactly what kind of chaos he was about to walk into. "So," Darcy drawled, glancing at Rick's face before looking at the boys. "I take it he didn't win?"

"Not even close." Sam grinned, then, almost absentmindedly, slipped his hand into Rick's. "It's okay, Dad. You don't have to be good at this ride."

Rick raised a brow. "Oh? And why's that?"

Walter rolled his eyes, slipping his phone back into his pocket. "Because you're already our superhero. Duh."

Rick's breath hitched for half a second, caught off guard by the simple but weighty statement.

Sam nodded. "Yeah. We don't need you to win a game. You already won where it matters."

As the laughter died down and the boys walked ahead, Rick lingered for a moment, watching them go. His heart was full—fuller than it had been in years. He wasn't sure if he'd ever get tired of hearing them call him their superhero. But all superheroes needed to refuel, and at this point, a dinner break sounded like the next best adventure.

Adjusting Ellie's juice cup, Rick glanced up—and for a fleeting second, the bustling noise of the dining hall seemed to soften. Marianne wove through the tables with ease, her eyes scanning until they landed on them. When they did, her smile brightened—not just polite, not just friendly, but something warmer.

As soon as the kids spotted Marianne, they greeted her with excited waves as Caroline asked about work, and Darcy pulled up an extra chair.

Rick, still holding Ellie's cup, found himself smiling too. That same quiet sense of joy remained with him later as they made their way to the long line for the character meet-and-greet he and Lily had been dreaming about for months. She had talked about this moment for so long, clinging to the promise he had made her in the cellar. Now, here they were.

Minutes later, when it was finally their turn, Lily's squeal of pure, unfiltered joy could probably be heard across the park as she practically ran into the yellow dog's waiting arms, hugging him tight as he wagged his tail and patted her head.

"Daddy said when we were free, we'd get to see you," she exclaimed, looking up at him.

Pluto gave an exaggerated gasp, covering his floppy ears with both paws before wagging excitedly. He tilted his head, playfully curious, as Lily continued.

"You know what I love most about your stories?" she asked, bouncing on her toes. "You get to run around without a leash because you're free!"

Pluto nodded enthusiastically, giving her a big thumbs-up before scratching at his ear like an untamed pup.

Lily hesitated for just a moment before nudging down the edge of her sock, revealing the delicate silver anklet resting just above the scars that remained. "I don't need my chain anymore either," she whispered, pride soft but unwavering. "See? I'm free too."

Rick's breath caught. He had known this moment would mean something to Lily, but he hadn't realized how much it would mean to him. Watching her stand there, proud and unafraid, showing the world she was free—it did something to him.

Pluto froze, tilting his head as if really seeing her. Then, the costumed dog bent slightly, tapping his paw gently against his own foot in understanding before wagging his tail even harder. With a dramatic flourish, he pointed to her anklet, then to himself, before tracing a big heart over his chest.

Lily's grin stretched wide. "You like it? My Auntie Caroline gave it to me when I was in the hospital. She said I could wear something pretty there instead of my chains."

Pluto clapped his paws together in celebration before reaching down and tapping the anklet again, giving her a playful salute.

Lily straightened proudly. "Yep! No more chains. No more being locked up. Just like you, Pluto!"

Pluto mimed wiping away a tear, then opened his arms wide for another hug. Lily threw herself into it without hesitation, and Rick had to swallow the lump rising in his throat.

A familiar laugh rang out from behind them. "Well, if it isn't my favorite VIP family!"

Rick turned, startled, and broke into a grin as he spotted Adrian—rainbow hair as vibrant as ever under a fabulous light-up headband.

Lily gasped, her eyes lighting up. "Adrian!"

Adrian crouched to her level with an exaggerated gasp. "Lily-bean! Look at you! No oxygen tank, no IV pole—just a princess at the happiest place on Earth!" He glanced up at Rick, his smile turning knowing. "And you—out in the real world, no hospital bed in sight. Didn't I tell you the adventure was just beginning?"

Rick shook his head, chuckling. "You did. And for once, I'm glad you were right."

"Ah, music to my ears," Adrian teased before giving Darcy a once-over. "And I see the world's most overprotective best friend is still standing guard. You let him breathe at all, Mr. Darcy?"

Darcy smirked. "Only when I'm too busy making sure he's hydrated."

Adrian let out a dramatic sigh. "Well, at least he's consistent."

A cast member cleared their throat. "Would you like a family picture?"

Darcy, grinning, handed over his phone. "We absolutely need documentation of this historic moment."

Rick knelt beside Lily, resting a hand on her shoulder as the kids gathered around. Sam stood beside him, hugging his side. And for the first time in a long time, Rick didn't have to remind himself to smile.

"Adrian," Rick called. "Join us for a picture, please."

As the camera clicked for a final time, the announcer came over the PA system, reminding guests that the fireworks would be starting in half an hour. Adrian clapped his hands together. "Ooh, perfect timing. Fireworks, sugar-high children, and a family full of survivors. What could be better?"

Rick exhaled, looking at the kids—at Lily's joy, at Walter's quiet confidence, at Sam's laughter, and Ellie's excited bouncing. He looked at Darcy beside him, always steady, and Marianne playfully rolling her eyes at Adrian's antics—until now.

Adrian, still chatting, waved a hand. "Oh, speaking of miracle recoveries, Marianne, I ran into Greg Willoughby, your old partner, last week. He and his wife just had their baby. A little girl. Would you believe that?"

Rick caught the shift in Marianne instantly. The easy joy in her expression disappeared, replaced by something guarded, her shoulders tensing ever so slightly. She dropped her gaze to the kids, brushing a stray curl from Ellie's forehead as if she hadn't heard.

Rick frowned slightly but didn't press. Instead, he glanced at Adrian, who—ever observant—had also noticed but kept his tone breezy. "Anyway, it's good to see you all. Glad to see how well you're all doing."

Rick filed that moment away, making a mental note. Something about Greg Willoughby had struck a nerve with Marianne.

As promised, minutes later the fireworks burst across the sky, brilliant reds and blues illuminating the night. Lily clutched her new stuffed dog, blinking sleepily up at Rick, and in that moment, he knew—this was more than just a holiday. This was their first Fourth of July as a family, truly free. No chains. No locked doors. Just open skies and the promise of tomorrow.

Rick watched as Lily hugged her new stuffed plush and blinked up at her beloved Uncle Darcy with tired but happy eyes. "This was the best day ever. Thanks for bringing us."

Darcy kissed her forehead. "I'm glad, Sweetheart."

An hour later, they were being dropped off by the bus at the parking lot. Farewells were brief as the younger kids barely managed to keep their eyes open. Caroline and Marianne headed off to Marianne's car while Darcy took the rest of them to his SUV.

Within minutes, the boys were asleep in the backseat— Sam curled up in his booster seat and Walter knocked out against the window—while their sisters were securely fastened in their car seat and booster seat in the middle row, Ellie's hand clasped in Lily's.

Rick leaned his head back against the headrest, exhaling slowly.

Darcy glanced at him, one hand on the wheel, the other adjusting the air conditioning. "You good?"

Rick nodded, staring out at the road. "Yeah."

A comfortable silence settled between them, the kind that only came with years of friendship, of knowing each other beyond words.

After a while, Darcy spoke again. "You know, back in the day, if someone told me you'd be a father of four, spending your Fourth of July at a theme park in a ridiculous fairytale t-shirt, I'd have laughed in their face."

Rick smirked. "Yeah, well, back in the day, if someone told me you'd voluntarily sit through a princess musical ride, I'd have thought they were insane."

Darcy sighed dramatically. "You owe me for that, by the way. Ellie must have sung that song at the top of her lungs the entire time we were in our clamshell."

Rick laughed, shaking his head.

The freeway stretched ahead, dark and open, the occasional car passing by.

Darcy tapped the steering wheel idly, then glanced over again, more serious this time. "You really are doing okay, aren't you?"

Rick hesitated for a second, then nodded. "Yeah. I mean, there are still moments. But today?" He exhaled. "Today was good. Really good."

Darcy nodded, his gaze fixed on the road. "Told you, man. Life's not over just because you went through hell."

Rick let the words sink in, feeling their weight, their truth. He glanced at Darcy. "Thanks for today."

Darcy smirked. "Hey, what are best friends for?"

Rick shook his head with a grin. "Apparently, expensive theme park tickets and emotional pep talks."

Darcy snorted. "You're lucky I like you."

Chapter 64

> Seeing my sons stand guard for Lily, their loyalty unwavering, fills my heart with indescribable pride, reassuring me that despite the darkness we've faced, the bonds of family, faith, and love remain our greatest strength.
> – Rick's Journal

The steady hum of activity around Rick—the clatter of keyboards, ringing phones, and murmured conversations—offered an odd sense of comfort. After a few months at Darcy's firm, he was slowly finding his rhythm in the routine. As he was sorting through a pile of mail for Darcy, his desk phone buzzed, lighting up with Caroline's name. A call during school hours was unexpected, and Rick's stomach tightened as he quickly answered.

"Caroline? What's wrong?" he asked, his voice edged with concern.

"Rick," Caroline began, her tone calm but serious, "Lily's in the principal's office. There was an incident on the playground. A boy was taunting her and saying awful things. Rick, she—fought back."

Rick's stomach clenched, heat surging through his veins. Lily was in the principal's office? On the first day of school? Someone had taunted his baby girl? His grip tightened around the phone. "Fought back?" His voice came out sharper than intended. His mind raced. "Is she okay?"

"She's shaken, but she's fine," Caroline reassured him. "Walter stepped in, too. The principal wants to talk to you. Can you come?"

Rick didn't hesitate. "I'm on my way," he said, already grabbing his jacket.

As he hung up, Darcy walked past his cubicle and stopped, noticing Rick's tense expression. "Everything okay?" he asked.

"Lily's in the principal's office," Rick said, running a hand through his hair. "Some kid was taunting her. Caroline says they're all in the office."

Darcy frowned. "Do you need me to come with you?"

Rick shook his head. "No, but thanks. Can I work on this stuff tomorrow?"

"Don't worry about it," Darcy said. "Take whatever time you need. I'll have Jennifer go through my mail. And Rick—if you need support, just call."

Rick nodded, appreciating the offer but knowing this was something he needed to face alone.

The office at Austen Academy buzzed with subdued first day activity as Rick stepped inside, scanning for familiar faces. Caroline was already there, standing near the reception desk, her expression calm but concerned. She stepped forward when she saw him.

"She's okay," Caroline said softly, placing a reassuring hand on his arm. "A little shaken, but she's holding it together. Walter's with her."

Rick exhaled slowly, some of the tension in his chest easing. "Thanks for being here," he said. "I appreciate it."

"Of course," Caroline replied. "They're family."

The receptionist directed them to the principal's office. Rick squared his shoulders as he stepped inside. It was only the first day, and already his kids were in the office.

Lily sat in a small chair, clutching Leo the Lion tightly, her cheeks flushed and her eyes red. Walter sat beside her, his arms crossed, a faint bruise darkening his cheek. Across the desk, the principal, Mrs. Weston, sat with an expression of professional calm tinged with compassion.

"Mr. Wentworth," she greeted, standing to shake his hand. "Thank you for coming. Please, have a seat."

Rick glanced at his children, his heart aching at their visible distress, before lowering himself into a chair. "What happened?" he asked, his voice steady despite the storm of emotions brewing inside him.

Mrs. Weston folded her hands on the desk. "There was an altercation on the playground," she began. "A student, Jason, was taunting Lily at recess. He made inappropriate comments about her, her situation, and you. Lily confronted him, and when he became more aggressive verbally and physically, she responded by pushing him. Walter stepped in to support her, and things escalated further."

Rick's jaw tightened. "What exactly did this boy Jason say?" he asked softly.

The principal hesitated, glancing at Lily. "According to the yard duty attendant, he mocked her for having a stuffed animal, calling her a baby and said she was too old for toys. There were some hurtful comments about the fact she was held back a grade, and he might have said that she was stupid and she didn't belong with normal kids. And when that didn't get a reaction, he brought you into it by saying you were weak and that real men don't let themselves get locked up."

Rick's fists clenched under the desk, anger burning through him. "Someone heard all this and didn't do anything?" He forced himself to take a steadying breath before he lost his temper further. "Lily fought back?"

"She told him to stop, and when he didn't, she pushed him," Principal Weston explained. "He shoved her in response, and Walter intervened."

Rick turned to his daughter, his voice soft. "Lily, is that what happened?"

Tears welled in her eyes as she nodded, clutching Leo tighter. "He wouldn't stop, Daddy," she said, her voice trembling. "He said mean things about you and about me."

Rick placed a gentle hand on her shoulder. "You were brave to stand up for yourself," he said. "But when we get home, we'll talk about other ways to handle these kinds of situations, okay?"

Lily nodded, her lip quivering. "Okay."

Rick shifted his attention to Walter, pride flickering in his chest. "Walter, you stepped in for your sister?"

Walter nodded, his jaw set. "Yeah, Dad. Jason was a bully. He even grabbed Lily's cane and threw it in the bushes! I wasn't going to let him keep saying and doing those things."

Rick rested a hand on Walter's shoulder. "Thank you for protecting her," he said. "That means the world to me."

The principal cleared her throat. "Mr. Wentworth, while I understand the circumstances, the school has a zero-tolerance policy for physical altercations. Both Lily and Walter will need to accept disciplinary action."

Rick nodded. "I understand, Mrs. Weston," he said. "But I hope Jason's behavior is being addressed as well."

"It is," the principal assured him. "His parents have been notified, and he will face consequences for his actions."

Rick felt a flicker of satisfaction then raised another concern. "Principal, I'm also concerned about the yard duty attendant who witnessed this harassment and didn't intervene. Has that been addressed as well?"

The principal paused, her cheeks coloring slightly as she realized the oversight. "I—that has not been addressed yet, Mr. Wentworth, but I assure you, we will look into it."

Caroline, who had been quietly observing the exchange, stepped forward, her tone stern and her demeanor resolute. "Principal Weston, given Lily's well-documented history and the trauma she's endured, it's deeply concerning that Harriet Smith failed to act. Lily's situation is not just any case; it's a public testament to what she's overcome. We can't let her down again by dismissing the lack of protection she received. It sounds as if it should never have escalated so far with the other kid stealing her cane. This should surely weigh into how the school considers the fairness and the severity of the punishment for all involved."

Mrs. Weston nodded, clearly embarrassed but recognizing the gravity of Caroline's words. "You're absolutely right, Miss Bingley. We will review our policies and staff responses immediately. And regarding the disciplinary actions for Lily and Walter, I think it's appropriate under these circumstances to reconsider the penalties they are facing. It's clear they were reacting to provocation and defending themselves from ongoing harassment. We will call you tonight after our board meeting if that is okay with you, Mr. Wentworth?"

Rick exhaled slowly, a mix of relief and gratitude evident. "Thank you, Principal Weston. That means a lot to us, knowing the school understands the context and is willing to consider it seriously."

As they drove away from the school, the car was quiet, the earlier tension still lingering. Walter and Sam talked in low voices in the back seat, while Lily sat in the middle row, her small hands clutching Leo tightly. Finally, she spoke, her voice hesitant.

"Daddy, am I too old for Leo?"

Rick glanced back at her, surprised. "Too old? What makes you ask that?"

Lily stared down at the stuffed lion, her fingers brushing over its frayed mane. "Jason said I was. He said nine-year-olds don't carry stuffed animals. And—maybe he's right. None of the other kids have them."

Rick pulled the car into a nearby parking lot and shifted into park, turning to face her. "Lily, do you know why most kids your age don't carry stuffed animals?"

Lily shook her head.

"It's because they've had dozens of them," Rick explained. "When they were little, they probably had piles of stuffed animals—different ones for different days or moods. Over time, they decided which ones they wanted to keep, and they outgrew the rest."

Lily looked up at him, her wide eyes filled with uncertainty. "But I didn't have that."

"No, Sweetheart, you didn't," Rick said softly. "You only had Bear Bear. He wasn't just a toy; he was your friend, your comfort when things were scary. And now you have Leo. He's not just a stuffed animal—he's part of the love and safety you deserve."

Lily's lip trembled. "So, it's okay to still need him?"

Rick smiled, brushing a tear from her cheek. "It's more than okay," he said. "Leo is special, just like you. In fact, do you know, there are adults who have stuffed animals they take to work?"

"Really?"

"Yes." Rick smiled. "There's a pretty awesome lawyer at Uncle Darcy's law firm who has a stuffed animal she keeps in her office. She calls it an emotional support stuffed animal. And if that kick-butt lawyer lady is able to have one, I don't see why you can't."

From his seat, Walter chimed in. "Jason's just a bully, Lily. He doesn't know anything."

"Yeah," Sam said, his voice stronger than usual. "Leo's awesome, and so are you."

Rick turned slightly, caught off guard. Sam had always been the quiet one, hesitant to pick sides, especially after visiting their mother up north a couple months earlier. But here he was, standing up for his sister without hesitation.

Chapter 65

> After ten years shadowed by Louisa's twisted semblance of
> affection, my first date with Marianne gently washed away the
> vestiges of confinement and renewed my belief in the possibility of
> pure, untainted love.
> – Rick's Journal

Rick stared at himself in the mirror, tugging at the collar of his button-up like it was a noose.

This was stupid. He felt stupid. He wasn't ready for this. Wasn't good at this. And yet—

A knock at the door interrupted his downward spiral. Before he could respond, Darcy strolled in with the confidence of someone who owned the place.

Rick sighed, rubbing his temples. "Ever heard of knocking and waiting?"

Darcy smirked. "Ever heard of locking your door?"

"What do you want?" Rick groaned, turning away from the mirror.

Darcy folded his arms, leaning against the doorframe with the same easy arrogance he always had. "Just here to make sure you don't completely self-destruct before your big date."

Rick scoffed. "It's not a big date."

Darcy arched a brow. "Oh, no? So, you're not taking a very beautiful, very patient woman out for coffee and cake for the first time since escaping the pit of despair?"

Rick glared. "Do not call my trauma 'the pit of despair.'"

Darcy ignored him. "And you're not about to have an internal meltdown over whether you deserve to be happy?"

Rick clenched his jaw. "I hate you."

"Right back at you, bud," Darcy quipped. Then he clapped his hands together. "All right, let's get serious. You're spiraling. So, let's cut to the chase. Why do you look like you're about to walk into an interrogation instead of a nice night out with a very lovely lady?"

Rick exhaled sharply, dragging a hand down his face. "Because I don't do this."

Darcy rolled his eyes. "Yeah, no kidding. But guess what? Neither does she."

Rick frowned. "What do you mean?"

Darcy shrugged. "I mean, Marianne isn't sitting there thinking, 'Wow, I hope Rick is the perfect man who has it all figured out and doesn't have a single issue to his name.' She knows what you've been through, man. The first time she saw you, you were in a dress with hair down to your waist, looking like you just crawled out of a gothic horror novel. And guess what? She still likes you."

Rick swallowed. "Yeah, but—"

"Nope." Darcy held up a hand. "Don't but me right now. This isn't about Louisa. This isn't about what she did to you. This is about you choosing to be something more than what she made you feel like."

Rick clenched his jaw. "And what if I can't be?"

Darcy's gaze softened just slightly. "Then you let someone love you anyway."

Rick inhaled sharply, the weight of those words settling into his chest.

Darcy exhaled, stepping closer. "Look, man. You survived something unimaginable. And now you get to have this moment. Here you have a choice. A chance at something good." His lips quirked. "So don't ruin it by being an idiot."

Rick huffed a quiet laugh, shaking his head. "That's your real advice?"

Darcy grinned. "If you want something profound, go read a devotional. I'm here to tell you to stop thinking and just go."

Rick rolled his eyes. "Fantastic."

Darcy clapped him on the shoulder. "That's what I'm here for."

Rick exhaled, glancing at his reflection again. Maybe he wasn't ready. Maybe he never would be. But maybe—just maybe—he didn't have to be.

He adjusted his collar one last time, turning to Darcy. "All right. Let's do this."

Darcy smirked. "Atta boy."

Rick took a step toward the door, then hesitated. "Maybe I should stay home with the kids?"

Darcy's smirk faded slightly, his expression steady. "They're good, Rick. Really."

Rick turned back to the mirror, nodding.

Darcy continued, "Lily likes Marianne, you know. She doesn't talk much about the night you were rescued, but she remembers Marianne. She says she made her feel safe."

Rick's throat tightened slightly.

Darcy went on, "Walter, too. He asked me today if you were nervous about tonight. He was smirking when he said it, so it's apparently made it onto his list of things to tease you about. That's progress."

Rick let out a slow breath.

Darcy leaned against the dresser. "And Sam? He's talking again. Not a lot, but more than before. He and Walter were actually playing video games together earlier. No arguing, no silent treatment. Just being brothers." He nudged Rick's shoulder. "That's on you, man. You got them through the worst of it."

Rick let that settle for a moment.

Darcy arched a brow. "So—are you gonna keep punishing yourself, or are you going to go have a good night with a woman who actually cares about you?"

Rick met his best friend's gaze in the mirror. "I'm working on it."

Darcy smirked. "Well, tonight's a good place to start."

Rick grabbed his jacket, squared his shoulders, and walked out the door.

By the time he reached Marianne's condo, the confidence he'd left with had started to unravel. Rick wiped his palms on his jeans for what felt like the hundredth time, pacing the length of the sidewalk outside Marianne's condo building. His watch ticked steadily, mocking him as 7:00 PM drew closer.

He had planned every detail meticulously, but his nerves twisted in his stomach like a storm. His phone buzzed. A text message from Darcy.

> Darcy: You're going to be great. Relax.

Rick let out a breath, a faint smile tugging at his lips. Darcy meant well, but the reassurance didn't completely settle the knots in his chest.

He had spent the entire week wrestling with doubt, questioning whether he was ready for this. Whether he deserved this. Truth was, he'd been struggling with his attraction to Marianne since his birthday bowling outing four months ago, trying to ignore the pull, to convince himself it didn't matter. But when he thought about Marianne—her warmth, her patience, the quiet way she had eased into his life—it felt right.

Even asking her out had taken more courage than he thought he had left. After church on Sunday, his heart had pounded in his ears as he approached her.

"Would you like to go out with me?" he had asked, forcing himself to meet her gaze. "Just the two of us. I'd really like to spend more time with you."

Her smile had been immediate, genuine. "I'd like that," she'd replied. "When?"

"Saturday," Rick had managed. "I'll pick you up at seven."

And now, here he was, pacing like a fool, second-guessing everything.

The last time he'd gone on a date, life had been infinitely simpler. He wasn't a single dad carrying the weight of years of trauma. He wasn't trying to balance healing with the hope of a future he barely dared to imagine.

Finally mustering the courage, Rick climbed the steps to Marianne's second-floor condo. His breath hitched when she appeared at the top of the stairs and met him half way.

A warm late-summer breeze stirred the air, the fabric of her dress swaying with her movements. Her dark hair framed her face in loose waves, and when she smiled at him, warm and amused, something inside him settled.

"I was starting to think you were running a marathon," she teased lightly. "You've been pacing the sidewalk for a solid ten minutes."

Rick froze. "You saw that?"

Her laughter was light, genuine. "I did. It was kind of cute, actually."

Rick huffed, a sheepish grin spreading across his face. "Well, now you know my pre-date ritual," he said, offering his arm with a slight bow. "Shall we?"

Marianne slipped her hand through his arm, her touch light but grounding. "Lead the way," she said, her voice soft with quiet confidence.

As they walked to his car, Rick felt his nerves relax, steadied by her presence.

The drive to the coffeehouse was filled with easy conversation, punctuated by laughter. When they arrived, the venue welcomed them with warm lighting and live acoustic music. The air smelled of espresso and cinnamon, and strings of lights twinkled along the exposed brick walls.

"This is lovely," Marianne said, her eyes taking in the eclectic décor, the vibrant energy of the place. "How did you find it?"

Rick leaned forward slightly in his seat, his voice warm. "Darcy mentioned it, but I thought of you when he described it. I know how much you appreciate art and creativity, and this place just felt—right."

Marianne's cheeks flushed faintly, her gaze softening. "You thought of me?" she asked, teasing but touched.

Rick nodded, a shy smile tugging at his lips. "Yeah. I figured you'd enjoy the atmosphere. It seemed like your kind of place."

Marianne's eyes lingered on his, her smile deepening. "You figured right," she said softly.

When the friendly waitress greeted them, they ordered coffee and chose to share a decadent slice of their famous three-layer chocolate cake. As had become the norm during their friendship, the conversation flowed as effortlessly as the coffee.

"Hey," Rick said, stirring his coffee absently as something tugged at his memory, "back at Disneyland, Adrian mentioned a paramedic named Greg Willoughby. Was he the other medic from the night I was rescued?"

Marianne visibly tensed. The easy light in her eyes flickered, replaced by something guarded.

Rick frowned, setting his spoon down. "Marianne?"

She exhaled, her fingers tracing the rim of her cup before finally meeting his gaze. "Greg is my ex-boyfriend," she finally said, her voice steady but reflective. "I thought he was my future. But he—wasn't the man I thought he was."

Rick's brow furrowed. "What happened?"

She sighed, her fingers playing with the edge of her napkin. "He cheated," she said simply. "And made sure I found out in the most humiliating way possible. It ended badly. You heard about the baby? For a long time, I thought it was my fault."

Rick clenched his jaw. "It wasn't." His voice was firm, conviction ringing in every syllable. "You didn't deserve that, Marianne."

She smiled faintly, though it didn't quite reach her eyes. "Thank you. I've spent a lot of time learning to trust again. It's not easy."

Rick nodded, his chest tightening at the vulnerability in her voice. He understood that. Maybe more than she realized.

The open mic portion of the evening started soon after, and when Rick's name was called, Marianne's curious gaze followed him. "You didn't tell me you signed up," she said, surprised but intrigued.

Rick shrugged, his smile a little sheepish. "I thought I'd give it a try. Wish me luck."

At the mic, he searched the audience until he found Marianne's face. Her supportive smile gave him the courage he needed.

"Hi, everyone. I'm Rick Wentworth, and this is something I wrote after a counseling session this week. It's about second chances."

He pulled out the journal Darcy had given him on his birthday. Taking a deep breath, he began to read.

"Second Chances
I stood among the ruins bare,
A man once lost in deep despair.
Each breath a ghost, each step unsure,
A past that lingers, wounds unpure.

The weight of years, the loss, the pain,
The echoes calling back again—
To chains once worn, to prayers denied,
To nights I thought I'd surely die.

Yet through the dark, a whisper grew,
Not mine alone—God's promise true.
It called me soft, it called me near,

Through guilt, through doubt, through every tear.

"I have not left, nor turned away,
Through every trial, I have stayed."
Not earned, not won, nor bought, nor sold,
But grace unbroken—strong and bold.

I cried for help, and light broke through,
A voice, a hand, a heart so true.
She pulled me from the dust and stone,
A stranger's strength—yet not alone.

Her hands were steady, warm yet sure,
A healer's touch, both firm and pure.
She saw the wounds I tried to hide,
Yet never turned, nor cast aside.

She whispered hope, she steadied me,
She saw beyond captivity.
She led me through the fractured night,
A lantern lit—a guiding light.

And though I walk with weary feet,
Through valleys dark where sorrows meet,
A whisper calls, a fire remains,
A love relentless, free of chains.

Second chances—could it be true?
Not just from man, but God's hand too?
For all I lost, for all I gave,
Could grace reach past an open grave?

So here I stand, though not yet free,
A man remade, yet still not me.
Yet hope remains, a spark, a light,
A voice that calls me through the night.

Hands once gentle, scarred yet kind,
A soul that sees yet does not bind.
Dark eyes searching, quiet and deep,

Seeing the wounds I swore to keep.

She did not save—God did through her,
A mercy fierce, a love so sure.
Not mending—merely standing near,
Could love still find me—even here?"

When he finished, silence hung in the air, stretching just long enough to make his chest tighten. Then, the room erupted into applause.

Rick's gaze instinctively sought Marianne. Her eyes glistened, her hands clasped tightly in front of her, but it was the quiet understanding in her expression that made his pulse stutter.

As he returned to their table, she reached for his hand, her touch warm and steady. "That was beautiful, Rick," she murmured, her voice soft yet certain. "I don't think I'll ever forget it."

Rick felt heat rise to his cheeks. "Thank you," he said, his voice quieter than he intended. "It's not something I ever thought I'd do, but—you helped inspire me."

Marianne's fingers curled slightly around his. "I could tell," she said, her smile tinged with something deeper. "You weren't just telling a story—you were telling your truth. And I heard it."

Rick swallowed, the weight of her gaze settling over him. She had noticed.

"It's not just about second chances, is it?" she continued, her voice quieter now. "It's about grace, yes? The kind you don't earn, the kind that finds you even when you think you're too far gone."

His throat tightened. He hadn't said those words exactly, but somehow, she had understood.

Marianne gave his hand a gentle squeeze. "I don't think it was just my hands that pulled you out of that cellar, Rick," she said. "I think God was already reaching for you. I just got to be there to see it."

Rick let out a slow breath, somewhere between humbled and unsteady.

"I'm honored, Rick," she continued, her voice steady, certain. "Not just to hear your words but to witness what they mean."

Several hours later, Darcy strolled into the kitchen, looking far too smug for someone who had just spent the night wrangling

286

four kids, and dropped into the chair across from Rick and stretched his legs out with a dramatic sigh. "Well," he announced, grinning like a man who had won a battle, "your kids are officially obsessed with me."

Rick smirked over the rim of his mug. "You say that now. Wait until they start calling you for every little thing."

Darcy snorted. "Please. If those little monsters call me at three a.m. for anything short of a fire, I'm blocking them."

Rick chuckled, shaking his head. "They had fun?"

"Oh, yeah. Fries, burgers, ice cream—Lily even talked the guy at the counter into giving her an extra cherry for her sundae."

Rick raised an eyebrow. "She did?"

Darcy nodded, grinning. "Total Sweetheart move too—tilted her head, gave the guy these big, brown puppy-dog eyes and said, 'Please, sir, may I have another?'"

Rick huffed a quiet laugh. "She's been watching too many old movies."

"Probably." Darcy stole a sip of Rick's coffee, then turned more serious. "But, hey, she was okay, you know? She had a moment at first where she was worried about you being away from us, but once she got focused on dinner, she was okay. I think it was good for her to see you going out without the family or me."

Rick nodded slowly, processing that. "She's trying," he murmured. "She's still struggling, but she's trying."

Darcy set the mug down with a thud. "Speaking of struggling—" He leaned forward, leveling Rick with a pointed look. "Did you kiss her?"

Rick stared in shock. "What?"

"Marianne." Darcy waggled his eyebrows. "The woman you are allegedly dating. Did you kiss?"

Rick groaned, rubbing a hand over his face. "I knew I shouldn't have confided in you."

"You really shouldn't have." Darcy smirked. "So—did you?"

Rick hesitated, then sighed. "No. I didn't."

Darcy tilted his head. "Because of Lily?"

Rick hesitated again before nodding. "No. I mean, yeah. I don't know." He exhaled, setting his mug down. "She still doesn't get it. Not fully. Earlier this week, when the boys teased about me kissing Marianne, she got upset. Really upset."

Darcy frowned, running a hand over his jaw. "Yeah. I figured this would be a thing after the whole Caroline-on-top-of-me fiasco."

Rick huffed a humorless laugh. "She's nine, Darcy. Nine, and she's never seen healthy affection. The only physical interactions she's ever known are Louisa forcing herself on me or watching her hurt me." He swallowed hard. "So, yeah. She hears 'kissing,' and her first instinct is to protect me."

Darcy's face darkened. "That's not fair," he muttered.

Rick shook his head. "No, it's not. But it's where we are."

Darcy exhaled sharply. "So, what's the plan? You just never kiss Marianne? Hope Lily magically figures out that kissing isn't an attack?"

Rick rubbed his face, suddenly feeling exhausted. "I don't know. I just know that right now, it's too soon and not just for her. I have only been kissed by Louisa for the last ten years. This is a huge adjustment. Lily and I both need time."

Darcy nodded, mulling it over. Then, with a casual shrug, he said, "Well, I'll just have to kiss Caroline more often in front of her, then."

Rick stared at him. "What?"

"You heard me." Darcy grinned. "If Lily has only ever seen affection used as a weapon, then it's time we show her something else. Something normal. Something good."

Rick blinked. "That's actually not a terrible idea."

Darcy snorted. "You sound surprised."

"I am."

Darcy kicked him under the table. "Shut up."

Rick chuckled, then sobered again. "I just don't want to push her."

"We won't," Darcy said, suddenly serious. "But we'll let her see it. We'll let her be around it. She doesn't have to understand it all right away, but one day, she will."

Rick took a slow breath, letting that settle. Maybe Darcy was right. Maybe it wasn't about shielding Lily from the idea of affection. It was about showing her a different version of it.

Maybe one day, when he finally did kiss Marianne, Lily wouldn't be afraid. For now, though, baby steps.

Rick patted Darcy's shoulder. "Appreciate the help."

Darcy grinned. "Hey, that's what I'm here for. Teaching your daughter how to con waiters and normalize kissing? I am the MVP of this family."

Rick shook his head, smiling despite himself. "Yeah, yeah. Just don't go overboard."

"No promises."

Chapter 66

> Today I received a gentle reminder that love can indeed be sweet
> and pure, a stark contrast to the shadows of the cellar.
> – Rick's Journal

Lily was lounging on the couch, her legs tucked underneath her, the wedding magazine open in her lap. Her fingers ran absentmindedly over the glossy pages, eyes scanning over the pictures of lavish gowns, her face thoughtful. But she wasn't really reading—she was absorbed in the world of fantasy, the world of dresses and beauty that had once seemed so out of reach for her.

Caroline sat beside her, scrolling on her phone, while Darcy leaned against the kitchen counter, mug in hand, as usual. Rick had just returned from settling Ellie down for her nap when it happened.

The moment was simple, one that should have passed unnoticed. Darcy walked over to Caroline, bent down with a teasing grin, and pressed a kiss to her cheek. Before he could pull away, Caroline laughed, grabbed his shirt, and pulled him down for a proper kiss—quick, sure, and filled with affection.

Lily froze.

Rick noticed it immediately. The sudden stiffening of her body. Her eyes locked onto the kiss, wide and unblinking. Her small hands curled tightly into the couch cushions, the wedding magazine now forgotten on the floor. She was trembling.

Rick's stomach twisted.

"Lily?" Caroline asked, her voice gentle, noticing the change in the room. She reached out to touch Lily's arm, but her movements were slow, careful.

Lily blinked rapidly, her breath catching. Then, in a small, trembling voice, she whispered, "Why did you hurt Uncle Darcy?"

The words landed like a punch. In that moment, the room seemed to stop. Darcy's smirk dropped. Caroline's face turned pale. Rick's heart splintered into a thousand pieces.

"Sweetheart, no one is hurting me," Darcy said, crouching down, his voice soft and soothing. He held up his hands in a calm, reassuring gesture. "Caroline wasn't hurting me, Lily. I promise you."

But Lily's body was rigid, her chest rising and falling erratically. Her eyes darted between the adults, confusion, and fear written all over her face. Rick saw it in her—she didn't understand. She couldn't. She had seen too much, learned too much too early.

Rick moved toward her, kneeling down beside her. He placed a steady hand on her shoulder, his voice firm but kind. "Lily, Sweetheart, listen to me," he said, holding her gaze. "Kisses are supposed to be good. They're supposed to be shared between people who care about each other. But I know it's hard to understand that right now. You've only seen kisses used to hurt people. But not every kiss is like that."

Her hands tightened around Leo the Lion, her eyes still wide. Rick could see her trying to process the words, trying to make sense of something that had always been twisted in her mind.

Caroline shifted slightly, her tone still gentle but insistent. "Lily, I care for your Uncle Darcy. I love him. And we kiss because we choose to. Because we want to. It's not like before. It's not the same."

Lily's eyes flickered back to Caroline, still unsure. Her lip trembled, and Rick felt it deep in his chest, the weight of her confusion. Caroline waited patiently, holding Lily's gaze, not rushing her. The room was filled with a kind of heavy silence, the kind that only comes from a child struggling to untangle trauma.

Finally, Lily's voice broke the stillness. "So… kisses aren't always bad?"

Rick's chest tightened. His heart ached for her.

Caroline nodded slowly, brushing a strand of hair behind Lily's ear. "No, Sweetheart. Kisses aren't always bad. They're good when they come from a place of love."

Darcy, sensing the fragile moment, chimed in with his usual lightness, but with a softness that matched the mood. "Unless it's an old lady with too much lipstick," he teased. "Then, yeah, run."

Lily blinked, her face shifting for a moment as the corners of her mouth twitched, almost smiling.

Rick exhaled, feeling the tension slip away as Lily's giggle filled the room. It wasn't everything, but it was a start. It was a sign that, maybe—just maybe—she was beginning to understand, piece by piece.

Her giggles slowed, and her mind began turning once more, contemplating the new information she had just processed. She glanced at Darcy with a tilt of her head, her voice small but serious. "Are you gonna give Daddy a safe kiss too?" she asked innocently.

The room went still.

Rick froze, feeling the color drain from his face. Caroline's eyes widened. Darcy, though, merely grinned, his face lighting up with mischievous amusement.

Lily, completely unaware of the shock she had just caused, continued. "I mean, you love Daddy too, right? And he only gets kisses from me, Ellie, Walter, and Sam," she added, looking up at Rick with wide eyes. "You never get nice grown-up kisses, Daddy."

Rick groaned, the blood rushing to his face. "Lily—" he started, but Darcy, with his trademark grin, leaned in, barely suppressing his laughter.

"Aw, Rick," Darcy drawled, his voice low and teasing. "Didn't know you felt neglected."

Rick glared, his embarrassment growing by the second. "Don't you dare."

Darcy laughed and leaned over to plant a loud, exaggerated kiss on Rick's lips.

Lily's face lit up. "Yay! Now Daddy got a safe kiss too!" she exclaimed with glee.

Rick sighed dramatically, feeling his face burn as he rubbed at his mouth. "Great. I feel so much better."

Darcy patted him on the shoulder, a playful smirk still tugging at his lips. "Always here for you, man."

Caroline, wiping tears of laughter from her eyes, spoke up. "Lily, Sweetheart, I think Daddy might want his nice kisses to come from Miss Marianne."

Lily's face brightened. She glanced at Rick, her voice filled with genuine curiosity. "Is that true, Daddy?"

Rick, feeling trapped, but with a faint smile tugging at his lips, cleared his throat. "Uh—maybe," he said, trying to avoid Darcy's gaze.

Darcy's grin grew wider. "Make that more like definitely," he teased.

Lily's face lit up, her excitement palpable. "Oh! Maybe she'll give you a safe kiss soon!"

Darcy, ever the instigator, pulled out his phone, swiping at the screen. "You know what? Let's ask her."

Rick's eyes widened. "Darcy—"

But it was too late. Darcy had already dialed Marianne's number, hitting speakerphone before Rick could protest.

The phone rang twice before Marianne's cheerful voice filled the room. "Marianne Dashwood speaking."

Lily, all too eager, leaned in. "Hi, Miss Marianne! It's Lily!"

Marianne laughed warmly. "Hi, Sweetheart! Did you have fun shopping today?"

Lily bounced excitedly, then grew serious. "Miss Marianne?"

"Yes, honey?"

Lily took a deep breath, then declared, "I just wanted to tell you that I give you permission."

Rick froze. His heart stopped for a second.

Caroline, unable to contain her laughter, shook her head. Darcy grinned, looking like he'd just won a prize.

Marianne, sounding confused, asked, "Oh! Um—for what, Sweetheart?"

Lily nodded sagely, as if this was a declaration of monumental importance. "For safe kisses with Daddy. But you have to promise you won't kiss him unless he wants it. Only safe kisses."

Rick's face turned a deep shade of crimson.

Darcy was practically choking with laughter, and Marianne's response came out in a burst of hilarity. "Oh—oh wow. Well, that's very generous of you, Lily. I promise I will only give your daddy safe kisses if he wants them."

Lily grinned. "You're welcome! I just wanted to tell you."

Rick, mortified, grabbed the phone from Darcy. "Okay, we're done here."

Marianne, still laughing, said, "Are we? Because I think this is a very important moment."

Darcy, full of mischief, leaned in. "Yeah, Rick. This is monumental."

Rick sighed deeply, rubbing his temples. "You all are enjoying this way too much."

Lily, snuggling against him, beamed. "I just want you to be happy, Daddy."

Rick's heart softened immediately. He kissed the top of her head, his voice quiet with emotion. "I am, baby girl."

Marianne's voice came through once more, teasing yet gentle. "Just think, Rick, with Lily's permission, we're practically halfway to matrimony!"

Darcy elbowed him lightly. "One double wedding coming right up!"

Rick rolled his eyes, but the smile on his face couldn't be hidden. "You're insufferable."

Caroline laughed, shaking her head. "And yet, you'd be lost without him."

Rick chuckled quietly, shaking his head. "All right, I'm hanging up, Marianne. I'll see you tonight." He ended the call, his heart lighter than it had been in days.

Lily beamed up at him, her smile pure and innocent, her joy untainted. And Rick, for the first time in a long while, felt something truly new inside of him.

They were healing. They were whole. They were moving forward. Together.

Chapter 67

> I'm learning to lean not on my own understanding but to trust that
> God's justice transcends earthly courts.
> – Rick's Journal

The soft glow of morning sunlight seeped through the blinds in Darcy's office, casting long slants of light across the polished wood desk. Shelves lined with legal tomes and framed degrees framed the room, a testament to Darcy's precision and discipline. The air smelled of leather, paper, and the faint trace of coffee that had long since gone cold.

Rick sat stiffly, a lukewarm cup in his hands, its warmth faded, much like his patience. Across from him, Darcy leaned back in his chair, his sharp blue eyes steady, his expression unreadable. "I got some news this morning," Darcy said, his voice measured but serious. "Louisa's lawyers and the district attorney have reached an agreement. She's pleading not guilty by reason of insanity."

Rick's grip tightened around the cup. His stomach churned.

"What does that mean?" he asked, his voice low, clipped.

Darcy's gaze didn't waver. "It means she's accepting some responsibility, but she won't serve prison time. Instead, she's agreed to court-mandated psychiatric care at the state hospital for the next ten years."

Rick set the cup down with a sharp clink. His jaw locked. "Ten years?" His voice rose. "That's it? After everything she's done?"

Darcy nodded solemnly. "I know it doesn't feel like enough, and I agree with you. But this deal spares you and the kids from having to testify in court. No cross-examinations. No reliving the worst moments of your lives in front of a jury and the media."

Rick leaned forward, his hands gripping the edge of the desk. "So, she gets to avoid prison because she's claiming insanity? What about accountability? What about justice?"

Darcy met his gaze without flinching. "This is the justice system, Rick," he said. "It's not perfect. But the state hospital isn't a spa retreat. She'll be under strict supervision, undergoing treatment, and unable to harm anyone else."

Rick exhaled sharply, his mind tangled in a web of anger, frustration, and an aching sense of unfinished business. He wanted to believe it was enough. That ten years in a psychiatric facility meant something. But it felt like another escape, another way for Louisa to evade the full weight of what she'd done.

"So—that's it?" His voice was quieter now, strained. "That's how it ends?"

Darcy shook his head. "Not entirely. There's still the option of a civil suit."

Rick frowned, the thought both appealing and overwhelming. "What would that even accomplish? She's already being sent away. What's left?"

Darcy leaned forward, folding his hands on the desk. "Accountability," he said. "And financial support for you and the kids as you rebuild your lives. This isn't about revenge. It's about making sure your family has what they need—therapy, education, stability."

Rick hesitated, the weight of the decision pressing down on him. "But wouldn't that drag everything out?" He ran a hand through his hair, exhausted at the thought of another legal battle. "Haven't we been through enough?"

"It could," Darcy admitted. "But if her lawyers are willing to settle, it could mean closure and resources for your family without a long fight. We wouldn't pursue it unless it was in your best interest."

Rick rubbed his temples, his thoughts colliding. The kids had come so far—Lily no longer flinched at loud voices, Walter was learning to trust him, and Sam had finally started opening up. Did he really want to risk reopening old wounds?

"I don't want to drag the kids through this," he said at last. "They've already been through enough."

Darcy's expression was steady, his voice quiet. "I get it. But think about what this could mean for them in the long run. This isn't just about holding Louisa accountable. It's about ensuring your family's future."

Rick stared at the desk, his jaw tight. He didn't want another battle. But he had spent too many years just surviving. Maybe it was time to start building something instead. He looked up. "Do you really think it's worth it?"

Darcy met his gaze without hesitation. "I do. And you wouldn't be doing it alone. I'd be with you every step of the way."

Rick exhaled slowly, his shoulders sagging under the weight of it all. "I'll think about it," he said. "But if we do this—it's for the kids. Not for me."

Darcy nodded, a faint smile tugging at his lips. "That's all I'd expect. And Rick, no matter what you decide, you're already doing everything you can for your family. That's what matters."

Rick leaned back in his chair, his mind still heavy but a little clearer. "Thanks, Darcy," he said quietly. "For everything."

Darcy stood and extended a hand, his grip firm, steady. "You don't have to thank me. That's what friends are for."

As Rick clasped his hand, he felt a flicker of relief amid the uncertainty. He wasn't alone in this—whatever this turned out to be.

As Rick left Darcy's office, the weight of the conversation still pressing on his chest, he found himself dialing Marianne's number before he could second-guess it. If there was anyone who could help him untangle the mess in his head—and maybe even make him forget it for a little while—it was her.

The café was warm, the scent of cinnamon and freshly brewed coffee wrapping around Rick like a quiet reassurance. He sat across from Marianne, fingers curled around a ceramic mug, the heat pressing into his skin. Across from him, she studied him with quiet concern, her dark almond eyes searching his face.

"You've been quiet," she said gently, tilting her head slightly. "Even for you."

Rick exhaled, staring down at his coffee. He had spent the entire afternoon replaying his conversation with Darcy, wrestling with the weight of Louisa's fate, the civil suit, and everything that came with it. But here, with Marianne, the urge to speak won out over his usual instinct to lock it all inside.

"I got news today," he said finally, his voice low. "Louisa took a deal. She's going to a psychiatric hospital for the next ten years."

Marianne blinked, absorbing the words. "And how do you feel about that?"

Rick let out a dry laugh, shaking his head. "That's the question, isn't it? I should be relieved. It means no court battles, no dragging the kids into testimony, no endless public scrutiny." He ran a hand through his hair. "But ten years feels—light. She did horrible things. And she gets to avoid prison because she's 'insane'?"

Marianne's eyes softened, her fingers tracing the rim of her cup. "Rick, you've been fighting for so long. I know it doesn't feel like enough, but maybe this is still justice. Maybe it's not about how much time she serves but the fact that she's away, that she can't hurt you or the kids ever again."

Rick studied her, the way her voice held both certainty and care, the way she didn't try to push him in one direction but simply offered a different way to look at it. He wasn't used to that—wasn't used to being seen like this.

"Darcy wants me to file a civil suit," he admitted. "For financial support, accountability—closure, I guess."

Marianne nodded, watching him carefully. "And what do you want?"

Rick sighed, leaning back against his chair. "I don't know. I just know I'm tired." He rubbed his face. "I'm tired of fighting. Tired of thinking about her, about what she did. I just want to live my life without her shadow looming over it."

Marianne reached across the table, hesitating just a second before placing her hand over his. Her fingers were warm, grounding. "You deserve that," she said softly. "And you don't have to make a decision tonight. Just—let yourself breathe."

Rick swallowed past the lump in his throat. "Easier said than done."

A small smile played on her lips. "Lucky for you, I'm stubborn. I'll remind you as many times as you need."

He huffed a quiet laugh, shaking his head. "You really are something else, Marianne Dashwood."

She smirked. "I try."

The moment stretched, the air between them shifting. He was too aware of her, of the warmth of her hand still resting over his, of the way she tilted her head slightly as if she were waiting for something. And suddenly, Rick found himself wondering what it would be like to kiss her.

The thought knocked the breath out of him. It wasn't like he hadn't considered it before. He wasn't blind. Marianne was beautiful. But it had always been an abstract thought, something he'd never let himself dwell on.

Now? Sitting across from her, the soft glow of the café lights reflecting in her eyes, her lips just barely curved into that teasing smile—it didn't feel abstract anymore. His throat went dry. He needed to get out of his own head. Fast.

"Marianne," he said, his voice a little rougher than he intended, "if you keep looking at me like that, I'm going to start thinking you're up to something."

Marianne arched a brow, entirely unfazed. "And what exactly do you think I'm up to, Rick Wentworth?"

He exhaled, shaking his head, trying to smother the heat creeping up his neck. "I don't know, but you've got that look."

She grinned, all warmth and mischief. "You mean my I'm about to win an argument look?"

"Exactly," he muttered, making her laugh.

She tilted her head slightly, still watching him like she knew exactly what was going through his mind. Then, as if the thought had just hit her, her grin widened. "Wait a second." She gasped, mock-scandalized. "Rick Wentworth—did you just think about kissing me?"

Rick choked on his own coffee.

Marianne cackled, sitting back in her chair, clearly delighted by his reaction.

Rick wiped his mouth, scowling at her. "I don't know where you got that idea."

"Oh, come on," she teased, still grinning. "You got all quiet and serious for a second, and then your ears went red. That's basically a confession."

Rick groaned, rubbing a hand over his face. "I hate that you're a paramedic. You notice everything."

Marianne propped her chin on her hand, looking far too pleased with herself. "You love that about me."

Rick gave her a long, unimpressed look. "That remains to be determined."

She let out a soft hum, watching him. Then, in a voice far too innocent, she asked, "Well? Does it count?"

Rick frowned. "Does what count?"

Marianne leaned in slightly, her lips twitching. "As a safe kiss."

He froze.

Marianne barely held back her laughter. "I mean, technically, you didn't kiss me, so I suppose Lily won't be needing to launch an official investigation. But the intent was definitely there."

Rick groaned again, dropping his head into his hands. "I'm never going to live this down, am I?"

Marianne grinned, sipping her coffee. "Not a chance."

Rick shook his head, but he was smiling now. It was ridiculous. She was ridiculous. And for the first time all day, the weight in his chest didn't feel quite as crushing.

As they finished their coffee, Rick glanced at her, a quiet warmth settling in his chest. Maybe he wasn't ready for everything yet. But this? This was a start.

And maybe, just maybe, he wasn't as alone in it as he thought.

Chapter 68

> Under the glow of the Halloween moon, I knew, without a word spoken, that I had irreversibly fallen for the grace that is Marianne.
> – Rick's Journal

The church lobby hummed with post-service chatter as Rick ushered his kids through the crowd. Walter and Sam were deep in debate over who would get the biggest haul of candy on Halloween, while Ellie clutched Quackers, her other small hand securely in Rick's.

"Daddy, can we say hi to Miss Marianne?" Lily asked, tugging on his sleeve. Her voice was hopeful, her eyes sparkling with excitement.

Rick hesitated but nodded. "Okay, but let's not take up too much of her time," he said, following them as they rushed toward Marianne, who stood manning the merchandise table, chatting with Pastor Fanny.

Marianne spotted them and smiled warmly, crouching down to greet the kids. "Hi, everyone! How are my favorite soccer players and princesses today?"

Ellie beamed, holding Quackers up proudly. "Quackers wants to say hi, too!"

Marianne laughed, gently patting the bunny's head. "Hello, Quackers. It's lovely to see you."

Sam stepped forward, his usual boldness on full display. "Miss Marianne, do you like pizza?"

Marianne tilted her head, her smile unwavering. "I love pizza. Why do you ask?"

"We're having pizza on Halloween after trick-or-treating," Sam declared. "You should come!"

Rick's face flushed as he stepped in quickly. "Sam, I'm sure Miss Marianne has her own plans."

"I don't have any plans," Marianne said, cutting him off gently. Her gaze shifted to Rick, her smile softening. "But only if it's okay with your dad."

Lily chimed in, her voice quiet but insistent. "Please, Daddy? She's so nice. And she saved me."

Rick's throat tightened at Lily's words. He glanced at Marianne, who gave him a reassuring smile. He hesitated, caught between surprise and something dangerously close to relief. He should have expected this—the kids adored Marianne. Yet, hearing them so openly claim her as part of their world sent an unexpected warmth through him. And yet, it unsettled him too. It wasn't just that they wanted her here for Halloween. It was the way Sam had said it. Like she belonged. Like she fit in a space Rick hadn't dared acknowledge was empty.

"If you're sure," he said carefully, then cleared his throat. "The kids—I mean, we—would love to have you."

"I'd love to join," Marianne replied, her eyes bright. "Thank you for inviting me."

Ellie clapped her hands, her excitement contagious. "Quackers says yay, too!"

Caroline appeared beside them, her sly smile instantly making Rick wary. "I think it's a fantastic idea," she said lightly. "After all, the more, the merrier."

Rick shot her a pointed look, but Caroline only shrugged with feigned innocence, her eyes glinting with amusement as she curled into Darcy's side.

Pastor Fanny chuckled as Lily and Ellie wrapped her in warm hugs. "Seems like you're outnumbered, Rick," she said with a wink.

As they walked to the car, the kids chattered excitedly about costumes, candy, and whether Marianne would wear a crown to match Lily's. The energy carried home with them, the anticipation building as the sky deepened into evening.

On Halloween, the doorbell rang just as Rick finished adjusting the cuffs of his borrowed costume—a princely ensemble that Darcy had dug out from a theater gala years ago. The velvet jacket felt a little too formal for him, but when Lily had asked him to be her prince, there was no way he could say no.

Sam bolted toward the door, yelling, "I'll get it!"

"Sam, wait—" Rick called, but the boy had already flung the door open.

"Whoa! You're a fairy!" Sam exclaimed, his eyes wide.

Marianne stood in the doorway, her delicate costume glowing in the porch light. She wore a flowing dress of pale green and silver, its embroidery reminiscent of the intricate patterns found in a hanbok, delicate yet regal. Her dark hair, sleek and shining, cascaded over her shoulders, a flowered crown nestled among the soft waves. The warm glow of the porch lights reflected in her dark eyes, turning them luminous as she smiled. In her hand, she held a wand tipped with glittering stars, her presence both ethereal and timeless, like something out of a moonlit folktale.

Rick joined her by the door, pausing longer than he meant to. The shimmer of her wings caught the porch light, a soft glow tracing the delicate edges of her costume. She looked—magical. And not just in the playful, storybook way Lily saw her. Something about her presence, her warmth, made the night feel different.

"Marianne," he said, finally finding his voice. A smile tugged at his lips. "You look—stunning."

Marianne laughed lightly, her eyes sparkling. "Thank you, Rick," she said. "And I see you're quite dashing as a prince tonight. Very fitting."

Rick chuckled, rubbing the back of his neck. "It's all for Lily," he admitted. "She insisted."

"And she was right," Marianne teased, leaning in slightly to kiss his cheek. "You wear it well."

Rick felt his face warm, his breath hitching for just a second. It was just a kiss on the cheek—simple, casual—but it sent something unexpected through him. Before he could process it, he cleared his throat and quickly glanced away. "Kids," he called over his shoulder, his voice just a little rougher than before. "Marianne's here!"

A chorus of cheers rang through the house as the kids came racing toward the door, admiration clear in their wide-eyed stares at Marianne's shimmering costume. Rick barely had time to grab their coats before they were already bouncing toward the porch, eager to start their adventure.

The night was alive with the magic of firsts.

Lily twirled in her wings, her hand clasped firmly in Rick's. Walter and Sam dashed ahead, racing from house to house. Ellie, dressed adorably in denim overalls, a red-and-white checkered shirt, and tiny brown boots, hung back near Rick's side. Her wide-brimmed cowgirl hat sat slightly askew on her head, the string dangling beneath her chin. She twirled the string absently around her small fingers, her eyes darting between the rushing children and the glowing porch lights. The laughter, the swirling costumes, the crisp scent of fallen leaves—it was all new. Why just a year ago, she'd been in the cellar with him and Lily. He had to remind himself this wasn't just Lily's first-time trick-or-treating. It was Ellie's too.

At the first house, Ellie hesitated, watching the Walter, Sam, and Lily rush up to the front door. Her tiny hands fidgeted with the brim of her hat.

Rick knelt beside her. "Go ahead, Sweetheart," he encouraged. "It's okay."

Ellie glanced at him, then at Marianne, who smiled warmly. "I'll go with you," Marianne said gently, holding out a hand.

Ellie hesitated for only a second before slipping her tiny hand into Marianne's. Together, they walked up to the door, and Ellie proudly held out her pumpkin-shaped bucket. "Trick or treat!" she said, her voice small but brave.

Rick's throat tightened. His girls were trusting the world for the first time. And thankfully the world was responding with kindness.

As the night carried on, the kids' candy bags grew heavier, their footsteps lighter with excitement. By the time they made their way back home to Darcy's house, Ellie's earlier hesitation had vanished. She trotted alongside Sam and Walter and Lily, her cowgirl boots clicking against the pavement as she proudly showed off her growing collection of candy. At one point, she let out a delighted "Yeehaw!" as she twirled her hat string, fully embracing the fun.

Rick sighed contently as he squeezed Marianne's hand in appreciation as they walked behind the children taking in the joy of the night.

For years, Halloween had been about survival. Finding small pockets of light in the dark. Making something out of nothing. Now, it was different. Now, the light surrounded them. It was filled with love, laughter, and the promise of something more.

And maybe—just maybe—this was one of those moments where God wasn't just leading him somewhere better. He was showing him it was already here.

Chapter 69

> I was reminded today that our chains of anger can be unlocked not through forgetting but by entrusting our wounds to God's care.
> – Rick's Journal

The hallway outside the pastor offices at church was quiet except for the distant hum of voices from a Bible study down the hall when Rick walked in with all four kids, Ellie balanced on his hip, her stuffed duck tucked securely under her chin. Lily walked beside him, gripping Leo the Lion, while Sam and Walter trailed slightly behind, their expressions unreadable.

Waiting near the doors stood Pastor Eddie, Pastor Ned, Pastor Fanny—and, to Rick's surprise, Darcy. Rick frowned slightly, shifting Ellie in his arms. "Darcy? What are you doing here?"

Darcy smirked, though it was softer than usual. "Got a request at breakfast this morning."

Rick turned to his sons, his heart kicking up a notch. "You asked him to come?"

Walter nodded. "You were already bringing us, but we wanted Uncle Darcy here, too."

Sam hesitated before adding, "He was with us when we saw Mama in June. He knows."

Rick's throat tightened. He looked to Darcy, who gave a small nod of understanding.

"Of course, guys," Rick said, his voice steady. "Whatever you need."

Darcy clapped a hand on Rick's shoulder. "Come on, Wentworth. I couldn't let you have all the fun."

Rick let out a short chuckle, then followed as Pastor Eddie opened the door to his office. They all filed into the familiar room. Ellie climbed onto Rick's lap without hesitation, Quackers held securely under her chin, while Lily sat beside him, leaning into his side. Walter and Sam took their usual spots across from the pastors, though something about their posture felt different today—tense, but determined. Darcy sat beside them, his presence steady, solid.

Pastor Eddie settled into his chair, his warm gaze sweeping over them. After an opening prayer, he cut straight to the matter at hand. "I can tell you've got something on your minds. What's up?"

Walter shifted in his seat before speaking. "We've been thinking about Mama a lot. About how she made us feel bad for liking Dad. How she made us think we had to pick her."

Rick stiffened, forcing himself to remain still, letting them speak.

Sam fidgeted with the hem of his shirt. "We've realized she's been trying for years to make us think she was the only one who really loved us."

Walter swallowed hard. "I think I knew something was wrong, but I didn't wanna see it."

Rick exhaled slowly, his chest tightening. He wanted to reach for them, to pull them into his arms and tell them none of this was their fault. But something told him to wait. They needed to get there on their own.

Pastor Eddie leaned forward. "That's not your fault, boys."

Sam frowned. "Feels like it."

Pastor Ned shook his head. "You were children. You still are children. Your mom controlled the story for years, and it's only now that you're stepping away from it that you can see the full picture."

Sam hesitated, then glanced between Rick, Darcy, and the pastors. "We just believed her, you know? That our dad left 'cause he was a pathetic sissy."

The room froze.

Rick stiffened, his breath catching in his chest. Pastor Eddie's jaw tightened. Pastor Ned sucked in a sharp breath, while Pastor Fanny flinched outright. Even Lily gasped, her expression darkening with fury.

Ellie, sensing the sudden change in the room, frowned, looking from face to face. "What's wrong?" she asked, hugging Quackers tighter.

Darcy, who had been leaning back casually, suddenly sat up straight. His expression—normally so controlled—turned to stone.

Pastor Ned cleared his throat, his voice tight. "Sam, where did you hear that word?"

Sam frowned, confused at the reaction. "Mama said it all the time."

Walter nodded. "She'd say stuff like, 'Your dad's a pathetic sissy who ran away from real life.'"

Lily made an outraged sound in the back of her throat. "She lied!"

Darcy let out a sharp breath, muttering something under his breath before dragging a hand down his face.

"It's not that big a deal," Walter muttered as he shifted in his seat. "All the boys say it. It doesn't mean anything really."

Rick forced himself to stay still, though his hands clenched into fists against his knees.

Pastor Eddie's expression darkened, though his voice remained steady. "Boys, that word—sissy—it's meant to insult a man, to say he's weak. It's a way to strip him of his dignity. It's a cruel insult you don't want to say to another man even in jest."

Walter frowned. "So—Mama was cruel?"

Pastor Ned leaned forward, his voice gentle but firm. "I know that's hard to hear, but yes. Twisting the truth to make you believe something false about your father—that was cruel."

Pastor Eddie sighed, his voice heavy with sadness. "Do you see how she wanted you to believe your dad wasn't someone worth respecting?"

Sam's brows knitted together, his voice hesitant. "But— she wasn't cruel. She's our Mama."

Lily's hands curled into fists. "This is the stupidest thing I've ever heard!" she burst out, her voice shaking with fury. "Daddy's the strongest man in the whole world!"

Rick exhaled sharply, reaching for her hand. "Lily—"

But she wasn't done.

"She lied to you! She made you think bad things about Daddy, but she was the bad one! You're just now figuring it out?"

Sam shrank back slightly. "Lily—"

"You should feel bad," Lily interrupted, shaking her head. "But not because you love her. Because you believed her when Daddy was the one who was really hurting!"

Her voice wavered, but she pushed forward.

"She took you away from Daddy. He took care of you when you were babies! And then she just—just ripped you away from him!"

Sam's mouth fell open.

Lily's hands curled into fists. "If she had locked you in the basement instead of me, would you still believe her?"

The silence that followed was deafening.

Pastor Fanny's voice broke through the tension, gentle but firm. "Lily, Sweetheart," she said, leaning forward, her expression filled with warmth, "it's okay to feel upset. That's part of healing. But Jesus tells us that anger can trap us just like chains. Do you remember what He says about forgiveness?"

Lily bit her lip, her shoulders tense.

Pastor Fanny continued. "Ephesians 4:31-32 says, 'Let all bitterness and wrath and anger and clamor and slander be put away from you, along with all malice. Be kind to one another, tenderhearted, forgiving one another, as God in Christ forgave you.'"

Lily sniffled, looking down. "I don't want to forgive her."

Pastor Fanny reached out, gently squeezing her hand. "That's a normal feeling, Sweetheart, but forgiveness isn't saying what she did was okay. It's saying you won't let your anger control you anymore. It's you giving God your pain and trusting Him to take care of everything."

Lily was quiet for a long moment before she whispered, "I guess but—I just don't want my brothers to love her more than Daddy."

Rick's heart clenched.

Walter spoke first. "Lily, we don't." His voice was sure. "We love Dad."

Sam nodded. "And we don't want him to think we're picking Mama over him."

Rick barely managed to hold himself together as he pulled them both into a hug. He exhaled slowly, his chest tightening as he looked at his sons. "Listen to me," he said, his voice steady but thick with emotion. "You don't have to figure all of this out today. You don't have to pretend it doesn't hurt. But you do need to know this—you are not betraying me by loving your mother. I will never ask you to stop loving her. I just want you to see the truth for what it is."

Walter swallowed hard, his face tense. "But what do we do now?"

Pastor Ned leaned forward, his voice warm and sure. "You keep walking in the truth. You keep learning what it means to love with wisdom. And you keep honoring your father."

Sam shifted beside Walter, biting his lip. "But—how do we do that? How do we honor Dad and walk in faith?"

Pastor Ned smiled gently. "By doing exactly what you're doing now—asking questions, seeking wisdom, and trusting that God will lead you forward." He let the words settle before adding, "Why don't we pray together?"

Rick nodded, his throat tight. "Yeah," he said quietly. "I'd like that."

Pastor Ned bowed his head, and the room followed. "Father, we come before You today, grateful for Your truth, even when it's hard. Thank You for revealing wisdom to these children, for softening their hearts to seek what is right. We ask for clarity, for strength, and for peace as they continue this journey. Let them learn to honor their father and mother as You command, and let them walk in faith without fear. Give Rick continued strength as he leads his family in truth. Jesus, we also ask you to please speak to these children's mother through the darkness and restore her soul. And above all, Lord, remind them that they are never alone. In Jesus' name, Amen."

As they lifted their heads, Walter let out a breath. Sam wiped at his eyes quickly, avoiding eye contact, while Lily leaned into Rick's side, calmer.

Rick met his kids' gazes and gave them a reassuring nod. "We'll figure it out. Together."

Walter nodded back. "Okay, Dad."

Sam sniffed and leaned slightly into Rick's side. "Yeah. Together."

Darcy exhaled dramatically, breaking the heavy moment. "Whew. That was intense. Who's up for ice cream?"

Rick rolled his eyes, but the corner of his mouth twitched. "Subtle, Darcy."

Darcy grinned. "Hey, I have a reputation to uphold. I'm here for the deep talks, but I'm also here for the post-biblical counseling sugar rush."

The tension in the room finally cracked as Walter let out a small laugh. Sam smirked. Even Lily softened, reaching for Ellie's hand.

Rick stood, shifting Ellie onto his hip as he looked at the pastors. "Thank you," he said sincerely. "For everything."

Pastor Eddie smiled. "That's what we're here for."

An hour later, after leaving the children at the ice cream shop with Darcy, Rick paced outside Marianne's condo, his hands shoved deep into the pockets of his jacket. The cool autumn air nipped at his skin, but the chill barely registered. His pulse hammered, his mind replaying every moment from earlier that afternoon in the counseling office. His boys had unknowingly unraveled him with their words.

Pathetic sissy. He had thought he had moved past those years, that Louisa no longer held power over him. But hearing that word from his son's mouth—his son, who had no idea the weight of it—had sent a sharp blade straight into his ribs.

Even now, his throat tightened. The conversation had ended with healing, with resolution, but his heart still felt unsteady. And for some reason he found himself arriving outside Marianne's door uninvited. He felt about to take another step into something unknown, something he wasn't sure he deserved.

Before he could talk himself out of it, he knocked.

The door opened, revealing Marianne in a simple sweater and dark jeans, her long hair cascading over her shoulders. She smiled instantly, warmth reaching her dark almond-shaped eyes. "You're a sight for sore eyes," she teased lightly.

Rick exhaled a breath he hadn't realized he was holding. "I know we didn't have a date, but I was hoping—Are you free?"

Her smile deepened, but she didn't tease him further. "You don't ever need an invitation, Rick." She stepped aside, gesturing for him to come in. "What's wrong?"

Rick hesitated. He could lie. Say yes. Keep everything buried, keep this light and easy like it was supposed to be. Or he could tell the truth.

He stepped into her arms, letting the door shut behind him. "I need you."

Marianne's arms wrapped around him without hesitation—strong, steady, like she'd always been waiting to hold him up. The warmth of her touch settled something deep in his chest, like an anchor dropping into place. For a long moment, he just stood there, breathing her in, letting the quiet of her space wrap around him.

"What happened?"

Rick ran a hand down his face, then laughed without humor as he burrowed his head into her shoulder. "Biblical counseling was intense."

She waited, patient as ever, giving him the time to say what he needed to.

Rick let out a slow breath and forced himself to meet her gaze. "Sam called me a pathetic sissy today."

Marianne inhaled sharply. "Oh, Rick—"

"He didn't know what it meant," Rick said quickly, shaking his head. "He wasn't trying to hurt me. He just repeated something Louisa used to say about me."

Marianne's expression softened, but there was fire in her eyes. "I hate that she twisted their minds like that."

"Me too," Rick admitted, rubbing the back of his neck as he sank down onto her couch. "It hit me harder than I expected."

"You know it's not true," Marianne said softly as she curled up next to him on the couch.

Rick swallowed past the lump in his throat. "Yeah," he said, though his voice felt hollow. "I know."

She saw through him instantly. "Rick."

His jaw clenched. "I do. But sometimes—sometimes the past doesn't care what you know. It just sneaks up on you and takes you down."

She studied him for a long moment before murmuring, "So what are we going to do about that?"

Rick blinked. "We?"

She nodded. "You think I'm going to let you walk through this alone?"

Rick let out a breathless chuckle, shaking his head. "You're something else, Marianne Dashwood."

She smiled. "I try."

Something shifted in the air between them. The silence stretched, not uncomfortable but heavy with something unspoken. Rick felt his pulse pick up, his heart pounding against his ribs.

He knew this feeling. He had spent months trying to ignore it, trying to push it aside. But tonight, sitting here in the dim glow of her living room, after a day that had left him emotionally raw, he couldn't deny it any longer.

He loved her.

It wasn't just gratitude. It wasn't just admiration. It was something deeper, something he hadn't dared hope for.

"Marianne." His voice was hoarse, thick with everything he wanted to say.

She tilted her head slightly. "Yes?"

Rick took her slender hand in his shaking hands. "I need to tell you something."

Marianne searched his face, her expression softening as if she already knew. "Okay."

He hesitated, then took a breath and went for it. "I love you."

The words hung in the air, heavy and real. Marianne's breath hitched, her lips parting slightly in surprise.

Rick shook his head, exhaling a quiet laugh. "I think I've loved you for a while. I just—I was too afraid to admit it. Too afraid of what it might mean."

Marianne reached up, brushing a strand of hair away from his forehead. "And now?"

His throat tightened. "Now, I don't want to be afraid anymore."

A slow smile spread across her face, warmth radiating from her eyes. "Good," she murmured. "Because I love you too."

Rick barely had time to react before she reached up, cupping his face with gentle hands. His breath caught, his entire body locking up for a moment before he let himself lean into her touch.

And then, slowly, carefully, she pressed her lips to his.

The kiss was soft, lingering, filled with the quiet promise of something neither of them had been ready to admit until now. It wasn't rushed, wasn't desperate—it was steady, sure. Like an anchor in the storm.

When they finally pulled away, Rick exhaled, resting his forehead against hers. "I don't deserve you," he murmured.

Marianne pulled back just enough to meet his eyes. "You do," she said firmly. "And I'll remind you of that as many times as it takes."

Rick let out a breathless laugh, his chest feeling lighter than it had in years. "Careful, Marianne. You're signing up for a lifetime commitment with a stubborn man."

She smirked. "Good thing I'm just as stubborn, then."

He chuckled, shaking his head, before wrapping his arms around her and pulling her close.

For the first time in his life, he wasn't just surviving. He was living.

Chapter 70

> As the chill of November whispers of Thanksgiving, I am profoundly grateful for the journey from agony to hope, for it has led me to a place of warmth and light I once feared lost forever.
> – Rick's Journal

The aroma of roasted turkey, baked bread, and spiced pumpkin pie filled the air as Rick set the final dish on the dining room table. Marianne entered moments later, carrying a basket of homemade rolls. She wore a simple autumn-inspired dress, and her raven black hair shimmered under the chandelier. Rick caught her eye and smiled, his heart swelling as she effortlessly blended into their world.

"Dinner smells amazing," she said, placing the basket on the table. "It's like something out of a magazine."

Rick chuckled, stepping closer to give her a gentle kiss. "You should've seen the chaos in the kitchen an hour ago," he said. "Not so magazine-worthy."

Marianne laughed softly, her eyes glowing. "Well, it looks perfect now," she said, taking in the beautifully set table. "But where is everyone?"

Rick grinned. "Good question. Are we starting Thanksgiving dinner alone, or is everyone joining us?"

Before Marianne could answer, Darcy's booming voice echoed from the hallway. "Hold your horses! We're coming! And don't touch the turkey—it's a family event!"

Moments later, Darcy entered, leading the kids in a dramatic procession. Caroline followed, phone in hand, recording every step. Walter carried the carving knife on a decorative platter like a royal scepter, while Sam held the carving fork with exaggerated seriousness. Ellie toddled in clutching her faithful Quackers, and Lily trailed behind, her eyes bright with excitement.

"We have arrived!" Darcy declared, sweeping his arms wide. "Let the carving commence!"

Rick laughed, standing to greet them. "You're making a bigger deal out of this than it is," he teased, gesturing to the beautifully roasted turkey on the table.

"Not true," Darcy countered, clapping Rick on the shoulder. "This is tradition. And as the guest of honor, you are in charge of the carving, my friend."

Rick raised an eyebrow, looking at the kids. "What do you think? Should we carve the turkey together?"

The kids erupted in cheers, and Caroline smiled, her phone capturing the moment. "This is going in the family archives," she said. "Everyone, gather in! I need this on video."

Rick held up the carving knife. "Okay, team effort," he said, his tone playful. "Walter, you guide the knife. Sam, you've got the fork. Lily, hold the platter steady. And Ellie and Marianne— cheer us on."

Ellie squeezed Quackers tightly, her face lighting up. "You got this, Daddy!" she cheered.

Marianne clapped her hands, her laughter adding to the warmth of the room. "Go, Team Wentworth! You're doing great!"

Rick laughed as Walter stepped up beside him, steadying the knife with his small hands. Sam hovered nearby, poised with the fork like a knight ready for battle. Lily carefully held the platter, her expression a mix of concentration and excitement.

"First slice!" Darcy announced dramatically. "A clean cut, folks. The crowd goes wild!"

The kids burst into laughter, their cheers growing louder with every slice. Marianne clapped along, her smile matching the joy filling the room.

"Great teamwork!" Caroline called out, her phone capturing the moment. "Lily, you're a pro with that platter. Walter, steady hands. Sam, excellent fork skills!"

"Don't forget Ellie!" Darcy added, pointing to the youngest, who bounced in her seat. "She's clearly the team's moral support."

Ellie grinned, waving Quackers in the air. "Marianne, Quackers, and I are the cheerleaders!"

As the turkey was carved and passed around, the room filled with laughter and camaraderie. Rick glanced at Marianne, watching her take in the scene with serene delight. Their eyes met, and for a moment, everything else faded. This sense of family, love, and light was everything Rick had hoped to rebuild.

"Turkey's ready!" Rick announced, placing the final slice on the platter.

"Well done, team," Darcy said, raising his glass in mock celebration. "To the best turkey-carving squad this house has ever seen."

"To family," Marianne added softly, her voice full of sincerity.

"To family," Rick echoed, his voice steady with gratitude.

With the carving finished, Marianne stepped closer, placing a gentle hand on Rick's arm. "That was impressive," she said softly. "You make a great team."

Rick looked at her, his heart full. "We're getting there," he said. "One step at a time."

Caroline lowered her phone, her expression teasing. "So, Rick, when's your next performance? This could be the start of a whole new career."

Rick rolled his eyes but smiled. "Let's just focus on getting this meal to the table," he said, gesturing to the kids. "Everyone, grab your seats!"

As the family settled around the table, Rick took a moment, his chest swelling with gratitude. This moment—filled with laughter, love, and new beginnings—was everything he had fought for. When they joined hands for grace, Rick's voice trembled as he gave thanks, feeling deeply that they were exactly where they were meant to be.

As the meal began, Darcy excused himself briefly, returning moments later with a manila folder in hand. He cleared his throat, catching everyone's attention. "Rick," Darcy began, his tone shifting to something more formal yet warm, "I have something for you."

Rick set down his fork, his brow furrowing. "What's this?" he asked as Darcy handed him the folder.

"It's the settlement papers," Darcy explained, sliding the folder across the table. "Louisa's lawyers have offered a very generous agreement. It's more than we expected—enough to provide long-term stability for you and the kids. The house and property are officially yours, and the financial support ensures your family is secure."

Rick's hands trembled slightly as he opened the folder, his eyes scanning the neatly typed lines. His heart pounded with each word that sank in. The house. Stability. A future.

"Darcy—" Rick's voice faltered, thick with emotion, as he looked up. "I don't even know what to say."

"You don't have to say anything," Darcy replied, his tone steady and warm. "Just know that you've earned this. You and the kids deserve every bit of it."

Tears pricked at Rick's eyes, blurring his vision. He closed the folder with care, setting it aside as his emotions threatened to overwhelm him. "Thank you," he said quietly, his voice low but rich with gratitude.

"Rick," Darcy continued, his expression softening as he caught the mood at the table, "there's more good news." He paused, ensuring he had everyone's attention. "Now, we can start the process of legally changing Walter, Sam, and Ellie's surname to Wentworth, just as they've been hoping for."

A whoop of delight erupted from the kids, their cheers filling the room with vibrant energy. All of his children exchanged excited glances and high-fives, their faces alight with joy and anticipation of this new chapter in their lives sharing his last name.

Rick looked around at his children's beaming faces, feeling a surge of pride and relief that washed over him like a warm wave. "Looks like it's really happening," he said with a broad smile, his heart swelling with hope and the promise of new beginnings.

Beside him, Lily reached out, her small hand resting gently on his arm. "We're going to be okay now, right, Daddy?" she asked, her voice carrying a fragile but unmistakable hope.

Rick turned to her, his smile soft and full of love. He placed his hand over hers, giving it a gentle squeeze. "Yeah, Sweetheart," he said, his voice steady despite the lump in his throat. "We're going to be just fine."

Later, the table buzzed with the warm hum of conversation as plates were cleared, and the aroma of pie and coffee replaced the scent of turkey and stuffing. Darcy stood once again, tapping his glass with a fork to gather everyone's attention. "All right, everyone," he said with a broad smile, his voice carrying over the hum of contented conversation. "Before the turkey-induced food comas hit, let's take a moment to share what we're thankful for. No interruptions, no rushed answers—let's savor this, like dessert."

The kids cheered, eager to take part, as Darcy explained the rules for going around the table giving thanks for what everyone was grateful for. Ellie bounced in her seat, raising her hand. "Me first!" she exclaimed, her voice bubbling with excitement.

Rick chuckled, gesturing for her to begin. Ellie hugged Quackers tightly, her eyes sparkling. "I'm thankful for Quackers, for my brothers and Lily, and for pizza nights with extra cheese!"

Laughter filled the room, but Sam leaned toward her with a teasing smirk. "What about Dad?" he asked, his tone playful but sincere.

Ellie paused, thinking. Rick waved his hand lightly, trying to let her off the hook. "It's okay, Ellie. You don't have to—"

But Ellie's voice rang out, firm and sincere. "And Daddy! I'm thankful for Daddy 'cause he gives the best hugs, he makes me laugh, and he always keeps me safe."

Rick's throat tightened, his heart swelling. He brushed her hair gently. "Thank you, Little Love," he said softly, his voice thick with emotion.

Sam eagerly jumped in, his eyes sparkling with mischief. "I'm thankful for candy, soccer, and never having to eat those gross Brussels sprouts Mom used to make us eat."

The table burst into laughter, and Walter added, "He's not wrong about the Brussels sprouts."

Sam's tone grew more thoughtful as he looked at Rick. "And, of course, I'm thankful for Dad. And for all of us being together."

Rick squeezed Sam's hand, his heart swelling with pride.

Walter sat up straighter, his tone earnest. "I'm thankful for Uncle Darcy letting us live with him and for us all being together again. And I'm thankful for Dad—for never giving up on us, no matter what."

Rick's composure wavered as he met Walter's steady gaze. "I'm thankful for you too, son," he said quietly.

Finally, all eyes turned to Lily, who clutched Leo the Lion tightly in her lap. She hesitated, her fingers tracing the plush mane as she looked down at the table. Taking a deep breath, she lifted her gaze, her voice soft but clear.

"I'm thankful I don't have to wear the chain anymore," she said, her words heavy with emotion. "And I'm thankful for Daddy—for keeping his promise that we'd get out of the cellar." She paused, her eyes glancing around the table at the warmth and love surrounding her. "And for this. My first Thanksgiving with turkey, mashed potatoes, and pie. It's better than I ever dreamed."

Ellie, ever curious, piped up with a question only a three-year-old could ask. "What did you have last year for Thanksgiving with Daddy in the cellar?"

"You, Daddy, and I had a can of chicken noodle soup," she said matter-of-factly before sorrow filled her voice. "That was just before Mama came down and took you upstairs."

The room fell silent, the weight of Lily's words settling over everyone. Caroline dabbed her eyes, and Marianne reached for Rick's hand under the table, giving it a supportive squeeze. The contrast between their warm meal now and the memories of what they endured in the cellar hit everyone hard.

Darcy cleared his throat, his voice thick with emotion. "Well," he said, raising his glass, "I'm thankful for resilience—everything this family has overcome. I'm thankful for Rick, for being a dad who inspires me every day. I'm thankful to Caroline for agreeing to marry me. And I'm thankful for this table full of laughter, love, and second chances."

Caroline smiled warmly, placing her hand on Darcy's. "I'm thankful for all of you," she said. "For the joy you've brought into my life and for reminding me what family really means."

Rick turned to Marianne, his heart full. "Marianne, what about you?"

She hesitated, her eyes shimmering. "I'm thankful for courage," she said. "For finding the strength to leave behind the parts of my life that weren't healthy and for starting over here. I'm thankful for all of you—for showing me what love and hope really look like."

Her words touched everyone deeply. Rick gave her hand a gentle squeeze as he kissed her for the first time in front of his children, slow and gentle.

Finally, all eyes waited for Rick. He cleared his throat, feeling the weight of their attention. "I'd like to share something a little different," he began, reaching into his pocket. He pulled out the journal Darcy had gifted him on his birthday, the edges already worn from frequent use.

"This year, Darcy gave me this journal and told me I should write," Rick said, his voice steady despite the emotions welling up inside him. "I didn't know if I had much to say, but it turns out I do. I wrote something I'd like to share with all of you. It's a poem. A reflection, I guess. I call it Half Agony, Half Hope."

The room quieted as Rick opened the journal, his fingers brushing over the page. He took a deep breath and began to read:

"From shadows deep, where silence reigned,
Where every breath ached, every step constrained,
I cried out, unseen, unheard, alone,
In a world of agony, carved from stone.

But even in the depths, a flicker remained,
A whisper of hope, though battered and strained.
A voice unseen, yet steady and clear,
Promised redemption, held me near.

In the agony, I was shaped and refined,
Though darkness sought to consume my mind.
Each tear a prayer, each wound a plea,
That grace might come and set me free.

And then, a crack—a light broke through,
The dawn of hope, a love renewed.
Chains that bound me crumbled to dust,
In His mercy, I placed my trust.

Now I stand, no longer confined,
With children's laughter and peace in my mind.
The love of family, the warmth of the sun,
Reminders that the battle's been won.

Half agony, yes, for the scars still ache,
But half hope, for the steps I take.
Each one leads me farther from despair,
To a life rebuilt with love and care.

For in the dark, He held my hand,
In the light, He helps me stand.
Half agony, half hope, I've learned,
Through Him, my strength and faith returned.

So today, I give thanks, my heart made whole,

For the grace that healed my weary soul.
Half agony, half hope, but wholly free,
A testament to His love for me."

As Rick's voice faded, the room remained silent for a beat before erupting into applause. Darcy was the first to stand, clapping with a wide grin. Caroline dabbed at her eyes with a napkin, her expression radiant with emotion. Marianne leaned forward, her smile soft but her eyes shining with unshed tears.

"That was beautiful, Rick," Marianne said softly, her eyes shining. "Thank you for sharing that."

Rick sat down, his hand lingering on the journal as he glanced around the room at the faces of those he cherished. "Thank you," he said simply, his voice filled with quiet sincerity. "For everything."

Darcy raised his glass, his expression steady and full of warmth. "To family," he said. "To second chances. And to hope."

"To hope," everyone echoed, their glasses meeting in a symphony of celebration.

Later, after dinner, as the last of the plates were cleared, Rick sat back in his chair, a deep contentment settling over him. The house was alive with laughter, warmth, and the promise of new beginnings. Marianne, sitting beside him, reached for his hand, lacing her fingers through his.

"You know," she said softly, "I was thinking about something."

Rick turned to her, curiosity flickering in his eyes. "Yes?"

Marianne hesitated, then reached into the bag she had brought with her and pulled out a worn notebook. It was his first journal from his time in the cellar that she had asked to read. She held it like something precious. "I think you should publish this," she said.

Rick blinked. "What?"

"Your journals. Your poems. Everything you've written about your journey," Marianne explained, her voice gentle but insistent. "Rick, your words are powerful. They're raw, real, and filled with hope. I think people need to read them."

Darcy, who had been eavesdropping from across the room, perked up. "Oh, I love this idea," he declared, already pulling out his phone. "Rick Wentworth, bestselling author. I can see it now."

Rick groaned. "Darcy, don't—"

"Too late," Darcy grinned, typing rapidly. "I'm already looking up publishers."

Rick rubbed his temples. "You guys are ridiculous."

Marianne laughed, squeezing his hand. "Maybe. But I mean it, Rick. Your story matters. It's time to share it."

Rick glanced at the journal, his mind racing. The idea of exposing his most personal thoughts, his pain and healing, to the world was terrifying. But looking into Marianne's eyes, he saw nothing but certainty. Trust. Faith in him.

He exhaled, rubbing the back of his neck. "I'll think about it," he said finally.

Darcy smirked. "That's Rick-speak for 'I'll let Darcy drag me into it eventually.'"

Rick rolled his eyes, but he was smiling.

Just then, Lily climbed onto Rick's lap, resting her head against his chest. "Daddy?" she murmured sleepily.

"Yeah, Sweetheart?"

Lily peeked up at him, then glanced at Marianne. "I think you should keep her," she said simply, before snuggling closer.

Marianne's breath caught, and Rick's heart clenched with overwhelming love. He met Marianne's gaze, something deep and unspoken passing between them.

Rick pressed a kiss to Lily's forehead. "I think you might be right," he whispered.

Darcy clapped his hands together. "Well, folks, looks like that's settled! I expect a wedding invitation in the near future."

Caroline elbowed him. "Give them time, Darcy."

Rick shook his head, chuckling. "One step at a time."

Marianne leaned in, resting her head lightly against his shoulder. "I'm in no rush," she murmured. "As long as we get there together."

Rick smiled, pressing another soft kiss to her lips. "Yeah," he said. "Together."

To Be Continued—

Did You Like This Book?

If Half Agony, Half Hope moved you, encouraged you, or simply kept you turning pages late into the night—would you consider leaving a review?

Your words matter more than you know. Reviews help other readers discover this story and give indie authors like me the chance to keep writing, sharing, and growing.

Whether it's a sentence or a full reflection, your voice makes a difference.

Leave a review on Amazon, Goodreads, or wherever you buy your books.

Thank you for reading. Thank you for feeling. Thank you for sharing.

With gratitude,
Joy Michelle Austin

Acknowledgements

Writing *Half Agony, Half Hope* has been a journey of faith, perseverance, and healing—one that I could not have walked alone.

To WS Deming and Kimberly Coghlan—your editorial insight and wisdom helped shape this book into what it was meant to be. Thank you for your guidance, your honesty, and your belief in this story.

To Mom, Dad, and my friends—your unwavering support, prayers, and encouragement have been my anchor. You believed in me when I struggled to believe in myself. I am beyond grateful for your love and faithfulness.

To the late Mrs. Sandy Sanders (1943–2018)—you walked with me through my own agony after my assault, showing me that healing was possible. Your kindness and wisdom still resonate in my heart. Thank you for being a light in my darkest moments. This book would not exist without the strength you helped me find.

To Professor Buchanan and Dr. Malandra from Biola University—thank you for shaping me into the writer I am today. From the moment I was a wide-eyed English student in your classes, your encouragement and passion for literature inspired me to pursue my calling. Your words and lessons have stayed with me through the years, and I am forever grateful.

And above all, to God Almighty, the great Healer and Rescuer—this story, this journey, my very life, belongs to You. Thank You for never leaving me in the darkness, for redeeming my pain, and for turning ashes into something beautiful. Every word I write is for Your glory.

With deepest gratitude,
Joy Michelle Austin

About the Author

 Joy Michelle Austin is a storyteller, blogger, and debut novelist whose passion for literature led her to earn an English degree in creative writing. A lifelong admirer of Jane Austen, she brings together her passions for Jane Austen, true crime, and faith in *Half Agony, Half Hope* and the Jane Austen's Men series—gritty, emotionally charged stories of faith, redemption, and romance.

Beyond fiction, Joy has been a dedicated blogger at The Joyous Living, where she has collaborated with brands such as Disney, Affirm Films, Amazon, Segerstrom Center for the Arts, bestselling author Tracie Peterson, and more. Her work spans film, literature, and performing arts, always with a heart for storytelling that inspires and uplifts.

To connect with Joy and stay updated on her latest projects, visit:

www.thejoyousliving.com
www.facebook.com/thejoyousliving
www.instagram.com/thejoyousauthor
www.pinterest.com/thejoyousliving

Books by Joy Michelle Austin

📖 *Half Agony, Half Hope* – May 5, 2025

📖 *Half Agony, Half Hope, But Wholly Free: A Companion Devotional* –
Coming Soon
   A devotional journey inspired by Rick Wentworth's
struggles and triumphs, offering reflections on faith, endurance,
and God's unwavering grace.

📖 *Rick's Journals: Poetry & Reflections on Love, Loss, and Redemption* –
Coming Soon
   Raw. Honest. Beautifully broken. Rick Wentworth's
journals capture his decade of captivity, his fight to reclaim himself,
and the love that gave him hope. A deeply personal collection of
poetry and reflections straight from Rick's pen.

📖 *Darcy's Story: A Season of Change – Coming Soon*
   With his wedding on the horizon, Fitz Darcy faces doubts,
expectations, and the world's misconceptions about his fiancée,
Caroline Bingley. Meanwhile, Rick Wentworth navigates new love
with Marianne Dashwood in this compelling continuation of the
Jane Austen's Men series.

   The Jane Austen's Men series continues beyond Rick and
Darcy's journeys, exploring the lives of other men who must
confront their pasts, their faith, and the true meaning of love. Stay
tuned for stories of broken men seeking wholeness, of faith tested
in fire, and of second chances that arrive when least expected.

   For updates, exclusive content, and behind-the-scenes
looks at the Jane Austen's Men series, visit
www.thejoyousliving.com/the-joyous-author.